LOVE WAS HER PATH TO SUCCESS— AND ONE MAN WAS HER GOAL

Kate Shaughnessy knew about men and her power over them early, as her voluptuous beauty burst into flower, and her hunger grew for everything that poverty denied her.

But never had Kate known a man like John Wilton . . . the one man who gave her pleasure, not profit . . . the one man who could take her and then just as easily leave her alone.

Kate vowed to possess this man, even as he rose from a penniless newcomer to all-powerful cattle baron.

Kate vowed to make that climb, too, man by man, seduction by seduction, until she could meet John Wilton on his lofty level—and join with him at the peak of a passion that knew no limits and would pay any price. . . .

THE WILTONS

Great Reading from SIGNET

THE
WILTONS

Eden Hughes

A SIGNET BOOK
NEW AMERICAN LIBRARY
TIMES MIRROR

NAL BOOKS ARE AVAILABLE AT QUANTITY DISCOUNTS WHEN USED TO PROMOTE PRODUCTS OR SERVICES. FOR INFORMATION PLEASE WRITE TO PREMIUM MARKETING DIVISION, THE NEW AMERICAN LIBRARY, INC., 1633 BROADWAY, NEW YORK, NEW YORK 10019.

SIGNET TRADEMARK REG. U.S. PAT. OFF. AND FOREIGN COUNTRIES
REGISTERED TRADEMARK—MARCA REGISTRADA
HECHO EN CHICAGO, U.S.A.

SIGNET, SIGNET CLASSICS, MENTOR, PLUME, MERIDIAN AND NAL Books are published by The New American Library, Inc., 1633 Broadway, New York, New York 10019

First Printing, December, 1980

1 2 3 4 5 6 7 8 9

PRINTED IN THE UNITED STATES OF AMERICA

PART ONE

1

She thought it would take him at least an hour and a half, perhaps longer, to get free. There was no need for haste. She needed to bathe. The weather was unseasonably warm and humid for May, and the Royal and Imperial Opera House, across the street from the Sacher Hotel, had been stifling. And so had been the private dining room downstairs, to which they had gone afterward for a late supper.

Margaret Wilton was traveling without her maid, as was her custom, even if it raised a few eyebrows in Victorian London, and since she didn't like strangers in her bath, she dismissed the hotel maid after the woman had drawn the water, and undressed herself, hanging her gown on a hanger in the wardrobe. Feeling delightfully wicked, she walked around the suite naked, arranging things until the water in the tin tub cooled enough.

She had even examined herself shamelessly, in the mirrored doors of the wardrobe. Margaret was thirty-eight years old and had carried two children and she didn't look it. The breasts weren't very large, but on the other hand, neither were they pendulous. There was no sag at the belly, no flabby flesh hanging from the upper arms; if anything, she could use a few pounds.

She entered the bathtub, washed carefully, but didn't soak. Soaking sometimes debilitated her, and she wanted all her strength tonight. She emerged, dried herself, sprayed herself with French perfume, then slipped into a dressing gown. She went to the head of the bed, pulled the floor-waiter cord, then went to the door to await his arrival.

"Please take care of the bathwater," she said. "And then bring the wine. And some cheese, I think, and some grapes, too. Can you arrange that?"

"It will be done, Frau Grafin," the waiter said.

Margaret smiled at that. She wasn't a countess. She was a second daughter married to a second son. She was simply "the honorable," which was rather funny, when you got right down to it. There was nothing in the titles of the nobility suggesting morality. They were simply ranks. If you had no rank, it was presumed that you must have morality and honor.

The floor waiter returned with a bellboy to help him with the bathwater, and with a cooler with the wine in it.

"I thought perhaps the Gnadige Frau Grafin would like a little wine now," he said.

"How thoughtful of you," Margaret said.

She picked up a glass while he opened the bottle and then held it out to him while he poured. Then she went into the parlor of the suite and sat down at the piano and played, from memory, some of the Johann Strauss she had heard in the last few days, picking the melody out with the fingers of her right hand, frowning at her lack of ability to make it sound cheerful.

She had gone back into the parlor to make sure everything was in order before she dressed to receive him, when she heard the door to the entrance foyer open.

"The cheese, Gnadige Frau Grafin," the floor waiter said. "A nice little Emmentaler. And I have taken the liberty of bringing another bottle of wine. Just in case . . ."

"You are so very thoughtful," Margaret said. "Thank you very much. And that will be all, I think, for the evening."

"The Gnadige Frau Grafin is most gracious," the floor waiter said. She turned as he bowed his way out of the foyer. She heard the door close and then open again, and she turned in some annoyance, wondering what in the world the man wanted now. But it wasn't the floor waiter. It was him.

"Oh, damn," she said. "I'm not dressed."

"I readily forgive you," he said. He had half a dozen long-stemmed roses clutched in his white-gloved left hand. "I

2

come bearing gifts." He handed her the flowers, then walked back and locked the door.

He was in white tie and tails. The uniform was gone, and there were no decorations at all on his evening dress.

"I have been thinking about this for three weeks," he said. "Ever since I heard you were coming to Vienna. And I have been thinking about it for the past three days, from the moment I actually saw you, to the exclusion of everything else."

Margaret smiled and sniffed the flowers and laid them down and looked up and met his eyes.

"Me, too," she said. "It's been a very long time."

He opened his arms and she went into them, putting her face against the stiffness of his shirtfront. He held her tightly for a moment, then reached down and put his fingers under her chin, raising it.

"Hello, Maggie," he said.

"Hello, Arthur," she said.

He kissed her. She felt his tongue pushing into her mouth. She pressed against his body, met his tongue.

His hand fumbled with the cord on her dressing gown. She pulled away from him far enough so that he could unfasten it, and when he had it open and his hand on her breast, she shrugged her shoulders and slipped out of it.

"I hoped you would do that," he said, hugging her to him, "when I was thinking about this. I love to have you quite naked."

"I know," she said.

"Oh, Maggie, Maggie."

"Put it in me, darling," she said. "I want to have you in me."

She didn't know how long they'd been dozing, but suddenly she was wide awake, sitting up, supporting herself on one arm. Someone was knocking at the door. She frowned down at Arthur; in sleep, he didn't look like a prince of the realm, the Prince of Wales's younger brother, such a stern, respected man. She got out of bed and walked naked from the bedroom to the sitting room, picked up the dressing gown where she had thrown it onto the carpet, wrapped it around her, and went to the door.

"Who is it?"

3

"Colonel Price-Cunningham, ma'am," the familiar voice said softly. She closed her eyes for a moment, then unlatched the door.

"Forgive me, ma'am," he said, "for the intrusion. I wouldn't be here if it wasn't necessary."

Margaret went to the bedroom. Arthur had slid up against the headboard, propping himself up with pillows.

"It's Price-Cunningham," she said.

"What the hell does he want?" Arthur said, annoyed.

She shrugged. "This is when I feel like a slut. When your equerry comes to take you back where you belong."

"Don't be a bloody fool," he said angrily. He got out of bed, pulled on his trousers, arranging the suspenders over his naked chest, and walked barefoot out of the bedroom, not closing the door after him.

"Well?" she heard him snap.

"There has been a cable from London, your Highness," Colonel Price-Cunningham said. "I took the liberty to bring it here."

"It bloody well had better be important," Arthur said.

There was a moment's silence; then Arthur spoke again. "Are there copies of this?"

"No, sir."

"Well, then, wait just a moment, please. And then you can run it over to Princess Beatrice. I'm sure that she would like to have this information as soon as possible."

Arthur came back into the bedroom, this time closing the door behind him.

"There is some bad news, I fear," he said, and handed her the telegram. Philip St. Claire Wilton, Margaret Wilton's husband and the man she hated most in the world, was dead.

"By his own hand," the telegram said. "This afternoon, while temporarily deranged."

"I'm terribly sorry," Arthur said.

"Suicide?" she asked rather numbly.

"I suppose he was found out," Arthur said. "And took that way out."

"It's hardly been a secret. Why now?"

"I don't know," he said. "You'd better give that back to me. I'll have Price-Cunningham run it over to my sister. She

4

will want to tell you herself." He gently tugged the cable from her fingers, turned, and left the bedroom.

"You will tell Princess Beatrice," she heard Arthur say, "that you and I were having a late supper together when this cable came into your hands, and that I have instructed you to make the necessary arrangements to return Lady Margaret to London as soon as possible."

"Yes, sir. By your leave, sir?"

"Thank you again, Price-Cunningham," Arthur said.

He went back into the bedroom. He sat down on the bed and pulled his socks and shoes on, then the dress shirt. She rose and tied his white tie.

"I'm sorry for you, darling," Arthur said. "But I won't be a bloody hypocrite and say I'm sorry for him. I never could stand the bugger."

"If he hadn't been . . . that way," Maggie said. "We would never have had what we have had."

"I violently dislike having to leave you," he said.

"I know."

"I feel so . . . so bloody *impotent*!"

"Not that," she said with a little laugh. "Not that!"

He wrapped his arms around her, hugged her to him, and then left her. She waited until she heard the door close. Then she went through the suite and emptied the ashtrays of his cigars, dumping them into the wine coolers. She rang for the floor waiter and had him take the coolers, and then she went into the bedroom, took off the dressing gown, put on a flannel nightgown, and waited for Princess Beatrice to come to tell her that her husband was dead.

2

The Marquess of Haverford, Margaret's oldest brother, who had acceded to the title five years before, on the death of their father, met Margaret's train at Waterloo Station. Whenever she saw him—and she didn't see much of him, for he preferred to spend his time on his Northumberland estates—she was instantly reminded of their father. The physical resemblance was astonishing. The character resemblance was practically nonexistent.

Their father had had, beneath the same stern, even dour, sharp-featured face, a shy smile and a rather ribald sense of humor. How much nicer, Margaret thought, it would be if he were still alive, and meeting her, rather than Francis.

Francis tipped his top hat to her as she approached. There was no smile on his face, not even a polite one. "I'm very sorry about all this, Maggie," he said. "I want you to know that."

"That's very kind of you, Francis," she said. "Eleanor and the children are all right, I trust?"

"Quite well, thank you," he said. "I'll have someone take care of the baggage, if you'll give me the stubs."

"Why can't we just take it in the carriage with us?" she said.

The duke has asked that you call, right off."

"Can't that wait?" she asked. She was really in no mood to face her husband's father.

"I think not," her brother said, and held his arm for her to take. They walked through the station. A brougham behind a matched pair of sorrels waited at the curb. On the polished wood of the door was the crest of the Wiltons. A footman held open the door for Margaret and she climbed aboard. Francis handed him her baggage stubs and a coin. "See to Lady Wilton's luggage, will you, my good man?"

"Very good, m'lord," the footman said. Francis stepped into the carriage, and the footman closed it after him. The driver looked over his shoulder to wait until Francis was seated across from Margaret, facing forward, and then he put the horses into motion.

"Is Thomas at Chester Square?" Margaret asked. Her father-in-law, the Duke of Chesterly, maintained a town house at Chester Square.

"He didn't come down from school," Francis said. "Under the circumstances, we thought that best."

Margaret bit off the reply that came to her lips. It was done, and flashing at Francis would accomplish nothing. And perhaps it had been the right decision. There very well might have been whispering at the funeral. At seventeen, her son Thomas was old enough to understand that kind of talk.

The duke was seated on a couch placed at a right angle to the fireplace, and it seemed to Margaret that he was staring unseeing into the empty fireplace. In mourning? It would be a shock to any father to have a son die before him, and in this case, under these circumstances, Margaret felt a wave of sympathy for the old man.

And then he heard them, and stood up. He looked, Margaret thought, very old.

"I trust your trip went well?" the duke said. He made no move to extend arms to her, nor even to offer his hand. "Would you like tea, Margaret? Or sherry? Or perhaps spirits?"

"I would very much like a brandy," Margaret said.

"I think we could all use a brandy," her brother said. He turned to the butler. "Will you fetch some, please, Kenner, and then see that we're not disturbed?"

Margaret was beginning to have a sense of misgiving. Whatever this was all about, this being delivered to the duke right off the train, it was not going to be a ritual expression of condolences.

She already knew what had happened. Lieutenant Colonel Price-Cunningham had been on the first train out of Vienna the morning after the telegram had come. And he had been waiting for her when she got off the channel steamer. On the train to London, he had told her the sordid details.

Philip had become involved with his batman, to the extent that he'd rented a flat for him. Not content with that, he'd put the batman out to solicit boys for him. One of the boys had been a runaway. His father had come after him. The police had arrested the batman, and, terrified, the man had told the police all.

Aware that the affair had come officially to the attention of the Household Cavalry, Philip had put his service revolver in his mouth and blown the back of his head off in his own flat. He had been found there by the officers sent to inform him of the charges being brought against him and to place him under close arrest.

Price-Cunningham, himself a member of the Household Cavalry, had been able to find out that, under the circumstances, there would be no further investigation of the allegations made by Trooper Devine, who had been given his option of a posting to the King's Own African Rifles or a discharge and migration to Australia.

Margaret had felt sorry for Price-Cunningham's embarrassment as he relayed the story to her, though the truth of the matter was, she was a good deal closer to Price-Cunningham than she was either to her brother or to her father-in-law. For one thing, Price-Cunningham had known for years that she shared Prince Arthur's bed. And Price-Cunningham, who was a clever man as well as a discreet one, certainly knew about her sons, John and Thomas.

"For the life of me," the duke now said, "I don't know how to begin. I find the whole business not only beyond credibility, but quite distasteful."

"I don't know what you're talking about," Margaret said. "Is there something you're trying to tell me?"

She had wanted to make it easy for him. For her efforts, she got a withering glance from the duke, and when she looked at her brother, his face was even more cold.

8

"It isn't the sort of thing I'm accustomed to discussing with women," the duke said.

"I'm a married woman," Margaret said. "Not a child. Please say whatever it is you wish to say."

"I'm afraid," the duke said quickly, as if he hoped to be finished with what he had to say before she could protest again, "that I must ask you certain questions regarding your physical relationship with Philip."

Margaret flared. "I have no intention of discussing that with you, sir."

"I am very much afraid, madam," the duke said, "that we must discuss it."

Margaret felt a chill. This conversation, this *confrontation*, had assumed a menacing character. It was not to be simply a recitation of the facts concerning Philip's death. She looked at her brother. He was sitting with his hands before him, fingers spread, nervously tapping them together. And she knew that he was here, not as her brother, not as her advocate, not even as the senior male of her line, but as part of this inquisition.

"If you are asking if I was aware Philip had . . . had inverted tendencies," Margaret said, "I will tell you that I did. I can see no reason to discuss the matter any further."

The duke looked at her, and nodded, as if registering her reply, then went on. "When this was put to him, to avoid bringing disgrace to his name, and to the Household Cavalry, he saw fit to take his life."

She resisted the temptation to speak, to tell him to get to the point.

"Philip left a letter," the duke said slowly, so slowly that Margaret knew he was having difficulty maintaining his calm. "Addressed to me. Unfortunately, it came into the hands of Scotland Yard before it was turned over to me. In the letter, I'm afraid, he made certain statements."

"What kind of statements?"

"Concerning John and Thomas," the duke said. "Specifically, he referred to them as your 'bastards' and made the statement that there was no possibility that either of them is his issue."

"I refuse to listen to one more word of this," Margaret said. She stood up. "Francis, will you see me home?"

9

Her brother looked right at her. "'Please sit down, Margaret," he said. "This must be resolved."

"Philip was deranged," Margaret said. "I refuse to comment on a letter written while he was out of his mind."

"My eldest son is without issue," the duke said. "My title would thus pass to Philip's eldest son. I will not see a bastard bearing my title."

Margaret was surprised at herself. She really hadn't thought about that at all. What she had thought was that she would inherit Philip's property, enough to support her. She had not thought about John becoming heir to the dukedom.

"I want you, on behalf of your sons, to renounce their claim to the dukedom," the duke said. "And to leave England."

"I have no intention of doing anything of the kind," Margaret said.

"In that event, I would be left with no alternative but to bring the matter before the House of Lords."

Margaret now lost her temper. "In that event, you would look like a foolish, vindictive old man," she said. "And the whole story would come out."

"Margaret," her brother said, "there is nothing else for you to do."

"I would be forced to take that action without considering what it would do to me, or others," the duke said, as if it were a speech he had memorized. "Whatever scandal came to light, involving yourself, or the boys, or Price-Cunningham, would be on your shoulders."

"You would publicly brand your son a degenerate?"

"A scandal involving Lieutenant Colonel Price-Cunningham," her brother said, "would embarrass Prince Arthur."

The duke had mentioned Price-Cunningham. Did he think that Price-Cunningham was John and Thomas' father? Had Philip really not known?

"I am prepared to swear," she said, "that Colonel Price-Cunningham is not the father of my sons."

"The both of you would be banished from court," her brother said. "The queen would certainly do that. At least that."

"I see, Francis," Margaret said, "that you have tried and

convicted me." But even as she spoke, she realized that she had lost the battle. Arthur would of course provide for her. But if this came out, he would not be able to see her again. It was all over. She fought back the lump in her throat. "And am I just supposed to pack a bag and vanish, is that it?" she asked.

"Arrangements will be made for you, of course," the duke said.

"What sort of arrangements?" Margaret asked. "A monthly check to pay for a flat in some obscure Spanish town?"

New questions came into her mind. What was she going to tell the boys? What humiliation was this going to cause them?

"I was thinking more along the lines of a settlement," the duke said. "Some cash, and title to some property I own in America. Enough to provide for your needs and those of your sons. You would be able to make a new life for yourself."

"You have the whole thing planned, don't you?" she asked, aware that she was on the edge of losing control. "Have you had this plan in mind ever since you married off your son to me, knowing full well what he was?"

The duke looked at her from hurt eyes. "There is no cause for you to be abusive, madam," he said.

Margaret walked to the door.

"We have not concluded our business," the duke said.

"We have, until I can get the advice of a good solicitor," Margaret said.

3

The first thing Margaret Wilton did on arrival in Philadelphia was to take a public carriage to the brand-new Bellevue-Stratford Hotel, where she had telegraphed for a reservation for a three-room suite for an indefinite period.

The second thing she did was cross South Broad Street from the hotel to the First Philadelphia Bank & Trust Company. She had never heard of the First Philadelphia until she looked out of her hotel window and saw its sign, written vertically above an enormous clock. It looked substantial, she decided immediately, and she was going to need a bank. If she didn't like what she saw inside, she could look for another.

A doorman pulled open the door for Margaret and her son Thomas and she stepped inside. It was unlike banks with which she was familiar in England. It was a huge, high-ceilinged room, around three corners of which was a counter topped by a gilt-metal grille. There were tallish tables, the purpose of which she could not imagine, in the open space. Beside each was a brass spittoon, which she found distasteful.

She had no idea what to do next.

Finally she got in line before one of the windows. She was the only woman in line. Ultimately she reached the window.

"Yes, ma'am?" the clerk behind it asked.

"Whom would I see with regard to opening an account?"

"That would be the window that says 'New Accounts,' "

12

the clerk said. He had an Irish accent, thick, Londonderry, she guessed. She felt like a fool.

There was no one at the 'New Accounts' window, and she stood there with Thomas beside her for a minute or two before another clerk, another Irishman, came to it.

"You'll excuse me, ma'am," he said, "for not being here when ye came up. How may I be of help to ye?"

"I am interested in opening an account."

"Yes, ma'am," he said. "Then you've come to the right place." He handed her a small piece of cardboard. "If you'll just fill this out and bring it back to me," he said. "If you please." He nodded toward the tables in the center of the room. She understood now. They were sort of stand-up desks.

"Margaret Wilton," she wrote. "Bellevue-Stratford Hotel . . . Philip St. C. Wilton, deceased . . . Army officer" She had no credit references. And she had no idea how much money she wanted to deposit. She thought about that a moment, left the blanks unfilled, and returned to the window.

The Irish clerk looked at the card. "You're thinking of a household account, ma'am?" he asked.

"Yes," she said. "Precisely."

"You haven't listed any credit references."

"I have just arrived here," she said. "I have none to offer."

"I see," he said, not liking that at all. "And how much were you thinking of depositing, if I may ask?"

"One thousand," she said. "Pounds sterling," she added. "I have a letter of credit from the Bank of England."

"If you'll just wait here a moment, ma'am," the clerk said. He left his little cubicle and disappeared. She turned and smiled at Thomas. He was frowning. He was taking the sudden uprooting very badly, although there hadn't been many outward manifestations.

A middle-aged man in a frock coat suddenly appeared at her elbow. "Good afternoon, madam," he said. "My name is Ledderman, and I am the assistant cashier."

"How do you do?" she said. "My name is Wilton, and I wish to open an account."

"So I understand," he said. "And how are you, young fellow?"

"Quite well, thank you," Thomas said rather coldly.

"Did I understand the teller to say you had a letter of credit?"

"That is correct."

"Would you please come with me, ma'am? Step into my office?"

Thomas muttered something.

"What did you say, darling?" she asked.

He was, even though he had only turned seventeen, already taller than his mother. He bent slightly over her, held his hand to conceal his mouth, and whispered, "High time, I would say, that someone paid attention to us."

"Thomas!" she said, chastising him. But she realized he was right. Her step was more sure now than it would have been had Thomas not put things in perspective.

When she had been bowed into a chair, she started the conversation.

"I would like to open an account in the amount of one thousand pounds," she said. "The equivalent amount in dollars, I mean, of course."

"We'd be very happy to accommodate you, I'm sure. Mr. O'Malley mentioned something about a letter of credit?"

She took it from her purse, a document eight by eleven inches, ornately printed, with a gold seal and a red ribbon. The Bank of England would guarantee drafts against this document up to the amount of five thousand pounds sterling. Corresponding banks were requested to mark on the certificate the amounts advanced, and to present their drafts to Messrs. Morgan & Company of New York for payment.

"Precisely how much is that in dollars?" Margaret asked.

"Four thousand, two hundred dollars," Thomas replied.

"I was asking this gentleman," Margaret said.

"The lad is correct, Mrs. Wilton," the banker said. "Are you planning to be in Philadelphia long?" he asked.

"Permanently," she replied.

"Well, I hope this marks the beginning of a long and fruitful relationship."

"Tell us about your interest-bearing certificates of deposit," Thomas suddenly said.

"Well, I'd be happy to do just that, young fellow. The bank will pay an interest of three percent per annum for any funds you might care to entrust to us for at least one year," Mr. Ledderman said.

"And if we take the money out before the year is up, then what?"

"Then I'm afraid we couldn't pay the interest."

"But there would be no penalty?"

"No."

"Then that would be to our advantage far more than simply converting the letter of credit into dollars, wouldn't it?" Thomas asked.

"Yes, it would," he admitted. "Clever little chap, isn't he?"

"Yes, he is," she said.

"Mother, why don't you just open an account for, say, one thousand dollars, and then put the rest in an interest-bearing account?"

"Will one thousand dollars provide for your needs?" Ledderman said.

"If it doesn't, we can always take money out of the interest-bearing account," Thomas said. "We stand to loose nothing by doing that. And for every hundred dollars we don't need, there would be a hundred and three at the end of the year. Isn't that the way it works?"

"Yes, it is."

"I read the back of one of your deposit slips while Mother was filling out that form," Thomas explained. "The proposition this gentleman offered, of merely keeping the money against demand, would have seen that money go either to the Bank of England, if you didn't cash the letter of credit, or to this bank, if you did." There was the slightest hint of accusation in Thomas' voice.

"Well, then, Mrs. Wilton," Ledderman said quickly, "shall we say we open an account for one thousand dollars and place the rest in an interest-bearing account?"

"I suppose," she said, slightly hesitant, "that would be the thing to do."

"It would," Thomas Wilton said firmly and surely.

The third thing Margaret did in Philadelphia was walk with Thomas down South Broad Street to Strawbridge & Clothier's Department Store. There Thomas was outfitted in an entirely new wardrobe, costing very nearly two hundred dollars. It was men's clothing. It would have been unthinkable to dress a seventeen-year-old that way in England, but this wasn't England, and Thomas was not acting like a boy. He was acting like a man, and she realized that it wouldn't hurt a thing for him, under the circumstances, to appear older than he was.

He looked so darling in his suit, with the silk tie and the bowler, that she had a photograph of him made, and without thinking, ordered six copies. There was no one at all to send copies of the photograph to. She didn't have an address for her older son, John, and she certainly couldn't send any to England. For the first time, she realized how alone she was.

The hotel was outrageously priced. Nine dollars a day for the three rooms, $270 a month, reduced to $250 on a monthly basis. Food came to nearly four dollars a day, another $120 a month.

The obvious thing to do was to get a flat, or even a house.

On her third day in Philadelphia, after having made inquiries about enrolling Thomas at the University of Pennsylvania in the fall, Margaret got in touch with a rental agent.

Half a dozen blocks from the hotel, up toward the Schuylkill River, she was shown a brownstone house at 14 Rittenhouse Square that seemed to be precisely what she needed. There was something about the house, and the square itself, that made her feel less than a traveler in a strange and alien land. The park in the square itself was open to the public, something she felt was rather odd, but aside from that, it looked like a proper square.

The asking price of the four-story brownstone was $7,500, which Thomas quickly translated for her to mean nearly eighteen hundred pounds sterling. She was convinced that the price was negotiable downward. It seemed, she thought, from what little she knew of American property values, to be a fair price. Still, it was a great deal of money, and only the knowledge that she would have ample income from property settled on her enabled her to agree to it.

She had been perversely rather pleased to see how anxious the Duke of Chesterly was to get rid of her, and the boys, if the settlement was to be the criterion by which this could be judged.

There had been a moment almost of exulation when she had seen the official description of the Anglo-American Land

& Cattle Company, of which she was now the sole owner: "the assets of which may be described as comprising 115,000 acres, more or less, located in the state of Texas and in the New Mexican territories in the United States of America, together with all residences, farm buildings, timber and subterranean minerals, horses, livestock, fowl, and game, farm equipment, accoutrements, and supplies, all held in fee simple and without lien or other indebtedness."

One hundred fifteen *thousand* acres was equivalent to more than thirteen *square miles*. It was obviously an enormous estate. Trying as hard as she could to be the devil's advocate, she had asked herself why the duke had been willing to part with it. Part of his reason, of course, was that he had steeled himself to pay dearly to get her out of England. Another part of it was that the duke, getting on in years, had enough to do with the management of his own vast estates in England. And finally, Margaret had decided, it *was* in the American Southwest. It wasn't nearly as valuable a property as one-half, or even one-quarter, that much land would represent in England. By the duke's standards, it was something he could well afford to give up. By her standards, even placing its value at *one-tenth* of what that much land would be worth in England, it would, beyond question, provide an income more than adequate for her needs.

The property description of Lennai Mills, Inc., had been similarly succinct and encouraging: "the assets of which may be described as consisting of 160 acres, more or less, in the township of Lennai, County of Delaware, Commonwealth of Pennsylvania, in the United States of America, on which are situated a manufactory building complex containing twenty-four looms for the manufacture of wool and cotton cloth, together with 120 worker homes, together with miscellaneous equipment for the aforesaid manufacture."

There was, of course, no amount of money or property which could properly compensate either John or Thomas for the humiliation they would be forced to face. She had had to agree that she would not, and would see that her sons did not, at any time, in any way, communicate or attempt to communicate either with her family or that of the duke, or with "any persons with whom they had been associated in any part whatsoever of the British Empire," and that "she

17

would deny any familiar connection with any of them, excepting solely the late Lieutenant Colonel Philip St. C. Wilton."

He had even tried to get her to change her name. She had refused to do that. She would live up to her end of the bargain. She would deny any association with the Duke of Chesterly, the Marquess of Haverford, or anything connected with her former life. But she would not change her name. It would not be difficult for her to discreetly paint a picture of herself as the widow of an army officer, a lieutenant colonel, who had left her rather well fixed. But she was not going to allow anyone to think that she was someone's discharged mistress.

At the desk of the Bellevue-Stratford, she made inquiries regarding a visit to the Lennai Mills, Inc. Feeling quite the self-sufficient woman, she had decided that although the general manager, a Mr. T. Dawton, whose name had been given to her, would certainly be more than delighted to make whatever arrangements were necessary to show her, the new owner, the property, it might just well be in her best interests to show up unannounced. She would take the early train, the one that left at 5:25 in the morning.

The next day began badly. She had left a call for 4:15 and the maid who was supposed to appear at that hour with the tea failed to do so. Margaret woke up at five minutes to five, and there had been barely enough time to wake Thomas, dress hurriedly, and practically run to the railroad station, at Broad and Market, and find the proper track in that enormous and quite ugly building.

The train made good speed, however, and she consoled herself for the missed breakfast: When Mr. T. Dawton, as he certainly would, offered her "a little something" in his office, she would accept with alacrity. He would have in mind a cup of tea. *She* had in mind eggs, sausage, and toast.

There was no sign of life at the Lennai station, no one even came to collect a canvas sack marked "U.S. Mail" that had been thrown from the train. There was nothing in sight whatever except a boxcar sitting on a spur, and a dirt road leading over a rise. Since it was the only road leading anywhere, it followed that the Lennai Mills would be at the far end of it.

As the sun came out, Margaret regretted not having carried her parasol. The day was already hot and muggy, and if the muddy road was any indication, there would be rain. It was half a mile, perhaps a bit more, from the station to the gate to the mills, and by the time she came to the corner of the board fence, the hem of her skirt was soaked and mud-streaked. Thomas was sweating, and grimly silent beside her.

When she got to the gate itself, she was even annoyed and felt the first pangs of worry. There was no one in the gatekeeper's shack, and from the look of it, no one had been in it for a long time. When she looked up at the sign over the gate, she saw that letters were missing. It now said "LE NA M LS."

She looked at Thomas. He had taken in everything she had, but still had chosen to say nothing. His lips were slightly pursed, a look she remembered from his babyhood. It signified that he didn't like something, but was afraid to say so.

Margaret walked into the millyard. There were four buildings, she thought, but then looked closer and saw that it was but one building, with four steeply angled roofs. They looked like sawteeth, she thought, and then she understood the reasoning behind their design. The slanted part of the roof was glassed, to permit light to enter the factory. As she drew closer, she saw that she was right, but that the windows had gone so long without cleaning that they were now, if not opaque, then at best dimly translucent.

And when they got very close, she saw that there was no activity whatever within the first, or the second, or the third quarter. Only in the last section of the building, the one of which a portion had been set aside, according to a sign, for "MILL OFFICE," was there the sound of a loom moving its shuttle back and forth.

She pushed open the door to the mill room itself. There were four looms in it, but only two of them were apparently in use. A burly red-headed Irishman, sweating, and with lint stuck to his body with the sweat, was sitting on the stone floor, tools in hand, doing something to one of the looms.

Margaret walked over to where he worked. Four feet away, she could smell him. He paid no attention to her whatever.

"I say," Thomas suddenly said. "My good man."

The burly Irishman looked up, a look of displeasure on his

face. Then he let the tool drop to the floor and pushed himself backward with the palms of his hands, far enough so that he could stand up.

"I'm not your good man, sonny," he said. "But what can I do for you?"

"Who might you be?" Thomas demanded imperiously.

"I wonder," Margaret Wilton said with a smile on her face, "if you could tell me where we might find Mr. T. Dawton?"

The man looked them both over carefully. "Why should I be answering your questions?" he asked.

"Are you an employee of the mills?" Thomas asked.

"I don't know, lad, whether that's any business of yours or not," the man said.

"My name is Wilton," Margaret said. "Mrs. Margaret Wilton."

The name obviously meant nothing to him, but he put out his hand and gave her his name. She took his hand with what she hoped was grace; she didn't want to touch him.

"Mr. Finley," she said. "I've recently come into the ownership of Lennai Mills."

He pursed his lips. "And ye've come to tell us we have to get out, is that it?"

She sensed both repressed anger and resigned frustration. It was an emotion she recognized. She had been cornered and resentful and angry herself, from the moment she had walked into the Duke of Chesterly's morning room and seen him staring into the unlit fire.

"My dear ma—" Thomas began.

"Shut up, Thomas," Margaret Wilton said. He looked at her, pained, his eyebrows raised, his mouth open. "Please, dear," she said, softening it.

"My husband is recently dead, Mr. Finley," she heard herself saying. "Thomas has been taking his new responsibilities very seriously."

"Aye," the Irishman said. The one word said that he understood.

"The mills came to me as part of my inheritance from my late husband," Margaret said. "I had been led to believe they were fully in operation."

"I'm sorry to tell you then, mum," Mr. Finley said, "that someone's been lying to ye."

dead men. One could not really imagine being killed. But one

4

Many thousands of miles from Lennai Mills, Margaret Wilton's older son, John, nineteen years old and bone-weary, was fighting to stay alive in the barren, dusty mountains of northern India. A lieutenant in the Prince of Wales's Own Bengal Light Cavalry, John and his men had been on routine patrol when ambushed by rebellious mountain tribesmen. Eight of the troopers and one of the English sergeants were dead. The other sergeant and four more of the twenty-two troopers were wounded.

By the time the search party found Wilton, two more of the Englishmen had died and six others were wounded. Wilton himself, his khaki tunic shredded by rock, was using the carcass of his dead mount as support for the Lee-Enfield rifle with which he was returning the tribesmen's fire.

The captain of the search party put his two-pounder cannon into action immediately. The English had learned the hard way that the cannon's grapeshot, ricocheting murderously off the bare granite, was the only quick way to assure the mountain tribesmen's departure.

As they rode back to Tezpur at a walk, the captain saw how very much a boy Lieutenant John W. F. Wilton still was. Now that the pressure was gone, shock was setting in. He was having time to consider how close to death he had come. An ambush in the hills of the North-East Frontier was not at all like the glorious pictures of the cavalry painted for budding officers at Sandhurst. There were no trumpets, no guidons flashing at lance tips. There was heat and dust and thirst and death.

Mail in India being what it was, John Wilton had not yet heard of his father's sudden death nor of his mother's and brother's move to America.

Two weeks later, John Wilton was informed by his squadron commanding officer that he was to leave forthwith for Calcutta, where he was to attend ceremonies honoring HRH Prince Arthur, by special invitation of the royal family. The commanding officer was suitably impressed by the fact that the mother of one of his junior officers, Margaret Wilton, was lady-in-waiting to Princess Beatrice.

The smell of Calcutta and its squalor appalled John Wilton. He felt a moment's righteous indignation. England was bringing to these people a hope for a better life, and look at the bloody place! Whatever else was wrong with Tezpur and the hills of the North-East Frontier, it wasn't as bad as this indescribable poverty and filth. He was greatly relieved to step inside the clean, luxurious anteroom of the royal residence. A liveried footman led him into the library.

And there, in a sack suit, getting out of a chair was Prince Arthur.

"Your Highness," Wilton said, inclining his head.

"Ah, Wilton. Good to see you again," Prince Arthur said. "We've been getting splendid reports on you."

There were two others with him, one in the uniform of a lieutenant colonel of the Household Cavalry, and another man, older, in a morning coat.

Wilton bowed his head to each in turn. Prince Arthur had walked up to him, hand extended. His handshake was warm and firm.

"Your host, Sir William Montedale," Prince Arthur said. "And my aide-de-camp, Colonel Price-Cunningham.

"I so much want to hear, from someone actually involved, what's going on on the North-East Frontier," Prince Arthur went on. "But first, I'm sure you can use a whiskey."

"Very good of you, sir."

"Come sit down here," the prince said, pointing to the

chair facing the one he had just vacated. "Can we get this chap a cigar, Sir William?"

They spent an hour and a half together before Prince Arthur pulled a watch from his vest and announced that he would have to be going.

"May God preserve and keep you, my boy," he said, his voice suddenly thick. Then he let go of Wilton's hand, clasped him on either arm, and looked into his face. For a moment Wilton thought that he was actually about to be embraced.

"Well," Prince Arthur said. "Well. As I said, I have to be going. And you're going to have to change." He and Sir William marched out of the room. Colonel Price-Cunningham stayed behind. That was odd, Wilton thought.

"I would have a word with you, John," Colonel Price-Cunningham said, using his Christian name. "Perhaps we could talk while you're changing."

"Whatever you say, sir."

When they were in the large high-ceilinged bedroom which had been assigned to him, and John began to change his uniform, Price-Cunningham said, "I bear the fond wishes of your mother, John."

"That's very good of you, sir," Wilton said, thinking that explained everything. Price-Cunningham was a friend of his father's. He had seen to it that he had come to the attention of Prince Arthur.

"And a message of the sort one cannot put on paper," Price-Cunningham said.

"Sir?"

"She deeply regrets the circumstances, and begs you to believe they were otherwise."

"I don't follow you, sir."

"Have you wondered why you haven't heard from your mother recently?" Price-Cunningham asked.

"Yes, sir."

"Your mother has found it necessary to leave England," Price-Cunningham said. "Permanently. She and Thomas are now in the United States of America, specifically in Philadelphia, Pennsylvania. Your father . . . your father has regrettably passed on. My deepest condolences."

John Wilton sat, too stunned to reply. He had never felt

close to his father, had scarcely seen him all his life, yet his death shocked him. And his mother and brother in America? What did it mean?

"I have several documents for you," Price-Cunningham went on, and handed over two envelopes. One contained five hundred pounds in five-pound notes.

"That's for your traveling expenses once you reach America," Price-Cunningham said. "Your passage on the *Benjamin Franklin*, sailing at ten tomorrow for San Francisco, has been paid."

"Forgive me, sir, but I don't understand . . ."

"Your mother thought you might wish to inspect some property she owns in Texas and New Mexico on your way to Philadelphia," Price-Cunningham plunged on, visibly nervous. "Your assessment of it will certainly have an important bearing on her future plans."

"What are you talking about?" Wilton demanded.

"Among the property which came into your mother's hands," Price-Cunningham said, responding to a narrow question, rather than what Wilton knew he understood to be the larger one, "is the Anglo-American Land & Cattle Company. About the only assets, I'm afraid, are the lands in Texas and New Mexico, along their borders."

"With all respect, sir, what's going on?"

"Very well," Price-Cunningham said. "Certain events have transpired which make it impossible for your mother and brother to remain in Great Britain, and for you, I'm afraid, to remain one of her majesty's serving officers. I'm not at liberty to discuss the details."

"Has this something to do with Prince Arthur?"

"The second envelope you hold in your hand is your resignation," Price-Cunningham said.

"Resignation be damned!" Wilton said, but he opened the envelope. It was neatly typed on stationery of the King's Counsel's Residence.

Calcutta
3rd July 1890

To The Colonel Commanding
The Prince of Wales's Own Bengal Light Cavalry

Sir,
I have the honor to submit herewith my resignation, effective immediately.

John F. W. Wilton, MC
Lieutenant, 2 Squadron

"I'm afraid you have no choice in the matter," Price-Cunningham said. "As your mother had no choice in the matter. As Colonel Wilton had no choice in the matter."

Price-Cunningham went to a writing desk and pulled the chair out for Wilton to sit down.

"In good time, John, not only will this seem a good deal less painful than it does now, but you will understand," he said.

Wilton scrawled his signature on the resignation. "It says 'MC' on here," he said. "I don't have a Military Cross."

"You will at half-past six," Price-Cunningham said.

5

In Philadelphia, Paul T. MacSwain had just posted a letter to Mrs. Margaret Wilton regarding a business proposition about the Lennai Mills.

When there was no reply in a week, he sent another letter. And when a week passed without a reply to the second correspondence, he somewhat impulsively ordered round his cabriolet and told the driver to carry him to 14 Rittenhouse Square.

There was already a coach parked by the curb when he got there. He walked up the stone steps and twisted the doorbell. It was answered in a moment by an Irish maid.

"Good day to ye, sir," she said in a brogue that suggested she had gotten off the boat from County Derry a week before.

"Would you be good enough to give Mrs. Wilton my card?" he said. "And inform her that I would be most grateful for the courtesy of being received?"

The maid took his card, and, completely unbashed, read it and allowed her eyebrows to rise. The card read, "The Philadelphia and Norristown Interurban Rapid Transit Company. Paul T. MacSwain, President."

The card wasn't exactly representative of his position. He felt a slight pang of remorse as he handed it over. True, he had been president of the Philadelphia and Norristown Interurban Rapid Transit Company. He had, in fact, owned 90 percent of its stock. But he had, six months before, sold out.

The price had been right, and once he'd got the thing going, and running efficiently, he had wanted out.

He intended to do something new, the concept of which rather pleased him. There was going to be a market, long before anyone he knew dreamed there would be, for horseless wagons. These would be powered by electric storage batteries, and be used for in-city deliveries. There were some already running in such places as Paris, France, and London, England. They weren't quite practical yet, but it was MacSwain's judgment that was because the Europeans weren't quite as up on modern things as the Americans.

For several reasons—including the fact, frankly, that he didn't want his friends mocking him in personal and business matters—he intended to build his manufactory far enough outside Philadelphia so that visiting it would be difficult or impossible without advance warning.

He had set his people looking for a suitable small plant, with sufficient acreage to expand when that became necessary. They had come up, rather quickly, with the Lennai Mills. It met both the physical requirements he had established, and far more important, it had gone under. Or was so close to going under that it was one and the same thing.

He had attempted to make a deal with the English owners, who apparently were cut from a different bolt of cloth, and replied vaguely, if at all, to his London agent's inquiries. And then he had learned, both from his English agent and from friends in the First Philadelphia Bank & Trust Company, that title to the mills had come into the possession, somehow, of a widow named Margaret Wilton. Widow Wilton (who probably had been sold a bill of goods, but that was no skin off his nose) had come to the United States to supervise their operation.

A tall, pale boy in his teens, but dressed like a man, stood in the foyer when the door was opened again by the Irish maid. He tapped the card in his hand. "Mr. MacSwain, is it?" he asked.

"Yes, my boy, it is."

"I'm afraid I don't quite understand," the boy said, and MacSwain was both infuriated and unnerved by his awareness that he was being regarded with great suspicion by this child.

"You don't understand what?" he demanded.

"I was reading, just yesterday, that the Philadelphia and Norristown Interurban Rapid Transit Company, that is, its cars, were no more. That they had all been repainted to reflect their new ownership."

MacSwain's face colored. He was furious with himself. "I am the *former* president, the former majority stockholder." he said lamely, aware of how foolish he sounded. "I just haven't got round to having new cards made up."

"I see," the boy said. "And precisely what is it you wish with my mother?"

"I'll discuss that with her, if you don't mind," MacSwain flared.

"I'm afraid that you'll have to discuss it with me first," the boy said.

"I want to buy her damned mills."

"Oh?"

"And I'm prepared to pay a good price for them."

The boy had the insufferable arrogance to stand there tapping MacSwain's card against his cheek while he made up his mind.

"Very well, Mr. MacSwain," he said finally. "Mother is having morning tea. Perhaps you would be good enough to follow me?"

MacSwain had to restrain himself from storming away. But he had long ago learned that whenever he lost his temper, he lost money. He nodded, not trusting himself to speak, and took off his hat.

The maid looked at him with frank curiosity and made no move to take his hat. He stood there, he thought, like a damned beggar.

"Mary," the boy said, "you must, as I've told you and told you, take gentlemen's hats when they enter. Please try to remember that."

MacSwain's response to this was not gratitude. He would have eagerly given five dollars to any charity in exchange for permission to boot this arrogant young fop where he sat.

The boy led him across the foyer and slid open a door.

"Mother," he said. "A Mr. MacSwain to see you."

Widow Wilton was not the gray-haired lady of advanced years that Paul MacSwain expected. She was a blond lady

28

who looked hardly old enough to be the mother of the young dandy. She was sitting on one of two settees before a fireplace, in the process of pouring tea. On the other settee sat the Reverend Dr. Lawton Steele Houghton of Saint Mark's Episcopal Church.

"Mr. MacSwain," this stunning blond said, extending her hand.

MacSwain went to it. He had the odd notion that she expected her hand to be kissed. Instead, making what he recognized to be an awkward little bow, he took it and shook it gently. That seemed to amuse her.

"By chance," she said in a voice he thought sounded like a bell, "do you gentlemen know each other?"

"Indeed we do," the Reverend Dr. Lawton Steele Houghton said, "Mr. MacSwain is one of our more distinguished citizens. How good to see you, sir."

MacSwain had the distinct feeling that the reverend gentleman was lying through his teeth.

"It is always a pleasure, Dr. Houghton," MacSwain said.

"How nice," Mrs. Wilton said. "Milk and sugar, Mr. MacSwain?"

He looked at her and bit off what came to his lips ("Neither, thank you, I can't stand tea") just in time.

"Lemon, please," he said.

"Sugar?" she asked.

"One lump."

"Are you perchance one of Dr. Houghton's parishioners?" she asked.

"No," MacSwain said.

"Mr. MacSwain is a Presbyterian," Dr. Houghton said. "A traveler, as I like to think of it, with the same destination, by a different road."

"But that would presume, wouldn't it," Margaret Wilton asked innocently, "that you both wish to go to the same place?"

"Don't we all?" Dr. Houghton asked, surprised.

"I sometimes wonder," Mrs. Wilton said. "I for one would dread being in a Methodist heaven, with no cards to play. Or, for that matter, in a Roman Catholic one, where unless one knew Latin, one would be rather hard pressed for light conversation."

29

Dr. Houghton looked pained. MacSwain was aware that he was smiling. Houghton drained his tea and announced that he had to be going, that he would see Mrs. Wilton and Thomas at Sunday worship.

"Thank you for calling, Dr. Houghton," Mrs. Wilton said, omitting the near-ritual expression of regret that her caller had to leave so soon. "Thomas will see you to the door."

There was no conversation until the boy returned to the room and settled himself in an upholstered armchair.

"Now, Mr. MacSwain, what precisely is it that you wish from me?" she said. She looked right at him, out of light blue eyes that seemed to see right through him. He was disconcerted.

"I wrote a letter," MacSwain began, immediately correcting himself. "I wrote two letters, to which you did not see fit to reply."

"I did not consider a reply necessary," Mrs. Wilton said. "I thought you would take the point. That I was not interested in your business proposition." Her smile suggested that she was carefully explaining something very simple to someone who was not quite bright enough to grasp it.

"But you haven't even heard it," MacSwain said.

"You are a very determined man, aren't you?" she replied. This came across as a compliment. "Very well." She was now waiting for his proposition.

"If you will have the property assessed, appraised, by someone of your choosing," MacSwain said, "and I'm sure the bank would be happy to recommend a number of reputable appraisers, I will pay that figure plus ten percent."

"No, thank you," she said. "And now, if you'll excuse me . . . ?"

She got up and walked to the door, pausing for a moment to smile at him. And then she was gone. He still had his full cup of tea balanced precariously on his knee.

The boy stood up and waited wordlessly for MacSwain to put the tea down and leave.

MacSwain went directly from Rittenhouse Square to the First Philadelphia Bank & Trust Company. After exchanging masculine courtesies with its first vice-president, he asked for, and was given, the bank's records of its relationship with the Lennai Mills, Inc., and with Mrs. Margaret Wilton. Thirty minutes later, he knew in precise detail what the vice-president had told him in general terms.

Lennai Mills, Inc., through its manager, Mr. Thomas Dawton, had not only gone through essentially all of its operating capital, but had obtained a series of loans, secured by the mills and the property surrounding them, which were about to fall due. The recent expenses of the company had been limited to Mr. Thomas Dawton's generous salary and even more generous expense allowance. There had been no revenue at all for more than eighteen months.

That left two possibilities, both of which were quite credible. First, that Mrs. Wilton had additional funds of which the bank was not aware, funds sufficient to pay off the loans. Second, that she was a fool who didn't know the trouble she was in.

Paul MacSwain's driver was instructed to return to 14 Rittenhouse Square.

As he approached the house, MacSwain saw Margaret Wilton and that overdressed son of hers come down the stairs and cross the street into the square itself. Striking woman, he thought; magnificent carriage. He ordered the cabriolet to the curb and got off. Feeling somewhat foolish, he walked very quickly, nearly trotted, down one side of the square, and then turned right, finally slowing as he entered the walkway on which Mrs. Wilton and her son could be encountered.

There was, he thought, a faint sign of recognition when she saw him. He tipped his hat.

"Mrs. Wilton."

"Mr. MacSwain," she replied, exposing her dazzling teeth momentarily. She kept walking. He turned and caught up with her.

"What a pleasant coincidence," he said. "I had hoped to have another conversation with you."

"So I surmised when I saw you running around the square," she said.

"Madam, you exasperate me!"

"I can't imagine why," she said. "I'm very sorry if I do, however."

"I am a man of few words," he said. "I believe in getting directly to the point."

"Please do."

"I . . . uh . . ." MacSwain began, and then said something he had had no intention, or, for that matter, the wildest idea of saying. "I would be very honored, Mrs. Wilton, if you would take dinner with me."

The boy actually sniffed as if he smelled something distasteful.

Margaret Wilton looked at MacSwain and then at her son, and then back at MacSwain. He was about, he knew, to suffer some sort of incredibly painful humiliation at the hands of this blond Englishwoman.

"That is very kind of you, Mr. MacSwain," she said. He waited for the "but" he felt was as sure to follow as the night follows the day. It did not come. He realized, belatedly, that she was waiting for him to continue. As he struggled to put his confused thoughts into words, she did speak. "Did you have a date in mind?"

"Tonight," he blurted. "Would tonight be all right?"

"I am not very skilled at deception, Mr. MacSwain," she said. "I cannot be a hypocrite, or a liar, and say that I regret I have other plans for this evening. I do not, and I would be delighted to dine with you."

"Eight o'clock?" he asked. "Would eight o'clock be all right?"

"Eight o'clock would be fine, Mr. MacSwain. I'll expect you then. And thank you."

She began to move again. MacSwain stayed rooted where he stood. He heard the boy speak incredulously to his mother: "Why did you do that?"

"Because I wanted to, Thomas," Margaret Wilton said.

Paul MacSwain went directly from Rittenhouse Square to the Union League Club on South Broad Street. He had a sudden and quite unusual hunger not only for familiar surroundings in which he felt sure of himself but also for a drink, or possibly two drinks, of strong whiskey.

He stood at the long mahogany bar and ordered a Scotch whiskey with a slice of lemon. Surprising himself, he tossed it down neat and slid the glass back to the barman.

The whiskey seemed to clear his mind. Infatuated, that's what he was. There was something in that woman's chemistry that had kindled—kindled, hell, *ignited*—his own. It was a perfectly natural thing to have happened, if you considered the circumstances. Since he had lost Beth, not only had there been no other women, there had been no desire for one.

Beth's death had killed part of him, and for the very good reason that he was responsible for it. It was all very well to say that it was part of God's plan, but the inarguable fact was that if she hadn't borne his son, she would not have died in childbirth. He had come very close to taking his own life in the weeks that followed. There had been very little to live for. All his accomplishments seemed to have lost their value.

As he tipped the second Scotch to his lips, Paul MacSwain saw it all quite clearly. He had gone through, understandably, a period of great shock. He had first started to come out of it when he began thinking about electrical motors for delivery wagons. By God, at first he hadn't even shaved or dressed, just stayed in their bedroom and read, and—be honest with yourself, man—got entirely too cozy with John Barleycorn.

That had passed. He had come off a three-day bender and taken a look at himself in the mirror, unshaven, haggard, and told himself he owed his son more than that. So he'd stopped drinking, and that had been the first step. And the second step had been a rekindled interest in business, a desire to do something, to work. And the third and final step had been what had happened today. He had experienced a rekindling of the physical desires he had believed extinguished forever when Beth passed on.

And then Paul MacSwain had a shaming thought. The boy. My God, what was he doing here when the boy was home feverish and down with God alone knows what? He snapped his fingers for the bar tab, scribbled his initials on it with a pencil, and walked quickly away.

On the announcement board by the side of the wide stairway to the second floor was an announcement: "WEDNESDAY. MAIN DINING ROOM. LADIES' EVENING."

It was, he thought, as he hurried down the stairs to South Broad Street, beckoning to his driver, a very interesting coincidence.

6

The evening began badly and steadily proceeded to grow worse. He told the driver to have the cabriolet at his door at 7:45, and being a man of punctuality, Paul T. MacSwain was standing on his marble steps at 7:40, taking a few minutes to puff on a cigar (the Englishwoman probably would not like cigars) and to remind himself that he was in a position where he could very easily make a fool of himself with her.

The cabriolet did not appear at 7:45. It did not appear at all. The driver, puffing hard from the exertion of running all the way, appeared at five past eight to announce that as he crossed Cherry Street, he had run over a dislodged cobblestone, which had shattered the rim and two spokes in the right wheel.

He could—and did—telephone immediately to the stable to have a hack dispatched from the livery, but he could not telephone Mrs. Wilton because, for reasons he suspected had to do with her awful financial condition, she had not had a telephone connected.

It was 8:45 when he arrived at 14 Rittenhouse Square. He had gone there directly once the hack had shown up, and had not (as he had originally intended) stopped at a florist's shop to bring her some flowers.

The Irish maid, the one who had to be told to take his hat, answered the door. "Missus is eating," she announced.

"Would you please be good enough to tell Mrs. Wilton that I am here?" MacSwain said icily.

34

"What did you say your name was," she asked.

He was left standing like an errand boy on the stairway, the door closed in his face, for a good three minutes (which seemed to him much longer) until Margaret Wilton appeared.

"You'll forgive me," she said. "When it became apparent that you were unavoidably detained, in such circumstances that you couldn't send round a note, I decided to eat with Thomas."

"My coachman ran over a stone and broke a wheel," he said. "I apologize for any inconvenience."

"I see," she said. "Well, perhaps we can dine another time."

She started to close the door in his face.

"Mrs. Wilton," he said, suddenly furious, "it's not my fault the idiot ran over a damned stone!"

"You needn't swear at me," she said.

"Oh, God!"

"There you go again," she said, and then she laughed. "Do I provoke you that much?"

"Indeed you do, madam," he said. He tipped his hat to her and started down the stairs.

"Mr. MacSwain," she called after him. "We're having a simple supper here, which we would be delighted to share with you."

Instead of telling her what she could do with her simple little supper, he again found himself saying something he had no intention of saying. "I'd rather have you on my own ground," he said.

"I beg your pardon?" she asked, her eyes smiling.

"Tonight's Ladies' Night at the League," he said. "The Union League, on South Broad Street."

"I know nothing of Philadelphia," she said. "Is it the sort of place a woman of my position can be seen?"

"I assure you it is."

"Very well, then. Give me a moment to get my hat and coat."

She then closed the door in his face, giving him another three minutes to consider what an ass he was making of himself. Here she was, about to go down the drain, with no way out of it that he could see, save marrying a well-to-do man, and she was treating him as if he was trying to take her to some place of ill-repute.

Was she that clever? Had she already set her eyes on him? That damned Episcopal minister had said something about him being a prominent citizen. Was this her technique to snare him? By playing hard-to-get?

Well, he would fix her wagon. He'd take her to damned dinner and let her see precisely how prominent a citizen he was, and then he would take her home, and tip his hat, and that would be the last she saw of him. Period.

When she opened the door and swept past him down the stairs, he got a nose full of her scent. It was absolutely wicked. Very likely French. Well, as far as he was concerned, she could drench herself with it, and it wouldn't do her a bit of good.

The scent filled the hack on the way to the Union League. He defiantly put a large cigar in his mouth and lit it. The smell of a good Cuban cigar would not only overwhelm the scent, but would annoy her, and annoying her was precisely what he wished to do.

"I love the smell of a good cigar," she said, and smiled at him, and he found himself looking into those damned blue eyes again. "I sometimes wish I were Dutch."

What the hell did she mean by that? "Dutch? Why would you want to be Dutch?"

"Dutchwomen can smoke cigars," she said. "I had a . . . friend . . . who smoked cigars, and sometimes I've taken a puff or two."

"I'll be damned!" he said. "I've never heard anything like that before."

"I have shocked you," she said. "I'm sorry."

"You have not shocked me," he said firmly.

"I beg your pardon."

As they walked up the stairs of the Union League, she said, "This is rather nice, quite lovely actually."

"You didn't expect it to be?"

"I thought it was somehow connected with the labor movement."

What the hell did she mean by that?

"*Union* League," she said. "I thought perhaps it was a clubhouse for coal miners or some such."

"I can assure you it is not," he said. "The Union League . . . it makes reference to the Union. The United States union."

"It is rather a poor choice for a name, then, isn't it?" she asked, gently chiding him.

When the doorman held open the door for them, he took her arm and propelled her by the cloak room and then up the stairs to the main dining room.

The meal was ordered, but before it could be served, while he was sitting there wearing a stiff smile, the steward appeared. "Telephone, Mr. MacSwain," he said. "Your housekeeper."

MacSwain took the call in the steward's office.

The boy had a terrible fever. She was unable to reach Dr. McGrory on the telephone. She thought she had best notify him.

"I'll be right there," he said. "Send one of the maids round to McGory's house. Try to reach him at Hanneman Hospital."

MacSwain returned to the table. Margaret Wilton looked at him with concern in her eyes.

"I'm very sorry," he said. "But my little boy is ill, and I'm going to have to go to him. We're going to have to leave, I'm afraid."

"Of course," she said without hesitation, picking up her purse and standing even before he had finished speaking. As they quickly left the dining room, causing, of course, interested stares from others, she took his arm. It looked as if they were running away from something. What they all think, he thought, is that we have just been warned her husband is on the way here.

"Mrs. Wilton," he said, once they were in the hired hack, "would you very much mind being sent home alone? I realize that it's bad manners—"

"Don't be silly," she said. "You do what you have to do."

He ordered the hack to his house, and practically jumped out of it when they got there. He ran up the steps, unlocked the door, and then ran upstairs to the child's room. The housekeeper and the nurse were standing over the boy's bed. There was the smell of vomit in the room, and the child suddenly convulsed and threw up again as MacSwain looked at him.

The doorbell rang, and MacSwain felt a sense of immense relief.

"Well," he snapped at the nurse, "let the doctor in, for God's sake!" She scurried out of the room.

But when the door to the boy's room was opened again, Margaret Wilton swept into the room, not Dr. McGrory.

"It occurred to me that you might need me," she said. "That the child would."

She went to the boy, put her hand on his head, felt his neck, began to undress him.

"You'd better find a doctor, and you'd better find one right now," she said. And then she turned to the housekeeper and started to issue orders: she wanted wet sheets. She wanted sweet spirits of niter. She wanted an ounce of whiskey mixed with an ounce of water and a teaspoon of sugar.

"Move, woman!" she ordered.

When the boy was nauseous again, she picked him from the bed, carried him to a chair, and held him while he vomited into a basin.

Patrick J. McGrory, M.D., appeared at nearly midnight, deeply apologetic, and almost immediately confirmed Mrs. Wilton's diagnosis of scarlet fever.

"Have you any sweet spirits of niter in the house?" he asked. "And we'll need some spirits, too."

"I've already done that, doctor," Margaret Wilton said.

"You've had experience with scarlet fever, madam?"

"Both my sons have suffered from it."

"Then you understand the degree of contagion?" Dr. McGrory asked.

"Yes, of course," she said.

"I don't," MacSwain said.

"Well, Paul, everyone who has been exposed to the child will be quarantined for at least two weeks. You, this lady, the servants. The Board of Health will be around in the morning to put a sign on the door."

"My God!"

"And I'll arrange for around-the-clock nurses," Dr. McGrory said.

"That won't be necessary," Margaret Wilton said. "I can

manage with the housekeeper and the maids. Let them go to bed. They can relieve me in the morning."

"I don't know what to say to you," MacSwain said.

"There's nothing to say," she replied. "I like to think of myself as a Christian woman. I know I'm a mother, and that's what this tyke needs. A mother."

Tears welled in MacSwain's eyes.

Three days later, Paul T. MacSwain was himself stricken. And so was the housekeeper. The house was turned into an isolation ward. Food and other supplies were delivered to the rear entrance of the house and left before the closed door, which was not opened until the deliveryman had left.

MacSwain was quite ill, semidelirious. He had vague memories of being bathed, of being wrapped in wet blankets, of having his head held up so that he could take a little soup, of having his head held while he vomited seemingly without end. His glands swelled painfully so that any movement was painful. The room was kept in near-darkness. He had, however, a very clear memory of Margaret Wilton, little Edward riding on her hip, looking down at him.

And then, late one afternoon, the infection, or whatever it was that had kept him flat on his back, groggy, half-asleep, seemed to pass. The fever was gone, and most of the swelling. He lay there for about an hour, wondering what in the world he was going to say to her when she came in.

She did not come in. A nurse he could not remember having seen before arrived in the room, gave him something to drink, asked if he thought he could have some soup to build up his strength.

"Where is Mrs. Wilton?"

"She left this morning, sir," the nurse said. "When it became apparent that you were over the worst of it."

"And the boy?"

"She took the boy with her," the nurse said. "He's still pretty weak, and she thought that would be better for him."

Dr. McGrory appeared shortly afterward; he had been making two visits a day to the house. MacSwain wondered if this was because he had been so ill, or whether McGrory was trying to make amends for not having been available at first.

McGrory told him that he had been quite ill, which MacSwain interpreted to mean that he had come close to death. He also held a mirror up for MacSwain to see himself. His skin was peeling off; he looked, he thought, like a leper.

The boy, McGrory said, was in fine shape. He had gone by the Wilton home just before coming. "He's far better off there. Thomas has already had the fever, so there's no danger of infection. She sent the servants home, to protect them. And you're in no condition, Paul, to do anything but lie there until you recover. You look a fright."

MacSwain, having seen his reflection in the mirror, did not need to be told about his appearance, and he did not need to be told that he was in Margaret Wilton's debt.

"I have to use the telephone," he said. "How am I going to do that?"

"You don't have to do anything but stay in bed."

"Then get me a damned telephone in here!"

That was resolved by having a wheelchair delivered to the house that same afternoon. He was rolled to the top of the stairs. Two nurses helped him down the stairs, then reinstalled him in the wheelchair. He rolled to the corridor from the foyer to the butler's pantry, where the telephone had been mounted on the wall.

He called the bank's number, gave his name, and was connected with the president. Sitting in the wheelchair, he could not reach close enough to the speaking microphone to make himself heard. The nurses held him erect.

"Now, listen carefully to me, Fred. I stand behind any business indebtedness of Lennai Mills and any personal indebtedness of Mrs. Margaret Wilton. You understand what I'm saying to you?"

Margaret Wilton appeared in his bedroom that night. He had been sleeping, and somehow sensed that someone was in the room with him. He opened his eyes and found hers on him.

"I have taken care of things, everything, at the bank for you," he said.

"I don't quite know what you mean."

"I told them I stand behind your indebtedness, that's what I mean."

"You had no right," she said indignantly, "to intrude upon my personal affairs."

Goddamned exasperating woman!

"I came to assure you that Edward has recovered," she said, and he could see just how legitimately, honestly, inexplicably furious she was. "Having done so, I will say good night."

It was a full week before he felt well enough to get out of bed, ten days before he got dressed and had himself driven to Rittenhouse Square to reclaim his son. He took with him a nurse, a new one, a trained registered nurse, rather than someone who simply took care of children and called herself a nurse.

The Irish maid let him in, annnouncing that "Missus was bathing the baby" and not making a move to take his hat. He and the nurse followed her upstairs in the house. She flung open a door. Margaret Wilton, hair mussed, wearing only a skirt and blouse with the sleeves turned up, was on her knees beside a galvanized-iron bathtub. A pint of water and a delighted laugh erupted from the tub.

Margaret saw him. "Mr. MacSwain." she said coldly, "if you will give me just a moment, we'll finish our bath and get dressed."

Edward MacSwain, quite naked, emerged from his bath laughing and kicking. He was deposited on a dresser, dried with skill, and diapered. He was dressed in a nightshirt, and then he had his hair brushed. Margaret Wilton swung him easily over her hip (like a damned Indian, MacSwain thought) and walked toward them.

The baby was clinging to her with delight. MacSwain saw, and was shamed by his immediately flaming interest, that the water the baby had splashed on Margaret Wilton had soaked her blouse over her bosom. The effect was to make the fine cloth translucent, almost transparent. He could see her surprisingly large and dark nipples.

Margaret grabbed the boy under his shoulders and swung him playfully toward the nurse, finally handing him over. His smile vanished. His face contorted. He started to cry, then scream, and pushed at the nurse.

"He acts as if he's forgotten her," Margaret Wilton said.

"She's new," MacSwain said. "A real registered nurse."

Margaret Wilton snatched the baby back from the nurse.

He immediately clung tightly to her again, and stopped crying.

"That wasn't very smart of you, was it?" Margaret Wilton demanded. She comforted the baby, and then tried to give him to his father. The boy would have none of it. He acted as if his father were Satan himself. "Well, we know where we got that hard head, don't we?" Margaret Wilton said. She looked at MacSwain, the again instantly contented child riding on her hip, her nipple staring him in the eye. "We seem to have an impasse," she said.

"Yes, we seem to have an impasse," he said, aware that he sounded like a fool.

"Ordinarily I'd warm his bottom and give him something to cry about," Margaret said. "But he's still a bit weak, and I'm afraid we're going to have to give in to his hardheaded Scots temperament, at least until he decides to go to sleep."

He nodded.

"Why don't we have tea?" she asked. "He usually goes to sleep right after his gin."

Did she say "right after his *gin*"? "Did I understand you to say after his *gin*?" MacSwain asked.

"A slice of orange soaked in gin," she said, unabashed. "He's teething, you see."

"And you give him gin?"

"What do you think is the principal ingredient in teething medicine?" she asked, as if marveling once again at his overwhelming ignorance.

"I have no idea," he heard himself say.

"Alcohol, of course, and generally a narcotic of some sort. I think babies should not have narcotics. And he takes the orange slices like candy."

"I guess he would," MacSwain said. He then docilely followed her downstairs and watched her feed his son a slice of orange that she first carefully dipped in a glass of gin.

MacSwain took his tea from the Irish maid and looked at Margaret Wilton. So what, he decided, if she has set her cap for me? Even if the worst is true, even if she purposely set out to place me deeply in her debt, I could do a whole lot worse. Anything that baby wants and that I can provide is certainly my duty to provide. I could hire ten registered nurses and all of them together couldn't give him what she's giving him.

"Is there something wrong with my blouse, Mr. Mac-Swain?" Margaret Wilton asked. "You seem to be staring at it."

"Nothing at all, nothing at all," he said. He realized both that he had been unable to say six words coherently and that his face was flushing.

And then he looked at her, and saw that her face was probably just as red as his. After a long moment she said very softly, "I am sure that you must be aware that I was dressed to give Edward his bath, not receive gentlemen callers."

By God, he thought with something close to triumph, I have her off balance. It's about damned time.

"Margaret," he said, and it was the first time he had used her Christian name, "I have never seen anything quite so beautiful as you sitting there holding my boy."

And he saw with both triumph and warmth that those pale white cheeks flushed again.

7

John F. W. Wilton learned the American game of poker between Manila and Honolulu. At one time, he had been down nearly two hundred and fifty pounds, or more than a thousand dollars in U.S. of A. money. But by the time they had sailed into Pearl Harbor he had come, as he thought of it, to understand the philosophy of the game, and he was up five hundred dollars, most of it from the master, whose fault, John F. W. Wilton saw, was that his masculine concept of himself forced him to challenge a somewhat effete Englishman when challenging the value of his cards was not wise.

The master had taken his losses well. Wilton came to regard him as a gentleman, despite the man's obviously humble background. Wilton had been interested to learn from him that it was not at all uncommon in what he thought of as the American merchant navy, for a boy to go to sea at fourteen, and within ten years become a master, and, as in the case of Captain Connor, a high-ranking officer of the shipping concern itself.

Connor had come to think of himself as a friend to young Wilton, a friend close enough to offer almost paternal advice.

"You did the right thing, John," he had said. "In chucking the army and coming to America. A bright young fellow like you can go a lot further here than you could have where you was. There's no limit to what you can make of yourself."

The question, John F. W. Wilton thought privately, was not how high he could rise in the United States of America, but how low he had fallen. Something quite extraordinary had occurred in England. Obviously, it centered around his father's death. It had become increasingly obvious to him that his father's suicide (as he had later learned it to be, from his mother's long-delayed letter) had not been the result of his being temporarily bereft of his senses.

He had had plenty of time, as the *Benjamin Franklin* crossed the Pacific, to concoct a dozen different situations, arranging and rearranging in his mind what few facts he knew: that his father had committed suicide; his mother and brother had permanently left England; Prince Arthur and Colonel Price-Cunningham were not only aware of the circumstances, but felt sympathy, even pity, for his mother and himself. He could not imagine his mother voluntarily becoming an expatriate, but neither could he imagine his mother being involved in anything that would require her to give up her life, and her position, in England. It was certainly clear that Prince Arthur, which meant the royal family itself, was aware of what had transpired. Prince Arthur's own aide-de-camp had been the one to hand him his filled-out resignation.

Had his mother become involved with Price-Cunningham? Unlikely. With Prince Arthur himself? That was unthinkable, but what about the remark his highness had made at the investiture? That he was the son of the dearest friend he had ever had. At the time, Wilton had assumed naturally that his highness was speaking of his father.

Had his father committed suicide when he had learned that his wife, the mother of his sons, was having an affair with a prince of the realm? That was a likely set of circumstances, but it didn't really fit either.

Captain Connor had other advice to offer, and John Wilton had taken it. When he debarked from the *Benjamin Franklin*, he climbed into a carriage sent to dockside to pick up passengers with reservations at the Palace Hotel. He had no such reservations.

"You walk in there, John, and announce that you have reservations for a suite, and they'll find one. You mark my words."

He spent two days in San Francisco, long enough to have his laundry done and to make reservations on the Atchison, Topeka & Sante Fe Railroad to Loving, New Mexico Territory, and to send a telegram to his mother, announcing his arrival in America.

Wilton was quite impressed with Union Station when he went to board his train. It was spotless and had an aura of efficiency. Compared to the station in Calcutta, with its squalor, Union Station looked to him as symbolic of this *new* country in which he was apparently destined to spend the next part of his life.

He took the best accommodations available, what the Americans called a drawing-room compartment. It consisted of a sleeping room with private toilet and a connecting room equipped with plush-upholstered seating for four. The train pulled out of the station precisely on time at 12:04, and almost immediately a porter knocked at his door to announce that luncheon was being served.

A maître d'hôtel smilingly greeted him at the door to the dining car and showed him to a table set for four with crisp linen, shining flatware, and gleaming crystal. There was even a rosebud in a vase. An African steward in a crisply starched white jacket immediately presented him with a large menu card and poured iced water in a glass.

What happened next was quite as astonishing. Without so much as a by-your-leave, the maître d'hôtel showed first a couple and then another single gentleman to the empty places at Wilton's table.

The single gentleman, in his fifties, a chap with a bushy mustache, would have been a welcome companion, someone to speak to, but the couple was something else again. There was something about the man, something cheap and flashy, that he immediately disliked, and the man's wife, if that's what she was, while more than attractive, was obviously an Irish peasant.

The man insisted on offering both his hand and his name, and there was nothing to do but take the hand. He did not introduce the woman, but subsequently referred to her as "Katy here" and volunteered the information that they were bound for someplace called Pittsburgh, Pee-Aye, which after a long moment Wilton came to understand was a vernacular reference to Pennsylvania.

The man expressed an entirely uncalled-for interest in Wilton's destination, and announced that he could tell right off that he was English.

Wilton was aware that he had offered more information about himself than he intended. And as the food was served, Wilton's snap judgment of the man was confirmed. His table manners were actually offensive. He slurped his soup, and when he had his fillet, he rested his knife, when not in use, by clutching it, blade upward, in his fist, the fist resting on the table.

Try as he could to remind himself that he was in a new country, with different social standards, and that it would well behoove him to forget that he was born a gentleman, the couple nevertheless ruined Wilton's lunch. He excused himself as quickly as he could, and even forced himself to smile when the man said it had been a pleasure to make his acquaintance and would see him later.

About three-thirty in the afternoon, the mustachioed gentleman who had also been at the table knocked at Wilton's door. "Forgive the intrusion," he said. "I wondered if you played poker. It's a good way to pass the time."

"I have played some at poker," Wilton said.

"We could probably pick up some others in the parlor car," the gentleman said. "And there we'd have the steward to bring us drinks."

"I'll be right with you," Wilton said.

Within thirty minutes there were four at poker, the two additional players being chaps who identified themselves as "drummers," which confused Wilton somewhat.

Wilton was not surprised when they removed their jackets and turned up their shirt cuffs. He had learned from Captain Connor, aboard the *Benjamin Franklin*, that this was standard practice among poker players, demonstrating that those handling the cards had not slipped any up their sleeves.

After several hours, the stakes in the game, which had begun with five-cent and ten-cent coins "nickels" and "dimes", had risen tenfold. "Pots" now contained as much as three or even four dollars.

There was an announcement of dinner. No one seemed hungry. Wilton had been losing at first, had in fact lost more than he had won, but since he had begun to win more as the stakes had gone up, was now ahead about fifteen dollars. He didn't want to quit, and apparently, neither did any of the others.

The unsavory chap and his woman appeared among the kibitzers, greeting him and the other gentleman as long-lost friends and suggesting they have dinner together. Wilton was relieved that the other gentleman answered for him.

"Not now, thank you, we're playing cards."

Forty-five minutes later the unsavory chap was back. This time, again without invitation, he pulled up a chair and informed the man handling the cards to "deal me in."

The game was now growing more intense. A "cut" was made from the "pot," and a steward dispatched to the dining car for sandwiches. They would play through dinner.

The stakes continued to rise. Nickels and dimes were no longer in play. Pots and bets consisted of silver dollars and paper money. Mildly ashamed at his feelings, Wilton saw that the unsavory chap was an impulsive, that is to say, bad, player and lost steadily. A newcomer to the game seemed to be a consistent winner, and gradually Wilton began to wonder if he was cheating. He seemed to display an extraordinary facility when cutting, shuffling, and dealing the cards. It was entirely possible that he was a professional gambler. Connor had told him that there were men who made their living riding the cars and playing at cards. And if that were true, it was entirely possible that he was what Connor had referred to as a "mechanic," a mechanic being someone who could deal the cards to his advantage.

At a few minutes before ten, the unsavory chap, after waging a final bet of $7.50 on three queens, and losing to Wilton's full house of three sevens and a pair of fours, left the game as Wilton rather expected him to, expressing frustration with a foul vulgarity, clearly audible to the Irishwoman with him, and without regard for her gender. Although Wilton had not expected him to behave as a gentleman, he was still annoyed and quite glad to be rid of him.

The game lasted another thirty minutes. There were two winners. The man Wilton distrusted, who took, Wilton judged, about $175 from the game, and himself. He had won about $45. It had been a pleasant way to pass the hours.

He had just returned to his compartment, marveling at the complexity of the water closets aboard these American Pullman cars (the WC's on Royal Indian Railway sleepers were simply holes; attendants periodically flushed them down with buckets of water; on the Pullmans, each was equipped with its own automatic water supply), when he heard a knock at his door.

He opened it to find the unsavory chap and his Irish-woman standing in the passageway.

"I'd like a moment of your time, John," the man said. "If you don't mind."

John F. W. Wilton was offended at the man's use of his given name; he had given him no signal that he wished to be so addressed. And he certainly didn't want to talk to him.

"Just a moment of your time," the man pursued, and Wilton pulled the door open to him. The woman, averting her eyes, followed him into the compartment. "You just go in there, Katy," the man said. "While I have a word with John."

Wilton didn't like the woman being ordered into his sleeping compartment, either.

"What is this all about?" he asked rather coldly.

The man got to his point rather deviously, making reference to himself and John as fellow sportsmen who understood that sometimes the cards went your way and sometimes they didn't. The thing was, he had not only had a bad run of cards, but had been so sure that his luck had turned when he'd drawn the three queens, one after the other, that he'd bet a bit more than he should have, in an attempt to recoup his losses. He'd bet, in fact, just about his last dime, and John, as a fellow sportsman, knew well how that sometimes happened.

Was this fellow actually asking for his money back? Good God!

"I don't quite understand what it is you wish of me," Wilton said.

There followed another devious explanation of what the bounder had in mind, so diverse, with its references to the length of their journey, and how Katy had spotted him right off as a real gent, that it took Wilton some time before he finally realized that this scoundrel was actually—for a "temporary loan of twenty dollars"—offering Wilton his woman.

"No, thank you," John F. W. Wilton said, aware that he was at the edge of his temper.

"She'd give you a good time, John," the man said. "Anything you'd want, if you know what I mean."

Wilton, fighting to retain control, glanced into his sleeping compartment. He met the eyes of the woman, who returned his look without expression.

"Take off your blouse, Kate," the man said. "'Show John what you've got."

The woman exhaled, a long, resigned sigh, and put her hands to the button of her blouse.

Wilton, who had his arms folded behind him, was suddenly aware that he was shaking with rage, that he had his jaws clenched so tightly they hurt.

"By God!" he said, the words exploding from his throat. He grabbed the man by the lapels of his coat and picked him off the floor. He slammed him against the door, and then, holding him with one hand, cocked his fist back to smash him in the face.

"Oh, God, please don't," the woman said, and he felt the pressure of her hands on his poised arm. He looked down at her. "Please," she repeated, and then again, "please don't. Just let him go."

Wilton, trembling, finally lowered his fist. He moved the man to one side, pulled open the door, and threw him violently into the corridor. The woman squeezed past him. He closed the door and leaned against it, suddenly exhausted.

It took him a moment to regain control of himself, to consider his options. His first impulse was to summon the conductor and apprise him of the facts. But that would harm not only the cad and scoundrel, but the woman as well. She was obviously under the man's influence. Whatever happened to the man, he would take it out on the woman. The thing to do, rather than create a sticky situation, was simply put the whole business out of his mind.

Wilton went to the lavatory and splashed water on his face and combed his hair. Then he checked his cravat in the mirror and walked to the door. He pulled it open, half-expecting to find the rotten whoremonger where he'd thrown him into the aisle.

But the aisle was deserted. The man had fled. At this very moment, Wilton thought, he was in his compartment waiting nervously for the rap of the conductor's knuckles at his door.

The thought of that pleased Wilton, and he walked toward the parlor car.

He had a cigar and two glasses of brandy with two gentlemen from the poker game. He decided, after some thought, that he would not mention anything about what had transpired in his compartment. They spent the next few hours congenially playing craps, and Wilton found himself winning over one hundred dollars.

It was one o'clock when he made his way back to his compartment. Remembering one more thing Captain Connor had told him—sleep on your wallet—Wilton laid it on the plush upholstery as he undressed down to his linen. He carried the billfold in his hand as he entered his sleeping compartment, intending to slip it into the pillowcase before shedding his linen and putting on his nightshirt. He bent down for the pillow, and then there was a sudden blinding pain at the base of his neck, and he felt himself falling forward.

He never completely lost consciousness. There were sensations of being manhandled, and waves of pain, accompanied by a sense of the color red, and then a sensation of being paralyzed.

And then, quite clearly, he saw a woman's face close to his. He tried to speak but could not; something was in his mouth.

"Los Angeles," she said. "Los Angeles." He had no idea what that meant, but he recognized her as the Irishwoman.

"What did you say?" He heard a man's voice, and then Katy's face suddenly vanished, as if she had been pushed away. "Oh, you're awake, are you?" the bastard said, and Wilton had a fleeting glimpse of something in the scoundrel's hand as it flashed toward his head. There was a moment's pain, again the sense of the color red, and then a final smashing blow, accompanied by an explosion of light in his brain, and then blackness.

8

John F. W. Wilton became gradually aware that his hands and feet were painfully asleep, and then of something, a soggy mass of cloth, in his mouth. He coughed and choked, and for a moment had a frightening belief that he was about to die, but then the force of his exertions loosened mucus in his nose, and with effort he was able to swallow it and breathe through one nostril. With a massive effort he forced his lungs full, and then exhaled. More mucus was expelled, but it was a full minute before he had his breath.

At that moment, the train began to move. He was lying on his side, his arms tied behind him. The upper arms were tied around his chest, and the wrists, lashed together, were also tied to his lashed-together feet, which had been drawn up behind him tightly.

He tried to roll over on his back. The pain, as his arms pulled against the sockets, was excruciating. He let himself fall on his side again. He was tempted for a moment to just lie there and wait for someone, the steward or the conductor, to discover him. But whatever it was with which he was bound had been placed so tightly that his circulation had been cut off. If he didn't manage to get free, it was entirely possible that he would lose his hands.

In Bengal, the Pathan mountain tribesmen had often, with their exquisite sense of cruelty, done intentionally just this to captive native troopers. Handless, or footless, prisoners set loose were far more effective a means to create terror than dead men. One could not really imagine being killed. But one could vicariously experience being handless. Wilton had no intention of permitting that to happen to him.

He wiggled and squirmed, and finally reached the edge of his bed. If he continued, he would fall over the side. If he fell wrong, he would land on his back, and stressed as they were, either pull his arms from their sockets or break them.

It would be necessary to roll over, so that he landed on his chest and face. This took a good deal of effort, doubly difficult because of the trouble he had breathing around the mass of cloth in his mouth and his mucus-clogged nasal passages, and once he got on his back, the pain was even more excruciating than he thought it would be. But it was also proof that if he had landed on his back he would have seriously injured himself.

With one mighty heave he hurled himself over the edge. He had hoped to hit on his chest. He hit, instead, on his face, and he felt blood begin to fill his nostrils. If he continued to struggle, to make his way to the door, he would very likely choke on his own blood. The only thing to do was to stay as immobile as he could, his head raised as high as he could hold it, so that the blood would drip out of his nostrils until it naturally coagulated.

Eventually he reached the door. Very deliberately he positioned himself sideward to it, and then began to bang his head against the wooden panel above the baseboard. Every time he banged his head, the base of his neck sent a wave of pain down his spine.

And then, suddenly, there was someone in the corridor.

There came two raps at the door. "Suh? Suh?"

The porter. He banged on the door again with his head. "Suh?"

He smashed his head against the panel again. There was a click, and then the door shoved painfully against him.

"Sweet Jesus!" the porter said. "Lord, Sweet Jesus!"

The porter stepped around him and knelt down. He tried for a moment to untie whatever it was holding the cloth against Wilton's mouth, and then gave up. He reached in his boot and came out with a glistening straight razor.

"You just hold still one second, suh, and I'll have you out of this."

53

Something fell away from his face. Wilton pushed at the mass in his mouth with his tongue. It fell out. He was racked by coughing, every cough causing pain in the back of his head and in his shoulder sockets.

"Cut the damned ropes free!" he finally managed to blurt out.

"I'm working on it, suh," the man said. All of a sudden his bent-double legs were set free. They slammed painfully onto the floor. He felt the man working on his wrists. When the pressure of what he learned a moment later were rawhide leather thongs was released, he thought he would scream with pain as the blood surged into his hands.

"Let me help you into the seat, suh," the porter said. "And I'll get the conductor."

Effortlessly the porter picked him up and set him on the plush upholstery in the drawing room. Wilton's arms were still tied to his sides, around his chest. The porter cut these thongs away, looked for a moment at him, and then left.

Wilton forced his hands in front of him. They were swollen to twice their normal size, and almost black. With an effort of will he first spread the fingers, the pain making him light-headed, and then made as much of a fist as he could.

"What happened to you, young fella?" the conductor said, coming into the room.

"I've been attacked and tied and robbed," Wilton exploded.

"Do you know who did it?"

"A man accompanied by an Irish trollop," Wilton said, painfully working his hands from spread to fist.

"There was a gentleman and a red-haired lady got off at Yuma," the porter said. "They was ticketed to Phoenix."

"Too bad, son," the conductor said. "By now they're long gone."

"Where is Los Angeles?" Wilton asked.

"A little fishing town on the California coast," the conductor replied. "If you think they've gone there, we can send a wire at the next stop. But we're going to have to have a better description of them than the one you gave us."

Wilton had enough feeling in his legs to try to stand up. He stood and collapsed against the porter. He hung on him and made his way to the washroom. He looked awful. There was an angry two-inch-wide bruise on his face, apparently from the last time he had been struck. His lower chin was covered with dark, drying blood. For some reason, his left eye socket was dark.

"He really worked you over, didn't he?" the porter said with something like awe in his voice.

"When," Wilton asked, "is the next train from Yuma to Los Angeles?"

At Kofa, Arizona, Atchison, Topeka & Sante Fe Number 117, was flagged to an unscheduled stop. A tall young man, showing every evidence of recently having undergone a severe beating, got aboard. He had in his possession a pass from the conductor of the *San Antonio*, authorizing him to travel anywhere on the AT&SF, courtesy of the line, for the next fourteen days. The *San Francisco* conductor noticed that while he didn't have any luggage, the young man did have a large, strange-looking revolver stuck in the waistband of his trousers.

At exactly 7:15, on schedule, the *San Francisco*, having easily made up the five minutes the unscheduled stop at Kofa had cost, pulled into Yuma, Arizona. Wilton's assailant and the woman were standing on the platform waiting to board the train.

Wilton, who had been standing on the stairs of his car, was sure the woman had seen him, and when the train had finally slowed enough for him to jump safely from it, he was surprised to see that she was still standing beside the man.

He had his Webley out of his trousers now, holding it, muzzle downward, in his hand. He walked slowly toward them. The woman was looking squarely at him now, but still she didn't warn her companion. But the man sensed that she was looking at something, and turned and looked over his shoulder. It took him a moment to realize that it was indeed Wilton, and then he started to run. Wilton started to run after him. In ten yards, it was evident that he wouldn't be able to catch him.

He stopped running. He held the Webley over his head and fired. The sound of the cartridge going off was remarkably loud. But it didn't stop the man. If anything, he picked up speed.

Wilton, without really thinking about what he was doing,

stood erect, turned his right side toward the fleeing figure. It was the classic, formal stance of pistol marksmanship he had been taught at the junior officers' school at Jamshadpur.

He fired. The Webley rose in recoil. He thought he saw the man stumble. But then he began to run again. Wilton aligned the sights and fired again. The man fell forward onto his face.

Wilton ran after him, aware first of the red-headed woman, who looked at him with terror in her eyes as he ran up to and then past her. And then he became aware of the people on the platform, either standing rooted in place, as the woman was, or scattering out of his way.

He ran closer to the man, and then stopped. He had shot him in the leg, the upper right leg. The man was clutching it with both his hands, in some agony.

Something poked Wilton painfully in the back. He turned in anger and surprise and saw a man in railroad uniform backing away from him, holding a shotgun at his shoulder.

"I don't want to kill you," the man said. "So you just bend down and put your pistol on the ground."

"That man," Wilton said, "robbed me."

"Put the goddamned pistol down, goddammit!"

The man was obviously very nervous. Wilton very slowly laid the Webley .455 on the ground.

The man on the ground looked at Wilton. "You son of a bitch," he said indignantly. "What did you have to do that for?"

A law-enforcement official of some sort, not in uniform, a sheriff, appeared.

"The man you shot said he never saw you before in his life," the sheriff said after he'd made a preliminary inquiry into the affair.

"I have told you, my good man," Wilton said, with the righteous indignation only a wronged upper-class Englishman can muster, "that he robbed me and left me trussed up on the railway cars."

"But how do I know that?" the sheriff demanded.

"Unless he has had the opportunity to sell it, I think you will find him in possession of my watch, in addition to my money," Wilton said. "The watch is a Perrigaux, in a hunting case, and it will be engraved, within the case, 'From Lieutenant Colonel Wilton to Subaltern Wilton, Sandhurst, May 1888.' "

The man had the watch, engraved as described, in his pocket. The sheriff, who had picked up and been holding the Webley .455, handed it back to Wilton.

"And the woman with him," the sheriff asked. "Was she involved in it?"

Wilton had quite forgotten about her. A short, bald, muscular man with a badge pinned to his leather vest was holding her firmly by the arm. There was fear in her eyes, the look of a trapped animal.

"Well?" the sheriff asked. Wilton looked back at him. He was going through the wounded man's pockets, emptying their contents onto the ground.

"No," Wilton said. "I never saw her before."

The sheriff nodded. "How much money did he steal from you?"

"Two thousand, four-hundred-odd dollars," Wilton replied.

The sheriff nodded again. "You come with me, please, sir," he said, "and we'll get your statement written down."

The administrative details of the affair were explained to Wilton in the sheriff's office, once he had written down an account of his assault and robbery. Armed robbery aboard a train in the Arizona Territory was a federal offense. The man would be held for the United States marshal, who would appear in Yuma again in about three weeks. Wilton's statement, plus that of the sheriff and other witnesses, would be sufficient to bind the man over to the territorial grand jury, which sat in Phoenix every month. In the sheriff's opinion, the grand jury would return an indictment, which would bring the man to trial. At that point, Wilton's presence, to give personal testimony, would be required.

"But I won't be here," Wilton said.

"In that case, they'll have to turn him loose," the sheriff said. "You really shouldn't have told me that. Now I'm supposed to hold you as a material witness."

"And are you?"

"I didn't hear what you said," the sheriff said.

The sheriff was obliging in other ways. He returned Wilton's money, permitting the polite fiction that by the time he had arrived on the scene, Wilton had already reclaimed his property, except for the watch. The watch he could return without question, since it bore Wilton's name.

Wilton had a good deal of time to pass, nearly sixteen hours, before the next day's train arrived in Yuma. He took a room in the crude hotel and managed to sleep several hours before the pain in his face and at the base of his neck woke him. He went to the bar and drank a good bit of whiskey, to deaden the pain, and then he walked around the town, examining with interest the adobe construction of the buildings, the Spanish influence on the architecture, if it indeed could be called architecture.

He came across a Mexican saddlery, and studied with fascination the construction of the saddles, so different from an English saddle, and their silver decoration. And then he permitted the craftsman to make him a holster for the Webley. He didn't think much of the American holster design, a soft leather socket with a covering flap from which it would be quite difficult to hurriedly remove the weapon. He understood the necessity for the covering flap in this dusty environment, but he thought the design faulty. On a scrap of paper he drew a pencil sketch of what he wanted the man to make. An inch-and-a-half strap over the left shoulder held the holster under his left arm, butt forward. A second, half-inch strap held the holster against his side by circling his body. The holster itself was of saddle leather, rather than thinner, flexible material. The pistol was held in the holster by gravity and the pressure of his arm.

The Mexican craftsman, after some confusion, finally understood, and bubbling enthusiastically, went to work, cutting and stitching the leather with a skill and facility that would have earned him a master saddler's spot anywhere in London. And when he was finished and Wilton put the device on, not only was he nearly unaware of the weight of the .455 Webley, but with his coat in place there was no sign whatever that he was armed.

He returned to the hotel and had supper in its dining room. The food left a good deal to be desired, and he was momentarily humiliated when he took a large bite of a small green pepper and found that not only did his eyes water from the heat, but that he was rendered dumb and had to gesture for water to put out the fire.

After another night's rest, Wilton was feeling rather sprite despite the throbbing pain in his face and neck, and boarded the train with quick, light steps. He removed his jacket and cravat and unstrapped his Webley .455 in its new holster as the train pulled out of Yuma. There came a discreet knock at his door. Wilton opened it grandly, finding himself face to face with the red-headed woman.

"What can I do for you?" he asked after some moments' pause. She didn't look quite as frightened, as desperate, as *desolate* as she had the last time he had seen her, with the deputy holding firmly to her. But there was still something about her that reminded him of a frightened small animal, a gazelle, perhaps, or a young doe, startled by a sound in the bush.

"You can let me in before the conductor asks me for a ticket," she said quickly. "I don't have one."

Wilton stepped back into the compartment. She entered and closed the door.

"What are you doing here?" he asked. "What is it you wish of me?"

"I couldn't stay there."

"Isn't that your place?" Wilton said. "He is your husband," he said, and it was more of a challenge.

"Huh!" she snorted. "Husband!"

"If he is not your husband, then what were you doing with him?"

"What did it look like?" she asked.

"Oh," Wilton said. "I see. Quite."

"Oh," she mocked. "I see. Quite." She put her fingers on his face where the man had struck him with his bludgeon. "God, he really did a job on your face, didn't he?"

"While you watched," Wilton said.

"What was I supposed to do? I did what I could. I wasn't going to get myself killed because of you. I never saw you before in my life."

"I suppose you have a point," Wilton said.

"You got back your money," she said. "If it wasn't for me, you wouldn't have it."

"If it wasn't for me, you would be in the prison in Yuma." Wilton really found her quite annoying.

"But if it wasn't for me," she said determinedly, "you wouldn't have gotten your money back."

He understood that she had carefully thought out this line of reasoning, perhaps even rehearsed it.

"What I was hoping was that you could see your way clear to letting me have enough money to get back to Philadelphia."

"Why should I do that?" he asked. Her cheek was really incredible.

"Because without me, you wouldn't have gotten your money back," she said again. "My baby's in Philadelphia," she explained. "With the nuns." She put her hand to her face, rubbed it, and then looked at it. "Jesus, I'm filthy!" She saw his look and went on, "And so would you be, if you'd spent all day trying to stay out of the sun in that stinking little village."

"Why . . ." Wilton began, intending to ask why she hadn't gone to the hotel, and then knowing, and being shamed by the obvious answer: she didn't have any money.

She looked at him. "Why what?"

"Why don't you go in the facility?" Wilton asked. "And wash up, I mean."

"Then I can stay?" she asked, jumping at the opportunity.

There was no way in the world he could say anything but what he did. "Yes, you may stay." He added, "In here. I have no intention of giving you my bed."

She nodded, then, moving past him, walked into the facility, closing the door.

9

When the red-haired woman came out, a good ten minutes later, she was wearing only her blouse and skirt. She had removed her jacket and hat.

"I'm going to have to do something about clothes," she said. "Mine were in his bags, and I couldn't hardly go ask that sheriff for them, could I?"

She was far less unattractive now that she had washed the dust off. Her skin was white, and here and there lightly freckled. Her red hair was freshly combed. That meant, he realized, that she had used his comb, for obviously she had none of her own.

"I don't suppose you have anything to eat, do you?" she said. "Or that you'd be willing to get something from the dining car? I haven't had a damned thing to eat in twenty-four hours."

How could he possibly think of himself as a Christian, or even a gentleman, and fail to respond to that?

He pushed the bell, summoning the porter.

"It would be best," Wilton said, "if you waited quietly in there." He handed her her hat and coat, and when she had gone into the bedroom, closed the connecting door after her.

"Yah, suh?" the porter said. "Something I can do for you?"

Wilton ordered the kind of dinner he felt someone who had spent a harrowing day would want. "I would like a steak, extra large, and some *pommes frites*, and several eggs," he said. "And coffee, plenty of it, and two slices of pie."

When the porter left, he opened the connecting door and motioned the woman out.

"You were telling me about Philadelphia," Wilton said, "You have a child there, you say?"

"With the good nuns at St. Philomena's," she said. "I'm going to get her and raise her. It's not her fault she's no father."

"No, of course not," Wilton said, taken aback yet again. "You have employment in Philadelphia?"

"I have employment, as you put it, wherever I am," she said. And then she was amused. "Or practically anywhere."

He caught her meaning.

"You don't seem at all embarrassed about it," he said, aware that he sounded quite prissy.

"You don't need to be embarrassed about things you can't help."

They were interrupted by the arrival of the food. The woman ate everything set before her, and then reached over without embarrassment and forked his half-eaten, obviously unwanted eggs, and ate that, too. Then, without saying a word, she began to take the dishes and bowls from the table and set them outside the compartment in the passageway. When she had finished, she helped herself to a small drink of Scotch whiskey.

"Well, that's one problem solved," she said.

Wilton said aloud what he had been thinking. "As near as I can figure, I won one hundred and seventy-five dollars from your . . . companion. I will give you that."

He took out his wallet and counted out the money. "That should be enough to get you through to Philadelphia," he said. "And perhaps to keep you going until you could find honest employment."

"Honest employment, ten hours a day, six days a week," she replied, "pays seven dollars and a half a week. I make that much on my back in four hours."

"And that doesn't shame you? That doesn't shame you at all?"

"I would rather be married to the Prince of Wales," she said. "Or the chap what owns the Norristown Interruban Rapid Transit, but they haven't asked for my hand."

"Surely there are men, good honest men, of your own class, who would be willing to marry you. You're a rather attractive woman."

"Well, thank you. I didn't think you'd noticed. But ye miss my point. *Why* would they want to marry me? To get me on my back, for sure. But also to cook their food, and wash their clothes, and all the rest of it, while they spend their money in barrooms. My trade isn't all that bad, I've learned. Particularly if you have ambition."

"Ambition?" he asked incredulously.

"My own house," she said. "A high-toned place, catering to gentlemen like yourself . . . you know what I mean." She stopped in embarrassment. "With girls, I mean. A clean place, with a regular clientele. I worked in a place in Philadelphia like that for a while. Before I let myself be talked out of it by him."

There was a moment's silence, in which it became evident that she didn't want to talk about this anymore.

Wilton also had had enough conversation. His head had begun to throb mercilessly, and there was an unbearably noisy ringing in his ears. He lay down on the bed and pulled the sheet up over him. He closed his eyes, and there was a terrible surge of pain, almost a flaming sensation, and he went under.

John Wilton woke up vaguely aware of something white, something painfully white, coming quickly up to him, and then of firm, gentle hands pushing him back down on the bed.

"Now, you just take it very easy," a female voice said to him. "You're going to be all right, by the grace of God."

He lost consciousness again.

When he woke the next time, he looked carefully around. He had difficulty focusing his eyes. The whiteness returned, and a female face, a nursing sister, to judge by her headgear, bent low over him and looked into his eyes. Fingers spread his eyelids.

"Can you hear me?" she asked.

"I can hear you," he said. "I'm thirsty."

A glass of water was tipped to his lips. He had never tasted anything quite so good. He wanted all he could get. The glass was removed.

"More!" he said.

"Not just yet," she said. "I'll have to go for Father. He'll give you some water, possibly."

She went away. Wilton raised his head, trying to focus. They fell upon a crucifix hanging on the wall. It wasn't an abstract sculpturing of Wilton's Lord and Savior. It looked like a little doll nailed to a wooden cross. It was plaster, and the plaster had been painted. Christ's beard was black. He had a white loincloth, a golden crown of thorns, and bright red blood dripped from his hands and feet.

A man in a long white, high-collared coat came and stood by the bed. "How do you feel?" he asked.

"Get me some water," Wilton said.

The man gestured to the nurse, who handed him a glass, which he then held to Wilton's lips.

"I am Father duKley," the man said. "I'm a doctor. Do you know your name?"

"Of course I know my name," Wilton said. "Where am I?"

"In the San Juan Hospital in Phoenix," the priest said. "What is your name?"

"John Francis William Wilton."

"And do you know what has happened to you?"

"I damned well do! I was bludgeoned twice."

"You may leave us, Sister," the priest said. "Have the kitchen boil a couple of eggs for Mr. Wilton."

The sound of the word seemed to trigger a response in Wilton. He felt his stomach churn. He was famished. He tried to sit up. The priest pushed him back down.

"You have a fractured skull," he said. "And you have experienced a concussion."

"How did I get here?" Wilton said.

"Your . . . uh . . . *friend* brought you," the priest said. "From the railroad station."

"I'll need to speak to some law-enforcement officer about her," Wilton said. "I want her prosecuted."

"Oh," the priest said. "I think I understand. You believe you were struck again."

"Wasn't I?"

"Not as I understand it," the priest said. "While you were

64

aboard the second train, the concussion made itself known. The . . . uh . . . tension of the situation finally brought it on. Your friend was quite upset."

"Where is she now?" Wilton asked.

"In the city. At the hotel. I managed to convince her, after the third day, that she was doing nothing around here except getting in our way. You have been here eight days."

Later that day, after he'd had something to eat, the priest told Wilton in more detail of his diagnosis and prognosis. The beating he had taken had both fractured his skull and caused the concussion. Blows such as he had suffered frequently caused death or blindness. However, now that Wilton had regained consciousness, the odds were that he would experience no further difficulty.

The woman—he remembered now her name was Kate— Kate had not absconded with his money. She was waiting for him in town. When he dressed and found that there was only about fifty dollars in his wallet, he was told she had taken it for safekeeping.

He would, Wilton decided, show his appreciation of this behavior by advancing her another $200 or $250.

He paid the hospital, a charge so small he was embarrassed to the point that he gave the priest an additional twenty-dollar gold piece for the poor, and then had himself driven into town, to the Marshall House Hotel.

After first making inquiries and finding that the next train to Loving, New Mexico Territory, would not be until the following morning, he asked as to the woman's location. With a knowing smile that Wilton could not quite understand, the desk clerk informed him that a woman meeting his description, a red-headed Irisher, could doubtless be found at Miss Allen's Boardinghouse.

She was probably, Wilton decided, conserving funds, so that there would be adequate money to get her child from the foundling home in Philadelphia. That was commendable. But he certainly had no intention of staying at a boardinghouse, which he understood to be the American equivalent of the European pension.

He took a room, the best the Marshall House had to offer. Since he had no baggage, payment of $1.50 was demanded in

advance. He paid it, trimmed his mustache, and then set out
to find Kate.

The first inkling that things were not as he had pictured
them came when he quite politely raised his hat and inquired
of a lady on the street if she would be good enough to give
him direction to Miss Allen's Boardinghouse.

She looked at him in shock, pursed her lips, and marched
off in high indignation. Wilton immediately grasped the situation. Kate was working. He remembered quite clearly what
she had said on the train about how much money she could
make on her back.

Miss Allen's Boardinghouse turned out to be an adobe
building, the only wood in which appeared to be the log timbers holding up the flat roof, the doors, and window shutters.
From the street it looked not unlike a fort, with its solid
walls, narrow door, and blank walls. All that it lacked were
battlements on top.

A fat Mexican woman opened the door to Wilton's knock,
smiled at him, and gestured for him to follow her inside.
There was a rough little room, incongruously furnished with
a grand piano and half a dozen straight-backed, velvet-uphol-
stered chairs and a matching love seat. There was a bar,
which Wilton saw was nothing more than a board between
sawhorses, covered with a clean tablecloth.

The Mexican woman left him, and in a minute a buxom
blond in a clean but well-worn dressing gown came into the
room.

"Hi ya, handsome," she said, flashing him a smile.

"I would like to see Kate," Wilton said stiffly.

"Kate? Big Kate?" she asked. "She ain't here no more."

"I am referring to a small woman," Wilton said, gesturing
with his hand to indicate his Kate's approximate height.
"With red hair."

"Oh, *Miss Katherine*," the woman said. "You heard about
her, huh? I think she's seeing a gentleman caller."

"I will wait," Wilton announced. "I have business with
her."

"So do most of the men in town," the woman said. "Even
if she can't do anything I can't do." She winked at him.

"Is she permitted to leave the premises?" Wilton asked. He

wanted to get his money, but there would be time for that. He wanted most of all to get out of this place.

"Can she leave, you mean?" the woman asked. "I don't know if she'd want to do that."

"Would you please tell her," Wilton began, and then Kate came into the room. She had on an evening dress, and looked quite attractive.

"The maid said there was a *caballero* in the parlor," Kate greeted him. "But I didn't know it was you."

He just looked at her. It was simply astonishing that a woman of such beauty would willingly be a prostitute.

"You've come for your money," she said.

"Correct," he said. "And to thank you for taking care of me when I fell ill."

"It was nothing" she said. "Your money is safe, don't worry about that. As safe as in a bank."

He nodded. "I appreciate your honesty."

"Look," she said, "why don't you go to the Marshall House and get a room? I'll be along about half-past two. You get a room and lay down and rest."

There was something about her attitude that made him uneasy. Was it possible that she didn't expect that he would suddenly emerge from the hospital and demand his money? Would she flee with it the minute he left this place?

That was unlikely. If she had intended to disappear, she would have left him either on the train or the minute she had seen him into the hospital.

"I'll be at the hotel," he said, "waiting for you." As he left the establishment, he encountered two men going in. They infuriated him. Damned woman—damned slut.

Two hours later, he paid his bill at the Marshall House bar and marched out, intending to go back to Miss Allen's and collect his money. He met her coming into the hotel lobby as he walked out of it. She was now dressed, as he thought of it, quite respectably, as opposed to the lurid lady-of-the-evening gown she had been wearing before.

She smiled, and took his arm, turning him around and marching him back through the lobby, past the smirking clerk, and up the wide staircase.

"What room did they give you?" she asked. Wordlessly he led her to it.

One would never know, to look at her, what she was. But of course, everyone knew, from the desk clerk onward. She closed the door and locked it after them.

"It took a little longer getting rid of the both of them than I thought it would," she announced matter-of-factly. She went to the dresser, and watching her reflection in the mirror, took off her hat. Then she unbuttoned the jacket of her dress and carefully hung it on the back of a chair.

"You say you have the money?" Wilton asked.

"I wanted to talk to you about that," she said. "I can't give you all of it."

"What do you mean?"

She went to her purse, opened it, and came up with a sheaf of bills. She walked up to him and handed him the money. He took it and started to count it.

"There's only about a thousand dollars here," he said.

"Eleven hundred and ten," she corrected him.

"Good God, woman!" he said. "Where the hell is the rest of my money?"

"I borrowed it, you might say," she said. "I bought Miss Allen's."

"You bought that brothel?" he asked incredulously. "With *my* money?"

"I gave her two thousand dollars," she said. "And I'm to pay her the rest as I make it. It was an opportunity I couldn't pass up."

"And it never occurred to you that I could go to the sheriff and tell him what you had done, and that he would put you in prison as a thief?"

"I thought about that, matter of fact," she said. "And I thought that you really wouldn't want to do that. And it's not as if I really stole your money. I mean, if I done that, I would have just left you on the train, wouldn't I, when everybody thought you were dying. I mean, if I had really stolen it, I wouldn't still be around, would I?"

She turned away from him and walked back to her purse, this time returning with a piece of paper.

"Here it is," she said, "All written down, properly."

Phoenix, Arizona Territory
15th September, 1890

I, Katherine Mary Shaughnessy, promise to pay to Mr. John Wilton the sum of $2,500 on demand. I pledge the property known as Miss Allen's Boardinghouse, Phoenix, Arizona Territory, as security for this loan.

Katherine Mary Shaughnessy

It was so outrageous that he was tempted to laugh. "Do you realize that this document means that I can demand the money right now, and that if you don't pay, I can take your . . . boardinghouse?"

"The lawyer told me that," she admitted. "But I told him I didn't think you would."

"And why shouldn't I?"

"Because we're friends," she said. "And because I don't think you'd want to own that place. I mean, own it so that people would know you own it."

"Good God! You talked over our relationship with a lawyer?"

"One of my gentleman callers," Kate said. "He wrote that up for me." She looked up at him and smiled. "Okay, John?"

"No, it is not okay, as you put it," he said. "It most definitely, decidedly is not okay."

"But you're not going to make trouble for me?" she asked, and there was again that look of the frightened doe in her eyes.

"I can't see what good that would do me," he said honestly. "Although I really would like to do something to you."

She chose to misinterpret that. She put her hand on him. "I hoped you would," she said. "But for a while, I wasn't sure."

"I am absolutely out of my mind," he said, looking down at her and meeting her eyes. "Absolutely."

"Me, too," she said. "Somebody in my business should never give it away."

"Good God!"

"But you're somebody special," she said, and now her fingers were moving softly downward. "And we got something special going, don't we?"

He put his hand to her breast, feeling the warmth of it.

"I wonder," she said, "if we'll be able to keep it up."

"Keep what up?" he asked idly, his attention now directed

69

to the buttons of her dress and the incredible perfection of her breasts coming before him.

"Being friends," she said.

"Time will tell, I suppose," John Wilton said as he realized, incredible as it might be, that was exactly how he felt about her, as a friend.

She giggled. "Katy Shaughnessy and John F. W. Wilton, friends and partners-in-bed."

He laughed out loud. "You are a bloody goddamned jewel," he said.

10

Lucille Stevens lay on her back on the double bed, the covers thrown down off the end, wearing only a chemise, fresh from her bath, but already losing the clean feeling the bath had given her.

It was summer-hot, Texas heat, turning El Paso into an oven with the first light of dawn, and she really hated the notion of getting dressed and going downstairs.

The French doors, on both sides of the corner of the third floor of the Parker House, had been opened just enough to admit the breeze, if any, while still blocking a view of the bed. Since the Parker House was the tallest building in El Paso, it was highly unlikely that anyone, even so inclinded, would be able to look through her windows. The truth of the matter was, and it embarrassed her, that she was always a bit uneasy in El Paso, population 10,006. It didn't do any good to tell herself that ten thousand people could be easily lost in New York or San Francisco or Saint Louis. By comparison with where she'd spent most of her days, El Paso was a teeming metropolis, the Big City. And in the Big City she was uneasy to have her windows open. God alone knew who was liable to look in.

She went to the French windows on bare feet, carefully keeping herself behind the translucent curtains that covered their glass panes, pushed them closed and locked them.

The room, with bright sunlight filtering through the curtains, now looked softer, less harsh, than it had a moment be-

71

fore. She pulled the chemise off over her head and stuffed it into a laundry bag. She went to the mirrored dresser and picked up a bottle of Mrs. Laudermann's Patented Skin Softener for Ladies and poured a thumb-sized glob of it into the palm of her hand. It looked, she thought, like mustard. Maybe mustard mixed with mayonnaise. Maybe that's all it really was, even if it cost fifty cents for the small bottle. She sniffed it. There was a faint oily smell. Well, whatever it was, she needed it. Her skin was too dry.

She saw that her skin was not only dry, it was of two colors. Halfway between her elbows and her shoulders, it suddenly turned pale white. She was suntanned from the mark down to her fingers. She looked at herself in the mirror, her hand to her throat. She was suntanned down her neck, too, almost to the swell of her bosom, a V-shaped area of darker skin, like the arms corresponding to the short-sleeved, open-neck blouses she normally wore at Rancho San Miguel.

Lucille knew that suntanned skin was considered unladylike. She would have preferred to be one color all over, but that was impossible. That would mean wearing blouses buttoned to the neck (which would still leave the face exposed to the sun) and the wrists (which would leave her with brown hands, anyway). Or, she could go riding about in her birthday suit. She smiled at the insane thought as she rubbed the mustard-colored concoction onto her arms and neck.

It didn't matter. No one ever saw her without her blouse.

She took a fresh chemise from a drawer in the dresser and pulled it over her head. She disliked being naked; she had since puberty. Before that, she hadn't been aware of nudity very much. There was a pool on Rancho San Miguel where she had gone swimming stark naked whenever she could get away from her parents.

That was a long time ago.

She put on linen underdrawers, and over them an underskirt. Then a blouse, stiffly starched white Irish linen. There was a tablecloth and napkins at the ranch cut from the same bolt of Irish linen. The blouse had wrist-length sleeves, and buttoned high at the neck.

Then she brushed her hair, and put it up, and fixed her hat on top with an eight-inch hat pin. Then she pinned the diamond brooch, a four-carat diamond, to the breast of her jacket. She put the jacket on, and only then pulled the skirt up over her hips, sucked in her breath, and fastened the snaps. She did not need a girdle. The height of fashion was supposed to be a waist that a man could circle with his hands. Hers wasn't that small, but on the other hand, there was no man on the horizon who was going to determine that by scientific experiment.

Hers was small enough so that she didn't have to be strapped into one of those things. She had one of them, of course, bought from an advertisement in *Harper's Magazine*, sent all the way from Boston. But she hadn't even brought it with her from the ranch. She's tried to put it on the day it arrived, laughed at herself (or perhaps the vanity of the female generally), and put it into a drawer.

She turned sideward, straightened the bustle, examined herself in profile. The bustle stuck out in back far more than her bosom did in front. Those waists were supposed to accentuate the bosom. What they did, she thought, was squeeze you in the middle like a sausage.

Lucille Stevens went to the door, then turned. She had forgotten scent. She took a bottle of French scent (like the waist, ordered from an advertisement in *Harper's*) and applied it behind her ears, on her neck, and then to her wrists.

There was little chance that it would overwhelm the smell of cigars, whiskey, and roasted meat in the dining room, but it pleased her nonetheless.

She went out of the room, locking it behind her, and then down the carpeted corridor to the wide stairway, and down that to the lobby of the Parker House. The room key was attached to a heavy brass plate with the number. After a moment, she decided against giving it to the desk clerk. When she dropped it into her purse, the brass plate clanged against the .41-caliber Remington derringer. The little purse was heavy. It held the derringer, two hundred dollars in gold coins, and now the heavy key. And a small Irish-linen handkerchief.

Lucille walked slowly back and forth in front of the door to the bar until, when she was just about ready to stand in the door, her father saw her. He smiled, looked surprised, took his watch from his vest, snapped open the cover, and looked at it. Then hurriedly and somewhat unsteadily he got to his feet, shook hands with the men at the small table with him, and walked out to her.

"Lucille," he said grandly, "you are the most stylish, and if I may say so, the most beautiful woman I have seen in many a day."

He was drunk. It wasn't a condemnation, it was a statement of fact.

He took her arm and they walked across the lobby to the dining room. The headwaiter snatched two menu cards from his stand-up desk. "Major Stevens," he said. "Ma'am."

"We will be two for dinner," her father said, carefully pronouncing each syllable.

"Right this way, sir," the headwaiter said. He led them to a table, held the chair for Lucille, and snapped his fingers for a busboy. Her father staggered against the table, rattling the silver and china. He was in worse condition than she had thought.

He forced a chuckle and sat down. A waiter appeared, and he ordered for them, not asking her what she would like, choosing turtle soup and roast beef and a bottle of wine.

"And while we're waiting," he said, "I do believe I could use another two inches of that fine Kentucky whiskey."

"How do you feel?" Lucille asked.

"I'll be all right," he said reassuringly.

She was not tactfully asking if he had had too much to drink; she was asking how he felt, which meant how bad was the pain. Her father was dying, slowly, painfully.

"I was thinking," he went on, not looking at her, "that there is no reason for us to stay here beyond tomorrow. Manuel knows the drive as well as I do."

Manuel was the foreman of Rancho San Miguel. They were in El Paso to take delivery of yearlings driven up from Mexico. There were four hundred head just outside Ciudad Juarez, on the Mexican side of the border, and four hundred more head were expected tomorrow or the day after. Once the beefs had arrived and been culled (as a general rule of thumb, one in four would be rejected), they would drive them the 150 miles to Rancho San Miguel, in the New Mexico Territory.

Lucille knew her father would never see the yearlings they were buying get to market. It would take two years for them to be ready, and he would die long before that. She looked away so he couldn't see the sudden dampness in her eyes.

"Lucille? You about ready to go home?"

"I'm really not finished shopping," she said carefully. She had to do this exactly right. There were several things that had to be done. First and foremost was getting him back to Rancho San Miguel. When he was "making business," either in El Paso or at the ranch, he didn't take his laudanum. He couldn't function when he was full of laudanum. And without the laudanum, he was in pain, horrible agony. Whiskey had never been very effective against the pain, and it was growing less and less so. Even when he drank himself into a stupor, he sometimes moaned.

"Well, in that case," her father said, "we'll just stay over another day or two, whatever it takes."

The man they were buying the yearlings from, Don Alejandro de Montayo y de Chala, wasn't as impressive physically as the elegant name suggested. He was a tiny, tense little man with an unsuccessful mustache. But he was a Spaniard, as opposed to a Mexican, and Manuel, as self-confident as Manuel was on the ranch, instantly reverted to being a Mexican peasant the moment he got close to Don Alejandro. Manuel would be unable to reject any animal if that meant incurring Don Alejandro's displeasure.

She was going to have to be there to go through the new herd, or they would wind up with every cripple on the Tex-Mex border. But her father wouldn't stand for that. Culling a driven herd was a man's job. It was unladylike for a woman to do that, particularly if it also meant that she was likely to have words with Don Alejandro over what was a fit yearling and what wasn't. Major Henry Stevens could not stand by while his daughter did a man's work.

"Father," Lucille said, "why can't Manuel cull the herd? You could go home on the morning train and let them know we're coming. And I'll just spend another day or two here, finishing my shopping."

"I hate to leave you alone," he said.

"All I'm going to do is go from the hotel to the shops," she said. "And I really much prefer taking my time when I shop, not making quick decisions because I'm pressed for time."

"You're a young woman, and you should not be left without protection."

"Don't be silly," she said. "I'll only be a day or two. And Manuel is here."

"Well, perhaps you're right," he said.

"Then it's settled."

He couldn't eat more than a couple of mouthfuls when the food came. But he had three more drinks. Going up the stairs to their rooms was an effort for him, and she recognized the signs of pain on his face. She wished, for his sake, that he would take the laudanum. But he wouldn't do that. Not here, where people could see him.

She saw him to his room, and then went to hers. She undressed, stuffing the sweat-soaked blouse and chemise and underdrawers into the already tightly packed laundry bag, put on a cotton nightdress, and lay in bed reading a Sir Walter Scott novel of knights and ladies in England until she grew tired and blew out the lamp.

She was afraid her father would change his mind, that he would wake up in the morning, sobered by pain and made mean by it, and announce he was staying, or that he'd thought it over and it wouldn't be seemly for her to stay alone in a public hotel by herself, and what did Manuel know anyway?

But that didn't happen. When she went to his room in the morning, his dilated pupils told her he had given in. He had taken the laudanum. She sent a Mexican boy to the boarding-house where Manuel was staying, and asked him which of the hands he felt should be sent on the train with the major, who was ill.

Manuel told her that the second herd of Don Alejandro's yearlings had arrived. She asked him to bring a horse with a sidesaddle to the railroad depot, and to keep it out of sight.

Semicoherent, Major Stevens still tried to deliver orders to Manuel. He was to cull the herd, when it arrived, as *el patrón* himself would cull it, and he should not be afraid of Don Alejandro. Manuel was visibly relieved to hear that Lucille would be there, too, and that she would bear the responsibility.

She kissed her father, loaded him on the train, and waved when it pulled out. Then she went behind the freight depot, where her sidesaddled horse waited for her. She would, she decided, ride sidesaddle as long as they were in El Paso, so that she would maintain the ladylike decorum Major Charles Stevens expected of his daughter.

With Manuel riding three yards behind her, she rode across the bridge into Ciudad Juarez to deal with Don Alejandro de Montayo y de Chala.

It wasn't until late that afternoon, when the herd had been culled and the tally made, that she thought about the bank draft. They had bought cattle from Don Alejandro (and others) for years. What happened next had become a ritual. Her father and whoever had sold them the cattle would ride back across the bridge into El Paso to the Ranchers & Merchants Bank. The bank was closed, but the banker, in courteous deference to Major Stevens, would be waiting behind the drawn curtains.

There would be handshaking and a drink of whiskey (sherry for Lucille), and then her father would write out a draft, and the banker would either credit it to the seller's account or issue him a bank check or make payment in gold, whatever the seller preferred.

If her father wasn't here, he obviously couldn't sign the bank draft.

As Lucille was thinking this (was he reading her mind?) Don Alejandro raised the question. "The major will meet us at the bank, Doña Lucille?"

"The major has returned to Rancho San Miguel, Don Alejandro," she replied. "I will go with you to the bank." She smiled at him and touched her riding crop to her horse.

The banker, Timothy Feeney, bowed them into his office and offered Don Alejandro the customary drink.

"And when may we expect the major, Miss Lucille?" he asked.

"The major has returned to Rancho San Miguel," she said.

"But he did leave you a draft? May I have it, ma'am?"

"I'll issue the draft," Lucille said.

Timothy Feeney didn't like that at all. Banking was a man's business. "Forgive me, Miss Lucille," he said, "but I don't believe you're authorized to issue drafts against your father's account."

"I don't know what you mean," she said. My God, what

was going to happen now? Don Alejandro wasn't going to wait for his money.

"I'm sure it was just an oversight on the major's part," Feeney said. "We'll just get you to sign the major's name, ma'am. I'm sure that will be fine."

Lucille surprised herself both with the anger that swept through her and with what she said. "I will not sign my father's name," she said firmly. "I'm not a child. I will sign my own name."

"Miss Lucille, I can't allow that. I can't accept your signature. You're your father's daughter, but that's all you are. Legally speaking, I mean. In a banking sense."

"You'll either accept it," Lucille said, "or as soon as I get a telegram back and forth to Rancho San Miguel, we'll take every last dime we have out of your bank."

"I'm sorry, Miss Lucille," Feeney said. "But I have my rules—"

Lucille stood up. She opened her purse and handed Don Alejandro the small suede bag with the two hundred dollars in gold coins. "I hope you will be willing to take this as earnest money. I will pay you the balance tomorrow, in gold, at my hotel."

"Well," Feeney said, having decided she was serious, "perhaps we can make an exception, just this one time, under the circumstances."

"No," Lucille said. "Not just an exception. Not just this one time. You'd better get used to the notion, if you want our business, that I'm running Rancho San Miguel, and that when I write a draft on the account, it will be honored."

She glowered at Feeney.

"I've got a draft right here, Miss Lucille," he said, pulling open a drawer in his desk. Then he stood up and held his high-backed chair for her to sit down and write.

She blotted the draft and handed it to Don Alejandro, as she had watched her father do a half-dozen times before. He bowed, and then handed the paper to Feeney.

"Thank you, sir," Timothy Feeney said. "How would you prefer payment?"

"In gold, please," Don Alejandro replied.

Lucille restrained a smile. Don Alejandro wanted to take no chance on Feeney changing his mind.

Feeney smiled uneasily, but then bent to work the combination on the five-foot-square safe against the wall.

I won that one, Lucille thought. But the feeling of victory faded quickly. It would have been so much nicer to be a spectator, sipping a glass of sherry, watching her father go through the routine of issuing the draft.

11

A month later, back on Rancho San Miguel in the New Mexico Territory, Lucille Stevens came out of her father's room wishing he would die. He wasn't really alive now. He was either drunk, or in a laudanum stupor, or in agony. And the agony of his consumption was gradually overwhelming the painkilling effects of the laudanum and the brandy.

He was wasted away to his bones. His flesh hung slack between the joints.

And he smelled. God forgive her, she couldn't stand the smell. It was the smell of death.

She was shamed at her wish that he would die, and wondered if the shame itself was selfish. For when the major died, there would be born—resurrected, really—the problem of Charles Broadhead. In deference to her feelings, Charley was not pressing her to marry him. He was biding his time. She thought she knew what he was thinking. That in her grief when her father died, her realization that she was a woman alone would drive her to gratefully marry him.

There didn't seem to be much of an alternative. She wasn't sure, in her own mind, that she could indeed run the ranch by herself. She *had* been running it for almost two years now, since her mother had died, from the time her father had drowned that grief in the brandy, when Lucille was only twenty-three. But there was a difference, and she knew it, between giving orders and making decisions in her father's name, and making them herself. The decision of a woman was suspect, even though it might be precisely the decision a man would make in identical circumstances. The question was not whether the decision was right, but whether she could enforce it.

The obvious answer was to marry Charley—Charles Lowell Broadhead, Esq., like Lucille, the offspring of defeated Confederates who had fled the Reconstruction South for the West. Randolph Broadhead had been an attorney before the War Between the States, and he had not prospered in postwar New Mexico Territory. Genteel poverty was the term. An office, so to speak, and infrequent appearance before the territory courts, augmented by what they could make out of their ranch.

Major Stevens and Randolph Broadhead were both transplanted Southern gentlemen surrounded by the lower classes. They were ranchers, and pretended to notice no difference between the Broadheads' two sections, 1,240 acres, and the 70,000 or more acres that made up Rancho San Miguel.

As one gentleman to another, Randolph Broadhead had offered the services of his son Charles "to help out" when the major had fallen ill. A man was obviously needed to take charge. In addition, Randolph Broadhead and his wife hoped and expected that proximity would result in marriage between Lucille and Charley.

Lucille Stevens was in the kitchen when the *muchacho* rushed in excitedly to report the arrival of a rider. She sent him to fetch Señor Charley, who was supervising calf branding, and then she climbed the ladder into the bell tower to have a look.

She could see a figure more than a mile off; he was following the road. He had some sort of tent affair over him, which she recognized after a while was a frock coat, buttoned into a cape, which he wore over his head.

The horse was walking slowly, and the impression she had was of great fatigue. It was obviously the Englishman, the man whose luggage had been mysteriously unloaded at Loving without its owner.

Charley had brought the luggage to the hacienda to keep it from being stolen by the Indians. There were only two trains that stopped at Loving on a weekly schedule, and there was no station agent. Charley had been returning from Dallas

81

when he found the luggage, and had simply brought it with him, leaving a message where it could be found.

She heard the sound of horse's hooves and turned and saw Charley coming up from the ramada. Charles Broadhead, Southern gentleman, had gone Mex. He wore a sombrero and a serape.

The rider was now in sight of the hacienda, but he didn't urge the horse on. It plodded slowly as before. She went down the ladder and found Charley waiting for her at the bottom. They waited for their visitor together.

The rider now had his frock coat on the way it was intended to be worn, with his arms through the sleeves. He was dust-covered, which was to be expected, in these last few days before the rains started, when everything was as dry as could be. He had made some effort, she saw, to knock the dust off, and had understandably failed. There was dust all over him, some of it turned to mud by having been mixed with sweat and then dried.

He took off his silk hat. "Good afternoon," he said, and bowed to her. "My name is John F. W. Wilton, and I have been led to believe that you have some knowledge of the location of my luggage."

Charley, she saw, was torn between responding to the newcomer's formal courtesy as one gentleman to another and being what he was, a New Mexico Territory rancher who could not help but find the sight of a dust-covered dude, complete to silk top hat, more than a little amusing. The gentleman won out.

"My name, sir, is Charles Broadhead," he said, putting out his hand. "And this is Miss Lucille Stevens, mistress of Rancho San Miguel."

The dust-covered Englishman bowed to Lucille again. "Ma'am," he said.

"Come on in the house," Charles Broadhead said, "and we'll get you something to drink, and then we'll arrange for you to wash some of that dust off. Little sandstorm, was there, while you stopped?"

"I didn't expect the heat," the man said.

"Juan," Lucille ordered, "bring some water."

"You look a little stiff, sir," Charley said, slightly mockingly, as he led Wilton into the living room. "Not used to the saddle, I take it?"

"I've never seen a saddle like that before," Wilton said.

"It shows," Charley said, and Lucille frowned at him. "No offense intended."

"None taken," Wilton said.

"Where did you spend the night?"

"I rode straight through," Wilton said. "I left Loving at seven this morning."

"You mean you came out without supplies?" Charley said.

Wilton took the glass of water from Juan. Lucille was a little nervous. If he drank deeply, there was a fifty-fifty chance he'd throw it up. But he didn't gulp the water. He took a small sip and sloshed it around in his mouth. Lucille sensed this man had been around dry, hot country before.

"As I was saying, the man in Loving was quite reluctant to have me come out here at all. By myself, I mean."

"This can be pretty rough country," Charley said.

"So I have noticed," the man said, and took a little more water. "Did I understand you to offer a bath?"

"Whenever you would like to have a bath," Charley said, slightly mocking the English broad *a*, "we shall see that you have one. We've had your things put in a room for you."

"I appreciate your hospitality," John Wilton said. "The thought of riding back to Loving today, even in a wagon—I hope to rent a wagon from you—is not very attractive."

Lucille Stevens decided that the Englishman had been prepared to return if need be, regardless of what he said. A tough character, she decided.

"You're welcome . . . more than welcome, to stay as long as you want. We're always glad to have visitors out here," she said. "I suppose you've come about the ranch?"

"The Anglo-American Land & Cattle Company properties," Wilton said. "My mother has recently come into possession of them."

"If you're planning on selling out," Lucille said, "I'd like the chance to match any offers. These lands abut mine."

Lucille sensed that Charley hadn't liked her saying this. Because it wasn't her place, because it wasn't ladylike to make a business offer? Or because he had already begun to think of Rancho San Miguel as his?

83

"I think Mother plans to continue to operate them," Wilton said. Charley didn't say anything, but Wilton saw something in his face. "You seem surprised," he added.

"There's nothing to operate," Charley said. "I'm sorry to tell you that, but that's the way it is."

"I don't quite understand."

"I could break the bad news to you better after you've had a bath and a drink," Charley said. "Or would you rather have it now?"

"Now, please," Wilton said.

"The place has been deserted for three years," Charley said. "Before that, they went broke. There's not much out there but the stone walls of the buildings."

"I see," Wilton said.

"Forgive me," Lucille heard herself say. "I don't think you do. Why don't we just suspend this discussion until you can see the property for yourself?"

"I think perhaps we should, Miss Stevens," the Englishman said.

"Come on, Mr. Wilton, we'll get some of that New Mexican dust washed off you," Charley said.

The Englishman bowed again to Lucille and followed Charley toward the rooms in the left wing of the house reserved for visitors. The Englishman had been given the best of these, his social status having been judged by his luggage. The stickers had announced that he had come from India as a first-class passenger on an ocean liner. Lucille had never seen an ocean, nor an ocean liner, but she read *Harper's Magazine,* sent out from New York, and she had seen the drawings of prominent people and the vessels on which they sailed.

Charley came into the drawing room in just a few minutes. He smiled at her. "Well, we don't see many like that out here, do we?"

"He seems very nice."

Charley said. "He's lucky he made it out here."

She had to smile. Charley was right. The Englishman was a real city slicker; his long ride alone had been foolhardy. It was funny to think of it now, as Charley did, to scorn a dehydrated, saddle-sore dude, but only because he had arrived alive.

Lucille thought something else. Charley didn't seem at all concerned that instead of the middle-aged Englishman they had expected, he had turned out to be a young man, a potential rival. Was it because he was so sure of her?

When Wilton reappeared, three-quarters of an hour later, that was again the first thing she thought of, and she believed she knew why Charley had been so unconcerned. With the dust gone, and his face shaved, and despite the mustache, it was immediately apparent to Lucille that the Englishman was nothing more than a large boy. Charley, obviously, had seen that right off.

The Englishman was well dressed, and Charley saw that, too, and responded to it, thinking of his parents. "Perhaps while you're here, Mr. Wilton, you will be able to dine at my home," he said. "I'm sure that my parents would be delighted to receive you. We have so few visitors out here."

"Charles," Lucille said, "why don't you send a *muchacho* to ask your mother and father to come here for a few days?"

"I think I'll do just that," Charles said. "I'm sure Mr. Wilton would not look forward to another long ride."

"I never thought I would be happy to see a saddle," Wilton said, smiling.

"Sir?" Charley asked, confused.

"I have a saddle in my luggage," Wilton said. "The sort I'm used to."

Juanita, the housekeeper, came into the room and stood with her hands folded over her ample stomach until Lucille walked over to her. The major had somehow learned of the presence of a guest in his house; he wanted to see him.

Lucille nodded. She really didn't want to subject this boy, for that is how she now thought of him, to the horrible specter in the master bedroom. But then she was shamed. Her father was entitled to whatever he wanted.

Lucille had been born in the last days of the Civil War. She remembered nothing of it, but she had heard so much about it that it was quite real to her. She had heard, over and over, in the last days of her mother's life, how her father "had come home."

Home was no longer a plantation in Georgia. That had gone up in smoke during the March to the Sea. Home was an

85

adobe hovel outside Loving, to which her mother had brought her as a babe in arms.

"I smelled like a pig, Lucy," her father had said, and her mother had nodded fondly. "My clothes in tatters, even the soles of my boots gone."

He smelled like death now, she thought.

"Your father went from the prison camp, when the Yankees released him," her mother had said, "to the old place in Georgia. And there was nothing there, of course, except the shell of the house. The darkies were gone, and the fields were grown over, and all he knew was that I had gone west with Marybelle. You remember Marybelle, honey, rest her soul? She died when you were about five. She stayed with us to the end of her days."

"God guided my steps, Lucy," her father said. "There's no other explanation. I told myself that I was going to California, but I knew that I would find you and your mother before I got there."

"It was the eleventh day of May, 1866," her mother said. "And I looked up at the door. I was changing you. I remember that clearly. And there was your father, his hat in his hand. I knew it was him, of course, but he didn't recognize me. 'Madam,' he said. 'Forgive the intrusion.'"

"She wasn't quite the girl I'd left behind me, Lucy," her father said.

"And I said, 'Oh, Henry, you're nothing but skin and bones,'" her mother said. "And when I put my arms around him, Lucille, you started to scream and carry on something awful."

"And that brought Marybelle on the run," her father said. "She'd been outside, cutting wood or something, and when she heard her baby screaming, she came running, and then she saw me, and she said, 'My God, Master Henry, you look awful.' And I suppose I did."

"You didn't look awful, Henry," her mother said. "You were thin . . ."

"And I wept, Lucy," her father said. "Like a little child. I wept because I had found my family, and I wept because I didn't know what I was going to do, now that I had found them. I didn't have a French sou, nothing but the clothes on my back and a Remington revolver and a worn-out horse.

And here we were in the middle of the desert." He took out his handkerchief and blew his nose. "So they gave me you to hold, Lucy honey, and Marybelle started making something for me to eat, and your mother got down on her hands and knees on the dirt floor in front of the fireplace, and started digging it up."

"You can still see where that house was in Loving, Lucy," her mother said. "It's falling down now. Hasn't been used in years, not even by Mexicans, but it's there. I've shown it to you."

"And what she dug up from the floor in front of the fireplace, some gold money and her jewelry, which she had brought all the way from Georgia, was what got us started out here, Lucille. I dread to think what would have happened to us if it hadn't been for those valuables your mother brought out here with her, all alone, all the way from Georgia."

Among the valuables her mother had brought was the four-carat stone from the center of the ring Mr. Henry Stevens of Belle Fontaine Plantation had given to Miss Elizabeth Ann Howeley of Oak Forest Plantation on the occasion of their engagement to be married. The other jewels had been sold, turned into land and supplies and cash to pay the ranch hands, but not that stone.

It was now a brooch on the breast of Lucille Stevens. She fingered it. She had thought about having it reset as a ring when she married Charles. God knows, he didn't have enough money to buy her a stone that large.

"Mr. Wilton," she said, and he looked at her out of his boyish eyes, so childlike, she thought, "my father, who is very ill, has learned that you are here."

He didn't say anything, just looked at her, waiting for her to go on.

"He would like to see you," Lucille said. Charles gave her a strange look. He made regular dutiful calls on her father, suppressing his revulsion. But it was not the sort of thing to which you subjected a guest. "I must warn you that he is a very sick man."

"I would be honored, ma'am," Wilton said.

The devil with him, Lucille decided. Let a little revulsion be the price he paid for having his luggage cared for, for

87

learning the true condition of Anglo-American Land & Cattle. Her father was entitled to what little pleasure she could give him.

She made a gesture toward the door, and he walked out of it ahead of her. She sensed, rather than saw, that Charles had decided to come along.

12

When she pushed open the door to her father's room, she saw that he had had himself propped up against the back of the bed, supporting himself with pillows. The smell was there, but he didn't look as bad as she thought he would. The pupils of his eyes were dilated, and his eyes looked glazed. His face was flushed. It was a drunkard's face, she realized, the cheeks and nose red with ruptured blood vessels.

He forced a smile on his face when he saw the door open.

"Father, this is our guest, Mr. Wilton," she said. "Mr. Wilton, my father, Major Henry Stevens."

Wilton walked to the bed, took the major's limply lifted hand. "John Wilton, sir," he said. "Late lieutenant, the Prince of Wales's Own Bengal Light Cavalry."

"Your servant, sir," the major said. "You must forgive me for not being able to entertain you. I've been ill."

What had he said? Lieutenant? The Prince of Wales's Cavalry?

"It is very kind of you to have me in your home, Major," Wilton said.

"Cavalry, you say? I was once cavalry. Second Georgia Cavalry. And then we were down to eating our mounts," the major said. And then the laudanum or the brandy, or both, got to him. His eyes rolled, and the lids closed. His body went slack.

"I think, perhaps," Wilton said, "we should lay him flat." Without waiting for permission, he leaned over the bed and

89

slid the old man flat on his back, pulling over the covers. Then he marched out of the room stiffly. In the corridor she could hear him trying to stem his nausea.

But he helped my father first, she thought.

Charley went out after him, and when Lucille went into the corridor herself, they were both gone. She found them in the drawing room, with a bottle of brandy between them. She walked to the table and helped herself to a glass of brandy, drinking it straight down, like medicine.

"Thank you," she said to John Wilton.

"My pleasure, ma'am," he said.

Damn, she thought. Why does he have to be a boy? Why did he have to come here at all? Having anything to do with him was obviously out of the question, but as unquestionably, he made Charley seem less desirable simply because he proved there were other men in the world. Unfortunately, none of them seemed to be in New Mexico.

When Charley, an hour later, announced that he'd better be getting cleaned up for dinner, the Englishman misinterpreted this as a subtle announcement that he was expected to dress. She felt sorry for him when he appeared in evening dress, to find Charley changed into nothing more formal than a clean cravatless shirt. Charley had the decency to go find a coat, and when he returned wearing it, she excused herself and put on a nice dress.

After dinner, when John Wilton lit a long, thin black stogie, Lucille thought he really was adorable in the sense that an appealing child is. He was a little boy, playing man. The mustache was really absurd. Someone like Charley could get away with a mustache, but not someone whose soft, pink cheeks would have been quite at home on a woman. She wondered if he really shaved closely, for she could find no suggestion of whiskers on his cheeks, or whether there was really nothing there to shave, and he had been cultivating the hair on his lip for years.

It was agreed at dinner that Charley would ride out with Wilton in the morning to the Anglo-American Land & Cattle property. Lucille announced that she would ride along, which surprised her, for it would not be a pleasant trip, and she was surprised by her decision that she would ride sidesaddle, which would make the whole thing even less pleasant. She normally rode astride, but for some reason it was important that tomorrow she ride as a lady was supposed to.

After the way he had dressed—overdressed—for dinner, Lucille would not have been surprised if the next morning John Wilton had come out onto the porch in a coat, tie, and high hat. He came out, instead, wearing rough clothes cut out of canvas, and with the silliest-looking hat Lucille had ever seen, a brimmed canvas cap with a tail on it, down over the neck. He had a funny-looking revolver, a six-shooter, in an equally funny-looking holster under his arm, and in one hand a rifle in a canvas bag, and in the other, one of those strange saddles that were hardly more than a pad of leather on either side of the horse's backbone.

"You really going to try to put that on one of our animals?" Charley asked.

"I would be very grateful if you permit me to do so," the Englishman said. "I ache in muscles—forgive me, Miss Stevens—I didn't know I had, from yesterday's ride."

Charley loosened the belt band and pulled the saddle from the back of the piebald he had picked out for Wilton, and then stood aside. Lucille was surprised at how quickly the Englishman got his saddle on the feisty little piebald. He had been around horses. Probably nothing like this, but around horses.

The Englishman had half a leg up when the piebald decided to find out who was going to be the boss. He shied away, and turned his head to bite. Lucille thought that the bite was more than playful. She wondered if the animal disliked essence of sweet roses or whatever it was the Englishman had soaked himself with after shaving. She expected it would take the Englishman at least three tries to mount the piebald, and then they would see if he'd ever been on a bucking horse before.

But the Englishman was ready for the shying, and he was ready for the rearing, and the piebald didn't even buck. The piebald was smart enough to figure out that anyone so secure in the saddle to reach forward and stroke him comfortingly when he was in the very act of rearing on his hind legs probably knew all about riding down a cow pony.

"Spirited, isn't he?" the Englishman said with a bright smile of appreciation.

"English John," Charley Broadhead said approvingly, "you're all right." Then he touched the spurs to his stallion and they trotted away from the hacienda.

Over the next three hours, as they rode abreast, John F. W. Wilton in the center, across the rolling ground toward what had been the ranch house of the Anglo-American Land & Cattle Company, Charley gave Wilton an explanation of what it took to raise cattle successfully (two to three acres of land per head was the amazing basic statistic) and sheep (one acre per animal) in the dry terrain.

He told him why, in his judgment, the English had gone wrong and then broke, and what had happened to the vast sums of money that the English had poured into the failed project. Essentially, they had grossly underestimated the acreage necessary to sustain a herd. They had overgrazed, and then underestimated the painfully slow recovery time for the grazing land. Their cattle had literally starved to death; what cattle they had been able to get to market had been salable only at sacrifice prices, less than the cost of raising the animals.

Lucy could find nothing wrong with Charley's assessment of the situation. And that reminded her that he was what she needed. A knowledgeable rancher, a man of stability. A good and decent man. Why didn't she want him? What was wrong with her?

John saw the farm buildings forty-five minutes before they reached them. There were half a dozen slightly rolling hills between the top of the first rise where he saw the buildings themselves. He lost sight of them then, descending a rise, and saw them again closer, topping the next. At first, the main building looked intact. It was a long, low structure sitting atop a gentle rise, with a shallow sloped roof.

As they rode closer, however, he saw that the roof was sagging inward, and when he got close enough, he saw that there had been a porch, now gone.

When they reined up outside, John swung down from the saddle and walked to the building. It was a ruin, or very nearly. The only thing that held it up was the quality of the masonry work. The walls had been built of the flat stones which, if he were able to judge from the strata he had seen crossing creeks, underlay the thin overburden of earth, flat jagged stone, no wider than six inches, as if a solid structure had been shattered by some sort of explosion.

There was a doorway in the wall, five feet off the ground. Pillars of the stone masonry showed where a wooden porch had once been. He was able to climb up the wall and look inside. The floor had apparently been of wood, too, for that was gone. Someone had even taken structural timbers from the walls, leaving roughly squarish holes. All the wooden door and window framing had been ripped out.

"Well, there you have it," Charley Broadhead said. "That's all that's left."

"What happened to the wood?" Wilton asked. "Termites? Army ants?"

Lucille laughed. "Two-legged termites," she said. "Wood is in very short supply out here. I suppose the wood was gone from here within a month after the last Englishman cleared out. The people who took it didn't think of it as stealing. They thought of it as salvage."

"And the same happened to the livestock?"

Charley shook his head. "People get hung out here for 'salvaging' cattle. I suppose you've got a couple of hundred head of branded cattle around. Don't look for any yearlings, though. They're already wearing someone else's brand. The sheep, of course, are long gone."

"There's two hundred head left?"

"Maybe a few more. They'll last until they die of natural causes. It would cost you more, if that's what you're thinking, to round them up than they'd bring at auction."

"I was thinking of rebuilding the herd," Wilton said. He grabbed the horse's reins and walked him around the rear of the house, where the ground and the doorway were even. Charley and Lucille walked their horses after him.

Wilton, admitting that he knew practically nothing about ranching, realized it would take an enormous amount of money to get this place in operation again, fifteen, perhaps twenty thousand dollars. Perhaps even more. He wondered if his mother had that kind of money, and if she would be willing to invest it in an operation which had already failed once. The sensible thing, obviously, was to sell it to Major Stevens.

On the other hand, selling out would mean the loss of an enormous piece of land, so large that it literally staggered the imagination. The potential was obvious. For some odd reason, he felt quite at home here. In his mind's eye, he had already rebuilt this building.

A trio of rusty iron rods, looking not unlike arrows sticking out of a quiver, caught his eye. He went to them and tugged. They were securely stuck in the ground, in the dried mud. For some reason, it was important that he free whatever it was. He put both gloved hands on one of the iron shafts and gave a mighty tug. The ground cracked and all the iron shafts came free. There was something oddly shaped at the end. He held it up to Broadhead, a question on his face.

"That's what you call a branding iron," Broadhead said, amused.

Wilton looked carefully at the end of the iron, and saw, reversed, like printer's type, two of the letter A set inside a C. Anglo-American Cattle. It was easy to figure out.

"They called it the Double-A C," Broadhead said.

"Yes, I see," Wilton said. "And the idea, I gather, is that this thing is heated, and then pressed against the flanks of the animal?"

"That's the idea," Broadhead said, the expert dealing with the novice.

"Charley, look," Lucille said, and both men turned to look at her, and then where she pointed. A deer, a buck, with a large rack was making its way, at a walk, along a ridge line about 250 yards away.

"I'd like him for the pot," Broadhead said. "God, would I like him for the pot."

"Why don't you take him, then?" Wilton asked.

Both the girl and Broadhead looked at Wilton, surprised that he should have to ask.

"By the time we got close enough for a shot, he'd be in Arizona," Lucille said.

"Would you mind if I had a go at him?" Wilton asked.

"Help yourself," Broadhead said, this time not troubling to hide a sarcastic chuckle. "It's your land, and if you want to make noise, that's your business."

Lucille looked at Charley in surprise. That had been an unkind remark, unfriendly, out of character for Charley.

When she looked at him, she found that he was looking at her. It took a moment for her to realize what was going on.

Charley was annoyed with Wilton, even angry. Since the Englishman had done nothing, said nothing, that justified anger or even annoyance, there was only one possible explanation: Charley had finally seen John Wilton as another man, a possible contender for her. What had made him think that, all of a sudden? Lucille wondered if Charley had decided that she was being a little too friendly to Wilton. That was absurd, of course, but at the same time, it wasn't entirely unpleasant to have Charley think that, to stop taking her so much for granted.

Lucille watched as Wilton unsheathed his rifle from the canvas scabbard on the piebald. She had never seen anything like it before. She was familiar with rifles. She had received a specially engraved Spencer .32-caliber carbine for her fourteenth birthday and had taken deer with it from the day she'd gotten it. Today she had taken a Winchester Model 1873 lever-action .44-40 from the gun cabinet in the house and slipped it into the leather scabbard tied to her saddle as routinely as she had put on gloves to protect her hands. When you hit a deer with a .44-40 bullet, he generally went down. The word used, aptly, was "nailed." When you shot a deer with a .44-40, he was nailed down where he stood. Within range, of course. And this buck was well out of range.

Instead of a lever to chamber cartridges, Wilton's rifle had a handle, which was turned up, pulled straight back, and then pushed forward. There was a strange, fragile-appearing rear sight, a thin piece of metal which rose straight up from the rear of the receiver.

"How far do you think he is?" Wilton asked Charley.

"Two hundred yards," Charley replied immediately, flatly.

"I'd say closer to two-fifty," Lucille said almost argumentatively. "Maybe even three hundred."

The Englishman looked at her and smiled. Lucille knew that he agreed with her estimate of the range. He twisted something on the rear sight, and she realized that it was not only adjustable, but readily adjustable. What a good idea, she thought. How much better than Kentucky windage.

Wilton's rifle had what she had first thought was a leather carrying strap. But when he dropped to the ground, he used the strap to hold the butt of his rifle against his shoulder. A good idea, she realized. She thought almost triumphantly that he seemed to know precisely what he was doing, that he was not simply going "to make noise" when he fired, as Charley had so rudely said.

The rifle discharged, and Lucille just had time to notice that the sound of the firing gave off a much sharper crack than a Winchester or a Sharps, when she heard the unmistakable thu-whack of the bullet striking home.

"Well, you wounded him," Charley said, a hint of disgust in his voice. Charley, like her father, like herself, really hated to see an animal wounded so that it would run away to die in agony. Charley swung easily into his saddle, spurred the animal, and as it broke into a gallop, reached down and took his Winchester from its scabbard. He was going to correct the Englishman's mistake by running the buck down and finishing it off.

Wilton, who had risen from his prone position and was working the handle of his rifle to eject the spent cartridge, looked up at her.

"Where's he going?"

"To finish off the buck," Lucille said.

"I hit him square in the forequarter," Wilton said. "That should have put him down."

For a moment, his calm self-assurance, his arrogance, raised a flare of resentment in Lucille. And as suddenly, it was displaced by amusement. Charley was riding grandly off to do something that didn't need to be done.

Wilton stood up, and with the rifle held easily in his hand, watched as Charley galloped up to where the buck had last been seen. He reined up and slid off the horse and waved.

"I thought so," Wilton said, and went to his piebald and put the rifle back in the scabbard.

"That was a fine shot," Lucille said.

"It's the rifle, not the marksman," Wilton said. He swung onto the piebald and spurred him into a canter. Lucille got on her horse and trotted after him.

The buck, a magnificent animal, had died where he had been shot. He had really nailed him, Lucille thought. How about that, Charles Broadhead?

Charley and Wilton, grunting with the effort, hoisted the

animal onto Charley's horse, and when Wilton had remounted, Charley swung into the saddle behind them. They rode back to the ranch house, and grunting again with the exertion, hung the buck up to gut him, hanging him from one of the branding irons jammed into the masonry of the building.

Charley's ill-will seemed to have disappeared with his honest appreciation of Wilton's marksmanship. He dug into the forequarter with his knife until he found the bullet.

"That's some rifle," he said, all approval. "Look at the way the bullet mushroomed!"

When he had wiped his hands, he walked to Wilton's horse and wordlessly asked if he could look at the weapon. "I never saw one like this before," he said. "English, obviously."

"It's the Lee-Enfield Magazine Rifle, Cavalry Carbine model," Wilton explained. "Caliber .303 inches."

"What's this box on the bottom?" Charley asked, turning the rifle over. "The magazine?"

Wilton nodded. "The sight goes to five hundred yards. Beyond that you have to mentally adjust for the bullet droppage."

"I've got to have one of these," Charley said. "I'll pay you time and a half what you paid for it, and be grateful to you."

"It's yours," Wilton said.

"Why the hell would you want to do that?"

"As a small token of my gradidute for your courtesy and hospitality."

"I'd rather pay you for it," Charley said.

"I know you would," Wilton said. "That's why it gives me such pleasure to give it to you."

For some reason, inexplicable, Lucille now suddenly disliked both of them.

"How are we going to get him back to the ranch?" she demanded, aware that she wanted to break up what she now recognized as a mutual-admiration society. I really am terrible, she thought; I liked it better when Charley was trying to be nasty.

The two men considered the problem. Charley came up with the final answer. The deer would be lashed to Lucille's mare. Since Wilton's piebald was the larger mount, she would, he was sorry to say, have to ride double with Wilton.

So much, she thought angrily, for my sidesaddle, ladylike behavior.

When they had the buck lashed to her mare, Wilton got on the piebald and extended his hand to her. He pulled her on with his hand wrapped around her wrist as she with absolutely no grace whatever pulled her bulky skirt up high enough so that she could straddle the horse behind him.

13

Mr. and Mrs. Randolph Broadhead were on the porch of the main house at Rancho San Miguel when Charley, Wilton, and Lucille finally rode up to it. She had forgotten her suggestion to Charley that he send a *muchacho* to ask them over.

Lucille slid off Wilton's horse without his help, and fixing a smile on her face, walked up to the porch. Charley led her mare around to the rear of the house, to put the buck up in the cellar to hang.

"A little luck, I see," Charley's father said, getting to his feet, taking his hat off.

"My dear," Charley's mother said, an expression of ladylike sypathy for her having to ride double with a man.

"I'm so glad you could come," Lucille said. "May I present our guest? Mr. John Wilton."

As soon as she could, she excused herself and went to her room and ordered Juanita to fill the bathtub. Juanita reported with a sad face that Señor Broadhead had already ordered her to take the tub to Señor Wilton in the guest room.

"As soon as he has his bath," Lucille snapped, "bring it in here."

Mr. Broadhead spent dinner telling Wilton what he knew of the legal problems of the Anglo-American Cattle Company, including something she hadn't known, that there was federal tax trouble. He gave Wilton the name of a lawyer,

99

Albert Dennison, in Dallas, who could probably be of great assistance to him.

The next day Wilton rode into Loving, then took the train to Dallas. Lucille put him—permanently, she was quite sure—from her mind, and went down to look in on her father.

In Dallas, Wilton took a room at the Harlingen House, an apparently brand-new hostelry, four floors of rooms behind a wide porch, topped by spires and ornate scrollwork, with more scroll work on the roof over the porch.

He started to write his mother a letter, and then decided that a telegram would have more impact. He telegraphed that the property looked promising, despite obvious neglect; that he was meeting with an attorney to clear up some minor tax matters; and that he would need five thousand dollars to pay the taxes and for other immediate expenses; would she please wire same immediately?

The telegram was so long that he considered changing it back to a letter, but finally decided against that. The sooner she had the information, the better. He proceeded to visit the lawyer Mr. Broadhead had recommended.

Albert Dennison occupied a suite of offices taking up the entire second floor of a three-story brick building on Second Street. The reception room was large, cluttered with heavy leather furniture, potted plants, and an enormous oil painting of the Battle of the Alamo.

Dennison himself was large, red-faced, already balding, and looked about thirty-five. He was tieless, his collar was open, and because he wore no jacket, Wilton was able to see the suspenders, of a woven material with a design of roses, which he thought set some new standard for bad taste.

"I'm Albert Dennison," the man said, and waved Wilton through the door to the inner office. The office was ornately furnished, and with the largest desk Wilton had ever seen. A stuffed moose head hung from a wall, the glass eyes staring balefully toward the desk. There was a low table between two overstuffed leather armchairs.

"Sit," Dennison said to him. Wilton sat.

Dennison bent over him a moment later and handed him a

water glass with about an inch and a half of dark brown fluid in it. "Tennessee sour mash," he said mysteriously. "Mellow as a maiden's milk."

He tipped his glass up and drained it. Wilton did likewise. The bourbon whiskey burned his throat.

Dennison read the letter of introduction. "You must have really made an impression on Major Stevens," he said, putting on his coat and motioning Wilton out of his office.

The United States marshal was visibly surprised to find Albert Dennison on the side of Anglo-American Land & Cattle, and very obliging. He'd be happy to take a bank draft and stop the sale of the property for overdue taxes.

"I . . . uh . . ." Wilton began with some embarrassment, "am not at the moment in a position to issue a bank draft. I am, in fact, awaiting the transfer of funds to me from Philadelphia."

He got a look of withering scorn, alloyed with suspicion, from Albert Dennison.

"I have about a thousand dollars in cash that I could give you right now," Wilton said. "Until the other funds arrive from Philadelphia."

The marshal looked at Dennison for his reaction.

"Have you picked a bank to put your money in when it comes from Philadelphia?" Dennison asked.

"No, I haven't," Wilton confessed.

Dennison recommended the First Republic Bank, where he kept his own funds. He then accepted from Wilton a bank draft on the First Republic for the $3,880.40 due for taxes in arrears. The check was postdated five days, more than time enough for Wilton's money to arrive from Philadelphia. Dennison wrote a bank draft on his own account, and received a receipt from the marshal.

Wilton, embarrassed that he couldn't issue a draft himself, was also nervous. What if his mother didn't have the money to send from Philadelphia? He was sure that severe penalties were provided for people who issued bank drafts they couldn't back with cash.

He had to remind himself that money *was* on the way from Philadelphia, and that the tax bill would have to be paid in any event, even if his mother decided to dispose of the property.

He drank a bit that night, and slept late the next morning.

It was noon when he asked for messages at the desk. He was handed a blue-and-white envelope. The words "Western Union" were printed on it. He felt an immense sense of relief; the money was here already. He should have known better. His mother was more reliable, more efficient than most men he'd known.

He tore open the envelope:

JOHN F. W. WILTON
HARLINGEN HOUSE HOTEL
DALLAS, TEXAS
THERE IS NO MONEY. COUNTING ON YOU TO DISPOSE OF
THE NEW MEXICAN PROPERTY AT BEST PRICE AS SOON AS
POSSIBLE. POWER OF ATTORNEY MAILED TO YOU TODAY.
LOVE MOTHER

Oh, my God!

John F. W. Wilton crushed the telegram in his hand and threw it into the spittoon by the desk. Then he walked into the bar of the Harlingen House, propped his foot on the brass rail, and leaned on it, supporting himself with both hands.

The bartender came to him. This was the kind of customer he preferred. A well-dressed gentleman whose suntanned face identified him as someone who spent long hours outdoors.

"Brandy, please," Wilton said. "French, if you have it."

The way he was standing, as if he needed the support of the bar to stay erect, also caused his frock coat to fall open. The bartender could see the butt of the huge Webley .455 poking out from under Wilton's arm.

"Yes, sir," he said, and scurried away to get a bottle of brandy, good brandy, real French Cognac. This was a gent, the genuine thing. The bartender's snap judgment of character was confirmed when he delivered the bottle and a glass. The gent said, "Leave it, if you please," and then casually laid two silver dollars on the bar, waving away the change.

Wilton was oblivious of the interest he had aroused. He was doing his best to adjust to his position; being, for the first time in his life, in a situation over which he had no control whatever, and for which he could see no solution. He was out of money, and had no prospects to get any. Worse, he had issued an absolutely worthless bank draft for $3,880.40 to Albert Dennison, a clearly criminal act. There was no use wiring his mother to explain the problem; there was no mistaking the wording of the telegram: there was no money.

Of course, eventually Albert Dennison would be repaid. The property was worth far more than $3,880.40. But Dennison now had the means to have him put in prison and make him appear a cad and a scoundrel and a fool before Major Stevens, his daughter, and before Charles Broadhead and his family, the first friends he had made in the United States of America. He would never be able to face any of them again. That was presuming he eventually got out of jail.

He could not even take the gentleman's way out, for even beyond his duty as a gentleman was his duty to his widowed mother. She expected him to sell the property, and he could hardly do that if he put a bullet through his temple. But how could he sell it if he was in prison?

What would it do to his mother when she learned, as she would, inevitably, what had taken place?

The first time the idea came to his mind, he immediately dismissed it as clutching at straws. But after the fourth glass of the brandy, which seemed to calm him somewhat, it seemed, actually, like a rather good idea. Putting aside for the moment the truism that one should never gamble when one needed to win, what other option did he have?

If he lost every penny he had in cash, he couldn't possibly be any worse off than he was now. And he had already displayed an unusual flair for cards. He had, in fact, won enough money at cards to permit him to go into partnership with Kate Shaughnessy. That triggered a moment's desperate hope. If he wired Kate, could Kate wire him the $2,500 she owed him, plus the loan of, say, another thousand?

The hope faded with his realization that no matter how many gentlemen callers Kate and her friends had entertained, there was no way she could have earned $2,500 in so short a period of time.

It was either play at cards or nothing.

"My good man," he said, flagging down the bartender, "is

there somewhere in Dallas where I might find a game of poker?"

"Madam Estelle's," the bartender said.

"Is it a . . .?" Wilton said.

"A sporting house," the bartender said.

"And where might I find it?" Wilton asked as he downed the dregs of his glass.

14

Madam Estelle's turned out to be a huge Victorian house on Park Street, three-storied, surrounded by a wide porch, the door to which was opened by a black woman in a French maid's uniform.

"Afternoon, suh," she said. "Madam Estelle will receive you in the drawing room."

The drawing room was large, and gave Wilton the impression of having been stuffed with furniture by someone with unlimited funds and almost incredibly bad taste. There were three men in the room, and a woman who could only be the proprietor of this ostentatious brothel. She was large, big-boned, with yellow hair piled high on top of her head. She wore a stomacher, the centerpiece of which was a ruby, and on most of the pudgy fingers with which she held a champagne glass were diamond and ruby rings.

When she saw Wilton standing somewhat awkwardly by the door, she walked over to him. He was aware that she was examining him appraisingly. And he sensed that he had not been found wanting.

"I don't believe I've had the pleasure," she said, grandly extending a jeweled hand. "What was the name?"

"John F. W. Wilton," he said.

"A pleasure, Mr. Wilton," Madam Estelle said. "A newcomer to our fair city, I gather?"

"Just passing through," Wilton said, taking her hand and

kissing it. He wondered why he had done that. Perhaps it was the brandy.

Madam Estelle beamed at him. "Might I offer you a small libation to welcome you to my establishment, Mr. Wilton?" she said.

"What I had in mind, ma'am," Wilton said formally, "is that I might find some convivial companions at cards."

She examined him appraisingly again; he wondered why.

"Forgive me for saying this," she said. "I mean nothing by it. But the stakes here are rather high. Are you prepared to lose several hundred dollars?"

"I am prepared to win at least that much," Wilton said, rather pleased with his spontaneous wit.

"And again forgive me, Mr. Wilton, but we haven't had the chance to really make your acquaintance, if you get my meaning. I must be sure in my own mind, before introducing a newcomer to my old friends, that he, in a word, has the cash."

"I have something over a thousand dollars on my person," Wilton said.

She didn't reply to that. After a moment, he realized that she was waiting to see his money. He took out his billfold and let her see the gold certificates.

"Right this way, Mr. Wilton," she said. "There's a game in progress in the upstairs parlor I'm sure you'll find to your liking."

He suddenly understood, for the first time, and chillingly, what hell those poor damned chaps one heard of—those who lost the regimental mess funds at cards, those who issued valueless checks, those who were cashiered, those who took the gentleman's way out—went through. For the first time, he wondered if that is what happened to his father. Was it possible that his father's suicide, while he was "temporarily bereft of his senses," had really been because he had gambled away his money?

I am dissolute, he thought, depraved. A rake. A scoundrel. About to gamble with the less than two thousand dollars that is all I own in the world, in debt beyond any capacity, or even hope, to pay, about to be exposed before the world.

Madam Estelle led him through the upstairs parlor to one

of the bedrooms. There, gathered around a table covered with green baize, sat four men in their shirtsleeves.

"Gentlemen," Madam Estelle said. "This is Mr. Wilton. He's looking for a little action. Mr. Wilton, this is Colonel Pope, Major Davis, Mr. Porter, and Mr. Winslow."

"You just got here in time, sir," Porter said. "I have just been wiped out." He stood up, apparently unconcerned about his bad luck, and held the chair out.

"I thought I might take a hand or two myself," Madam Estelle said. She exchanged glances with Colonel Pope, a stout, red-faced man. Aha, Wilton thought, rather pleased with his perception. I have just been pictured as a pigeon ready for the plucking. The pleased feeling was almost immediately replaced by the realization: that's what I probably am.

The colonel explained the rules of the game: "We call it table stakes, sir. No bet can exceed the amount in the pot. We take only one marker."

"Marker?"

"Indebtedness. If you run out of money during a hand, your marker is good for the bets in that hand only. If you lose that hand, you're out of the game, and you're expected to make the marker good within twenty-four hours. But you can't play on markers, except for the hand in which you run out of cash. Understand?"

"I understand," Wilton said.

Madam Estelle discarded the cards she had gathered to her, opened a fresh deck, went through them with amazing skill, discarding the jokers, and then shuffled them with professional facility.

"The game which most of us prefer, Mr. Wilton," she said, "is seven-card stud. Is that all right with you?"

"Yes, ma'am," Wilton said.

Wallets were produced, and money laid on the table. Wilton laid out five hundred dollars, and within a half an hour had to go back in the wallet for another five hundred.

I am either a gambler, he thought, in the crazy sense, convinced my luck is going to turn, or else I'm drunk enough to think that I've got these people figured out. I know that's the last time I'm going to have to dig into my wallet.

In the next three hands, he had cause to consider that he was proved a crazy fool, for he dropped three hundred and eighty of the five hundred. But on the next hand, correctly reading the colonel's tightening eyes as an indication that he wasn't nearly as convinced of the value of his cards as his hundred-dollar bets tried to suggest, he stayed with him and called and raised the final bet two hundred dollars.

The colonel looked at him very intently, and then slid his cards, facedown, into the center of the table.

"*L'audace, l'audace, tourjours l'audace*," Colonel Pope said. "That was an expensive lesson, sir, to learn that you play poker like a cavalryman."

Madam Estelle raked in the pot, counted it, stacked the bills and coins carefully, extracted the house's one percent, and slid it over to Wilton. "One thousand, four hundred and forty-eight dollars and fifty cents," she said.

Wilton nodded at her, and then dealt the cards. He had a sudden sure insight. Colonel Pope had completely misread him; he thought Wilton had bought the pot on a bluff. He hadn't been bluffing: he had had a full house, jacks and fives.

Two hands later, God or the laws of probability handed Wilton a pair of nines, facedown, with a queen as his first card faceup. That gave him the bet, and he bet a hundred dollars. Everybody stayed.

His second up card was a third nine. The bet went to the colonel, who had the ace of hearts as high card. The colonel bet another hundred, and again everyone stayed. The third card was a fourth nine, giving him a pair of nines showing.

His heart started to beat rapidly, and he was furious to know that his excitement must be showing. But something told him that the colonel (whom he regarded as his only real adversary) had misread his excitement. He *knew* the colonel thought he had two pairs, queens and nines, and was betting on a full house. He already had four of a kind.

Wilton pushed two hundred dollars into the pot.

"Your two and two more," the colonel said, when the bet got to him. Madam Estelle and Major Davis anted up. Wilton looked at the money before him.

"Do the rules of your game permit me to raise a raise?" he asked.

"Raise away, Lieutenant," the colonel said. Wilton raised another two hundred.

Colonel Pope drew a second ace, giving him the best

showing hand and the bet. Smiling directly at Wilton, he pushed four hundred dollars into the pot. Major Davis folded as the bet came to him. Wilton pushed in the four hundred. Madam Estelle looked between the two of them, and then turned over her cards.

Major Davis dealt the final card, facedown. Wilton turned it over. He smiled. Another queen. Which he didn't need. He looked at the colonel, to find the colonel looking at him.

"Five hundred to you, sir," the man said. Wilton looked at the colonel's exposed cards. There was no way the colonel could have a flush, and that's what he was going to need to beat the four nines.

"Your five hundred," Wilton said, and then he counted the money remaining in front of him. "And six hundred and forty-dollars more."

"Make that a thousand," the colonel replied. "We'll take your marker."

There was a moment's terror. Had he read everything wrong? Was he about to lose his cash, too? "You have my marker, sir," he said.

"Full house," the colonel said. "Aces over kings."

"Four nines, sir," Wilton said, turning them over.

"I'll be goddamned!" the colonel said.

Madam Estelle counted up the pot, took the house's percentage, and pushed the money over to Wilton. "Six thousand, eight hundred and thirty-one dollars," she said.

He was exultant.

Wilton thumbed through the money. He knew what he should do. He should take out enough to make good the bank draft before his luck turned. But that might turn his luck. And there was no way he could do that, as a gentleman, for it would suggest he was leaving the game without affording the others the chance to win their money back.

The cards were dealt, and another glass of champagne set beside him.

He woke in excruciating pain. He was lying on his stomach with his right arm hanging out of bed. The circulation had been cut off, and the arm hurt from the shoulder to the fingertips.

He remembered, suddenly, quite clearly, what he had said,

immediately before passing out. He had said, "That's it, I'm afraid, gentlemen, for me."

But what the hell had it meant?

He was in bed, with a mirror on the wall placed so that it could reflect the activity beneath it. He could focus his eyes enough to see his reflection. He looked like death warmed over.

What the hell had happened?

He located his clothing, neatly hung over a chair. He slid out of bed and crawled to it, sitting on the floor while he took his wallet from his coat. He took it out. It was empty.

Oh, God! He had played until he had lost the money he had won. He remembered the glass after glass of champagne, his drunken, *insane* notion that he couldn't lose, that tonight was his night, that there was no way he could do anything but win.

Obviously, the opposite had happened: he had lost everything back, and given his marker, and *then* said, "That's it, I'm afraid, gentlemen, for me." God only knows how large that marker was. It didn't matter. He couldn't have paid a marker if it were for two dollars.

"You'll be all right, suh," said a voice by the bedside, and a large man in a butler's striped apron put Wilton's arm over his shoulders and half-dragged and half-carried him down three flights of stairs, to the basement, and into a small room with a heavy door. He was lowered onto a rough wooden bench, and he became suddenly aware of an awful heat.

He raised his eyes in time to see the man throw a half-bucket of water on what looked like a pile of rocks. A cloud of steam erupted. What were they doing to him?

The obvious thing was to lie down, gather his strength, and make an attempt to break out when he had greater control of his faculties. He lay down and closed his eyes.

He was placed on a table, was roughly rolled over onto his stomach, and assaulted. An enormous black woman, her ample abdomen pressed against the side of the narrow table, beat him with the lower edge of her hands, starting at his neck and working very slowly down his backbone, over his rump, down his thighs and calves.

She rolled him over and repeated the mauling on the other side. And then she began again. She bent and twisted his limbs, starting with his feet, working up to his head, which she twisted violently from side to side and back and forth. Even his fingers didn't escape her.

Finally he was put into a dressing gown and set up in a barber chair.

"You just lean back now, suh," the woman said. "And we'll take care of your hair and mustache."

Wilton was too baffled and exhausted to protest. He closed his eyes and half-dozed as his face was lathered, and he felt the flick of a razor against his cheek and neck.

A hot towel was applied, and then a cold towel, and finally some sort of perfume was slapped onto his face and then vigorously rubbed in. He felt the chair being returned to a vertical position. He opened his eyes and looked in a mirror.

By God, he looked human! And, incredibly, he felt alive. His stomach was tied in a knot, and he still had a headache, but it was a question of comparing how he felt now with how he had felt when he woke up, and the difference between those extremes was astonishing.

The butler returned with an assortment of items on a tray. As Wilton watched with morbid curiosity, the man put the yolks of two eggs into a glass, added salt, Worcestershire sauce, two or three ounces of something that was probably an intoxicant, and finally shook drops of a red liquid from a small bottle into it. He stirred it vigorously with a fork and then handed the glass to Wilton.

"No, thank you," Wilton said firmly.

"You just drink that down, suh," the man said. "It be good for you."

"I don't want it, thank you," Wilton said quite formally.

The woman pinned him to the barber chair, the butler forced his jaws open and poured half of the contents of the glass into his open mouth. He had no choice but to swallow it. There was a burning sensation in his throat, moving down toward his stomach. He opened his mouth to complain, and the rest of the drink was poured into his mouth.

The second half didn't burn as the first had. Actually, there appeared to be something therapeutic in the concoction. A warm glow spread throughout his midsection, the tenseness in his muscles relaxed.

"That's what we call a New Orleans prairie oyster, suh," the man said. "Good for what ails you."

"Apparently," Wilton said. He pushed himself out of the chair. He could walk without staggering, he found. Actually, he felt rather good.

"Right this way, suh," the butler said. He held open a door for him and led him back up the stairs to the third floor. He indicated a door, and opened it for him.

Albert Dennison sat behind the desk in what was obviously the office of the establishment. "Good afternoon," he said. "Almost good evening. How do you feel?"

"More ashamed than I have ever felt in my life," Wilton said. "I don't know quite what to say."

"What you need is a drink," Dennison said. "Give you courage to face the evening."

"God, no!"

"That was quite a performance you put on last night," Dennison said. "It will be a long time before they forget it around here."

"May I ask how you found me here?"

"When you passed out, they went through your pockets. They found the envelope, addressed to me, of Randolph Broadhead's letter. A good thing for you they did."

"I am completely at your mercy," Wilton said. "If you will tell me what is expected of me, I'll do whatever I can to make things right. I realize that my word, under the circumstances, may be quite suspect, but I swear to you—"

"Jesus God, boy, you really are in bad shape, aren't you?" Dennison said, holding his hand toward Wilton, palm outward. "Now, whoa! Just a minute."

He reached in his frock-coat pocket and came out with three pieces of paper. "I don't quite know how to tell you this, Wilton," he said, "but believe me, this isn't some attempt to talk you out of what you won fair and square."

"I don't follow you."

"All I'm asking, as a friend of Colonel Pope and Major Davis, and recommending to you as your lawyer, is that you just extend them a little time to make these markers good."

Wilton didn't trust his ears. He walked to the desk and took the pieces of paper from Dennison's hand. He read their

112

short messages and then read them again, not quite willing to believe what he was reading.

Dallas, Texas,
    I promise to pay to John F. W. Wilton, Esq., on demand, the sum of $23,500.
September 22, 1890   Elton P. Pope

I promise to pay to JFW Wilton, on demand, the sum of $14,300.
                             Major George Davis
                         Dallas, Sept. 22, 1890

Dallas, Sept. 22, 1890.
    To Mr. J. F. W. Wilton. IOU $9,050, payable on demand.
                         Mrs. Estelle Monaghan

15

Paul MacSwain was standing beside Margaret Wilton on the Philadelphia station's platform, obviously waiting for someone on the incoming train. Suddenly Margaret put her hand over her mouth, then began to wave a handkerchief in great excitement. John Wilton removed his Stetson and waved it back.

"Hallo, Mother!" he shouted.

He leaped down the steps, ran to her, wrapping his arms around her in an exuberant gesture, and actually lifted her off the ground.

"Darling, I never would have recognized you," she said when he had set her down. "That mustache! And that spectacular hat! And since when have you been smoking cigars!"

"Mother, you look simply splendid!" John F. W. Wilton said.

"John, this is Mr. Paul MacSwain, who was good enough to come here with me. Thomas is at school."

"How do you do, sir?" Wilton said, taking the older man's hand.

"I expected, frankly," MacSwain said, for some reason seeming to be pleased, "a boy."

John Wilton smiled; a boy, indeed. He remembered how much of a man he had had to be in the last couple of days, winning at that insane poker game in Dallas, coolly depositing the money at the First Republic Bank, paying off Albert

Dennison, then allowing himself to be placed on a train to Philadelphia—for "your health," Dennison had said, until it could be proven that Wilton was really what he claimed, and not a professional gambler working the West.

"Come back in a couple of months," Dennison had said. "That is, if you turn out to be Lieutenant Wilton of Prince What's-his-name's Indian Royal Cavalry. Otherwise, I wouldn't go too far west of Philadelphia if I were you." Albert shook his head. "I like you, Wilton; I look forward to renewing our acquaintance."

"Have you had any lunch?" MacSwain asked now.

"On the train, thank you."

"Oh, and I have lunch waiting," Margaret said.

"In that case, Mother, I shall eat again. Where did you say Thomas is?"

"He's enrolled at the university," Margaret Wilton said. "In the School of Business Administration. He wanted to come meet you, of course, but I told him he could wait until this afternoon."

"Of course."

"I didn't ask how the trip was," Margaret Wilton said.

"Rather interesting, actually," her son replied. "I'm a bit sorry it's over."

John Wilton walked up the stairs of the Union League and handed his Stetson, his gloves, and his walking stick to the porter. "John F. W. Wilton, as the guest of Mr. Paul MacSwain," he announced. He followed the porter up a wide flight of marble stairs.

Paul MacSwain was sitting at a small table in the upstairs dining room. He got to his feet when he saw Wilton coming in. "I imagine it must be difficult for all of you, suddenly coming here," MacSwain said.

"I would suppose that it is more difficult for Mother," Wilton said. "I stand in your debt, sir, for your many courtesies to her. And to Thomas and to me."

"Thomas is a rather unusual lad," MacSwain said. "I like him very much."

"And he, you, sir," Wilton said. "He gave me—please don't mention it—a rather incredibly detailed report of your business accomplishments. He seems fascinated both with business and with you."

"He asks a lot of questions," MacSwain said. "And although I think of myself as closemouthed, I find myself answering them. I have come to look rather fondly upon him."

Wilton nodded.

"And I have come," MacSwain plunged ahead, "to regard your good mother with a great deal of respect and admiration."

"You will forgive me for saying, sir," Wilton said, "but when I came down to luncheon yesterday and found Mother feeding your son, I began to suspect that you had more in common than business interests."

"The change in that child since your mother has been looking after him is astonishing," MacSwain said. "He is happier than he's ever been." He paused. "I'm skirting the issue again," he said. "What I'm leading up to, of course, is the question of asking your mother to marry me. After a suitable period, of course."

"A suitable period?"

"Your mother is so recently widowed," MacSwain said.

"But she's no longer in London, either," Wilton said.

"You're suggesting that we needn't wait a suitable time, a year?"

"It would seem to me, Mr. MacSwain," Wilton said, "that in your circumstances, there is no reason to wait at all."

Paul T. MacSwain had a sudden and very unpleasant thought. Margaret had certainly told her son about her financial condition. The son had instantly decided that any man with the means to support his mother was a windfall. It wasn't that MacSwain minded at all marrying a penniless woman—by God, he'd marry her if he came across her mopping floors—but there was something disgusting about the way this young fop seemed to be throwing her at him. Getting rid of the responsibility for his mother, and finding himself a warm nest all at once.

"Is something wrong, Mr. MacSwain?" Wilton asked, still smiling.

MacSwain realized that he must have read something in his face. He put a smile on his face. "What are your plans, John?" he asked.

"I had hoped to have the opportunity to discuss them with you," Wilton said after a moment. "But not just yet."

"Why not now? Clear the decks between us, so to speak."

"Why not indeed?" Wilton said. "At the risk of betraying Mother's confidence, Mr. MacSwain, she rather anticipated the subject of our conversation."

"Oh, she did?"

"And she, uh, led me to believe that you intended to, as she put it, find a place for me with your new firm."

"Does that interest you?" MacSwain said, reminding himself to keep his control.

"With certainly no offense intended, sir, it does not."

"It does not?" MacSwain asked, surprised. There was bound to be a catch in that reply. What did he want, a cash settlement? To "borrow" money?

"What I had hoped, sir," Wilton said, a little uneasy, "after we had come to know one another better, was to enlist your support."

"To what end?"

"Mother is a rather determined woman," Wilton said. "And at the moment, she is determined that we dispose of the New Mexican property, and that I stay here in Philadelphia."

"I've been led to believe that the Anglo-American Land & Cattle Company is an empty shell," MacSwain said.

"It will take about thirty thousand dollars to get it back in operation," Wilton said. "And there will be no profits to speak of for at least three years. But the potential is there."

"Okay," MacSwain said. "You've got it."

"I beg your pardon?"

"I'll lend you the money, if that's what you want," MacSwain said. He told himself that he would not permit himself even to consider that Margaret had put the boy up to this.

"I wasn't asking to borrow any money."

"You weren't?" MacSwain asked, and then he lost control. "Then what are you up to, young man? You and I both know that it took your mother's last dime to keep the bank from repossessing the mills, and if you were out there, you know as well as I do, probably from Colonel Elton P. Pope, that the Anglo-American Land & Cattle Company is about to go on the auction block for unpaid taxes."

Wilton, his mouth open, looked at Paul T. MacSwain, literally struck dumb.

"Let me state my position clearly, once and for all," MacSwain said. "Making your mother happy is the one thing in my mind. I happen to be in a position where I can advance you whatever money is needed. But don't you ever think, you arrogant young pup, that I don't know what I'm doing and that I'm not two or three jumps ahead of you all the time."

Wilton shook his head in astonishment. He was smiling, which infuriated MacSwain. He stood up, bumping the table as he did so.

"You think over what I've said to you," he barked. "And at some other time we'll resume this discussion."

"Sit down, Mr. MacSwain," John Wilton said coldly. MacSwain looked at him in surprise. He was not used to having someone address him in that tone of voice. "You heard me, sir. Sit down!"

MacSwain fought the urge to storm out of the room, reminding himself just in time that the last thing he wanted to do was put Margaret in a position where she would be forced to choose between him and her son.

He sat down, actually trembling. "I have a tendency," he said, "to say things in heat that I later regret."

"Well, we have that much in common," Wilton said. "You mentioned Colonel Pope. I gather that when he made inquiries about me, they came to your attention. And what did you tell him?"

"I gave you, solely because of your mother, the benefit of the doubt," MacSwain said. "At my request, the First Philadelphia wired them that you were both known here as reputable people, but that without specific reason it was bank policy not to furnish financial information."

"What the colonel hoped to hear was that you had never heard of either of us," Wilton said. "Which would have permitted him to take what solace he could in knowing he had lost his money to a card sharp."

"Do you want to explain what that means?"

"I won thirty thousand dollars of the colonel's money at cards," Wilton said.

"Thirty thousand dollars? At cards? You must be crazy."

"I was drunk," Wilton said.

Paul MacSwain could not think of any reply to that. He picked up his glass of sour-mash whiskey and tossed it down.

16

On October 7, 1890, a special train departed from the Broad Street Station of the Pennsylvania Railroad. Immediately behind the locomotive was a brand-new passenger car, Pennsylvania Railroad Number 3408. Behind it was Dining Car (Pennsylvania 786) and Lounge Car (Pennsylvania 1005), both removed for this trip from their usual attachment to the *Congressional Limited*.

The train departed precisely at seven A.M. As soon as it began to move, Mr. and Mrs. C. Harold Tilley; Miss Martha Tilley; Mrs. Margaret Wilton; Mr. Paul T. MacSwain and Messrs. John F. W. And Thomas Wilton, entered the dining car and took their places at previously set and place-marked tables, beside each of which stood a private waiter. At the head of the table sat Mr. and Mrs. Nicholas Cadwallader Murray, he being president of the Pennsylvania Railroad and, along with Harold Tilley, one of Paul MacSwain's oldest friends. A photographer took pictures.

The conductor and several waiters scurried to open doors and windows to provide a draft so that the smoke from the photographer's flash powder would be quickly sucked out of the car, and then breakfast was served.

Martha Tilley spent most of her time trying not to look at John Wilton. She thought he was terrible.

He kept referring to her as "Little Miss Tilley," and otherwise treated her as if she were thirteen years old. It had been doubly infuriating because her parents had found nothing wrong with this. They had actually sent her from the room, as if she were a child, when the conversation seemed to be turning to subjects not fit for an innocent child's ears.

She was not a child, and to tell the truth, she was not exactly innocent, either. Phoebe Murray had come across, in the attic of their home, a rather extensive and practically unbelievable collection of glass photographic plates, the ownership of which was unknown, but probably that of her Uncle Philus, showing absolutely naked men and women doing all sorts of utterly nasty things. And Phoebe, who had an unbelievably nasty mind, had told Martha about a part of her body that she hadn't even dreamed about, and what happened when you touched it.

Worse than that, Martha had allowed Thomas Wilton to touch her breast, and if they hadn't been interrupted, she was going to let him put her hand on him, down there.

Thomas was from England, and things were different, more wicked, over there. He had told her he was in love with her, and more or less because it seemed to be an interesting thing to do, she had told him that she loved him too. She had not considered beforehand the possibility that Thomas would go on from there with the philosophical argument that if they were in love, they should make love. She agreed with his philosophy, truth to tell, but she wasn't in love with him. Besides, if she did that, he would certainly tell somebody about it, and that would absolutely ruin her.

The truth was, of course, that many girls her age, mostly among the Irish and Polish immigrants, were already mothers. She had everything they had, even if she hadn't used it yet, and the high-and-mighty John F. W. Wilton, with that absurd mustache and those loathsome cigars, had no right to treat her as if she were a mere child.

Up ahead in the dining car, as the train slowed for Paoli, she saw Thomas looking at her, and she knew what he was thinking, that sometime during the three days they would be at Paoli for the Rose Tree Hunt, they would be able to get together and be alone. She did not see John looking at her, and she had no way, of course, of knowing that, actually, John Wilton had indeed inspected her and found her quite appealing. He had tempered his assessment of her with the belief that she was just right for Thomas.

121

The train wheezed onto a siding in Paoli. A line of carriages of all shapes and descriptions, including an absolutely handsome coach drawn by four matched grays, was lined up waiting for them. On the door was a crest and the legend "THE ROSE TREE HUNT."

To John Wilton, the idea of these people riding to hounds was amusing. Not only did they seem to be shamelessly aping the very English customs they had staged a revolution against, but there was something rather funny about riding to hounds itself. The witticism of the English playright, son of Sir William Wilde, Mr. Oscar Wilde, concerning fox hunting (the unspeakable in hot pursuit of the uneatable) had quickly made its way around the world to her majesty's cavalry regiments. Wilton had thought it hilarious, although some of his brother officers had thought it rather bad taste.

There was an elaborate means of seating people in the line of carriages, one Wilton did not quite understand. He understood that he was being honored by being asked to ride on the hansom coach's driver's seat (Mr. Nicholas Cadwallader Murray rode beside him), but he didn't understand why the Americans felt the precarious perch so prestigious. In England, the footmen rode there.

It was a five-mile trip from the siding at Paoli to the Rose Tree Hunt Club, which meant that it would be a five-mile ride back that evening, and another five miles back in the morning, and so on. Wilton resolved to see if he couldn't prevail upon someone to give him the use of a mount. Ten miles a day in a carriage was a bit much.

The Rose Tree Hunt Club itself could have been transferred intact from England. There was a riding ring, fenced with whitewashed poles and rails, a canvas-shaded grandstand, booths serving food and drink, white-painted stables, a white-painted clubhouse, and behind the grandstand, what looked like a polo field, although it seemed unlikely to Wilton that the game, only recently introduced to England from India, would already have made its way over here.

The balance of the morning was given over, as Wilton thought of it, to women's affairs. There was what seemed like an endless procession of children, all correctly attired for equestrian events, although some of them looked barely out of the cradle, and a good half-dozen of whose riding dress showed large dark wet spots that couldn't possibly have been perspiration, riding around the circle, atop Shetland ponies and small horses, accompanied by mommies and sometimes grandmas.

As the morning wore on, the age of the participants went up, from preschoolers to school age, and from school age to a category described in the program as "juniors," an appellation Wilton decided was based on the fact that junior girls had bosoms.

Finally it ground to a halt and luncheon was served in the clubhouse. The board groaned, Wilton thought. The display of food was sinful. Telling himself that he hadn't forgotten his vow to behave himself, but that he was entitled to just a couple of little nips, he slipped off as soon as he could into the gentleman's saloon, found a table in the corner, and had the waiter bring him a glass of Chablis.

As Wilton walked into the gentleman's saloon of the clubhouse (that is, as his mother and MacSwain and the Tilleys and the others walked out to return to the grandstands for the afternoon's events), Martha Tilley and her friends walked into the dining hall, having just changed from their riding dress into afternoon frocks.

They were shown to a table, and almost immediately a waiter appeared and offered champagne.

"Thank you so much," Phoebe Murray replied immediately, for all of them.

They were not supposed to have champagne, but their parents were gone, and who would be the wiser? It wasn't as if they were still children. They were students at the University of Pennsylvania, after all.

And then Martha Tilley raised her head to look around for the source of the voice calling for "Mr. John Wilton. Mr. John Wilton, please!" She saw one of the servants, a boy of about her age, moving through the dining hall, followed by one of the polo players.

Wilton was not in the dining room.

Martha wondered what was going on. It took her a minute or two to get Phoebe to agree to leave the dining hall, but finally she succeeded, and the four girls, giggling somewhat, left to go to the clubhouse.

Wilton, who had been thinking about Lucille Stevens and how she could show these overprivileged girls what horsemanship was all about, heard his name being called, looked around, saw the boy, and raised his hand over his head and snapped his fingers.

The servant and the man in riding clothes came to his table. "Mr. Wilton, your mother tells me that you've played polo," the man said.

"I have," Wilton admitted.

"The thing is, we're short a player. Dickie Williams took a tumble and dislocated his shoulder."

"Well, I would be happy to oblige you, sir," Wilton said. "But I don't have any riding clothes with me."

"Oh, we can fix you up," the man said. "No problem at all about that."

"Well, let me check with Mother," Wilton said. "And if she has nothing scheduled for me . . . when are you going to play?"

"We're playing now. Dickie took a tumble just before the first chukker ended."

"Now?" Wilton said. "You mean, right now?"

"Right now," the man said, and reading into Wilton's obvious reluctance something that wasn't there, went on, "You *can* play polo, can't you? I mean, you've played before?"

"Yes, of course I have," Wilton said. He stood up, walked out of the Rose Tree Hunt Clubhouse to be outfitted.

Then he cantered onto the playing field.

Meanwhile, Martha Tilley, accompanied by her friends, had made her way to the polo field and found that a champagne bar had been set up under a canvas fly against the sun. She had just accepted a glass when she looked out at the field and saw John Wilton.

The casual seat Wilton displayed was that of a superb horseman, someone who felt as much at ease in a saddle as he did in an overstuffed chair. He rode effortlessly and, Martha admitted to herself, marvelously. Before the chukker was over, he had scored one goal, a 150-yard ride without assistance, and given assistance to two other goals, driving the ball to a teammate in such a manner that a six-year-old with a croquet mallet could have made the goal.

He was a wonder, Martha thought. Indeed, it was only right that she should tell Mr. Wilton she considered his playing wonderful. But she felt a little dizzy, and decided to sit and wait to feel better before she spoke to him.

A half-hour later she still felt faint; in fact, the sun and the chatter of her friends seemed to make matters worse. She excused herself, and asked one of the waiting servants to drive her back to the railroad cars to lie down. It would be nice and quiet there, and she wouldn't be embarrassed by anyone seeing her ill from the effects of the champagne.

She didn't know how long she'd been in her compartment when John Wilton rode by on a huge sorrel. He cantered past Martha's carriage, looked in, and bowed. He was still wearing the clothing he had worn to play polo, the shirt now open almost all the way down his chest. He laughed loudly, and she knew, and somehow the knowledge pleased her, that he was drunk.

She wondered where he was going, and then figured it out. He was going to his car to change clothing. She got up, splashed water on her face, smoothed her hair, and then walked out toward Wilton's compartment. She was having trouble breathing. Her heart was jumping out of her chest. What she was doing was insane!

She skipped the first door, and opened the second. There was no one in that compartment. And there was no one in the third, either, but when she opened the fourth door, she found what she was looking for. John Wilton, naked except for a towel around his waist, having had a shower, was shaving before a mirror. Martha felt her knees grow weak.

He saw her and turned, his eyebrows raised questioningly. "You have caught me at my toilet, Little Miss Tilley," he said.

"I saw you play polo," she said.

He laid the straight razor down and wiped the remaining soap from his face.

She saw that he was unsteady. Her eyes ran down his naked chest to the towel. "There's nobody on the train but you and me," Martha blurted.

He turned around from her, and she saw him put the razor in a felt-lined case. And she sensed that she was going to be dismissed, sent away, rejected. She walked to him, laid her face against his bare back, put her hands on his waist.

"Unless you're out of this compartment in fifteen seconds, Little Miss Tilley," John Wilton said, his voice strained, "we are both going to find out whether you're a woman or simply a foolish little girl playing with fire."

"I want you," she heard herself say. "I want you so much."

"I doubt if you even know what it is you think you want," Wilton said.

It took her a moment to understand his meaning. Then, very slowly she moved her hand from his waist, around in front, and slid her hand in the opening of his towel. "Put it in me," she whispered. "Put it in me."

He spun around, put his hands on her waist, picked her up, and carried her to the bed. He dropped her on it. She spread her legs apart and looked at him. He knelt between her legs, and she reached out and guided him into her.

It's supposed to hurt, she thought as she felt his weight on her. But it doesn't hurt. It's wonderful!

17

Martha Tilley lay beside John Wilton, her head against his arm, her face against his chest. She could hear his heart beating. He smells like a man, she thought, and I am now a woman.

"I'm glad," she whispered. "I'm not ashamed, I'm glad."

There was no response.

"I love you, John," she said, the very sound of her words thrilling her.

There was still no response.

"But what must you think of me?" she asked.

This time there was a response. A horrible gurgling noise, suddenly shut off, and then resuming in a lower pitch, then another moment's silence.

He was asleep and snoring!

"John!" she whispered fiercely, and when there was no response, she pushed at his ribs. He grunted.

"John!" she said. He grunted again, this time more like a groan. She took the flesh of his chest below his nipple between her fingers and pinched him as hard as she could.

He made a sound of surprised displeasure and rolled over on his side away from her. Absolutely furious now, she began to beat on his arm with both her fists.

That woke him. He rolled back onto his back and then sat up. He turned and looked at her. "Good God!" he said.

"You went to sleep," she accused.

"Good God!" he said again, this time almost fervently.

Whatever it was, Martha realized, it was not an announcement of undying love. "I knew I had too much to drink, and I knew you did too, but I had no idea . . ."

"What are you talking about?"

"This wasn't the smartest thing that you and I could have done, is it?" he said, looking at her. "Here, I mean? Good God, anybody could have walked in on us!"

She didn't quite believe what she was hearing. "John," she said tenderly, "that was the first time for me."

"Oh, come now," he said. "Let's not mawk it up."

"It was!" she said, now close to tears.

"Good God," he repeated. "Look, what's important now is for you to get out of here before someone finds out what happened."

She looked at him with loathing. The temptation to cry was gone. What she wanted to do was strike him. She wanted to kill him. She pushed herself away from him, moved into a kneeling position on the bed. She became aware that all she was wearing was her petticoat. "You . . . you . . . you are simply *rotten*!" she said.

"For God's sake," he replied, "if you *want* to attract the servants' attention, push the button, get them in here, and I'll explain it to them."

"I hate you!" she hissed, then fled out of his compartment. It was only when she reached the safety of her own compartment that the tears came. She flung herself onto the bed, crying with rage.

Margaret Wilton could not, of course, have declined to accompany Elizabeth Tilley when Liz made it plain that she wanted her to ride back to the train with Mrs. Murray.

When the coach carrying the ladies drove up to the train, she saw the large sorrel tied to the handrail of her own car. It looked vaguely familiar, and after a moment she remembered having seen John ride off on it. John had obviously returned to the cars parked on the siding to change his clothing after his polo game.

How fortunate it had been, if unfortunate for the young man who had fallen from his mount, that John had an opportunity to play, particularly since he played so well. It had obviously given him an *entrée* to Philadelphia society.

While Adela Murray changed her shirtwaist, Margaret saw Martha Tilley, strangely white-faced, leave her compartment. Somewhat unkindly, Margaret decided that Martha had been ill from too much champagne and returned to her car to recover.

Margaret went forward to have a word with John. She knocked at his door, and then pushed it open, only to withdraw in haste. Her elder son was sprawled facedown on his bunk, barely covered by a towel. He looked, she thought, somewhat shamed, rather drunk.

But a moment later, a dressing gown wrapped around him, John appeared at the door of his compartment as she was walking down the aisle.

"Mother?" he called after her, and she could instantly tell that he was both surprised and embarrassed to see her.

"Obviously," she said, "you need your sleep. Forgive me for disturbing you."

"I was just catching a few winks," he said, and he was, after all, her son, and she could see that he was really upset. "What brings you here?" The question was entirely too innocent.

Margaret turned and walked back to his compartment. By the time she got there, he was rummaging in his luggage for a flask of brandy. He was not, she realized, going after the brandy as a drunk would go after it, mindlessly. He was not drunk.

"Mrs. Murray wanted to come back," Margaret Wilton said. "I came with her and Mrs. Tilley."

She sniffed. There was the unmistakable odor of feminine scent in his compartment.

"Haven't you had quite enough of that?" she asked somewhat nastily, pointing to his brandy.

"Mother, I'm John," he said. "The one you may ask questions like that of is my younger brother."

"Spare me your sarcasm," she said. The question was, which one of the girls? She remembered Martha Tilley's subdued look. How could he? His brother's little friend?

Because he was not only male, but a drunken male. And, she thought wryly, his father's son.

"Forgive me, Mother," John said. "Would you like a little taste?"

"As a matter of fact, I would," Margaret Wilton said, walking to the table where he had set his brandy flask. She resolved that somehow she would see to it that John Wilton had no further opportunity to be alone with Martha Tilley, or, for that matter, with any of Thomas' friends.

She debated and decided against saying anything to him. That would only confirm what had best be left a suspicion.

"I had some of that fishhouse punch," she said. "Is that what you've been into?"

"My God, it kicks like a mule," he said. "But I gather that being offered some is the Philadelphia equivalent of being raised to the peerage."

She had to smile at that. "But they are nice, aren't they, John? I mean, you do really like Mr. MacSwain and his friends, don't you?"

"Mr. MacSwain is quite nice," John said. "But, and please don't take offense, I'm glad I'll be returning to the New Mexico Territory. I would hate to spend the rest of my life here."

God forgive me, she thought. I'm glad he's going away too. What kind of a mother am I? One, she decided, quite bright enough to realize what the alternative would mean.

18

The cold hard truth was that she had missed her time of the month, and it was the very first time that had happened since she was thirteen. The other girls sometimes missed a period, but Martha Tilley had not until now.

She didn't feel pregnant. She hadn't thrown up in the morning, or anything like that. She had just missed her period. There was a possibility that she had missed it solely because of the excitement. Maybe sex had stopped it. And maybe it hadn't. Then what?

She had prayed to God that she wouldn't be pregnant, but that seemed rather futile. If God wanted her to be pregnant, she would be. He wouldn't be at all interested in whether she wanted to be or not.

She would have three more weeks to see for sure. She could put off telling her mother at least that long. Oh, my God, she didn't want to have to tell her mother!

Mr. and Mrs. Tilley were having dinner at the Union League that evening with Paul MacSwain and Margaret Wilton, and Martha was surprised to see Thomas accompany his mother to the Tilley house.

"How are you, Martha?" he said rather formally. "I haven't seen you since the hunt, and thought I'd drop by."

"Would you like some coffee?" She offered like a good hostess when the adults had gone.

"I would like some tea," he said. "Thank you very much."

She rather liked ringing for the maid, but the good feeling disappeared when the maid arrived in her coat and hat, and instead of treating her like the mistress of the house, spoke to Martha like a child.

"I've got to go out," the woman said. "I'll be back in less than an hour."

"I would like some tea," Martha announced, trying to salvage her dignity.

"You know where the pot is," the maid said, and left.

Insufferable woman. Martha heard the oiled click as the front door closed and then locked. If her mother was home, she wouldn't dare leave by the front door.

Thomas walked to the windows overlooking the street, pushed the curtain open, looked out, and then turned around, assuming a hands-clasped-behind-his-back pose. He had seen someone, probably his brother, standing that way, Martha thought. He was, she thought, about as good-looking as his brother. Probably, when he was full grown, he would be better-looking.

She wondered, shamed and delighted at once at the thought, how his body would feel close to hers, and felt her face blush.

"We seem to be alone," Thomas announced quite unnecessarily.

"So it seems," Martha replied. "What would you like to do?"

The question had been asked in utter innocence, but he hadn't accepted it in that way. He gave her an absolutely wicked look, smiled, and said nothing.

"We have," Martha said, "some new slides for the stereopticon." She took the stereopticon from the piano and sat down on the couch. He walked over and sat beside her.

She put a slide in the machine, focused it, and handed it to him. He looked at it without comment and handed it back to her. They repeated the ritual four or five times, until Martha realized not only that he had put his arm on the back of the couch but also that his legs, from the knees up, were touching hers.

"Behave yourself, Thomas Wilton," Martha said, but she made no move to withdraw her leg.

132

"I love you," he said. "I've told you that. And you have told me that you love me."

She lowered her head, refusing to look at him. She felt her heart beating, felt that disturbing loose warmth at her middle, wondered why she didn't get up. After a moment, she raised her head and looked at him. He was breathing hard, and his eyes were excited, and he was shaking. He put his hand out to her face. She knew she should pull it away, but she didn't. He wanted to kiss her, and she wanted to be kissed. What I really want, she thought, as his face nervously approached hers, is to lie down and . . .

He kissed her gently, chastely, and withdrew. She opened her eyes and looked at him, and opened her mouth. He grabbed her hard this time, and she felt his teeth scraping against hers. And then she felt his hand on her bosom. She struggled to push him away. Her clenched fist slipped off the tight muscles of his leg. Her knuckles brushed against something warm and stiff. She felt her breast swell, opened her mouth under his, felt his breath in her mouth, and with a mind of its own, her hand opened and closed around him.

"Oh, my darling!" he said.

She felt his hand tearing at his trouser buttons; she felt him pull himself from her hand, and then she felt him pulling her hand down to it, felt her fingers close on it again.

"We have to stop!" she protested.

He had his hand inside her dress now, on her naked bosom.

"Oh, my darling," he repeated. He means it, she thought. He really loves me. And I must love him, for I don't want him to stop. She fell onto her back, felt his hand dip to her waist, find no opening, and then dip down to raise her skirt.

"Oh, darling!" she said. "We mustn't!"

He had his hand on her now, feeling her through her underthings. He tried to work his hand over the top, and failed, and then she felt him searching for the tie. He would never find it. He expected to find it in front, where a man's undergarments fastened. Martha lowered her hand to her hip and tugged loose the bow that held her underdrawers up. A moment later she felt his warm hand on the softness of her belly.

Now he won't stop, she thought.

"May God forgive us," Martha said into Thomas' ear. When he had trouble getting her pantaloons off her ankles, she kicked them free. And when he didn't seem to be able to find her, she reached down and guided him inside her body.

19

Lucille Stevens was on her knees on the tile floor of the kitchen of the big house, half-soaked in the brine that splashed over the top of the two-foot-tall ranch-made ceramic urns in which she and the cook and the cook's daughters were corning beef.

Charles Broadhead walked into the kitchen from the house. "I wondered where you were," he said.

She didn't even bother to reply.

"Well," Broadhead said. "He's back."

She felt her heart jump, and was furious with herself. "Who's back?" she asked. What she was thinking was that Wilton was in the sitting room right now, and that he might even come out and find her on her knees and smelling of brine. What in the world is the matter with me? He's nothing but a boy.

"English John Wilton," Broadhead said. "And he's got his mother and his brother, and a half-dozen Chinese and two freight cars full of stuff with him."

She stood up, after first seeing that the beef was jammed tight against the bottom of the urn, so that it wouldn't bob to the surface, and dried her hands and mopped at her face. "Where are they?" she asked.

"On the siding over at Land & Cattle," Broadhead said. "They've been there for two days. They're living in a boxcar until they can get the house roofed over."

A flood of questions filled Lucille's mind. What are they

135

going to use for wood to get the house roofed over? Chinese? A boxcar? His *mother* and his brother?

"I didn't know what to do," Charley said. "I figured you'd want to ask them to stay here until they got the house finished, but I wasn't sure if I should ask them."

"Of course I want them here," Lucille said. Charley should have asked them. But she was glad that he hadn't; it wasn't his place to ask. This was her place. He wasn't her husband, and he seemed to be getting the unspoken message that she didn't want him to be.

What I should do now, before things get out of hand, is get this foolishness out of mind. I am not a princess in a novel, living in a castle, in the sure and certain knowledge that a knight will ride up, swoon at the very sight of me, and carry me off to his castle. I am a twenty-six-year-old woman, an old maid, about to be quite alone in the world, who needs a good, calm, competent man to father her children, to run the ranch.

"Let me wash some of this brine off, Charley, and I'll ride over there with you." As she left the kitchen, she made the conscious effort to put her hand on his arm, a gesture at least of affection.

And their eyes met for a moment. And she looked into them, and saw that he knew.

"For your sake, I'm glad he came back," Charley said.

"Don't be absurd," she heard herself snap.

He met her eyes until she looked away, and then he said, "I thought maybe we'd better take a carriage with us. For his mother, I mean. If she's going to come back here."

"Oh, God, Charley, I wish you were my brother," she suddenly burst out.

She loved him and felt sorry for him at once. She put her arms around him and hugged him. She felt his hand tenderly caress her hair.

"Some things aren't meant to be," he said. "I guess that's what it is."

She resisted the temptation to kiss his cheek, pushed herself away, and left the room. She had a perversely angry thought. If you weren't such a good man, it wouldn't have turned out this way. If you had taken advantage of me when you had the chance, we would have been married when John Wilton came here the first time.

When she came down, dressed warmly for the ride in the chilling winds that swept down from the mountains in late November, Charley had the carriage, side curtains in place, filled with buffalo robes, waiting at the front of the house.

When she got into the carriage, he tied his horse to it and got in beside her.

"There's something I haven't told you," he said, taking the reins from her.

"What's that?"

"I knew a week ago he was coming back," Charley said. Lucille looked at him, wondering what he was leading up to. "The thing is, Lucille, he's made me, or his mother has, a business proposition."

He had not been, as he had led her to believe, conducting family business on his recent trip to Dallas. There had been a telegram from her father's friend Albert Dennison, saying that Dennison had a business proposition in connection with Anglo-American Land & Cattle, and that he woulld pay Broadhead's expenses if he would meet with Dennison confidentially in Dallas.

The proposition was right to the point. The reason Anglo-American Land & Cattle had failed in the first place was that they didn't know what they were doing. John Wilton and his mother knew nothing more than the English general manager had known about operating a cattle ranch. The obvious solution was to find someone to run the place who did. In exchange for Charles Broadhead's services as general manager, they would pay him $350 per month for a period of three years, and at the end of the three years, if Anglo-American Cattle was making a profit, there would be both a bonus equal to one year's pay and the option to buy as much Anglo-American land, at three-quarters the then appraised value, as the total sum of money paid to him in salary and bonus. If he did not choose to exercise that option, he could remain on as general manager, at $500 per month, plus 10 percent of net profits.

It was, Lucille saw, a great deal of money. She had been paying Charley $175 a month, exactly half as much, and the notion of a bonus had never entered her mind. Probably, she thought, because it had then been mutually understood that she, which meant the ranch, would ultimately be the bonus.

In a moment, she realized something else. The business proposition they had offered him was more than just an offer. The complex provisions had obviously been the result of negotiation. Charley had wanted more, they had offered him a little more; there had been a compromise.

And what was she supposed to do? Who was going to run Rancho San Miguel? The answer to that came immediately. She was going to run Rancho San Miguel. She didn't need a general manager, she needed a foreman. You could find a hundred foremen at a hundred dollars a month, and glad to get the work. She remembered, the memory somewhat shamingly pleasing her, that more than once, when issuing a bank draft for Charley's wages, she had thought he was getting paid just about twice what he was worth.

"And what did you tell them?" Lucille asked.

"I told them I'd talk it over with you," he said. "But what I was really going to do was wait until I saw you with John Wilton. I found out just now in the kitchen I didn't have to wait until I actually saw you together."

"The Wiltons made this proposition to you?"

"His mother made it," Charley said. "I had the feeling that he didn't like it any, but there was nothing he could do about it." He could not suppress a dig. "His mother treats him like a boy."

"Damn you, Charley!" Lucille snapped.

"You don't need me to manage your ranch, and you know it," Charley said. "It's an opportunity for me, Lucille. And what was I supposed to do, anyway? If you and him——"

"Shut up, Charley," Lucille said. "Just shut up. When we get back to the ranch, I'll give you a bank draft for your wages through the end of the year."

He said nothing. Lucille felt betrayed, maneuvered, helpless. She sat beside Charley for a moment longer, her arms wrapped under her bosom. Then suddenly she pushed the buffalo robe off her lap and reached for the reins. The pair of sorrels stopped. They and Charley looked at her in surprise.

"I'll ride ahead," she said, and climbed out of the carriage. She untied Charley's horse and swung into the saddle. The leather was like ice against her inner thighs, but she knew that would pass in a minute, when her body heat took the chill off the leather.

She kicked the roan with her heels, got him into a fast trot, and then reined him in. She was too good a horsewoman to let a horse unnecessarily work up a sweat in a chilling wind.

She rather liked the feeling of having taken over Charley's mount, leaving him to drive the carriage, trailing behind her. She was, after all, the *patrona*. Even Charley had known, had admitted, she didn't need him to manage Rancho San Miguel.

Thinking about it, she was glad John Wilton had brought his mother.

Lucille reached the siding before she came to the falling-down ranch house. Even from a distance she could see that it had taken on the appearance of a camp.

Smoke came out of four chimneys, moving immediately horizontal in the north wind. There were two chimneys coming out the roof of a boxcar and from each of two structures that were half-tent and half-building. For the Chinese, she thought. What were they doing with Chinese? Building another railroad?

A ramada had been erected, using, she noticed, fresh white lumber for upright posts, with a rope or a wire string between them, and with strips of cloth hanging from the wire, if that's what it was. She had never seen anything like that before, but now that she saw it, she realized that it worked.

The flapping pieces of cloth had probably spooked the animals it contained when they first saw them, but they had quickly learned it wasn't harmful. They avoided the edges of the ramada, but they grazed peacefully within it.

She rode up to the boxcar, saw that steps had been erected up to the partially open door, and saw that the opening was filled with a door and a doorframe, complete to doorknob and lock. She slid off the horse and walked up the stairs and knocked on the door. She glanced over her shoulder and saw that Charley was still a quarter of a mile off.

There was a scraping noise, and then the door opened. She found herself looking at a woman who did not, she realized, look very much older than she did.

"Mrs. Wilton," Lucille said. "I am Miss Lucille Stevens, your neighbor."

"Oh," Margaret said. "Won't you please come in?"

Lucille stepped into the boxcar. It looked like a room in a house. There was even a carpet on the floor, wider than the car's width, so that it curled up against the walls. Mrs. Wilton pushed a heavy box against the door to close it.

"I've come, of course, to bring you to Rancho San Miguel," Lucille said. "I can't imagine what John was thinking of, exposing you to something like this."

"John wanted me to stay in Dallas," Margaret Wilton said. "The rail car was my idea."

There was one overstuffed leather-upholstered chair in the room. Margaret insisted that Lucille sit in it.

"Our furniture will take some time to get here from Philadelphia," she said. "But I felt we should have at least one proper chair. I'll get us some tea."

"I had no idea that you were planning to come out here," Lucille said. "Until my . . ."—she paused, just noticeably—"foreman told me you'd hired him away."

"Is that how you see it?" Margaret said. "I'm truly sorry."

"How should I see it?"

"Mr. Dennison asked Mr. Broadhead to recommend someone for the position," Margaret Wilton said. "He nominated himself."

She was obviously telling the truth.

"I'm sure he'll do a very good job for you," Lucille said. "And I'm sorry if I misunderstood the situation."

"So am I," Margaret said. "If we are to be neighbors, I would like us to be friends."

"And the first friendly thing you can do, when the carriage gets here, is come and stay with my father and me until your house is ready."

"That's very kind of you. And, I'm sure, a terrible imposition." She paused. "John has told me your father is quite ill."

"There's nothing anyone can do for him, I'm afraid," Lucille said. "But there are servants."

"We have Chinese," Margaret Wilton said. "I feel that I'm on some exotic frontier."

Lucille felt sorry for her. A woman like that didn't belong out here. That thought was in her mind when there was a creaking noise, and she saw that someone was trying to force the door open against the box holding it shut.

Margaret Wilton rushed to the door, pushed the box out of the way, and John Wilton stepped inside. He had a Stetson hat on his head, and wore an ankle-length, skin-side-out sheepskin coat. He took the hat off and made an almost courtly bow. "Miss Stevens," he said.

Despite that, Lucille thought: He belongs out here. If he didn't have that accent, just to look at him you'd think he belonged out here. He held in his hand something she had never seen before, sort of a cane, with a large oblong handle, and with a pointed end.

"Mr. Wilton," she said. And then curiosity got the better of her. "What is that in your hand?"

He held it up like a sword. "A shooting stick," he said. "I've been up watching the Chinese put the house back together." That made no sense at all, and her confusion must have shown on her face.

"*Voilà*," he said. He spread the handle of the shooting stick, then jabbed the point into the carpet behind him. Then he sat on it. He held up his hands. "Instant seat, you see."

"John, the carpet," his mother said, chastising him as a small boy. The look on his face was that of a small boy having been chastised. He jumped erect, and looked chagrined, like a child.

"As soon as my foreman gets here with the carriage," Lucille said, and the word "foreman" came easily now, "I'm taking your mother back to Rancho San Miguel."

"Your foreman?" he asked, confused.

"Perhaps I should have said *your* foreman," Lucille said, tempering it with a smile.

"That was not my idea, Miss Stevens," Wilton said. "That was mother's idea."

"Where is Thomas?" Margaret Wilton asked.

"Riding as slowly as possible back from the house," Wilton said. "Absolutely wallowing in self-pity." He turned to Lucille and smiled at her. "My brother, who is seventeen, fancies himself deeply in love."

"I don't think that was at all called for," Margaret Wilton snapped at him.

"Charley should be here in just a moment," Lucille said. "And if we're to make it to the ranch while there's still any light at all, we'll have to get started."

"Mother," Wilton said, "you really would be much more comfortable with Miss Stevens."

"And I would so much like to have you," Lucille said. "It sometimes gets terribly lonely out here." The confession surprised her.

Except for the major, now permanently confined to his room, and the servants, Lucille and Margaret Wilton were alone in the big house at Rancho San Miguel for the next two days. After dinner the first night, Margaret asked if she might play the piano. She played light, cheerful music Lucille had never heard before, music from Vienna, Austria, written by a Johann Strauss. Somehow, it painted for Lucille a picture of another world, and she sensed it was a world that Margaret Wilton had not left willingly.

She tried to ask tactful questions about Mr. Wilton. Other than to have him described as Colonel Wilton, not much information was forthcoming. Margaret Wilton's sadness was not over the loss of her husband. Lucille did not want to press her further. She wondered if she was just being curious, or if her motives were a little more noble—that she wanted to comfort this woman. Once they were alone, Margaret Wilton seemed far less self-sufficient, far less formidable.

She was absolutely useless in the kitchen the next day. Obviously she had not done much cooking. But when they talked about business, she soaked up information like a sponge, asking pertinent intelligent questions.

They had a bottle of wine with their second dinner together, and then a second bottle. Lucille became giddy enough to confess that one day she really wanted to go to Europe, to see the grand cities, perhaps to catch a glimpse of a prince, even of Queen Victoria herself.

"She lives a life quite as lonely as this," Margaret Wilton said. "A rather simple, strong-willed woman, prohibited from remarriage by circumstance.

"You've seen her?" Lucille asked.

"Yes," Margaret said. "I was rather close to her daughter, Princess Beatrice."

Lucille was able only with great effort to refrain from asking what in the world Margaret Wilton was doing here. What was a woman who had been "rather close" to a princess doing here in the New Mexico Territory? She believed what Margaret Wilton had told her. She wasn't a woman speaking her fantasies; she hadn't claimed friendship with a queen; she was one woman feeling sorry for another.

As she, she realized, felt sorry for Margaret Wilton. Not because she was here, where she obviously didn't belong, but because there was something, a tragedy, a scandal, something that caused her suffering.

Margaret had never once mentioned Paul MacSwain. But he had not been far from her thoughts from the moment she left Philadelphia with John and Thomas. Margaret had felt it essential that she personally examine the Anglo-American Land & Cattle Company before a decision to hold on to it, as John so much wanted, was made. There was too much at stake—too much money, John's future, Thomas' continuing education—to settle on a simple yes or no in Philadelphia, thousands of miles away.

Paul had wanted to come too, but Margaret wouldn't hear of him disrupting his life for what she considered a necessary business trip of short duration. But she wouldn't set the wedding date until she knew where she stood in the New Mexico Territory—actually, where she stood, period. She and Paul had a terrible row, their first real fight, and he had not come to the railroad station to bid her good-bye. And now that she had assured herself John had made a wise decision and their lives would safely rest with the Anglo-American Land & Cattle, she didn't know if she would ever go back.

Lucille rose, as was her custom, at daybreak the next morning. She had her breakfast alone in the kitchen, and then went into her father's bedroom to check on him. He was nearly gone, hanging onto life in a laudanum stupor. Suddenly Lucille realized how much she wanted him to live. When he was gone, she would be totally alone.

Then she went into his office, and took out the books, and went over them, adjusting herself to the knowledge that this was the way it was going to be from now on. She felt relief that she would no longer have to go through the charade of discussing business with Charley, and then she wondered if the relief was genuine, or whether it was defiance. Had Charley's advice been necessary? Had it really been *unneces-*

sary? Had she made her decisions based on what she thought his would be?

Juanita pushed the heavy door open. "Señorita, a Butterfield is on the road," Jaunita said.

A Butterfield? A stagecoach? Coming here?

She walked out of her father's office and onto the porch. It was a stagecoach drawn by six horses, walking. They were two hundred miles from the nearest stage line. What was it doing here?

She stayed on the porch, unabashedly curious, leaning on a pillar, until the coach came up to the house. The curtains over the windows in the coach were closed against the chill. The driver pulled on the brake with a chilling squeal, and then climbed stiffly down.

"Morning, ma'am," he said. "I wonder if your husband's around?"

"What can I do for you?" Lucille asked.

Over his shoulder, Lucille could see several of the hands coming from the bunkhouse, as curious about the presence of a stagecoach as she was.

"I'd like to rent or buy some horses, ma'am," the driver said. "Could I speak to your husband about it?"

The door of the stagecoach opened, and a stout middle-aged man got out. He had obviously slept in his clothes, and he was as obviously a city man. He tipped his hat to her. "Good morning, madam," he said. He seemed somewhat embarrassed.

"You've been driving all night?" Lucille asked.

"Yes, ma'am," the driver said.

"Well, then, you're probably hungry. Come in the house, and we'll get something for you to eat, and then I'll see about horses for you. You can turn these animals loose and have them fed at the ramada."

"You are very kind, madam," the stout man said. He turned around and reached up into the stagecoach. A child, hardly more than a baby, was handed down to him, and he held it awkwardly. Then a woman got out of the stagecoach and reclaimed the child from him.

"Please come in the house," Lucille said. "That child must be exhausted."

The man looked shamed. "I'm very grateful to you," he said.

Lucille didn't reply. She spun around and walked into the house. The man and woman followed her.

Margaret Wilton, in a dressing gown, her hair still undone, hanging down far below her shoulders, apparently wakened by the sound of the stagecoach and its team, was standing at the end of the corridor by the foyer. Lucille smiled at her to assure her everything was all right.

Margaret's eyes were flashing angrily. "Paul, you bloody fool!" she snapped, and swept across the foyer and snatched the child from the woman's arms. "What were you thinking of, bringing him out here?"

The child obviously recognized Margaret. He cuddled close to her, and she held him almost ferociously protectively.

Lucille looked at the stout man. Tears were in his eyes.

"God, he's absolutely soaking!" Margaret said, her hands inside the child's robe. "What's the matter with you, anyway?" she snapped at the woman. "How long has he been wet?"

"Sorry, missus," the woman said in a thick Irish accent.

"Get a nappie and some fresh clothing," Margaret Wilton said. "Bring them to my room."

"Yes, missus," said the woman, who was obviously a maid, or a nurse, some kind of employee.

Margaret turned and headed for her room. At the entrance to the corridor, she turned, and with ice in every syllable, said, "Forgive me. May I present Miss Lucille Stevens? Lucille, this bloody damned fool is Paul MacSwain."

Then she stormed out of sight.

Lucille looked at the stout man.

"I'm terribly sorry about this," he said. Then he blurted, "The thing is, I'm out here to take Margaret back where she belongs. With me and the boy."

"If you will go into the dining room," Lucille said, nearly as icily as Margaret Wilton, "Juanita will see to your breakfast." Then she went down the corridor after Margaret Wilton.

By the time the Irishwoman knocked at the door, Margaret had stripped the child of his clothing, wiped and cleaned him,

145

wrapped him in a blanket, and was holding him, and he her. And there were tears in her eyes, too.

"There are times," Margaret said, "when the stupidity of the human male beggars description!"

Lucille blurted what came to her mind. "He brought that child with him because he knew you loved him, didn't he?"

"That's precisely what he did," Margaret said. "Precisely."

"He's adorable," Lucille said.

"The boy, you mean," Margaret Wilton said. "Yes, isn't he?" She rocked the child in her arms. "Poor little darling never knew his mother."

The maid had laid out diapers and fresh clothes on the bed.

Margaret dressed the boy, and then swung him onto her hip. "Come on, darling," she said. "And we'll go let your father know what a bloody fool I think he is."

She didn't have to go far. Paul MacSwain was standing at the bedroom door. There was a look on his face that made it quite plain he had won. Margaret Wilton was obviously never again going to turn little Edward's care over to anyone else.

Mrs. Wilton Weds
Mr. MacSwain

Phila., Dec. 16—(By Telegraph) The Philadelphia *Inquirer* has been exclusively informed by telegraph from the Pecos, Texas, *Intelligencer* that Mrs. Margaret Wilton, of this city, and Mr. Paul T. MacSwain, also of this city, were united in matrimony at Rancho San Miguel, in the New Mexico Territory, on Dec. 14.

According to information received, the ceremony was performed by the Right Reverend Stanley W. Dawson, DD, Protestant Episcopal bishop of Texas. Mrs. Wilton was given in marriage by her son Thomas Wilton, of Philadelphia. Following a wedding trip to New Orleans, Louisiana, and other cities in the South, Mr. and Mrs. MacSwain will make their home in Philadelphia.

20

John Wilton was at target practice. Thomas Wilton watched him with loathing and impatience from inside the house. It was Sunday. Six days shalt thou labor, Thomas thought, and on the seventh, thou shalt behave like an ass.

John, wearing an enormous, bulky sheepskin overcoat, galloped twice around the house. When he came around again to the veranda, he reined in his piebald stallion, took his new Mauser rifle from its scabbard, rapidly worked the bolt action, put it to his shoulder, took careful aim, supporting the fore end of the rifle on his fingertips, and fired.

Three hundred yards away was his target, a water-filled clay pot twelve inches wide and eighteen inches tall. He had rather smugly told Thomas that it represented the vital forequarter area of a deer.

There was a sharp crack. The water-filled clay pot was untouched.

"Damn," John said. He put the rifle back in the scabbard and spurred the stallion into motion. He galloped twice again around the house, reined up in front, pulled the Mauser from its scabbard, took aim again, fired again, missed again, and swore again.

The Mauser went back in the scabbard. The stallion was spurred into action, and he made another two trips at a gallop around the house. He reined in again, slipped the Mauser from the scabbard, worked the bolt action, and took aim.

There is no way he can possibly hit that damned jug, Thomas thought. For one thing, it was too far away. For another, he was perched atop a heavily breathing animal. There was no way to get a proper bead.

The Mauser fired. Three hundred yards away, the water-filled clay pot exploded. A look of smug, utter self-satisfaction came onto John's face. He looked at the house to see if anyone had witnessed his triumph. When he saw Thomas at the window, he held the Mauser in one hand over his head.

Bloody ass, Thomas thought. But he waved. Hypocritical or not, he needed something from his brother. Needed a good deal, and needed it desperately.

John ejected the spent cartridge, examined the magazine, and then reached inside the sheepskin overcoat and came out with another five shiny brass cartridges. He slipped them into the magazine one by one, put the rifle back in the scabbard, and spurred the stallion into motion.

Thomas, furious, went out onto the veranda. He saw for the first time that there were four more clay jugs out on the prairie. His brother came around the house, bent over the piebald, running him as fast as he would go. He smiled at his brother as he passed, and then disappeared around the corner of the house.

Thomas went inside. It was bitter cold here, and the wind coming off the mountains made it even worse. And he knew there was absolutely no way John was going to give up his childish little game until every last one of those damned jugs had been blown up.

It was an hour before John entered the house from the rear. Thomas heard him saying something to Sammy Long, the cook's thirteen-year-old son, in Spanish. The cook and her son were Chinese, and the boy and John were both learning Spanish. Sammy apparently got the message—to walk the piebald before putting him into the stable. Thomas decided that was because he had observed that one always walked animals that had exterted themselves, and not because John had been able to make the point in his ludicrous Spanish.

John came into the great room, the sheepskin overcoat unbuttoned and nearly dragging on the ground. His face was flushed from exertion, and his nose and ears were red from the cold.

He laid the rifle on the large wooden table that served as a desk, and then he hung the coat on a stout peg. "The trick," he announced as he reached for a cut-glass whiskey decanter, "is to attune yourself to the mount's breathing. There is just a moment, after he exhales, and before he inhales, when he's absolutely still. You have to fire just then."

He sipped appreciatively at the whiskey. "Would you like a spot of this?" he asked.

"John, I'm in rather desperate trouble," Thomas announced. "I really am."

John looked at him with a smile in his eyes. Thomas would have very much liked to shatter the whiskey decanter over his head.

"Which requires your immediate presence in Philadelphia, no doubt?" John asked tolerantly, smugly.

"Damn you, it does," Thomas said.

"The answer, brother, is no," John said. "Mother and MacSwain are cooing like the proverbial turtledoves. The last thing they need is a near-man to remind them that Mother is actually somewhat older than Juliet."

Thomas blurted it out. "My . . . fianceé," he said, "is in the family way."

"You don't actually expect me to believe that, Thomas, do you?" Wilton said.

Thomas walked to the desk, where John was in the process of removing the bolt from the Mauser rifle, and laid the letter on the desk.

John took the bolt from the rifle and then peered through the bore before laying the rifle down and picking up the letter.

"That came yesterday," Thomas said.

"I know," John said. "I saw the postmark and that feminine handwriting."

He took the single sheet of paper from the envelope and read it. It was succinct:

My Darling Thomas,
    I can only fervently pray to our Lord that you meant what you said about loving me, and wanting me for your wife, for God has seen fit to make me with child.

I anxiously and prayerfully await word that you are returning to your terrified and loving,

Martha

He looked at Thomas and a smile crossed his face.

"It is nothing to smile over," Thomas said.

"Who is your little paramour, anyway?" John asked. "And why, for God's sake, did you give her your right name?"

"It's Martha Tilley," Thomas said furiously. "Who did you *think* it was?"

"I had no idea it was Martha Tilley," John Wilton said, suddenly sober. He had an image of Martha Tilley thrusting her body against his in the railway car at Paoli.

"Thomas, the possibility exists that you're not the only one to have . . . uh . . . been with Martha."

"You are despicable."

"I'm also practical. Look at it this way, you damned fool. What if Martha has been carrying on, say, with someone else? And found herself in that condition. I mean, what I'm trying to say—"

"You have said quite enough, John," Thomas said. "I should have known to expect nothing better from you."

"Answer my question, Thomas," John said. "How many times were you with Martha Tilley?"

"Just that once," Thomas said, adding dramatically, "We lost control of ourselves."

"Oh, you bloody little fool," John said.

"There is nothing you can say to me that I haven't said to myself," Thomas said manfully, accepting his responsibilities. "The question is, what am I to do to set things right?"

"You're asking my advice?" John asked. He didn't wait for a reply. "You ignore the letter, that's what you do. And little Martha will then move down the list to the next potential husband."

"Can't you get it through your depraved mind that we're in love?" Thomas shouted, but it was still more a cry of pain than a cry of anger.

"What would you like to do?" John asked.

"Well, obviously she can no longer stay in Philadelphia," Thomas said. "I intend to marry her and bring her out here."

"Oh, for God's sake, that's absurd!" John said. "For one

thing, you're not old enough to marry, and . . ." He stopped. He had almost said he had no intention of having Martha Tilley nearby.

"I am obviously old enough to marry," Thomas said.

"What do you want from me, Thomas?"

"I want enough money to return to Philadelphia and to tide me over until I can find suitable employment." He paused. "Since I am obviously not welcome here."

"You're determined to marry this girl?" John asked.

"I am," Thomas said solemnly.

"I'll give you enough money to take an apartment and to live on," John said. "In exchange for your promise that you will remain in college."

"When can I go back?"

John pulled his watch from his trousers. "We don't have time to go to Loving," he said. "But perhaps we can flag down the train here."

"You mean right now?" Thomas said.

"In an hour and a half," John said.

For a moment Thomas seemed to wilt. Then he got control of himself. "I'm grateful to you, John," he said. "I knew that when the chips were down, I could count on you."

John shrugged. I am arranging for my brother to marry a woman who may just be carrying my child, he thought. But what was the alternative? There was none.

John stooped over and moved a carpet aside. He hooked his finger in a flush-mounted iron ring and lifted a section of the floor. Then he got down on his hands and knees and put a key in the padlock of the strongbox set in concrete.

He counted out a thousand dollars in fifty-dollar gold certificates, and then, after a moment's thought, counted out another thousand dollars.

Mr. and Mrs. Paul T. MacSwain had been at the house no longer than thirty minutes when the doorbell sounded.

"We are not at home, Mary," Margaret MacSwain called softly from the sitting room, where she had just served her husband a cup of coffee laced with brandy, and herself a cup of tea.

Mary, who had just earned twenty dollars from C. Harold Tilley for telephoning him the instant Mrs. MacSwain returned home, didn't quite know what was going to happen next. There was no question in her mind that the caller at the front door was Mr. Tilley, and probably Mrs. Tilley, too.

"Is Mrs. MacSwain at home?" Mrs. C. Harold Tilley formally inquired.

"Oh, for God's sake, Lizzy!" Mr. Tilley said. He walked into the house, propelling his wife along with his hand on her arm. "Where are they, Mary?"

"In the sitting room," Mary said. Mr. Tilley seemed to have forgotten her twenty dollars. She tried to gather her courage to ask for it, but now Mr. Tilley was sliding open the door to the sitting room.

"Well, what a pleasant surprise!" Margaret said when she saw the Tilleys march uninvited into her sitting room.

"Oh, Margaret . . ." Elizabeth Tilley began, and then burst into tears.

"Oh, for God's sake, Lizzy, shut up!" C. Harold Tilley said.

"Martha and your Thomas . . ." Elizabeth Tilley said, not about to be shut up, and then sobbed. "They've run off to Baltimore and gotten married," she sobbed again. "Three days ago."

"Is she in the family way?" Margaret blurted. Elizabeth Tilley stopped sobbing. She became a martyr. She dabbed at her eyes, then nodded her head.

Oh, my God, Margaret thought. And it's probably not even Thomas' child.

"Margaret, what are we going to do?" Elizabeth Tilley asked. "They're still children!" She was about to start wailing again.

"We're going to be grandparents, Lizzy," Margaret said. "I don't think that's something we need weep over."

"That little son of a bitch," Paul MacSwain said. "I never would have guessed." There was something almost close to approval in his voice. He turned and went to the liquor cabinet and picked up a bottle of brandy and waved it at C. Harold Tilley. Tilley walked over and held out his hand for the glass MacSwain offered. The two men looked at each other, and, smiling, shook their heads.

Their wives, for different reasons, looked at them angrily.

"Where are they now?" Margaret asked.

"In Wardman's Hotel in Washington, D.C.," Elizabeth

said. "I have no idea what they're doing for money. I know Martha didn't have any."

"You've talked to them, then?" Margaret asked.

"No," Elizabeth said. "We just had the telegram from Baltimore, and then there was a postcard today. We wanted to wait to talk to you, to see what we should do."

Mary appeared at the door. She walked to Margaret and handed her a telegram. Margaret opened it, read it, and then handed it to Elizabeth Tilley.

"Well, now we know what they're doing for money," she said. MacSwain walked across the room and read the telegram over Elizabeth's shoulder.

LOVING, NEW MEXICO TERRITORY

MR. AND MRS. THOMAS WILTON
14 RITTENHOUSE SQUARE
PHILADELPHIA, PENNA.

HEARTIEST CONGRATULATIONS AND BEST WISHES FOR A LONG AND HAPPY LIFE TOGETHER. NAME THE FIRST ONE AFTER ME.

JOHN F. W. WILTON

MacSwain chuckled.

"I don't think that's funny, Paul," Elizabeth said. "It's in very poor taste to say something like that."

"Yes it is," Margaret said. There was such a bitter tone in her voice that MacSwain looked at her curiously.

"Oh, come on, Maggie," he said. "That's just the way John is."

"It was in very bad taste," Margaret said firmly. "I don't think I will ever forgive him for it."

"Do you think he knows about the . . . child?" Elizabeth asked.

"How did you know?" Margaret countered.

"Martha left a letter for me," she said. "On her dressing-table mirror."

"Then what happened seems fairly evident," Margaret said. "Martha told Thomas, Thomas told John, and John gave him money to come back here and do the right thing."

"She should have come to me," Elizabeth said. "What's going to happen now?"

"I think the first thing we should do is sit down and compose a telegram of our own. They are probably just about now really terrified about what they've done."

The congratulatory telegram was slipped under the hotel-room door of Mr. and Mrs. Thomas Wilton three hours later in Washington. Mr. and Mrs. Wilton were occupied at the time, and it wasn't noticed until several hours later, when, having put their clothing on, they left their room to have dinner.

Thomas read it, and then handed it to Martha.

"I was just thinking," she said. "Now that she's married to Mr. MacSwain, your mother won't need the house on Rittenhouse Square. I wonder if she'll give it to us?"

"We're going to take a flat near the university," Thomas said. "I thought that was settled."

"Oh, don't be silly, Thomas," Martha said. "I don't want to live in a flat. What would people think? What would people say?" When it looked as if he were going to protest further, Martha said, "And we certainly can't have our baby in a flat, can we?"

"I'm not sure Mother is in a financial position—" Thomas began.

"Oh, don't be silly. Of course she is. She's married to Paul MacSwain, isn't she?"

He looked unhappy. Martha reached out her hand and patted his cheek. "Don't be such a worrier," she said. "Everything is going to be all right now."

21

Kate Shaughnessy posed something of a problem to the hotel community of Phoenix, Arizona. Under the proprietorship of Miss Allen, Miss Allen's Boardinghouse had been a boardinghouse in name only. No food had been served, and its sleeping accommodations had seldom been used for that purpose. It had provided one service only. Guests at Phoenix's respectable hotels might be justifiably suspected of visiting Miss Allen's establishment for an hour or so, but they took their meals and rested their heads in sleep in the several respectable establishments.

Under Miss Allen's proprietorship, it had been a perfectly satisfactory working relationship, but the new proprietress had, almost immediately upon taking over, begun to change all that. No sooner had she—a good deal sooner than Miss Allen expected her to—paid off her mortgage than she began to reinvest profit into upgrading the establishment.

The first thing she did was to follow the English and Irish custom of having a bar, a public house, divided into two classes. There was the public bar, and the first-class bar, with a corresponding price differential. At first, the hotel community thought this was rather funny, a foolish pretension. But they quickly saw they had laughed much too early. Guests who had previously had several drinks in the hotel bar, walked over to Miss Allen's for a half-hour visit, and then returned to the hotel bar for more drinking, now went directly to Miss Allen's first-class bar and spent the entire evening there, with a consequent loss of business to the hotel bars.

She next installed a Chinese cook in a rough shed erected behind the adobe building and began to serve simple meals. Nothing very elaborate, beef-and-potato pie for lunch, and the same plus beefsteaks and mutton chops from six in the evening onward. The prices were nominal, and they served to effectively divert the restaurant trade from the respectable establishments to hers.

It made little sense, as one hotelier pointed out, to walk three blocks from Miss Allen's to a hotel for dinner, when the same meal was available for a dime or twenty cents less at Miss Allen's. Particularly if you had the idea in the back of your head that you'd just as soon drink in her first-class bar as in the hotel. There were no women in the hotel bars.

The issue came to a head when a wagonload of adobe bricks was unhitched in the empty space behind Miss Allen's, and it became obvious that Kate Shaughnessy was about to enlarge her place of business. It was quickly learned that she intended to offer overnight accommodations, with at least one item on the room service the established hotels did not provide. And could not provide, since by long custom Jasimine Street served as the dividing line between respectability and debauchery, and they were on the respectable side of the street.

There was talk, of course, of running her out of town. There were two things wrong with that suggestion. For one thing, it would have been of questionable legality, even if she could be frightened. For another thing, Kate Shaughnessy's admirers included both the mayor and the sheriff, and it was unlikely that they would tolerate anything stronger than suggestion.

The obvious solution to the problem was to reinstall Miss Allen as the proprietor. She knew how to run a whorehouse, and she was not interested (or qualified) to run anything more complex. After consulting with Miss Allen, the mayor, and the sheriff, it was decided to raise sufficient funds among them to buy Kate Shaughnessy out and to reinstall Miss Allen as madam. Actually, the idea seemed better the more they thought about it. With themselves as silent partners, there would be a profit to be made.

Kate Shaughnessy was reluctant to sell out. She refused their initial offer, which would have served to double her investment. She was quite convinced that once she got the new building up, she would be able to turn a nice profit. The new building would be entirely devoted to the first-class establishment. The old building would be the pub, with victuals, drink, and women accordingly.

She refused the second offer as well. By then the walls were up, and two freight wagons—covered by canvas tarpaulins and guarded overnight by a shotgun-carrying off-duty deputy sheriff—carrying the very latest in elegant furnishings from Sears, Roebuck & Company in Chicago, Illinois, were parked on the lot.

The third offer she accepted. It was made with great courtesy, but there was an unmistakable threat as well. She had no cash reserves. Every spare dollar had gone into the expansion. If one of the wagons had gone up in flames one night, if there had been a sudden burst of virtue on the part of the city government, closing her down for a couple of weeks, she would be in deep trouble.

Six months after she arrived in Phoenix with the unconscious John Wilton, Kate Shaughnessy left town debt-free with $8,200 in gold and gold certificates in a leather purse, which, worn under her skirts, left her upper thighs both chafed and stained with tannic acid.

There was the matter of the $2,500 she had borrowed from John Wilton. She intended to make an effort to see him when she was in Philadelphia, claiming her baby back from the nuns. What she intended to do was pay him interest on the money, three percent, just like a bank (more, if he was difficult), and see if she couldn't hang on to the money a little longer, in order to reinvest it in another establishment.

Her six months in Phoenix had taught her two things. There was good money to be made operating a high-class house. She had proved that. But she had also learned that she didn't know nearly enough about what really made a high-class establishment. The reason the menu at Miss Allen's had been limited to beef-and-potato pie, steak, and mutton chops was that that was about the extent of Kate's culinary knowledge, that and knowing how to bake bread.

She had really been surprised to learn how many kinds of

wine there were. There was a good deal more to that than sweet and sour, red and white. And there was all kinds of champagne, too, and all kinds of different whiskey.

What she really should do, she came to understand, was associate herself with a high-class place and learn the business from the bottom up.

She already knew about all there was to know about men, and she had come to understand that there were two kinds of women in a house, those that work on their feet and those that work on their back. She had started turning down new gentlemen callers even before the hotel people had come to start talking about buying her out.

She had to pick someplace where, as in Phoenix, she could make the personal acquaintance of the men in charge. She heard about, and discussed, El Paso, San Antonio, and Dallas, Texas. El Paso and San Antonio were too close to Mexico for her tastes. Truth to tell, she couldn't tell the difference between Spaniards, who were supposed to have class, and Mexicans, provided the Mexicans wore shoes. Dallas was something else.

It had started like so many of the towns out here, as a railhead town. As the railroad was built across the country, every so often they set up sort of a supply place at the end of the tracks. For a while, businessmen would set up warehouses at the railhead, selling their stuff wholesale to retail businessmen in the area. Normally, when another hundred miles of line, or two hundred, had been laid, they would load their "warehouses" on the cars and move them to the new railhead.

For some reason (Kate had no idea why, but she knew it was significant), that hadn't happened at the Dallas railhead. Instead of loading their goods, and the tents built over them, onto the cars when the end of the line had moved westward, the merchants had stayed in Dallas and built regular warehouses for their goods.

It was still a small town, small enough so that she figured she could get to know the important men, and it was growing. The consensus was that the best house in Dallas was Madam Estelle's.

When Kate Shaughnessy boarded the train at Phoenix, she had in her purse a ticket to Philadelphia, via Dallas. When she got to Dallas, she told the hack driver to take her to the best hotel in town. He took her to the Harlingen House. After she'd had a bath, she got another hack and told him to take her to the biggest bank in town. He took her to the First Republic Bank & Trust, where she opened an account with all of her money, less two hundred dollars for immediate expenses and, after asking how she could get money in Philadelphia if she wanted it, a letter of credit for one thousand dollars. The assistant vice-president of the bank, who ushered her back into the waiting hack, was really surprised when he heard her order the driver to take her to Madam Estelle's.

Madam Estelle misread Kate Shaughnessy on first meeting too. When the maid told her there was an Irish lady wanted to see her, Estelle had thought, with reason, that she would be an applicant for employment. When she actually saw Kate, saw how she was dressed, she decided, again based on her experience, that Mrs. Shaughnessy was either a deserted wife or a widow, which was one and the same thing, since it meant there was no man around to support her. From the looks of her, there were no kids.

If she was a widow, Madam Estelle would offer her a job. She was a looker, there would be customers anxious for her. But not if her husband had run off on her. Runaway husbands sometimes came back, and they made trouble when they found their wives in a house. So far as they were concerned, wives could starve, but no wife of theirs, deserted or not, could go to work in a house.

Kate Shaughnessy knocked Madam Estelle slightly off balance with her calm attitude and with her very first words: "I heard it was elegant," she said. "But I didn't expect anything like this."

She didn't exhibit the nervousness, the shame, the fear of other women appearing in Madam Estelle's office to negotiate the rental of their bodies.

"What's on your mind, honey?" Madam Estelle asked, consciously putting a little steel into her tones.

"I'm looking for work," Kate said.

"Husband dead? Or did he just leave you?"

"I've never been married."

"You just woke up this morning and decided you'd like to

be a whore, is that it?" Madam Estelle said as nastily as she could.

"No," Kate Shaughnessy said. "I've been a whore, now I want to learn how to be a madam, like you."

Madam Estelle laughed, and some of the nastiness was gone. "Every girl I've got working for me thinks she should run the place," she said. "What makes you different?"

"I've been running a place in Phoenix," Kate said matter-of-factly.

"And you went broke?"

"No," Kate said. "I was bought out. I was just there long enough to learn I didn't really know enough to run a really high-class house."

"And that's why you want to work for me? So I can show you how? You really have your nerve, I'll say that for you."

"I want to make something of myself," Kate said. "Like you have."

"Everybody that works here, except me, has to be available," Madam Estelle said.

"Well, in that case, I guess I've wasted your time," Kate said, and started to leave. She got as far as the door, wondering if she had misread Madam Estelle. Then Madam Estelle called out after her, telling her to wait a minute, she hadn't said no. She was just checking. Neither the customers nor the girls would take orders from someone who had walked upstairs. If Kate was to work the parlor, she could not be available.

In the next two hours, Kate Shaughnessy learned not only how Madam Estelle's physical plant operated, but something about the high-class sporting-house business that came as a shock, even if it had been there right in front of her nose for her to see.

"I've got steady customers in here, Kate, who never go near one of the girls. They get their fun at the card table."

There were gambling places all over Dallas, Estelle explained, but they were for cowboys and ribbon clerks. The real gamblers didn't want to play against the house, and they didn't want to play with ribbon clerks. They wanted to play against each other.

"It's kind of hard to understand or explain, Kate," Estelle said. "Sometimes I don't think they play for the money. They play to *win*, and the only thing that money means is to let them know how much they've won. Who they beat."

The house took one percent of each pot. The house provided a private place to play, and it was understood that the food and drinks offered, or ordered, were on the house.

"There have been pots in here with twenty-five thousand dollars in them," Estelle said with visible pride. "Men have got up from my tables a hundred thousand dollars richer than when they sat down. Or poorer."

"But you don't play against them?" Kate said, to be sure she understood. "You aren't the house?"

"That's two questions, honey," Estelle said with a laugh. "They're not house games. But I do play. But as an individual, if you understand me."

Kate went to work that same day, in time for the afternoon trade. It took her two weeks to learn how to do what was expected of her, and another month to make herself as indispensable as possible. By that time, when Estelle got up shortly after noon and went to her office, she could expect to find a detailed report of the previous night's business—girls, bar, and food—on her desk, and the cash, checked to the last dime, in the office safe. Kate had been given the combination to the office safe. The gambling safe was upstairs.

Kate had a flair for dealing with both the customers and the girls. She wasn't as formidable physically as Estelle, but there was something about her, a cold flashing of her eyes when she was crossed, that kept the girls in line. She charmed the men with the oldest trick in the book. She remembered their names, and used these frequently when talking to them. That, coupled with what the men chose to believe was a certain vulnerability, made them treat her with an exaggerated courtesy. She was Miss Katherine to them, a lady, with whom they ritually exchanged small talk before ever so politely inquiring if Miss Lucy, or Miss Barbara, or one of the other fourteen women plying their trade at Madam Estelle's was receiving callers.

She stayed at the Harlingen House only two days, and then found a room in a respectable boardinghouse six blocks away. It was two weeks before the proprietor put two and two together and decided that Mrs. Shaughnessy wasn't what she seemed at first. By then, Kate had rented a small fur-

nished frame house on Elm Street, with an option to pur-
chase, and installed a Mexican woman as housekeeper. Kate
took all her meals at Madam Estelle's, and had most of her
laundry done by Madam Estelle's washerwoman. She went to
work dressed as a housewife, and changed into a ball gown
once she got there.

And then she told Madam Estelle that she was going to
have to have a week, possibly ten days, off.

Madam Estelle's first suspicion was that Kate had received
an offer from one of the customers to "visit" his ranch, so it
was necessary for Kate to tell her about the baby. Madam
Estelle didn't like that information much more than she
would have liked confirmation that Kate had decided to pick
up a fast hundred dollars with a man.

But Kate, whom she was paying fifteen dollars a week, had
worked out well. She had done a fine job working the parlor,
and she had taken a lot of the bookkeeping off Madam Estelle's shoulders, and given her more free time than she'd had
in years.

"How are you going to support a child on what I'm paying
you?" Madam Estelle asked.

"I've got money from selling out my place," Kate said.
"And I don't intend to work for you forever."

"You could do a lot worse," Estelle said. "I'll tell you
what. I'll give you another ten dollars a week, in exchange
for your promise that having your baby here won't interfere
with your work. Hire a Mex woman to take care of it."

Four days later, Kate got off the *Congressional Limited* in
Philadelphia. She got a hotel room, and then went to the
lobby to the telephone. Central told her there was a listing
for a Wilton on Rittenhouse Square.

When she was connected, a thick Irish female brogue announced, "The Wilton residence."

"Mr. Wilton, please," she said.

"He's not to home," the brogue announced.

"When could I call?"

"About five."

Kate walked out of the hotel and got in a hack and had
herself carried to the red-brick establishment operated by the
Little Sisters of the Poor. The last time she'd come here,

she'd been on foot, carrying everything she owned in a laundry bag, and six months pregnant.

She was still frightened by the place, and had to remind herself that she was no longer a housemaid, illegitimately pregnant and flat broke. She had two hundred in cash, and a letter of credit for a thousand dollars, and a whole lot more than that in the First Republic Bank & Trust in Dallas.

"I have come for my baby," she anounced to the sister superior. "Mary Elizabeth Shaughnessy."

The sister superior told her what she had aparently forgotten—that when she came for help in her hour of need, she had signed a document authorizing the sisters to act in the baby's best interests. The baby had been four months old before adopted by a good Irish Catholic couple, whom God in His wisdom had not seen fit to bless with a child of their own.

Yes, they had the right to do that. Here was the document Kate had signed. No, there was nothing she could do about it, even if she couldn't or wouldn't understand that what had happened was in the baby's best interests. If she insisted on being difficult, the sister superior would have no choice but to summon the police.

"You and your husband, Mrs. Shaughnessy," the sister superior said, "can certainly have children of your own. I know how you feel."

"You have no idea how I feel!" Kate shouted. "I'm going to—"

She found herself out of the sister superior's office and outside the walls in five minutes.

Kate walked all the way back to her hotel. At five, she telephoned the number central had given her, and again asked for Mr. Wilton.

"Who should I say is calling?"

"Mrs. Shaughnessy."

"This is Thomas Wilton," a young English voice said.

"I'm trying to get Mr. John Wilton."

"My brother is in the New Mexico Territory," Thomas told her.

She could not talk him out of his address, although she tried very hard. At least, she thought, as she walked up the stairs to her room to pack, she wouldn't have to worry about paying John Wilton back the $2,500 she owed him.

It never entered her mind to give up the baby, just because she had been adopted and the Little Sisters of the Poor refused her pleas. She had decided, even as she sat in the sister superior's office, that she was going to find out who had her child, and take her back.

But not now. If she started something now, they would be too ready to fight. And she didn't know how to go about it. Whatever she did would probably only make things worse. What she would do, she decided, was go back to Dallas and talk to a lawyer she'd met at Madam Estelle's, a man named Albert Dennison. He was supposed to be the best lawyer in Texas, and she knew he liked her.

She would go to Albert Dennison and tell him the whole story, and ask him what to do. She was not going to have her baby raised by strangers.

22

Kate Shaughnessy sensed that the only reason Albert Dennison smilingly told her that he would see her at his offices at eleven the next morning was that he had no alternative. She had taken him by surprise, and Dallas' smartest lawyer or not, his brain just hadn't been quick enough to come up with a good reason why that might be inadvisable.

She had set him up that way, first congratulating him on a victory in court, in which he had successfully sued the Texas & Pacific Railroad for criminal negligence in a derailment. She led quickly from that to questions concerning how much work was required of him; from that to his office hours; and then she pounced: "I would very much like to have you represent me in a personal matter. Might I come by your office late tomorrow morning?" When he paused, obviously searching for an excuse, she went on, "Would eleven be all right?"

She dressed as respectably as she could. Now that she had a little money in the bank, she was able to copy the styles of the proper ladies she saw in Dallas, the wives of the merchants and the professional men.

Albert Dennison's law clerk, who was not paid enough to be able to patronize Madam Estelle's, got quickly to his feet when she walked in the door. From his attitude, Kate knew that he was so surprised to see a married woman come to Dennison's office, it never entered his mind he was facing a scarlet woman.

165

"Mr. Dennison said he would receive me at eleven," Kate announced. "My name is Shaughnessy."

"Yes, ma'am," the clerk said. "I'll let him know you're here. Won't you please have a seat?"

Dennison's secretary looked at her curiously, but there was none of the tightened-mouth, nose-up-in-the-air attitude Kate had come to expect when ladies found themselves face to face with a whore.

"Good morning, Mrs. Shaughnessy," Albert Dennison said, greeting her with a warm, professional smile. "Please come in. I'll have Miss Harper get us some tea."

He waited until the tea had been served and Miss Harper had left the office.

"Okay, Kate, what can I do for you?"

She told him the whole story, from her arrival in the United States, through her seduction (it was more a rape) by her employer, to her confinement in the charity maternity ward of the Little Sisters of the Poor in Philadelphia. She glossed over her trip westward, and left out entirely her relationship with John Wilton. Dennison was a man, Kate decided, and therefore he had a dirty mind. He could imagine how she had wound up at Madam Estelle's without having the details.

"You're not going to like what I'm going to tell you, Kate," he said. "But you came here for my best advice, and I'm going to give it to you."

"That's why I'm here," she said.

"The only hope you have is that the people who adopted your baby are not fit parents. And I don't mean that *you* don't think they're fit parents, I mean that you're going to have to prove to the courts, and, as importantly, convince the Catholic Church that that is the case."

"What I had in mind," Kate said, "was finding my baby, and then just taking it."

"That's kidnapping," Dennison said. "If you got caught doing it in Pennsylvania, you'd go to jail. If you got away with it, and managed to get the child out here, and they found about it, they would simply take the child back."

"Because of where I work, you mean?"

He nodded. "There's only one chance," he said.

"What is it?"

"If you were married to some respectable man, and didn't work at Madam Estelle's, and were far from here, so nobody could remember you, and you somehow managed to get that baby back, and it took them a long time to find you, a year or more, then a court just might decide that the baby properly belonged with you. Presuming, of course, that you could show that the people who have it now were not providing as good a home for it as you were."

"The first step, then, would be to find out who has the baby," Kate said. "How do I go about that?"

"You hire a private detective agency, you pay them a lot of money, and they may or may not be able to help you."

"Can you take care of that for me?" she asked.

He didn't want to. Normally, he would have said he had no idea of how to go about something like that. But there was something about Kate Shaughnessy that got to him. He considered for a moment what that was, and decided it was less her physical attractions than her character. She was tough. She hadn't shed one tear, not so much as a sniffle, while telling him her story.

"I'll see what I can do, Kate," Albert Dennison said. "But you understand that I'll have nothing to do with you going there and just taking the child."

"You find out where she is, Mr. Dennison, and I'll take it from there."

She offered him money. He refused it, even though he knew that private detectives operated on a cash-on-the-barrelhead basis. He had decided, he realized, that he would ask for repayment of what he had laid out for her only if the private detectives reported that the kid wasn't well off. If they reported to him that the kid was being well cared for, he simply wouldn't be able to ask Kate to pay for that information.

"My final advice, Kate, is that you consider what's really best for your baby."

"I will, Mr. Dennison," Kate said. She got up. "Thank you for seeing me."

He walked with her to the door. "Good morning, Mrs. Shaughnessy," he said. "Thank you for coming to see me."

"Thank you for your time, Mr. Dennison," Kate Shaughnessy said.

She doesn't look like the madam of a whorehouse, he thought.

That thought never entered the mind of Luther W. Sawyer of Waxahachie. He thought he had never seen a more beautiful woman, with whiter skin, a more erect carriage, or such lines of character in her face.

Luther W. Sawyer of Waxahachie was originally from Galveston, where he had been in the shipping business, primarily cotton, for most of his life. He had first gone to sea at fourteen, as a cabin boy. He had first sailed on a blockade runner during the War of Secession, as a sixteen-year-old quartermaster, running between the Caribbean and the Atlantic and Gulf Coast ports. When the war was over, he had five thousand pounds sterling in the Midlands Bank of Liverpool, and he was twenty-years old, and he was Captain Sawyer, of the Brigantine *James Daly*.

He had gone into business as a cotton broker, and married Miss Patience Furrman, and he regarded both decisions as major errors in judgment. He should have put his money into a ship, if not the *Daly*, then another one, and he never should have married, especially not Patience Furrman, behind whose pale face and willowy frame there had been hidden a tyrant, a shrew, and a bitch.

Luther Sawyer had barely felt sorry when she was carried away by fever after her first and only confinement. The child had lived, and that, of course, had kept him from going back to sea. The child had been raised by Patience's maiden sister. It was a toss-up in Sawyer's mind who was the meaner woman, but the situation was out of his hands.

Once the girl, Faith, had reached puberty, she seemed to prove beyond any doubt that she was her mother's child. He had, the year before, given her in marriage, and when she asked for the house in which she had been born and raised as her dowry, he gave it over to her new husband willingly. The poor man was going to earn every last nail and board in the place.

He had, over the years, when land had come on the market at a good price, bought cotton acreage near Dallas. Six months before, he had decided to move to Waxahachie to supervise the cotton operation. He was too old to go back to sea now, and he felt restricted in the three-room suite he had taken on a yearly basis at the Galveston Plaza Hotel.

What he would do, he thought, was build a little house. He would get a cook and a housekeeper. He would not look for another woman to marry. He had gone through that business once.

"Who was that, Al?" he asked now.

"A client, Luke," Dennison said. "A lady with problems. Not like yours, but with problems."

"English, wasn't she? I heard her say good-bye."

"Irish," Dennison corrected him.

"You don't say," Sawyer said.

Dennison decided quickly not to tell Luther Sawyer how Kate Shaughnessy earned her living. Sawyer's visits to Dallas always included three things. A visit to his bank, a visit to his lawyer's, and a visit to Madam Estelle's. He was not a card player. He took care of what the Book of Common Prayer referred to as the sinful lusts of the flesh as methodically as he took care of his shipping invoices and demand drafts and contracts. He had one glass of whiskey, picked out the woman of his choice, and spent the next two hours with her. Then he would have a steam bath, a shave, and a haircut and ride back to his plantation in Waxahachie.

There was no question whatever in Albert Dennison's mind that Luther Sawyer would visit Madam Estelle's sometime during his visit, and that when he was there, he would run into Kate Shaughnessy.

He would feel like a fool, Dennison thought, to find the object of his admiration a madam, and at first he might be a little annoyed with Dennison for not having told him. But that would pass, and Sawyer would come to realize that to have told him would be a breach of ethics, legal and personal.

Dennison decided, however, that today he would forgo his customary visit to Madam Estelle's. He would have his afternoon pick-me-ups at the bar at the Harlingen House. It would be better not to run into Luther Sawyer at Madam Estelle's. It would be better to wait until Luther for sure had time to understand why Dennison hadn't volunteered information about Kate Shaughnessy.

As it happened, it was two days before Albert Dennison

got to Madam Estelle's. The next day, he was entertained at dinner by one of his clients, one of the few clients who didn't much care what his wife thought of Albert Dennison's reputation as a patron of houses of ill repute, and a man who would wager five hundred dollars on the turn of a card.

When he walked in the foyer of Madam Estelle's and glanced into the downstairs parlor as he handed his hat to the maid, Luther Sawyer was standing, one of a group of three men, beside Kate Shaughnessy. He held a glass of champagne in his hand. It was the first time Dennison had seen him drink anything but Scotch whiskey. Dennison hated Scotch—it tasted like medicine to him—but Sawyer had told him one time he'd learned to drink it during the War Between the States and when he tried to drink anything else now, it had no effect.

There was nothing to do but walk over and ask the obvious question: "What kept you in town, Luke?"

"Good afternoon, Mr. Dennison," Kate Shaughnessy said with a smile.

"You're looking as lovely as ever, Kate," Dennison said. "And what kept you in town, Luke?"

Sawyer's answer threw him: "Once I had the pleasure of making Mrs. Shaughnessy's acquaintance, Albert, I just didn't want to go back to Waxahachie."

"What Mr. Sawyer has been doing, Mr. Dennison," Kate said, "is advising me on investments. Do you think I should trust him?"

Sawyer looked genuinely hurt at what was at best gentle mocking.

"I trust him," Dennison said. "His word and his judgment."

"So, I think," Kate said, looking Dennison right in the eye, "do I."

Luther walked into the front parlor of Madam Estelle's at exactly three P.M. the following day, his jaw set, his face grim with determination. Kate saw him refuse to give his hat and coat over to the maid, and she could read his lips across the room.

"I won't be staying," he said, and then continued walking toward her.

"I want to talk to you, Katherine," Luther said. "And this is not the place to do it. Will you please come with me?"

"I'll get my coat," Kate said. She wasn't supposed to leave, but Luther's look brooked no argument.

He had a hack waiting outside. He handed her into it, and told the driver to take them to the Harlingen House. That surprised her, and worried her. She was not welcome in the Harlingen House. Men took their wives to the Harlingen House, and wives did not want to be in the same room with women like Kate Shaughnessy.

"Is that a good place for us to go?" she asked.

"I think so," Sawyer said. Kate could tell that he was quite tense; he had something on his mind. But why would he take her to the best hotel in town?

He led her into the dining room. The headwaiter gave her an icy look, and as soon as he had shown them to a table in an alcove, he marched out of the room. Kate suspected he was going to report to the manager that Luther Sawyer had just walked in with a madam.

"Doubtless you think me a fool," Luther said. "A man my age being infatuated with a woman young enough to be his daughter."

"I don't quite know what you're saying."

"Be that as it may," Luther plunged on, "the point is that I am prepared to do anything to have you. Albert tells me the only chance you have to get your child back is to have a husband."

"You'd marry me?" Kate asked.

"And I'll do everything in my power to get your baby back for you," Sawyer said. "Whatever it takes."

"But I'm a . . . you know what I am . . ." Kate said.

"We can put that behind us," Luther said.

"There's no way we could do that."

"We could try." Luther reached out and laid his hand on hers. "Neither one of us has anybody else, Kate. Maybe we could make something together."

She looked into his eyes. "You sure you know what you're doing?"

"I'll be good to you Kate," he said. "I'll give you no cause to regret anything."

And I, Kate decided, as she turned her hand over to

171

squeeze his, will be good to you. I'll be the best goddamned wife in the world.

"There's a train to Waxahachie at five-fifteen," Luther said. "Is there any reason we can't take it?"

"None at all," Kate said.

Luther dropped a silver dollar on the table and walked back out of the dining room, his hand possessively on Kate Shaughnessy's arm.

Kate spent that night in the guest bedroom of Luther's house on the Waxahachie plantation. At noon the next day, they were married by the circuit judge in his chambers at the Waxahachie County Courthouse. The witnesses were the clerk of the court and Sawyer's Mexican housekeeper.

23

On the morning of Kate Shaughnessy's wedding, Lucille Stevens walked into her father's room, as was her custom, and put her hand on his forehead; his skin felt cold.

He was dead.

Just like that.

She put her hand over her mouth, and stood looking down at him for a long moment, and then she reached down and pulled the sheet over him.

She went out of his room, sat down at his desk, and wrote the telegrams that would have to be sent.

She had not become hysterical. She hadn't even wept. She wondered about that. Was it because she knew he was really better off dead? Or was she in shock, and the tears would come later? Or was it that there was nobody around who could comort her?

She finished the telegrams, then called for Juanita, to tell her the major was dead, and to send someone to the Western Union office in Loving.

Because of the intense summer heat, they buried Major Stevens the next day. John Wilton was at the funeral, of course, along with Charley Broadhead and Mr. and Mrs. Broadhead, and the cream of what constituted local society. Only the bishop, an old friend of the major's, was missing, unable to get to the ranch in time, and in his majestic stead the pale, nervous Loving minister officiated at the simple service.

Lucille felt very proud that she didn't cry, not once, not while the coffin was lowered into the ground, not during the interminable hours afterward while everyone murmured about "the tragedy" and "how on earth will you manage now, my dear."

Finally, at about eight, the mourners began to leave, even a reluctant Mrs. Broadhead, having uttered her fourth invitation for Lucille to stay with them awhile.

John Wilton had his Stetson in one hand, the other extended to shake Lucille's right hand, when she stopped him. "Please," she said, "stay a minute. I need to talk to you."

Actually, she had nothing to say. What she wanted was his presence, his warmth, the comfort he seemed to exude. And when she saw the last person out the door, walked into the parlor, and saw Wilton sitting there, she went to him as if it were the most natural thing in the world, put her head on his broad chest, and began to cry. It started as a few small whimpers, but soon Lucille's whole body shook with sobs, as she let all her fears, her worries, all the pain of her father's illness pour out. Wilton's arms went about her, holding her gently, with care.

He smoothed her hair. "I know it's not considered proper, but should I stay here tonight? I don't know if you should be alone."

Lucille pulled a small white handkerchief from her pocket, wiping her eyes and nose. She sat up. "I don't know . . ." she said. "Maybe, if you could . . . there is the spare bedroom you used before."

"All right," Wilton said. "Then I'll stay."

Long after they'd said good night, Lucille lay in her bed, eyes wide open, mind in a whirl. Her father's death . . . the funeral . . . being alone . . . John Wilton in the house . . .

She got up as if she were sleepwalking, put on her pink robe, her long cotton nightgown swishing on the floor as she moved on bare feet. She hesitated a moment before Wilton's door, then quietly pushed it open.

She stood by the side of his bed. And then, very deliberately, she unfastened her robe and took it off. She thought a moment more, and then she pulled the cord at the neck of her nightgown loose, and then bent and pulled it over her head and dropped it on the floor. Very quietly she slid into the bed beside him.

She lay there a long time, her arms at her sides, her legs straight. After a very long time, she fell asleep.

She woke instantly when he rolled over on her in his sleep, his arm coming to rest on her side (she had also moved in her sleep, onto her side, facing away from him), his hand searching and finding her breast, his fingers closing gently, possessively on it. She felt her breast swell, felt the nipple stiffen, felt something warm and stiffening at the crack of her buttocks, realized what it was, was shamed and exhilarated at once.

And then he woke. And she knew from the way his fingers left her breast, and his arm gingerly lifted off her side, that he had embraced her in his sleep, and that he was now awake. She felt the mattress sag beneath them as he very slowly rolled over on his back away from her.

She heard him exhale, and then she knew somehow, without actually seeing him do it, or feeling the bed move, that he had shaken his head. He had found her in his bed, and he didn't understand that. She lay there feigning sleep, forcing herself to breathe slowly and regularly.

The excitement she had felt when his hand grabbed her bosom was gone. She felt chilly, shriveled, ashamed, and very frightened.

Having gone this far (and she was suddenly very much aware of how incredibly far she had gone), perhaps the thing for her to do was to roll over, in her sleep of course, and establish contact with him.

But she could not do that. What she wanted to do was jump from the bed and run from the room and bury herself in her bed. And never get up again.

"We couldn't just carry on, you realize," he said, and she knew that he knew she was awake. "That wouldn't do at all."

She abandoned pretense. "Carry on?" she asked.

"I wouldn't do that to you," he said. "Have you as a mistress. I just couldn't."

"What makes you think I'd be willing to be your mistress?" she said, more angrily than she intended.

The answer to that, she realized immediately, was self-evi-

175

dent. She was naked in his bed, and he knew he hadn't brought her there either by seduction or by violence.

"And if we did the other thing," Wilton went on, "it would generally be accepted that I married you for your father's estate, and that you had made a fool of yourself."

She closed her eyes so hard it hurt. She said nothing.

He chuckled, and she had a mental picture of him shaking his head.

"Don't you laugh at me," she said, a hissing whisper. "For God's sake, don't you laugh at me!"

He put out a hand and patted her arm. Like she was a dog. Or a child. "I was laughing at myself, old girl," he said.

She rolled over on her back, covering her bosom with her crossed arms, and looked up at him.

"This isn't the way I thought it would be at all," he said. "In my fantasy, I have no conscience whatever."

"Oh?" she said. She saw his eyes on her, saw them drop to the swelling of her bosom.

"Unless you cover yourself within the next ten seconds, the first noble urge I can ever recall will have passed."

As if it had a mind of its own, her left hand rose from her breast and reached up toward his face. She saw his eyes dart between her face and her now exposed right breast. Her nipple, she thought, was standing proudly erect; she was pleased. Most times it was just a round, flat circle of soft flesh.

She slid her hand down from his cheek to his neck, and then stretched her body just enough so that she could put her fingers on his neck and pull him down to her. She thought he would kiss her. But his attention was on her nipple. He put his mouth on it.

"Oh, my God, I can feel that right down my middle!"

He took his mouth from her breast. "I suppose in the morning," he said, "we can pretend this never happened."

"Will you shut up?" Lucille said. She pushed his face against her breast again.

She woke at first light. He was lying on his stomach, with his arm draped across her. She wormed her way out from under him, surprised, and then a little annoyed, that he didn't wake up. She pulled the nightgown over her head and then wrapped the robe around her and went to her room. The clock beside her bed said 5:15. That was too early. She decided to get an hour's sleep.

Juanita woke her. "His eminence the bishop is here," Juanita said. The clock on the bedside table now said 9:30.

When she dressed, putting on again the black dress she had worn for her father's funeral, she went out of her room and found the bishop with John in the sitting room.

They both rose solemnly to greet her. Wilton's behavior was obviously that of a neighbor, a distant friend who had simply spent the night in the house. He was giving her the option of forgetting what had happened the night before. She hated him for it.

The bishop would conduct another graveside service, and then he would conduct a memorial service at the cathedral.

Lucille nodded her understanding and her thanks.

They formed a little procession right then, and marched out to the gravesite, the bishop leading, Lucille on John Wilton's arm following, with Sammy Long and Juanita, bringing up the rear.

On the way back to the house, John spoke to the bishop. "Miss Stevens and I would be honored to have you unite us in holy matrimony."

"Why, of course," the bishop said, his smile wide in his face. "When had you planned to do that? I should think, under the circumstances, that a six months' mourning would be more than sufficient."

"What I had in mind," John said, "was today." He walked to Lucille and put his hand on her waist.

"Have you thought this through?" the bishop said. "Considered at length the significance of marriage? Asked God's guidance?"

"From the moment I first saw her," John said.

Oh, you hypocrite! Lucille thought. But she tightened her arm against John's hand and leaned against him.

24

The carriage of Mr. and Mrs. C. Harold Tilley arrived at the curbstone of 14 Rittenhouse Square about thirty seconds before the carriage carrying Mr. and Mrs. Paul MacSwain and Master Edward MacSwain.

Mrs. Tilley went to Mrs. MacSwain and fussed over the baby while Mr. Tilley shook Mr. MacSwain's hand and then climbed the brownstone steps to the door.

Mary Francis, who had been the upstairs maid at the Tilley residence before Martha married Thomas, opened the door to them. Mary Francis had moved to Rittenhouse Square when Mrs. MacSwain had turned over that house to her son and daughter-in-law. Mary had gone with her to the MacSwain house.

"Well, how are you, Mary Francis?" Mr. Tilley said. "I believe Mrs. Wilton expects us for dinner."

"Indeed she does," Mary Francis said. "And I got Bridget to show the girl here how to make your leg of lamb." Bridget was the Tilley cook.

The men waited until their wives climbed the stairs, and then bowed them through the outer and inner doors of the vestibule before them.

"Miss Martha's in the parlor," Mary Francis said.

"Mrs. Wilton, Mary Francis," Mrs. Tilley corrected her.

Martha Tilley Wilton, whose blooming belly did not show under her voluminous gown, was nevertheless determined to play the role of mother-to-be. She had quickly learned that her mother, her father, and most importantly, Tom, treated her with awe and respect because of her condition.

She was sitting on a love seat in the parlor, her hair parted severely in the middle, her face liberally dusted to give her what she thought was an appealing pallor.

"How do you feel, Maggie?" her father asked, walking to her, bending down, and kissing her forehead. She loathed being called Maggie. It made her sound like an Irish washerwoman.

"Just fine, Daddy," she said very faintly. And then she spotted Margaret MacSwain with that damned child in her arms.

"Why did you bring the baby?" Martha snapped.

Margaret was unshaken. She smiled tolerantly and said, "My son informed me this was a small family dinner. Edward's small, and he's family." She paused, and then inquired, "What's that you've got on your face?"

God Martha thought, I loathe that woman!

"I don't know what you're going to do with him at dinner," Martha snapped. "We don't have a maid to care for him."

"I'm going to feed him at dinner," Margaret said. "There's a high chair in the butler's pantry. Will you get it, Mary Francis?"

Mary Francis, without so much as looking at her mistress, scurried to obey Margaret MacSwain. Martha was furious; she would have a word with her maid when the guests were gone.

Thomas appeared, in a suit, looking nervous. He shook hands with the men formally, unsmiling, looked nervously at his wife, and kissed his mother as if he had suddenly remembered that was expected of him.

"Will you have sherry?" Martha asked somewhat regally.

"I'd rather have whiskey, Maggie," her father said.

"For me, too," Paul MacSwain said.

"We will all, I think, have a drink of whiskey," Margaret MacSwain said. "Eh, Lizzy?"

"It's supposed to be good for the appetite," Martha's mother replied.

Martha was furious: again she was being treated as a child. This was her home. Good manners required that guests accept or decline what was offered, not announce they would have something else.

"And how did you spend the day, Thomas?" Margaret asked. Thomas had declined offers from both C. Harold Tilley to go to work on the *Inquirer* and from Paul MacSwain to go into MacSwain's new MacSwain Wagon Company. He was learning the loom business, getting out of bed in the middle of the night to catch the 5:25 train to Lennai. Martha thought he was fool.

Thomas, the boy reporting to his mother, launched into a five-minute description of what he had that day learned from "Mr. Finley," an Irish peasant who had been engaged as works manager. He was the sort of person one addressed by his first name, although Thomas insisted on calling him Mr. Finley.

Margaret MacSwain waited until they were seated at table and had finished their turtle soup before making her announcement.

"I have some wonderful news about John," she said. "Which I thought you had best hear sitting down." She waited until all eyes, including her husband's, were on her. "There was a letter today," she went on, and fished it from a pocket in her skirt, handing it to Paul MacSwain.

"John has married Lucille Stephens," she said.

"Well, I'll be damned," Paul said. "Just like that, eh?"

"Her father passed on," Margaret continued, "and that apparently tipped the scales."

"She's a very fine person," Thomas said somewhat pompously. "He couldn't possibly have done better."

"Indeed she is," MacSwain said. "Just what that boy needs."

"Wasn't that in rather bad taste, to marry so soon after her father died?" Martha inquired.

"Her father was ill for a very long time, poor man," Margaret said. "In great pain. I suppose that drew John and Lucille together."

MacSwain finished reading the letter and passed it to Harold Tilley. "A good marriage, in the practical sense," MacSwain said. "Putting both ranches together, I mean."

"I suppose it is," Margaret said. "I hadn't thought about it, but obviously it is. They can put the herds together, and probably they can cut down on the number of people they have working."

There was silence while Mary Francis served the lamb, then the oven-roasted potatoes, and finally the buttered carrots.

"How does that affect us?" Martha suddenly asked. "Putting the farms together."

"They're ranches, dear," Margaret corrected her gently. "I don't know what you mean, how it would affect you."

"Isn't half that *farm*," Martha went on, "Thomas'?"

"Martha!" her father snapped.

"No, Martha," Margaret said, trying to keep her temper in check. "Half of it is not Thomas'. I've turned it over to John."

"But that's not fair!" Martha said.

"Martha," Mrs. Tilley said, "Mother MacSwain gave you and Tom this house."

"Only because she didn't need it," Martha said.

"Maggie," Harold Tilley said firmly, "I think you owe Mother MacSwain an apology."

Martha pushed herself away from the table, knocking her water glass over, and fled from the room.

There was a moment's silence; then Margaret said, "Thomas, go to your wife. In her condition, she needs you."

"I apologize for Maggie. That was, that was . . ." Elizabeth Tilley said.

"There's nothing to apologize for," Margaret said. "But I don't think this is the time to bring up moving John's Chinese boy in here as a boarder." There was a lilt in her voice that made both MacSwain and Harold Tilley chuckle.

"What are you talking about?"

Harold Tilley handed his wife John's letter.

And then, all of a sudden, Martha and Thomas reappeared. Martha was subdued; Thomas was tight-lipped.

"If I have said anything to offend you, Mother MacSwain, I'm sorry," she said.

"Not at all, my dear," Margaret said. She was surprised, and pleased. Thomas apparently could handle this little hellion.

"What were you saying before," Thomas asked, to change the subject, "about a Chinese boy?"

"John has arranged for Sammy Long to attend Episcopal Academy here," Margaret said. "And he—"

"Splendid idea," Thomas said. "Martha, he's an absolutely delightful little fellow. Smart as a whip . . ."

"And what?" Martha asked.

"John suggests that he might stay with you," Margaret said.

"A *Chinaman*, in *my* house?" Martha almost screamed. "He must have been really drunk to come up with an insane idea like that."

"Now, just take it easy, sweetheart . . ." her father said.

"Take it easy? I'm going to have a baby, and Thomas' drunken brother wants to move a Chinaman into my house, and you tell me to take it easy? You make me sick. You all make me sick. I wish you would all get out of my house. I want you *all* out of my house!"

No one moved or replied. Martha got to her feet again, and sobbing, ran from the dining room.

"I'll write to John, Mother," Thomas said shakily, "and tell him that Sammy will be more than welcome."

"*I'll* write to John," Margaret said, "and tell him that while you were perfectly willing to have the boy, I thought he would be better off with Paul and me." She looked at her husband. "All right, Paul?"

"Certainly," MacSwain said. "He can teach us to eat rice with sticks, the way they do."

Elizabeth Tilley laughed, far more loudly than she intended.

Thomas looked at the door through which his wife had just rushed. He seemed indecisive for a moment, and then he picked up his knife and fork. Martha did not reappear for the rest of the evening.

As they stood on the curb, Harold Tilley did something very out of character. He put his arm around Paul MacSwain's wife and kissed her on the cheek. "I just realized I love you, Mother MacSwain," he said. "I hope Paul understands."

"If you mean that, Harold," Margaret MacSwain said, "then I'll tell you something."

"Of course I mean it," he said.

"The next time you call me Mother MacSwain, I'm going to dump hot soup in your lap." She kissed him in the cheek and gave Edward to her husband so she could climb into their carriage.

"Good night, *Father* Tilley," Paul MacSwain said, laughing, and got in the carriage. As soon as the door was closed, he took his wife's hand. "God, I hope that child takes after your side of the family," he said. She chuckled, and that encouraged him. "With a little bit of luck," he said, "he could turn out like John. That would be sweet justice, wouldn't it?"

She didn't laugh, and he sensed a chill. He thought it was because he had said something against John.

"Now, honey, you know I like John," he said. "What I meant to say was . . ."

"I know what you meant, darling," Margaret said, and picked up his hand and held it against her cheek.

Mrs. Thomas Wilton, née Martha Tilley, of 14 Rittenhouse Square, was delivered of an eight-pound-ten-ounce boy. Despite a fourteen-hour labor, which the attending physician said was not at all uncommon with women Mrs. Wilton's age, the delivery was without incident, and the child was pronounced fit and hardy in all respects.

Margaret MacSwain thought Martha looked like a madonna with the child at her breast.

Margaret and Elizabeth Tilley spent alternate days at the house on Rittenhouse Square for the next ten days, until Martha felt strong enough to get out of bed. Margaret forced back thoughts that Martha had milked her pregnancy for all it was worth. She remembered that she herself had gotten out of bed three days after the birth of her sons.

When the Reverend Dr. Lawton Steele Houghton, rector of St. Mark's Episcopal Church, had paid his ritual visit to mother and child five days after the birth, to conduct the service of Thanksgiving for Women Having Passed Through Childbirth, he had ritually announced that it certainly was a fine-looking baby.

Tom, flushed with happiness and the magnitude of it all, had been excited enough (and boyish enough, and stupid enough) to make what he thought was a witty remark. "He is now, sir," he said, smiling from ear to ear, "but when he was born, he looked like a red rat."

Martha had instantly taken deep affront. She threw her

water pitcher at Thomas, ordered him from her room for all time, and began to weep.

And she proved that she was able to carry a grudge. Nothing would move her from her decision that she was not going to name her red rat after her husband.

Three weeks after the boy was born, the family gathered around the baptismal font of St. Mark's Church, and the Reverend Dr. Houghton, in all his splendiferous vestments, looked at the baby's father and in ringing tones demanded him to "name this child." Thomas swallowed and croaked, "John Francis William Wilton II."

At the reception that followed, it was agreed that it was a splendid gesture on the part of Thomas and Martha to name the child after his faraway uncle, a gesture that united the family despite the thousands of miles that separated them.

The child's namesake was represented at the reception by Master Samuel Francis Long. It had never entered anyone's mind to suggest to Martha that "John's little Chinaman" receive an invitation to the christening in the church. Martha managed to make "little Chinaman" sound obscene. But the reception was held at the residence of Mr. and Mrs. Paul MacSwain, and Margaret had never for a moment entertained the notion of not inviting Sammy, who was living with them on weekends, and who she felt was an adorable child. It was, after all, her house, and she would damned well invite whom she damned well pleased.

Sammy, dressed in the blazer-and-slacks uniform of the Episcopal Academy, and backed up by a tall, skinny curate from the school, was waiting inside the drawing room when the christening party arrived.

He and the curate each held a package. The larger package held the christening gift of Mr. and Mrs. John F. W. Wilton, a complete set of infant's silver—knife, fork, spoon, plate, cup, saucer—Mexican silver engraved with an ornate W and inlaid with gold and turquoise. The smaller package was from Sammy's parents, who remembered Thomas. It contained a Chinese doll Margaret MacSwain thought was exquisite.

When the reception was over, Martha gathered up all the christening gifts except the doll and had them loaded into a hack. Margaret found the doll in a wastebasket.

She quickly snatched it up and carried it to her bedroom.

Sammy would not ever be in her bedroom, and would not see it. Over the years, she often had occasion to regret her decision. Every time she looked at the doll sitting on the mantelpiece, she was reminded of her daughter-in-law's cruelty.

Kate Shaughnessy Sawyer told her husband of John Wilton in the first few days of their marriage. His only response was to suggest that she repay Wilton the $2,500 she owed him; he would tell Albert Dennison to write a check.

She learned that Wilton had married when she and Luther stopped by Dennison's office en route to Philadelphia to get her child. Albert wordlessly handed over John's response to the check: it was torn in two and pinned to the torn IOU she had given him in Phoenix, and both in turn were pinned to a note:

> Dear Al:
>   If I were not myself in the euphoric mood of the newly married, I probably would not be doing this. The odd thing seems to be that I truly wish Kate and her husband a long and happy marriage, and admire her character in offering to repay the money. I could not in good conscience spend it knowing that it could be put to better use to give Kate and her husband a start in life. As a matter of fact, if there is anything I can do to that end, please let me know. You would not have to tell her whence came any funds.
>
> John

"Arrogant bastard," Kate said with tears in her eyes. "He probably doesn't have a pot to . . ." She remembered that Luther didn't like her to talk, as he put it, earthily, except in their bedroom, and she stopped.

"He married well, Kate," Dennison said. "He can afford the gesture."

"We don't want his money, however well-intentioned," Luther Sawyer said.

"Then send him a wedding present," Dennison said. "I know John, and as long as you keep sending checks, he'll keep tearing them up."

"Make sure that he finds out Kate doesn't need a start in life," Sawyer said.

The Sawyers passed through New Orleans on their way to Philadelphia. In a jewelry store on Canal Street, where Luther bought his wife a two-carat emerald-cut diamond set in a platinum cotton blossom, they both saw, at the same time, a sterling-and-gold locomotive and coal tender. The price was $2,500. They were so taken with the jewel they never learned what it was supposed to be. They just told the pleasantly surprised jeweler to pack it up and send it to Mr. and Mrs. John F. W. Wilton with the best wishes of Mr. and Mrs. Luther W. Sawyer for a long and happy marriage.

Luther waited in their hotel while Kate did the rest of their shopping. She bought a complete wardrobe for an eighteen-month-old girl, and suitcases to carry it all.

The Pinkerton man was waiting in the lobby of the Belle-vue-Stratford Hotel in Philadelphia when they got there.

He had both bad news and good news. The bad news was that the child was being more than adequately cared for by her adopted parents. Furthermore, James F. Herlihy and his wife, Patricia, were not only highly thought-of members of the Philadelphia middle class, but showed every indication of further rise. Herlihy's bricklaying business was well managed, successful, and he was growing rich.

The good news was that after ten-o'clock Mass at St. Rose of Lima's Roman Catholic Church, the child, whom they had named after her adopted mother, Patricia, was left in the custody of her nurse, who walked the carriage in the park nearby while the parents took coffee at the rectory with the monsignor, who was Mr. Herlihy's uncle. Getting the child away from the nurse would be no problem, and they would go directly from St. Rose's to the Broad Street Station, in time to make the 11:30 *Congressional Express* to Washington and points south.

"In other words, Mr. Sawyer," the Pinkerton man said, "getting the child will be easy. But if they find out where you've taken it—and I must tell you that Herlihy has a good deal of political influence, and you're going to have to face the fact that he's going to put somebody, maybe even us, to work looking for the mother—you're going to have trouble keeping the child."

In the five weeks that they had been married, Kate had learned enough about Luther to know what he was thinking, even if he said nothing. He didn't like what she was doing, and not only because he didn't want to share her with a child or because he was afraid of any trouble the little girl might cause. He had concluded that what Kate was doing was wrong. He would stand by her, and do what she wanted, but that wouldn't make it right.

Kate told herself that it would be all right once they got the baby to Texas. And she promised herself that, as much as she was going to love the baby, she would never forget that Luther was responsible for getting her back.

What happened finally was that Patricia Mary Herlihy's nurse had the most astonishing thing happen to her in the park across from St. Rose's after ten-o'clock Mass while she was walking the child in her care.

A lady, a real lady—you could tell by her clothes, and she had a diamond brooch that would choke a large dog—came out of a carriage and first just looked down at the baby and said how pretty she was, and then, all of a sudden, without a by-your-leave or nothing, she bent down and took the baby and gave it a hug and kiss, and she started to cry, and put the baby back, the baby started to cry, and then she ran out of the park as if she was being chased by the devil himself and got in her carriage and drove off, and I never saw her again.

What it probably was, the nurse concluded, was the poor thing had probably lost a baby of her own, and seeing Patricia had just reminded her of her own lost child. She decided against saying anything to either Mr. or Mrs. Herlihy; they would ask why she let the lady pick up Patricia in the first place. As if she didn't love Patricia near as much as they did, and would lay down her life for her and be glad, if that's what it came to.

25

Lucille Stevens Wilton was not at all surprised when she saw her husband ride up from the stable shortly before five in the afternoon. There were at least two and probably three hours of light left in the day, but he wanted to play with his toy, and he had quit work early.

She thought her husband, late of the Prince of Wales's Own Bengal Light Cavalry, looked far more like a Spanish bandit than either an English officer or a rancher. He wore a sombrero, an enormous and not particularly attractive sombrero, sweat-soaked dark halfway up the crown. The brim was crooked, and it had been torn in several places. He wore a now sweaty and dust-and-dirt-stained white cotton shirt. He had on a pair of faded blue canvas pants—sailor pants, Lucille thought of them—made by a firm in San Francisco from the same material ship sails were made from. Over them, a battered set of leather chaps, protection against the cactus. His feet were in high-heeled Spanish-style boots. He had a Western saddle, all leather (she had ordered for him, so far a secret, a silver-trimmed saddle, for his birthday) and worn from use. His old army revolver hung in a holster on one side of the pommel, and his German rifle, butt upward, on the other side. Around his neck he had a filthy blue kerchief tied loosely enough to mop his face with it.

He was deeply tanned by the sun and the wind. His hair was nearly white, and the sun had bleached his eyebrows, too.

He was dirty, and, she thought, he was entirely capable of making himself just a little more dirty than necessary so as to properly test the efficacy of his new toy. His new toy was a shower bath.

He was constantly demonstrating to Lucille a fund of knowledge that was often astounding. He had known, for example, where to drill a well. She had humored him, thinking that if her father had believed there was a source of water that close to the house, he would have long ago drilled a well there, to avoid the long trip to the stream for household water.

There had been water, just where John said there would be water, and he was visibly pleased with himself. He erected a water tank thirty feet in the air, a height sufficient to provide adequate water pressure for the flowing water system he installed in the kitchen and in the bathroom. And he had a shower bath.

Lucille heard the sound of John pulling off his boots, and then the thump as (for some reason she could not comprehend) he threw them across the room and they hit the floor.

She knew he was standing up to peel off his trousers. She finished slicing the potato in her hands, wiped her hands on her apron, took it off, and walked down the corridor toward their bedroom.

John was standing, his back to her, stark naked, in the shower bath, his legs spread, his arms raised high above his head. Water cascaded down on him.

In a moment he turned around, a smile she thought boyish on his face. He turned around again and shut off the faucets.

"What are you up to?" he asked.

"I'm working in the kitchen," she said.

"No, you're in here looking at me," he said with inarguable logic. "And dinner isn't for hours." There was a plaintive look on his face she could not resist. She turned on her heel and walked back into the bedroom.

"Where are you going?" he called, disappointment in his voice.

"I can't get in there with my clothes on," she said over her shoulder.

"You could. But you'd get them all wet."

She took off her dress and her underclothes, and averting her eyes, went back into the bathroom.

"Now that you're here, I don't suppose you'd like to soap my back?" he said.

"Give me the soap," she said, and he turned around and she soaped his back. And then he turned around and took the soap from her. With an absolutely wicked look on his face he started to rub the bar of soap on her, starting at her neck and working downward, scrupulously avoiding her breasts for a long time, and then finally putting his soapy hands on them. "My God, what a splendid sensation."

"You're terrible," she said.

"And don't you love it?" he said. He moved his soapy hand downward. "Obviously," he said. "All the effort was quite worthwhile."

"Obviously," she said.

"Let's do it soaking wet."

"Why not?" She put her arms around him, her mouth to his ear.

He picked her off the tile floor by leaning slightly back and walked with her to the bed and lowered her onto it.

It was good. The odd, inarguable fact seemed to be that it got better almost every time. Sometimes, when he came in nearly exhausted, it was too quick and too matter-of-fact for Lucille, but at times like this, happy times, sex was wonderful.

He ran his hand down her hair and onto her back, the balls of his fingers on her vertebrae. "Is there any reason you couldn't come with me to New Orleans for a week or so?" he asked.

"New Orleans?"

"I have an idea," he said.

"What kind of an idea?"

"Will you come with me?" he asked. "Or is there some reason you can't?"

By that, she realized, he might be asking if she was pregnant. She wasn't. God knew she wished she were. The idea of having his child filled her with joy. She wanted to be a mother, and wanted a baby for him, too. Having a child, a son, was very important to men. That she understood. And

190

she thought that John must really want a child, a son, now that Thomas, nothing more than a boy, was the father of a son.

But it just hadn't happened. She had her menses like clockwork. They didn't seem to bother her as much now that she was a married woman, no cramps, not even much swelling, but that was the only change.

"I'm not in the family way, if that's what you're asking," she said softly.

"I wasn't actually."

"Tell me about your idea," she said quickly.

"I have been doing some thinking about efficiency."

"I don't understand what you're talking about."

"It started when the Mexicans laughed at the swine belonging to Sammy's father," he said. "He has them penned up rather closely. So far as the Mexicans are concerned, swine should be allowed to roam around and feed themselves. But the thing is, you see, his swine are much heavier than theirs. The question, then, is why. And the answer is equally obvious. They are not burning up energy looking for food."

"You want to start raising pigs?"

"No. The first thing I thought of was penning up the cattle and bringing food to them. But that would obviously require an excessive amount of work by the men. Because of the distances, you see."

"And?" Lucille still had no idea where his mind was going.

"Factor two," he said, "is that we are paid at the slaughterhouse, not here. We are, in effect, expending energy and foodstuffs to put weight on cattle that they either burn up looking for more food here or en route to the slaughterhouse."

"Go on," she said.

"Factor three is that the grasses really grow in the coastal south—Louisiana, Mississippi—in the summertime, because there is a good deal more rain there than there is here," John went on. Lucille was both amused and impressed at the way he was presenting his argument, even if she hadn't the faintest idea what that argument was. He paused now, as if waiting for her to raise an objection or at least ask a question. When it was obvious that she was going to do neither, he went on.

191

"The solution, obviously, is to take the cattle nearer to, one, the point of sale, and, two, a source of cheap food."

"Darling, I still don't understand."

"I propose to acquire land, not much, a thousand, perhaps fifteen hundred acres should do nicely, in the vicinity of New Orleans. We will ship beef there to fatten them."

Now his pause awaiting her response was both more obvious and longer. And still she said nothing. On the surface, the idea seemed sound.

"There is one problem," he said finally.

"What?"

"I don't have the money to buy any land."

"How much will it cost?" she asked, and realized that the flaw in his plan would be high-priced land, prohibitively high-priced land.

"I believe the going rate is between a dollar and a half and three dollars an acre," John said. "In addition to which, of course, there would be the cost of building feed pens. And buying feed from local farmers, to supplement the grass. The initial cost, to acquire the land, erect buildings and fencing, is twenty-five thousand dollars.

"There's a little over ten thousand in the Rancho account, above and beyond operating expenses. If we're out of cash, we could get the rest from the bank, I'm sure."

"You would be willing to go along with this?"

"Oh, John, of course," she said. "Was there ever any question in your mind?"

"I dislike touching your patrimony."

"My what?"

"The money you received from your father."

"That isn't my money," she said. "It's our money."

"Oh, I say, Lucille, that's decent of you!" he said, visibly touched and pleased.

"Far more *decent*, I would say," she said, gently mocking him, then kissing his chest, "than cavorting around naked with you in the middle of the afternoon."

"I rather liked that," he said. "Perhaps we should do that every day, rather than have tea. I *know* you don't like tea."

"I rather liked it too," she said. "The shower bath, of course."

"Of course," he said.

And maybe, Lucille thought, just maybe, this time it had worked. God, it should have. She was still glowing from it.

26

Lucille tried not to show it, for John would think she was a fool, but she was thrilled with the prospect of going to New Orleans. She had traveled very little. She had never been anywhere, really, except El Paso and Dallas, and she sometimes found it hard to believe that John had been to all the places he had. Not only San Francisco and Philadelphia but also Calcutta and London and Paris.

He regarded the train as a means to get from Point A to Point B; to her it was a movable palace, a magic carpet that had flown by her so many times, passing her by. She reminded herself that it was her money buying the tickets, her money that was going to be spent setting up John's feedlot operation, but it didn't do much good. John was the key opening the door to the magic carpet. Without him, even if she had married Charley Broadhead, she would have stayed at Rancho San Miguel.

John had been amused, and she had been a little hurt by it, at her preparations for the trip.

"I can't understand why you have to have clothing made here," he said, "when they offer it up as the latest fashion from New Orleans. Why don't you just wait until we get to New Orleans?"

He was incapable of understanding that she couldn't walk into a New Orleans dressmaker's dressed in the latest fashion from Loving, New Mexico Territory.

But he understood, bless him, that the trip was important

to her. He went to the extraordinary length of sending a telegram ordering a compartment aboard the Pullman car on the train, and formally requesting an unscheduled stop of the train itself at the ranch.

The train had no sooner begun to move than the porter and a waiter from the dining car appeared with a bottle of champagne and two dozen oysters on the half-shell.

"Oh, what's this?" Lucille asked.

"I thought, uh, since our honeymoon, uh, was rather abbreviated," John said, "that I should do what I could to make up for it now."

It was the first oyster Lucille had ever seen. It looked awful, she thought. Slimy. She drank three glasses of champagne before she could muster the courage to try one. She knew that John's amused eyes were on her. She got the oyster down, and forced a smile. "Delicious," she said.

"You are a terrible liar," he said. "Oysters are an acquired taste." His smile became mischievous. "They are, additionally, a well-known aphrodisiac."

"Now, that is just not true," Lucille said. "You are teasing me."

"I shall prove my statement," he said.

"You will not," she said, but the truth of the matter was she found the prospect very exciting. Making love behind closed doors and blinds on a railroad train hurtling through the night en route to New Orleans seemed positively wicked. She forked up another oyster. This time she chewed it before letting it slide down her throat.

John took off his jacket and hung it up. For the first time, she saw that he was wearing his .455 Webley in a shoulder holster. On the ranch, she thought nothing whatever about his going armed. On a ranch, a firearm was simply one more tool, like an ax. But here, in the paneled elegance of the Pullman car, against his sparkling white shirt and beige linen suit, it looked out of place, even frightening.

"Why did you bring that?" she asked.

"A man never needs a gun until he needs one badly."

"Certainly not on a Pullman car."

"On a Pullman car as anywhere else," he said. But—and she thought it was in deference to her—he unfastened the straps and put the revolver in his gladstone bag. Her eye fell on that again, and the sticker on it: "PACIFIC AND ORIENT LINE FIRST CLASS." The ink had faded somewhat, but she could still read the words that filled in the blanks: "Stateroom 23. Calcutta–Manila–Honolulu–San Francisco."

God had brought this man to her all the way from Calcutta.

The porter knocked at the door and then put his head inside. "You will be taking dinner in your compartment, Mr. Wilton, sir?"

"Yes, I think so," Wilton said.

"John!" she said. "I'd rather eat in the dining car."

"The dining car it will be," he said.

"You tell me what time, and I'll have a table waiting for you, Mr. Wilton, sir."

"Seven all right with you, Lucille?" Wilton asked, and when she nodded, he told the porter to bring another bottle of champagne.

"Yes, sir."

"And one more dozen oysters, if you please," Lucille said.

"It's a pity you're a married woman," John said. "You would have made a splendid mistress."

Lucille loved New Orleans. They had a large suite in a rambling hotel not far from the Mississippi River, within walking distance of the shops on Canal Street and the French Quarter. John took her to see her first opera. He fell asleep ten minutes into the first act, but she was so thrilled by what she was seeing that it didn't bother her at all. Cocktails (something else new to Lucille) were served during the intermission. She had what John had (something called a Sazerac) without thinking, and only afterward noticed that all the other ladies were drinking champagne, and that a Sazerac was a man's drink. She was momentarily humiliated, until her eyes fell upon an elegantly coiffured lady in her sixties, a tiara (the first one Lucille had ever seen) in her silver hair, who had her diamond-bedecked fingers also wrapped around a Sazerac and who smiled conspiratorially at Lucille.

They met with a real-estate agent recommended, John said, by Albert Dennison, who took them to a restaurant for lunch in the French Market. It was a New Orleans landmark. There was no menu. You ate what had been prepared that day, and it came, and it came and it came, one course after another. The only thing that Lucille recognized was the boiled beef. Everything else, from the soup to the petits fours for dessert, was new to her, and delicious.

The real-estate man had half a dozen properties that met their requirements, and they spent the next four days making trips away from New Orleans. Two of the trips were by water. The real-estate man chartered a small steam launch. It was Lucille's first trip on a boat like that, and she was awed by the size of the Mississippi River. One trip was by carriage, downriver from New Orleans, and the final trip, the one on which they found what John was looking for, was by rail, seventy miles from New Orleans, a mile from the Mississippi state line. There they found 1,280 acres for sale at $2.25 an acre, including several run-down farm buildings and a deteriorating wharf on the banks of a tributary (a bayou, it was called) that was connected with a river called the Bogue Chitto, which would permit shipment of cattle and supplies by water.

Lucille was overwhelmed by the vegetation. The whole area reminded her of what Africa, and its jungles, must look like. It was exactly the opposite of the New Mexico Territory. If it weren't for the heat and humidity, she would have considered it paradise. But with the weather conditions and the hordes of insects, it was closer to hell.

Her underclothing quickly became sweat-soaked. The moment they were in their rooms, John stripped to his underwear and sprawled spread-eagled on the bed. She was clearly unable to emulate him, so she suffered in silence, wearing only a cotton robe. Bathing helped, but two minutes after getting out of the tub, the sweating resumed.

It put from her mind the notion of spending any time here. The heat in New Mexico was bad enough—"hot as hell" didn't seem to be too much of an exaggeration—but there was no humidity there. As soon as sweat formed, most of it evaporated.

The real-estate agent was visibly surprised when they concluded their business arrangements to buy the property and Lucille wrote out a bank draft on the Republic Bank of Dallas.

John saw his surprise and was annoyed by it.

"Perhaps I should have told you, sir," he said almost viciously, "that my wife is undertaking this enterprise on her own."

"No offense, Mr. Wilton," the man said, "or to you, certainly, ma'am. The thing is, this is Louisiana, and we have laws based on the Napoleonic Code."

"I don't quite follow you," Lucille said.

"The law here, ma'am, is that a wife cannot hold property by herself. It has to be in her husband's name."

"But, my dear man," Wilton protested, "that's her money she is spending."

The real-estate agent shrugged his shoulders. He was not, he was saying, responsible for the law, but there it was, and there was nothing to be done about it.

Lucille hated him. But when the deed changed hands, the property was in the name of John F. W. Wilton, Esq.

Despite the knowledge that it promised relief from the heat and humidity, Lucille left New Orleans reluctantly. Her experience with the wide world had been all too brief. John, on the other hand, was visibly relieved to be going home. So far as he was concerned, he was taking the best of New Orleans back with him. Thirty cases of French wine were in the baggage car forward.

They stopped at Dallas to see Albert Dennison and the bankers. John (surprising and pleasing Lucille) almost immediately brought up the business about the deed to the Louisiana property being in her name. He wanted to set things immediately right, he said, and how could they go about putting it in Lucille's name?

They could, Dennison quickly said, but the gesture would be meaningless. In the event Lucille wanted to dispose of the property, since it was in Louisiana she would be required to have her husband's consent. It was absurd, but that's the way it was.

John frowned but let the matter drop. Lucille, however, suddenly hated all men, her husband and Albert Dennison included. It was absolutely unfair. She was as intelligent as any man, and in terms of specific knowledge, it had immediately become apparent to her in Louisiana that she knew more about land generally, and cattle-raising specifically, than either her husband or the so-called expert, the real-estate agent. More, she thought, smug and furious at once, than Albert Dennison, who asked John if he thought the land would do what he hoped to do with it.

Dennison showed them to the door of his office with a broad smile, his arm around John's shoulders. Then he glanced into the outer office, his smile flickered off for a moment, and then came back on, this time obviously quite artificial. Lucille looked where he had looked.

There was another couple, obviously waiting for their turn with Al Dennison: a well-dressed middle-aged man, visibly a member of the upper crust, and a much younger woman, red-haired, a brooch in the shape of a cotton blossom with a diamond the size of a quail egg on the lapel of her expensive suit.

The redhead was startled. John Wilton was shaken. Albert Dennison was uncomfortable.

"Ah, Luther," Albert Dennison said, recovering his poise. "And Mrs. Sawyer. I don't believe you've met Mr. and Mrs. Wilton. John, may I present Mr. Luther Sawyer?"

"How do you do, sir?" Wilton said. "I have, of course, the pleasure of knowing Mrs. Sawyer. How are you, Kate?"

"Very well, thank you, John," Kate Shaughnessy Sawyer said.

"And my wife, sir," Wilton said.

"A pleasure, ma'am," Luther said.

"We are so pleased with our locomotive," Lucille said. "Thank you so much."

"I'm glad you liked it," Luther said.

Lucille had, in fact, been much taken with the jewel, and by the Sawyers' thoughtfulness in sending it. As casually as he could, John had explained his relationship with Kate Shaughnessy, omitting the true nature of Miss Allen's Boardinghouse and, of course, not even hinting at that evening in his hotel room where the loan for the $2,500 had been so very personally secured.

Lucille was surprised by both Kate's youth and beauty, and a little hurt by John's pointed failure to mention them. But then she decided (or was it safer to pretend?) that he had simply not wanted to cause her undue jealousy—and they had only been business partners, right? And Kate had saved his life. So Lucille smiled at the Sawyers some more.

Luther looked at the women and then at John Wilton. Then he said, "If you're going to be in town overnight, perhaps we could have dinner."

"Why, we would love to," Lucille said. "Wouldn't we, dear?"

"As our guests, of course," John said.

"The Harlingen House at, say, half-past seven?" Luther asked.

"We'll see you there," Lucille said.

27

Mr. and Mrs. Edward Forbish Portman requested the honor of the presence of Mr. and Mrs. Thomas Wilton at dinner, at eight o'clock, Franklin Ballroom, the Bellevue-Stratford Hotel. White tie.

Martha was afraid that Thomas would find some excuse to send their regrets, and confided this in Margaret MacSwain the next time she saw her. Mother MacSwain said she thought Tom would be delighted to attend the dinner, but that if there was any problem, she would speak to him. It was time Martha started getting out, and it would be good for Tom, too, to forget Lennai Mills for an evening.

Tom surprised Martha. The only question he raised was clothing. He didn't have evening dress. So Harold Tilley had a word with his tailor, who was waiting at 14 Rittenhouse Square the next evening when Tom returned from Lennai.

Martha had never seen a man measured for a suit of clothing before; there was something rather interesting about it. It wasn't at all like one of her fittings. There was even something slightly erotic about it. The moment she left the sitting room, she heard the tailor ask Tom if he parted on the left or right, and that was a curious question, until she realized the tailor was talking about his thing, asking on which side of the crotch he wanted his penis swung.

She had permitted Tom back into her bed a month after little John was born, but to sleep only. He hadn't made any overtures to her, and she had certainly not encouraged any.

After what the baby had done to her female parts, she knew that it would be a very long time before they did anything like that again, even if the doctor had made it clear, with several veiled references, that marital relations could be resumed after a period of about six weeks.

John was almost two months old. They could, she supposed, make love if they wanted to. She didn't think she wanted to. As a matter of fact, until the tailor had brought up his question, the idea had never entered her mind.

Her own fitting went well. She had been close to tears when she realized that she could never again wear any of her gowns. The lithe young body was gone forever. Her mother told her she was wrong about that, that if she watched her diet, her body would naturally return to almost its former shape. But her mother had understood (it was odd how having the baby had brought her and her mother closer) and had insisted that she have not just a gown for the Portman dinner made up, but several others as well.

"And don't get rid of the old gowns, darling. You'll wear them again, you'll see."

The truth of the matter was, and Martha was quite sure that she wasn't fooling herself, she looked better ("more womanly" was perhaps the term) in her new white gown than she had before the baby. Her bosom was fuller, and she seemed to have filled out those horrid hollows where her neck met her upper torso.

Two days before the dinner, her mother gave her a pearl-jade-and-diamond brooch.

"Grandmother Lowell gave me this when I had you, darling, and it's time for me to pass it on to you."

Martha was extraordinarily pleased with the brooch, as much for what it signified as for its beauty (or value), and when, on the night of the dinner, as they stood in the foyer waiting for her father's carriage to pick them up, and she saw the reflection of Tom and herself in the mirror, she was extraordinarily pleased with that, too.

Even the mustache, which Tom had decided to grow so as to look older, and which she had previously ridiculed, pleased her. It seemed finally to have transformed itself from several dozen ludicrous hairs on his upper lip into a proper mustache. He looked more like John with the mustache, but she considered this only momentarily before forcing that thought from her mind. The less she thought about John F. W. Wilton, the better.

The thought of John, and what had happened between them, came back into her mind. So far as Martha was able to determine, the possibility that John II was not Tom's child had not occurred to anyone. Tom, obviously, the way he made a fool of himself over the baby, wouldn't believe it if someone had taken photographs. And the others, naturally, had no reason to suspect anything.

The only irrational thing she had done was name the baby after John, but everyone, fools all, had decided that had been a gesture of sisterly affection on her part.

Martha decided that although she had been unaware of it at the time, she had passed through a major crisis in her life and handled it well. There was a certain inarguable satisfaction in having done so. She had met two adult situations and handled them well. She was therefore obviously an adult, and she rather liked that.

She put her arm in Tom's when the carriage came, and walked with dignity down the brownstone stairs to the carriage at the curb.

"Baby," her father said, "you'll be the most beautiful woman at the dinner."

Martha swept into the Bellevue-Stratford and propelled her husband across the room to say hello to Margaret and Paul MacSwain. Mother MacSwain, she realized, looked like anything but a grandmother. The amount of bosom showing approached the indecent. But Martha was not upset about it. What she thought was that Mother MacSwain was still, at her advanced age, a fine-looking woman. I will look that well, Martha vowed, when I am that old, if I have to exist on soda crackers and water.

There was a final pleasant surprise. When they went in to dinner, she and Tom were seated at the head table. The MacSwains and the Tilleys were elsewhere in the ballroom. And Mr. and Mrs. Thomas Wilton were not even at the far end of the head table. They were halfway up, so close that Martha's dinner partner was her friend Penelope Portman's young man.,

203

"I have so looked forward to meeting you and your husband," Philip Harkins said.

"That's very kind," Martha said. "But I can't imagine why. We're just dull old married people."

He gave her a knowing look, said, "I will explain at some length later, but I cannot, I'm afraid, right now."

The mystery was explained after dinner when Edward Forbish Portman (who looked, Martha decided, as if he had helped himself too generously of the champagne) rose to his feet, tapped a silver water pitcher with a knife to gain attention, and then began a rambling speech about his being filled with joy to have all his friends with him on this momentous occasion, and ended with the introduction of Mr. Philip Harkins, who had, it appeared, asked for and been granted the hand of Miss Penelope Portman in holy wedlock.

"Now you know," Phillip Harkins said, sometime later, a little tipsy himself.

"I beg your pardon?" Martha asked.

"We had one hell of a time with the old man," Philip Harkins confided. "You and your husband were held out time and again as visible proof that a young couple could indeed marry."

"Oh, I see," Martha said. The announcement pleased her no end.

Even later in the evening, between dances, when she was in the ladies' room, Penelope signaled for her to remain behind.

"What do you think of him?" Penelope asked.

"He's charming," Martha replied. She could hardly reply that he was offensive, ugly, and obviously demented.

"I want you as matron of honor, of course," Penelope said.

"I'd be thrilled, Penny."

"And now that you know, can I come see you?"

Martha had no idea at all what Penny meant by that.

"Of course, but why?"

"I want you to tell me all about it."

"About what?" Martha asked automatically, the words coming out just as the realization of what Penny was talking about came to her.

"You *know*," Penny said, flushed and excited. "Is it really as thrilling as they say?"

"This is hardly the place, Penny," Mrs. Thomas Wilton,

wife and mother, said sternly. "You call me when you're free, and we'll have a little lunch. A very private little lunch."

"Oh, Martha, I'm so glad to have you!" Penny said, and kissed her dearest friend on the cheek. "There's so much I have to know, and I don't know who else to ask."

Martha smiled at her, wondering if perhaps she had just been insulted.

But then she saw the look in Penny's eyes, and knew that she had been complimented.

Then she left the ladies' room, went back to the ballroom, and danced, with her father, and with Penny's Philip, and with her husband. Thomas smelled of brandy and cigars. She didn't like it when he drank, and she thought that when he smoked a rare cigar, he was an ass, because he only did it as a masculine thing to do. But tonight the mingled aroma of his drinking and his smoking was pleasant to her.

Three hours later, after having carefully worked her night-gown up over her hips, Martha Tilley Wilton, in her sleep, rolled over, the movement causing the junction of her legs to rest upon her husband's leg.

Five minutes later (damn him, he really had been asleep!) she assured him that if he was very careful, it would probably be all right.

Mrs. Thomas Wilton's second child, named Olga Elizabeth, was born nine months later.

28

Lucille was more than a little annoyed with her husband's reaction to Martha Wilton's condition ("Regular little rabbit, isn't she?"), relayed to them via Margaret's letter, but her major reaction was unhappiness that she herself had been unable to conceive.

She had confided her concern in Kate Sawyer on a visit to Waxahachie; Kate said that sometimes happened, and then, in a burst of shared confidence, told Lucille that she at least had hope, whereas Kate had none. She had been told she could have no more children.

That she had had a child thus slipped out, and so Kate told Lucille of her little girl in Philadelphia, and how she had backed down at the last moment from taking it away. Lucille had gone to Kate for sympathy; she ended up giving it.

To John Wilton's surprise, the two women had become friends, as much out of mutual need for female companionship as shared interests.

Lucille had even discussed the problem of Charley Broadhead with Kate before she aproached John. Charley had not exercised his option to buy any Anglo-American Land & Cattle land, and neither had he spent the bonus money he had earned, nor invested it anywhere.

What he proposed now was the formation of a new company, Wilton Stockyards, in which he would have a 25-percent interest. There was no reason, he pointed out, to limit feedlot operation to cattle from Anglo-American and Rancho San Miguel herds. It just might be possible, he suggested, to buy cattle from other ranches, either in New Mexico or Texas, or for that matter right there in the Deep South, at distress prices. Doing that, since they had all the range land, would pose no problems. They could simply retain their cattle on the ranches (which were now, de facto, operated as one ranch, although the custom of referring to them separately persisted) until such time as it was to their advantage to ship them to Louisiana for final feeding and sale.

The first battle Lucille had with John was worse than she thought it would be. She wanted what she referred to as "the feedlot" to be a separate company, and she wanted the ownership to be divided among Anglo-American Land & Cattle, Rancho San Miguel, and Charley Broadhead.

"In other words," John had said to her, his displeasure evident in his raised eyebrow and his tone of voice, "what you're saying is that we should give Broadhead a third."

"Not give, John," she said. "He will contribute his full time and services, and contribute some capital. And we, in effect, will retain control, for combined, Anglo-American and Rancho San Miguel will own two-thirds of the stock."

"I don't seem to be in any position to argue. Financially, I mean," he said. That was a reference to the fact that her Rancho San Miguel's cash had provided the money they'd needed. He had gone through his cash (the expenses were necessary and wise, but they consumed his cash) resurrecting Anglo-American.

"I'm sorry you choose to put it that way," Lucille said. "But since this is not Louisiana, and my money is my money, that's the way it seems to be."

It was the first time she had ever defied him, and it should have bothered her, but it didn't. He was wrong and she was right. They needed a full-time trusted supervisor in New Orleans while John took care of business at home. Charley Broadhead was exactly right, and worth the price.

But John was offended. He pouted like a spoiled child, she thought, when she told him that she wanted the company to be called the Broadhead Stockyards.

"Whatever you think best, my dear," he said. "As you point out, I am the minor stockholder in this enterprise."

The next morning, he took off for the mountains with two of the ranch hands. He didn't return for two weeks, and she was growing frantic when he showed up, finally, freshly shaven but reeking of sweat and the smell of the hunt, leading four packhorses loaded down with deer carcasses.

He greeted her coldly, pointed out the meat, suggested with infinite politeness that he thought she might wish to consider salting some, and making that German dish—sour-something—from the rest.

He didn't kiss her, and he walked with majestic dignity and hurt pride into the house. He did everything, she thought, but sigh in noble agony.

She knew just how to deal with that. She waited until she heard the sound of his shower, and then she took off her dress and got under it with him.

They never mentioned Charley Broadhead's one-third interest in Broadhead Stockyards again.

Lucille corresponded regularly with Margaret MacSwain, and Margaret quite innocently made her jealous by reports of what were to her simple, certainly nonostentatious reports of their life. They had dined, as usual, with the Tilleys on the second Tuesday, and Tilley had had a most remarkable guest, a diplomat just back from Germany, who had reported that he had seen on the streets of Berlin and Frankfurt, self-propelled carriages, horseless, so to speak, powered by a motor that ran on a by-product of kerosene called gasoline. A man named Daimler had a factory employing eighty people making them. Paul MacSwain was so excited that he was going to take a quick trip to Germany to have a look for himself. Paul thought there was a market for horseless wagons for use in big cities.

Margaret reported that they were going to spend a month in Atlantic City, that the salt-water air was good for Martha's children. That they were going to the Pocono Mountains for two weeks for the same reason. That she had been elected to the Ladies' Guild of the Philadelphia Academy of Music, and they were having a ball for the benefit of the visiting Berlin

Philharmonic Orchestra. That they had spent the weekend in New York at the Horse Show.

Lucille had little to write in return, other than that she had returned from Dallas visiting friends. She felt a little dishonest writing that, but Waxahachie wasn't much compared to Atlantic City, the Pocono Mountains, and New York City.

She was able to write that the feedlot operation seemed to be, from the very beginning, a success. For some reason, cattle bred in the dry New Mexico Territory climate seemed to be perfectly adaptable to feeding in the humid South; it had taken neither as much time nor as much foodstuff to bring them up to market weight, and their only problem seemed to be getting enough head to satisfy the demand.

There had been an unexpected bonus. Timber, mostly pine, but some cedar, was available at very low prices in Louisiana, both on the feedlot property and in the area. They had found out (actually, Lucille had found out, but in dealing with her mother-in-law, for some reason she felt it unladylike to mention her active role in the business) that it was possible to rent railroad cars for specific periods of time rather than paying for the one-way use of a car. They had started out with one car, and were now up to six. The cars went to Louisiana loaded with cattle and returned loaded with timber. It was simpler to cut or buy timber in Louisiana and ship it all the way to the New Mexico Territory than it was to cut timber in the New Mexico Territory, and they had found a ready market for what they could not use.

And she wrote that John, having imported the necessary mallets and balls from Calcutta, was now teaching his friends to play polo. She did not mention that his polo-playing friends consisted of Chiricahua Apache, who played with great enthusiasm and wild skill, bareback, two or three of the Mexicans willing to ignore the unconcealed hysterical laughter of their peers, and herself, who rode wearing trousers, her hair tucked up under a Stetson hat. It was far better that Mother MacSwain have a picture of her daughter-in-law standing under a parasol watching the polo players at their strictly masculine sport. Even Kate had been scandalized at Lucille's polo playing.

Lucille had regularly, ritually, made some remark in her

letters that they hoped they would all one day soon get together. In 1891, the MacSwains and the Wiltons met in New Orleans and spent a pleasant week together. Although Tom and Martha had been heartbroken, Mother MacSwain reported, it had been impossible for them to come.

Tom had the Lennai Mills going strong, a remarkable accomplishment for someone his age, and it would have been difficult for him to get away in any event, especially with Martha in the family way again. (Little Johnny is a scamp, a little hellion, to tell the truth. He and Edward have learned the most scandalous language from the help—you know how those Irish are always blaspheming—and they use it, I am sure, to shock everyone. Olga is a precious little doll, who idolizes her father and her brother, and Edward too, even if they do treat her scandalously.)

One afternoon during the New Orlean's reunion when the men were away, Lucille found herself discussing her apparent sterility with her mother-in-law. She had been to three different doctors, and they all had said the same thing—that there was no physical reason she could not conceive. They had suggested that the fault might lie with John.

"I've always felt, truly felt," Margaret MacSwain said (Lucille had the feeling that she either didn't like to hear it suggested that her son was sterile or that she simply didn't believe it), "that children are God's will. I wouldn't dwell on it. You're still a fairly young woman."

Margaret MacSwain knew that John was capable of fathering a child. It would have been so easy to allow herself to think that she had been wrong about John and Martha, to prove this by the fact that he had been unable to make Lucille with child, but that was not the case. Little Johnny was the spitting image of John, and he had John's character. Martha's attempts to turn him into a little gentleman were doomed. He had already learned how to control his mother, to either bend her to his will or to infuriate her when he knew that because of the presence of his grandparents he was immune from punishment.

Perhaps, Margaret decided, this was the punishment of God for John's sin. Having done what he had done, he was to be denied the joy of acknowledged parenthood. But that was so much nonsense, she realized. She had sinned twice against the laws of God and man, and her punishment had been two splendid sons, a wonderful second husband and foster son, three beautiful grandchildren, and at least one marvelous daughter-in-law.

29

"What in the world are you talking about?" Lucille asked, a sick feeling in her stomach.

"Blowing up a man-of-war is clearly an act of war," John explained. "We certainly can't take that lying down!"

The battleship *Maine* had blown up in the harbor of Havana, Cuba, which until this moment had been as remote to Lucille as London and Calcutta.

"Perhaps not, darling," she said. "But what has it to do with you? You're not even an American."

"Well, that's certainly a hell of a thing for a man to have to hear from his own wife!" he said, visibly hurt. "And just for your information, my dear, I am an American citizen. I have been an American citizen for years."

"I didn't know that," she said lamely.

"More important, I am a trained officer. My duty is clear. I have already written to the territorial representative—what's his name, something German."

"Schulz," she said. "Mr. Schulz."

"Yes. I wrote this morning to him, in Washington, D.C., informing him that I am ready to serve in an appropriate capacity."

Lucille knew that whatever she said, it would be the wrong thing.

The idea of John going off to war, leaving her for any reason, was terrifying. She spent a very bad evening, and an even worse four hours lying beside him in their bed wide-awake, listening to him breathe, before reason returned.

For one thing, she didn't think there would be a war. Now that she had time to think about it, she remembered that the Spaniards, who owned Cuba, had been more than obliging. They had granted Cuba (an island, or a country, she wasn't quite sure which, located somewhere near Florida) autonomy, and seemed to be leaning over backward to appease the Americans.

On top of that, if there was a war, there would be an increase demand for food, for beef. John would be told that a rancher would be of far more value to any war effort raising and shipping beef than he would in a uniform.

But she realized that his ego was involved, and that when his offered services were rejected, it would be her duty to agree with him that the territorial representative and the government he represented were fools. She would have to share his disappointment and let him know that she agreed with his belief that he had a duty to become a soldier.

She felt a lot better.

Two weeks later there was a letter from the Honorable August Schulz, representative of the New Mexico Territory to the Congress of the United States. In the most polite language (John F. W. Wilton, Esq., fool or not, was the owner of Anglo-American Land & Cattle and husband of the owner of Rancho San Miguel) he first expressed his profound admiration for the sentiments that had caused Mr. Wilton to volunteer his services to his adopted country, and then his profound regret at having to inform him that although the War Department, too, appreciated his interest and patriotism, there was unfortunately no position presently available where Mr. Wilton could be profitably employed.

Lucille thanked God. And then went out on the porch and sat beside John while he drank almost a full quart of Tennessee sour-mash bourbon without uttering one word.

He drank another quart of whiskey on April 26, when the daily newspaper thrown from the train as it passed through the ranch reported by telegraph from Washington, D.C., that Congress, amidst cheers from both sides of the aisle, and an *a cappella* rendition of "Dixie," had declared that a state of

213

war existed between the United States of America and the Kingdom of Spain.

Perversely, even though she thought he was behaving like an idiot, she felt sorry for him.

The next day's newspaper reported that Colonel Leonard S. Wood would be in San Antonio, Texas, recruiting a regiment of volunteer cavalry, John immediately began to pack.

"Appearing in person, you see, letting this Wood chap know of my experience, will be something quite different from dealing through that idiot Schulz. I wouldn't recruit a water carrier on that man's recommendation. Going myself is an entirely different matter."

She was afraid the end result would be the same: he was going to be humiliated in person rather than with a politician's tact.

The next morning he kissed her passionately, caught up in the drama of the moment, told her that she had been the most important thing in his life, and that if it were God's will that he not return, he hoped she would find comfort in that.

The lieutenant colonel of the First United States Volunteer Cavalry, a squat, barrel-chested man in pince-nez, a bushy mustache hanging from his upper lip, looked up from a desk made of planks laid across empty wine barrels. His eyes widened at the apparition before him. What in the hell was this?

It saluted. A British salute, palm outward, and quivering at the temple.

"John F. W. Wilton, sir," it said. "Seeking a commission in the regiment."

A commission, no less? "I'm sorry, but that looks rather impossible just now." The lieutenant colonel's voice was high-pitched. Wilton thought he sounded rather funny.

"Might I inquire why?"

"Well, I appreciate your sentiments, sir, certainly applaud them. But we're limiting enlistment, not to mention commissions, to experienced people."

"Then I would be willing to serve in the ranks, as a sergeant, or a corporal, if necessary. I feel I should point out, sir, however, that I'm a trained cavalry officer."

"Trained where?"

"At Sandhurst, sir. And I was once privileged to serve as a lieutenant with the Prince of Wales's Own Bengal Light Cavalry."

"Well, of course, that would preclude your being an officer in the United States Army. Citizenship is required."

"I am a citizen, sir."

The lieutenant colonel looked at Wilton and shook his head. Then he got up from his wooden folding chair and walked to a flap in the tent. "Colonel Wood?" he asked. "Have you a moment?"

A tall, heavy, silver-haired man came into the front of the tent.

"What is it, Teddy?"

"I think you should meet this gentleman," Lieutenant Colonel Theodore Roosevelt said to the commanding officer of the First United States Volunteer Cavalry. "I rather like the cut of him. And he's brought with him his own horses and a railcar to move them. And he's Sandhurst, Colonel."

They were fighting dismounted. There had not been room for horses on the *Vizcaya* from Tampa. (The First U.S. Volunter Cavalry, now known as the Rough Riders, had taken the *Vizcaya* at pistol point; it was the only way that Colonel Roosevelt could be sure of transportation to the war. The horses that Wilton had brought from the ranch had been requisitioned by the army under emergency war powers. He hadn't been paid for them, either, and he had a nasty suspicion he had seen the last of his tack, too. That was in a warehouse in Tampa.)

It didn't really matter. This wasn't horse country. The vegetation was thick, and the Spaniards well-entrenched. Their Mauser rifles were far better, more accurate, a higher rate of fire, and of greater range than the Krag-Jorgensen rifles in the hands of the Americans.

The Americans had two weapons, a dynamite gun (a cannon that fired explosive shells) and the Gatling machine gun, that was infinitely superior to anything the Spaniards had. But it was an infantry and artillery war, not a cavalry war, and the Americans had suffered severely at Spanish hands.

The Rough Riders had stormed and taken a hill, Kettle Hill, from the top of which they could see Santiago de Cuba.

They had chased the Spaniards down the far side of the hill, and were in a line with Tenth Regular Cavalry to their left, and the Ninth Regular Cavalry to their right.

They were both black regiments, called buffalo soldiers by the Indians because of the texture of their hair.

The Spaniards' major defense position was a blockhouse on San Juan Hill. When Colonel Wood (now General Wood; Roosevelt had been promoted colonel to fill his vacancy) had been unable to establish contact with the officers of the Ninth Cavalry (it was subsequently learned that with the exception of one lieutenant, they were all either dead or wounded), he ordered Roosevelt to attack with his First Volunteers through the lines of the Ninth.

Lieutenant J.F.W. Wilton (his official commission having come through only six days before) was ordered to precede the main body of Rough Riders to the front lines of the Ninth Cavalry. He was to seek out an officer and relay General Wood's orders that the Rough Riders would pass through their lines. Failing to find an officer, he was to assume command of what troops he found, and conduct operations accordingly.

He found no officer. A gray-haired first sergeant of the Ninth Cavalry told him they were all out of action. The black cavalrymen were armed with one-shot carbines and six-shot revolvers.

"We are ordered to pass through this line," Wilton said. "Would your men follow me?"

"My men follow their first sergeant," the old warrior said. "And I'll follow the lieutenant."

"Pass the word, First Sergeant," Lieutenant Wilton said. "We will hold in position until the last of the officers of the First Volunteer Cavalry pass through our lines. Then, on my signal, we will advance."

Wordlessly the old soldier crawled away to pass the word.

Santiago de Cuba
12th July, 1898

Mrs. John F. W. Wilton,
Rancho San Miguel
New Mexico Territory

My Dear Mrs. Wilton:

By now I pray you have received word from the War Department correcting the first message, based on information available at that time, that you husband was missing and presumed dead in action on July 2.

I have just come from visiting him in field hospital, and am pleased to inform you that he is recovering well from his wounds, and in the opinion of the attending surgeon, will suffer no permanent impairment. He suffered a rifle-bullet wound to his upper right leg, and, sometime later, additional wounds about the chest and in the lower right arm, presumably from shrapnel fired by Spanish artillery. The latter wound has precluded his writing you himself.

It was my great privilege to award Lieutenant Wilton our nation's second-highest award for gallantry on the field of battle, the Distinguished Service Cross, and to promote him to the grade of brevet captain. A copy of the citation accompanying the Distinguished Service Cross is attached to this letter, as is the medal itself, which Captain Wilton asked me to send to you for safekeeping.

I am delighted to bring you the good news of his recovery, and offer my most profound apologies for the unfortunate misinformation you were given.

I am further sure that you can take great pride in your husband's valor. I consider it a distinct privilege to have had him as a comrade-in-arms.

Faithfully yours,
Theodore Roosevelt
Colonel, Commanding
First U.S. Volunteer Cavalry

30

On March 11, 1899, Kate Sawyer half-woke with the first light of day. She extended her knee to make contact with her husband. When there was no contact, she reached out with her hand, and at the same time lifted her head an inch off the pillow.

The bed was empty.

"Jesus, Mary, and Joseph," Kate said softly, because she knew Luther didn't like her to use what he thought of as blasphemy. In the last couple of weeks Luther had been having trouble sleeping, or rather in staying asleep. He went to bed early, long before Kate was ready to sleep, and since she considered it her duty to go to bed when he did, that meant she spent long minutes, sometimes hours, waiting for sleep to come.

Probably because he went to bed so early, he had been getting up very early. Kate considered it her duty to make him a cup of coffee when he got up. She didn't have to like it, she told herself, just do it.

She rolled over and put her legs out of her side of the bed. She ran her feet across the sheepskin rug, and then found her slippers. She slipped into those, and then reached for her robe. Sleepily she staggered across the floor to their bathroom, her eyes trying to focus on the buttons of her robe.

She pushed open the door to the bathroom.

Luther was lying between the toilet and the bathtub, on his back, one knee brought up as if he were about to kick something. His mouth sagged open, and his eyes seemed to be staring at the ceiling.

Kate knew, even before she knelt beside him and looked into his eyes, that he was dead. She sat on the toilet slumped against the water closet, her hand holding her robe closed at the neck. After a moment she looked down at Luther and then leaned over and pulled his eyelids down over his staring, unseeing eyes. She sighed deeply, closed her own eyes, sagged again against the cold procelain of the water closet. After a moment she began to weep very quietly.

Kate's leg was painfully asleep. She had without thinking bent it under her on the toilet seat. She stretched it out, and then stood up, supporting herself on the wall, as the circulation painfully restored itself.

I will have to send Albert Dennison a telegram, she thought. And then she remembered that they now had a telephone. Lucille Wilton had been furious with John about their telephone. The telephone was John's new toy. He had set up the Loving Bell Telephone Company, and at a cost of what Lucille described as "God alone knows how much," both Rancho San Miguel and the house on Anglo-American Land & Cattle had been equipped with this marvel of the electrical age.

And if John Wilton had a telephone for "God alone knows how much," nothing less would do for Luther Sawyer. Luther hadn't had to buy his own telephone company, becoming a major stockholder had been sufficient.

Kate walked on a stiff leg out of the bathroom, through the bedroom, and to the foyer, where the telephone hung on the paneled wall like some pagan holy object. She put the receiver to her ear and cranked the instrument.

There was no response, and it finally occurred to her that there was probably no operator on duty. She was just about to hang up when a sleepy voice came on the line. "Central."

"Could you put me through to Rancho San Miguel in the New Mexico Territory?"

"I don't think they have telephones out there, Miz Sawyer."

"Yes, they do," and from some dark recess of her mind (John had announced this at least twenty times) she recalled the number. "It's Loving 1234." ("How," John had rhetorically inquired, "could one possibly forget a number like that?" The number of the ranch house at Anglo-American was, inevitably, 5678.)

"I'll try it and ring you back, Miz Sawyer," central said. But Kate didn't hang up, and central left the line open. Kate heard Dallas come on the line, and then San Antonio, El Paso, and Roswell, in the territory. Finally, after a very long series of rings, a voice said, "Hello. Hello. John Wilton here. Are you there?"

"This is Kate, John."

"Well, hello, Kate," Wilton shouted. "Calling all the way from Texas, are you? Luther said he was going to have an instrument put in. Is he there with you?"

"John," Kate said, and then blurted it out. "Luther's dead."

"No!"

"He apparently got out of bed," Kate said, "and died in the bathroom!"

"My God!" John said. "Hold on just a moment, Kate. I'll get Lucille for you."

And in a moment, Lucille's sleepy but concerned voice: "Oh, Kate, is it true? I'm so sorry."

The women wept together over the long-distance lines, and then John came back on, very practical, telling her they would leave on the afternoon train, and that in the meantime she should of course get in touch with Al Dennison. And she would, he said, have to notify Luther's daughter, in Galveston.

It was the first time Kate had thought about that. Luther had seldom talked about his daughter; they had never gone to Galveston together, so she had never met her or her husband; and there had been, she now remembered, no wedding gift.

Kate had no trouble reaching Al Dennison on the telephone. He was able to catch the early-morning train, and arrived in Waxahachie before the undertaker had finished his work.

Dennison had tried to telephone Galveston, he said, but the arrogant maid who answered had refused to waken Mrs. Stanley, so he thought he would wait until he got here to try it again.

Mrs. Stanley. The embarrassing truth, Kate realized, was that until Albert mentioned the name, she hadn't known it.

She knew the first name, Faith, but on those rare occasions when Luther had mentioned his daughter, he had always referred to her by her first name, and the man she married as "Faith's husband."

The men from the undertaker's came down the stairs, wheezing under their load. Kate walked to the door of the parlor and leaned against the jamb of the sliding door and watched them carry Luther out. Then she walked out on the porch and watched them load the wicker basket onto the ornate black tassel-draped hearse. They carefully drew inside curtains over cut-glass windows (they would, she realized, be opened when they had Luther in a casket) and then mounted the wagon, tipped their hats to her, and drove off.

When she walked back in the house, Albert was standing in the dooray to the parlor. He extended a large squat glass to her. It was three-quarters full of whiskey.

She took it, and took a deep swallow. It was just what she needed. Albert knew that. And with Albert it wasn't even necessary to make ladylike protests.

"He was a good man, Kate," Dennison said. "And you gave him a lot of happiness."

She didn't reply.

Dennison walked past her, rested his whiskey glass on the shelf of the two-foot-tall telephone box, picked up the receiver, cranked the handle, and told central to connect him with the K. LaMar Stanley residence in Galveston. He didn't know the number.

Kate finished her drink, despite the size of it, and poured herself another. Poor Luther. He was a good man, and he had given her a lot of happiness. What next?

When Dennison came back into the room, he looked upset. He repeated that Luther was a good man, and then he added, "He left you everything, Kate. Everything. And there's a lot more than I think you know."

She woke once that night, and tried to touch Luther, and then wept again.

Lucille and John arrived on the early train from Dallas on the day of the funeral. Luther's daughter was due later.

At twenty past one the telephone rang. Kate was near it and answered.

It was Rundel, of Rundel & Jones, Undertakers. "Can I speak with Mr. Dennison, please?"

"This is Mrs. Sawyer," Kate said.

"I think maybe it would be better if I spoke to Mr. Dennison," Rundel said.

"If there is some problem," Kate said, a little annoyed, "I will have to make the decision. Now, what is it, Mr. Rundel?"

"The thing is . . ." he answered quickly, and then hesitated for a long moment. "I don't know how to tell you this, Miz Sawyer, but there's a fellow here with a court order, and the sheriff, and they want Mr. Sawyer's remains."

Kate had no idea what was going on. She made him repeat what he had said. She had heard right. "Al!" she called, anguished. Dennison came running, and John was on his heels. She handed Dennison the telephone. Rundel went through his story again.

LaMar Stanley could not understand his wife's insistence that they get her father's body away from Waxahachie and bury him beside his wife in Galveston.

So far as Stanley was concerned, it was an unnecessary waste. It would be just as effective, and far cheaper, to chisel the old man's name on the tombstone, and let him be buried where he died.

The same court order Faith had acquired from the judge in Galveston, ordering the mortal remains of Luther Sawyer, deceased, to be instantly and forthwith turned over to his sole heir, Mrs. K. LaMar Stanley, or her appointed agent, also ordered that all persons whatsoever who may have been living on the property of the aforesaid Luther Sawyer, deceased, forthwith and immediately vacate said property.

The last thing LaMar Stanley had expected was trouble, at least trouble that could not be easily handled by his traveling companion, Bryan T. Anderson, formerly of the Galveston Police Department and presently the chief agent of Pinkerton's detective agency in Galveston.

They had stopped by the livery stable and rented a wagon. They could carry the casket to the station and be gone before anybody knew what was happening.

The undertaker read the court order and then announced

he hadn't quite finished embalming the body; they would have to wait.

That seemed to be taking a long time. A very long time.

Two men came into the undertaking parlor. LaMar Stanley was surprised in that they seemed dressed like gentlemen. The taller of them had a black band around his right coat sleeve.

"What's this about a court order?" asked the shorter one.

"You're not taking Luther Sawyer's body anywhere," the taller one said.

"I am K. LaMar Stanley. Mr. Sawyer was my father-in-law. I have come to take his remains home for burial."

Anderson, the Pinkerton man, turned to face John Wilton. He put his hands on his hips. The movement served to spread his jacket, revealing a gold badge and the butt of a Colt Sheriff's Model revolver. Wilton's face did not change expression. Anderson glared at him for a moment until he was sure he was cowed, and then turned around.

"Let's go, Mr. Stanley," he said. "He's bound to be finished embalming the body by now."

He had just finished the sentence when Wilton tapped him on the shoulder. He turned in exasperation, his fists balled. He found himself staring into the barrel of Wilton's .455 Webley revolver. The hammer was cocked.

"He has a pistol," Wilton said. "Take it away from him, Al. I dislike being threatened with guns."

Dennison took the revolver from Anderson's waistband.

The judge came before anything else could happen, indeed, as Wilton was wondering what he should do now. He could hardly keep the man at pistol point indefinitely.

"What the hell's going on here?" the judge asked. "Kate Sawyer called up, near-hysterical, and said for me to come here to tell somebody she was married to Luther. Captain Wilton, what are you doing with that gun?"

"This man threatened me with his pistol," Wilton said righteously. "We have disarmed him."

Albert Dennison extended the Pinkerton man's Colt to the judge, holding the stock between his thumb and index fingers. The judge took it.

"I'm the deceased's son-in-law," LaMar Stanley said, handing the judge the court order.

"It refers to 'the woman Kate Shaughnessy, who may be

known to refer to herself as the lawful mate of the deceased,' " the judge said.

"That is correct," Stanley said. "And we are here, sir, to claim the remains. I am the husband of Mr. Sawyer's sole heir, his daughter, Faith."

"Well, Mr. Stanley," the judge said, "the reason Kate is known to refer to herself as the lawful mate of the deceased is because she was. I married them."

"And, as counsel to the deceased," Albert Dennison said, "I take great pleasure in informing you, sir, that not only is Mrs. Stanley not the sole heir of Luther Sawyer, deceased, she is not an heir, period."

The next day, Albert Dennison received a call from a fellow attorney in Houston.

"Al," the man said. "I've just been retained by Faith Sawyer Stanley. She's going to challenge her father's will."

"On what grounds?" Dennison said.

"Insanity," the lawyer said. "An elderly man who would defy the mores of the community to marry a known prostitute is obviously bereft of his senses." He paused. "I'm sorry. But if I didn't take it, somebody else would have."

"See you in court, counselor," Dennison replied.

The attorney who told Albert Dennison he had been retained by Luther Sawyer's daughter had told the truth, but not all of it. He was not the only lawyer hired to plead Mrs. Stanley's case. He had been retained as additional counsel by the largest, most prestigious law firm in Galveston.

The investments Luther had made established him as a very wealthy man. Faith Sawyer Stanley had grown up convinced that all of her father's money would come to her on his death. She was determined to get it.

Luther's will was probated in the county of his residence. So far as Mrs. Stanley's attorneys were concerned, his residence was not where he happened to be when death befell him, but where the bulk of his assets, including real estate, were. The value of the Waxahachie property was no more than $85,000. He owned real estate worth twenty times that figure in Galveston. Galveston was the site of his cotton-brokerage office. The bulk of his cash was in the Planters Bank of Galveston. He was, therefore, a Galvestonian.

The Court of Appeals of the state of Texas approved a

change of venue to Galveston from Waxahachie, and continued the original temporary injuction prohibiting the distribution of assets.

The Galveston attorneys retained by Mrs. Stanley drew up a document stating that in accepting $25,000 in cash, Kate Shaughnessy, aka Kate Sawyer, renounced all further claim to the estate of Luther Sawyer, deceased, and would, moreover, cease and desist henceforth and forevermore to use the name Sawyer in any manner whatsoever.

Mrs. Stanley's legal counsel ten days later opened a registered letter from Dennison, Willis & Monley to find a cashier's check on the Republic Bank of Dallas in the amount of $100,000, and a document to be executed by Mrs. K. LaMar Stanley in which she agreed to give up all further claim to the estate of Luther Sawyer, deceased, and further agreed to cease and desist now and forevermore to use the name Sawyer in any manner whatsoever.

The Pinkerton agency's services were enlisted to determine where the person calling herself Mrs. Sawyer had come into $100,000 in cash, and, if she was using someone else's funds (as was believed), who her benefactor might be.

They expected to hear that the check had been drawn against funds of Dennison, Willis & Monley. The Pinkerton report stated the check had been drawn against funds of the Anglo-American Land & Cattle Company, of the New Mexico Territory.

"Inasmuch," Mrs. Stanley's lawyers replied to Dennison, Willis & Monley, "as we regrettably have been unable to reach an amicable out-of-court settlement of this matter, it obviously will be necessary for us to proceed to seek redress at the bar."

The Pinkerton agency did a splendid job of research. They traced Kate Shaughnessy back to Philadelphia, to her ownership of the boardinghouse in Phoenix, to her employment at Madam Estelle's establishment in Dallas.

As a "professional courtesy," copies of the Pinkerton report were made available to Dennison, Willis & Monley. It was hoped that Albert Dennison would be more amenable now to an out-of-court resolution of their differences. They would be coming before a Galveston judge, and they must be aware that a Galveston judge was highly unlikely to award the estate of a Galveston gentleman and father of a pillar of Galveston society to a Dallas prostitute.

The legal maneuvering before the trial consumed nine months; it was December 15, 1899, before the parties to the dispute assembled in the courthouse in Galveston.

Mr. and Mrs. K. LaMar Stanley, Mrs. Stanley in a veil to conceal her discomfiture at being forced to put herself on display in connection with so sordid a matter, sat at plaintiff counsel's table on the left side of the courtroom. Until moments before his honor entered the court, the defendant's counsel table was occupied solely by a clerk of the Dennison, Willis & Monley firm.

But then two couples entered the courtroom from the rear door. Looking to neither side, the ladies, also veiled, took seats held for them by the man at the defendant's table.

"Mr. Dennison," said the judge, calling Albert to the bench. "By any chance does the gentleman with you happen to be Captain John Wilton?"

"Yes, sir, your Honor, Captain Wilton."

"I thought it was," the judge said. "I had the honor of meeting Captain Wilton at a reception in honor of Colonel, now Governor, Roosevelt in New York City. This court is honored, sir, to have in its presence a man who has served his country with such valor. And the lady with him, of course, is Mrs. Wilton."

"Yes, sir. And the other lady is my wife," Albert Dennison said.

"A pleasure, madam," the judge said. "And where is the defendant?"

"Your Honor," Dennison said, "I am afraid that I have chosen to ignore that hoary principle of the law that a lawyer who defends himself or his family has a fool for a client. My wife, your Honor, is the defendant in this matter."

The court, an hour or so later, accepted a motion by counsel for the defendant that the action brought by the plaintiff had no basis in law, and ordered that the last will and testament of Luther Sawyer, deceased, before the court be executed.

Two weeks later, over the objections of her friend John Wilton and her husband, Katherine Shaughnessy Sawyer

Dennison sent a cashier's check in the amount of $100,000 to Mrs. K. LaMar Stanley, who promptly cashed it.

There were fools, Kate Dennison had recently concluded, and then there were fools. Perhaps everyone was a fool. *Probably* everyone was a fool. It was a matter of degree.

The judge who awarded her Luther's estate was a fool, for it was quite clear that she was what Luther's daughter said she was, a former prostitute. And only a fool would defy the conventions of society and marry a scarlet woman. The judge had concluded that Kate Shaughnessy, a former madam, had been transformed into a respectable woman by her marriage to two fools, one after the other, and also because a genuinely respectable woman, Lucille Wilton, was willing to be identified as her friend.

And Albert Dennison was a fool for losing all of his money in one harebrained scheme after another, and an even greater fool for thinking that Kate had come to their wedding bed innocent of the knowledge that he was broke. Didn't he know that his financial condition was just another shameful secret laid bare in Madam Estelle's?

Did he think she was fool enough to believe he was marrying her to help her out, or because he had been secretly in love with her for years? Obviously, he was.

And John Wilton was a fool for keeping Charley Broadhead on his payroll. Kate thought that Lucille probably was the reason behind that, out of some misguided loyalty, the same kind of fool loyalty that had seen her excommunicate herself from "decent" women in Dallas and the territory by jumping to Kate's side.

Poor, sweet, loyal Lucille, the only friend Kate had, but still a fool for not seeing that her closest friend was in love with her husband.

But Kate was the greatest fool of all. What she should have done was take the money and run. There was a whole wide world out there, where a woman with a healthy bank account, widow of a successful businessman, could build a new life for herself.

But making a new life for herself in San Francisco or Chicago (or even returning to Ireland with a purse full of gold certificates—a delightful fantasy on occasion) posed one problem Kate was unwilling to face. It meant that she would never see John Wilton again.

There was simply no understanding her feelings for John. Certainly she had few illusions about him. Most of the time she could convince herself that she loved him as a brother, which was convenient and comforting. And he treated her, if not as a sister, then as a friend. He had never made a sexual overture to her—whether he found her unattractive now, or because of Lucille, she didn't know.

But she couldn't think of herself as one of the boys. When he came into physical contact with her, however innocently, or sometimes when she just saw him riding up on a horse, her heartbeat increased, and she felt weak, as if her loins were calling out to his with a will of their own. That was a possibility, too—that nature was involved. Nature, which recognized no pretenses of dignity or morality, was sending out a message that this was the male animal with whom she should couple. Nature, she thought, when dwelling on this theory, wanted this beautiful man for her.

Six months after they came back from Galveston, Albert came home (that is to say, to their suite in the Harlingen House) unexpectedly in the middle of the afternoon.

There had been an accident, he said. Kate had better throw a few things in a bag and take the afternoon train to Rancho San Miguel. Lucille, playing that fool game with John and the Indians, had been thrown from her horse. She had no feeling in her legs. John had called, ordering Albert, damn the expense, to get the best doctors in Dallas on the next train out there.

31

Lucille hadn't fallen from a horse; she had been fallen on by a horse. The horse, a heavy stallion who was quick-footed despite his size, had stepped into a prairie-dog hole as Lucille was turning him. He had writhed on the ground in his agony, and Lucille had been under him.

The animal was still lying where John had shot him on the polo field where he'd fallen, when Kate and the two doctors whom Dennison had been able to pressure into leaving Dallas immediately reached the ranch.

Lucille's leg had been broken in two places, badly broken, and the doctor from Loving had set it in an elaborate arrangement of ropes and pulleys. But the broken leg wasn't the problem. The problem was that she had damaged, nearly severed, her spinal column. There was no feeling in her lower body.

There was hope, they said—faint, but hope—that the body would regenerate itself in time, once the broken leg had time to knit. Lucille was weak, but not in pain. She was frightened, not only for her condition but also because she thought (as it turned out, correctly) that John would blame himself for what was an accident.

Before she was able to be moved, John had more doctors summoned from Saint Louis and even San Francisco. Their diagnoses were identical: probably irreparable damage to the spinal column, with attendant paralysis of the lower body.

Kate stayed at the ranch. Albert seemed to expect this of her, but she would have stayed no matter what he had to say. Albert Dennison was very busy investing her money, spending a good deal of time on the Gulf Coast of Texas, laying out housing developments, and speculating in the cotton market and in something about which he knew even less than cotton, petroleum. The population was growing, he said, the market for kerosene would grow beyond people's wildest imaginations. And in the North and in California, they were using oil to replace coal as a source of heat not only for industry but also for homes and locomotives.

Baltimore & Ohio Car Number One arrived at the Rancho San Miguel siding carrying three nurses and a doctor, the master stateroom turned into a hospital room. It would travel to Philadelphia by a circuitous route designed to provide the smoothest ride.

Lucille told Kate that she really didn't want to make the trip; there was no question in her mind that it would be fruitless, but she had to go for John's sake, to give him the opportunity to do something.

Kate went with Lucille to Philadelphia. The MacSwains and the Wiltons met the car at Broad Street Station. An ambulance was drawn up at the end of the platform. Two hospital attendants came aboard the train and carried Lucille in their arms off the car and put her into a wheelchair to roll her from the car to the ambulance. It was the first wheelchair she had ever seen.

Lucille took it a lot better than John. She waved the attendants away and moved herself around in the wheelchair, smiling with pleasure, as if with a toy. John Wilton broke down and wept shamelessly.

Kate was grateful to Paul MacSwain, who persuaded John to stay away from the hospital "until they have a chance to get Lucille settled," and then took him to the Union League and got him drunk.

Margaret and Kate spent long hours with Lucille in the hospital. They both seemed to understand that the whole business was an exercise in futility, but that they had to go through the motions.

To no one's surprise, which in no way diminished John Wilton's guilt and sorrow, the doctors at University Hospital confirmed the initial and all subsequent diagnoses: Lucille had permanently lost the use of her lower limbs; she would spend the rest of her life in a wheelchair.

Lucille took it very well. She said there was no questioning God's will, and no sense weeping over something that could not be controlled. She confided to Kate, in tears, that what really bothered her was that God had not seen fit to give her and John at least one child before this happened.

Now that they knew for sure, it was time to go home. Lucille flatly refused to be surrounded by nurses as if she were at death's door. One maid, to help her dress, was all that she needed, and all that she would accept.

And Kate was dismissed when the train passed through Dallas. Kate had done more than any human being could be expected to do, and it was time that she thought of her husband.

John was already sketching changes that would have to be made at the house to accommodate Lucille's wheelchair and give her as much mobility as possible. Lucille encouraged him with what she told Kate was obviously John's new toy.

The question of what John Wilton was going to do with his sex life ran through Kate's head. There was no question in her mind that sooner or later, and most probably sooner, he would have to overcome his guilt. What he would probably do, she realized, was bed one of the Mexican girls, develop some sort of discreet arrangement that would permit him to find quiet satisfaction.

In September, 1900, Kate went to Beaumont, Texas, with Albert. He had invested a good deal of "their" money in and around Beaumont. Kate thought his real-estate investments (based on the notion, which had no basis in any facts that Kate could discover, that Beaumont was destined to be the greatest city in the state) were foolish. She had been surprised when a brickyard he bought from a man with the odd name of Patrillo Higgins had almost immediately started to make money.

She had, with some effort, kept her mouth shut when a petroleum engineer from the United States Geological Survey in Washington had announced that, after an extensive investigation, conducted by both the Geological Survey and geologists from the Massachusetts Institute of Technology, it had been concluded that there was virtually no chance of petroleum being found in the area. Albert had invested more of their money in the wild notion that oil was going to make them all rich.

She had put her foot down, their first real confrontation, when he said he wanted to "unload the Waxahachie property" in order to get a little more capital for the oil investments. She was not all that fond of the place at Waxahachie (she had been back to it only once since the funeral; the land was being worked on shares), but Luther had loved it, and she was not about to see anything that Luther had loved thrown away on a fool scheme.

There hadn't been a fight. Albert, although willing to use her money in a manner she thought reckless, was apparently aware and a little ashamed that he was doing so. At least, he wasn't willing to fight.

Until she got to Beaumont, Kate had believed that Albert had stopped the land speculation. But there she found that her husband had gotten money from John Wilton. And she was ashamed of the reason Wilton had given it to him—a misguided sense of obligation. Mr. and Mrs. Dennison had been faithful, selfless friends in helping with Lucille's accident. If they needed money, it was clearly his privilege (not to mention duty) to provide it.

Kate was furious with Albert, but there was nothing she could do about it now, except the next time she saw John to explain the facts of life to him. But being in Beaumont—a rough, tough little city with nothing for her to do but stay in their room in the Beaumont Hotel for long hours—was something she didn't have to put up with. The summer heat was over, she told Albert, and she was going to New Orleans to shop. When he was ready to go back to Dallas, to stay there for more than a day or two at a time, he should send her a telegram at the hotel in New Orleans.

On her second day, coming back on foot from the shops on Canal Street to her hotel, she reached the door just as a carriage pulled up and discharged John Wilton and Charley Broadhead. She almost called out, when she stopped herself, and turned to pretend to look in a shop window, so in case he glanced her way, he would not see her.

Her behavior, she realized, was more than a little odd. Why shouldn't she greet him? That would at least get her dinner in his company, which would be a lot more pleasant than sitting alone in the hotel dining room, acting ladylike and making sure she didn't establish eye contact with any male.

She walked around the block, and entered the hotel from the other door. Then she did something else inexplicable. She stopped at the desk.

"How may I help you, Mrs. Dennison?" the desk clerk asked.

"I wonder if you could tell me if you have reservations for Mr. and Mrs. John Wilton."

He didn't have to check his reservation file for that. "Mr. Wilton is here in the house," the desk clerk said. "Four-oh-seven. I don't believe Mrs. Wilton is with him. Would you like me to see if he's in?"

"Oh, no," Kate said quickly. "Mrs. Wilton and I are friends. I would not like to bother him if he's here alone."

You knew he was here, and you knew Lucille was at Rancho San Miguel, so why did you do that?

She bought a copy of *Harper's Magazine* and established herself in an armchair in the lobby that gave her a clear if oblique view of the door to the men's bar. She sat there until an hour later when Charley Broadhead and John Wilton came out. She held the magazine in front of her face and watched as they walked out the door. She was tempted to follow, but while she was still making up her mind, John came back in the lobby. He walked toward the elevators, hesitated, changed his mind, and walked back into the bar.

He was in there another hour before coming out. It was now, according to the clock mounted on the wall behind the desk clerk, half-past seven. He walked across the lobby, passing within twenty feet of Kate, and entered the dining room.

She got up, and walked toward the dining-room entrance, planning appropriate gestures of pleased surprise at discovering John there. But at the last minute she turned abruptly, hurried to the elevator, and rode up to her room on the fifth floor.

She ordered a light supper, lamb chops and a salad, from room service, then ate slowly, forcing herself to read and reread *Harper's Magazine*. When she had finished, and the dishes were cleared away by the floor waiter, she made up her mind what she was going to do. She was going to go back to the lobby and sit there and hope he would see her; this time she would not hide behind her magazine.

When John Wilton came out of the dining room, he walked to the elevator and got on.

This was ridiculous, she thought. He was alone and she was alone, and they were friends, and there was no reason why she shouldn't just knock on his door and say, "Hi, there, John. Fancy meeting you here." He was, after all, an old friend.

She headed for the elevator, and then changed her mind and started up the stairs. She was slightly out of breath when she reached the fourth floor, and told herself it was for that reason that she paused on the landing rather than either going down the corridor or going up to the fifth floor.

From the landing she saw the elevator door open to discharge a bellboy, and she knew that he was headed for 407 even before he stopped at that door and knocked.

John was sending for whiskey.

No he wasn't. He always carried a bottle of Tennessee sour-mash bourbon and a bottle of brandy in his luggage. He called this his emergency field rations. What did he want from a bellboy?

When the bellboy, after no longer than two minutes, came out of 407 stuffing paper money into the crown of his circular little hat, Kate knew what had been ordered. Fifteen minutes later, Kate, stationed near the door to 407, saw a flashily well-dressed young woman emerge from the elevator. She had to look for room numbers to get her bearings. She avoided looking at Kate.

Kate, fumbling quickly in her purse, intercepted her. "Excuse me," she said. The young woman looked at her nervously. "You won't be needed," Kate said. "Something unexpected happened." She held out ten dollars. The young woman shrugged her shoulders and without a word walked back to the elevator. Kate waited until she saw her get on it, and then she rapped twice on the door of 407.

"Come in," John Wilton called. The door was unlocked. Kate stepped inside. Wilton, fully dressed, had his back to her. He was pouring drinks. When he turned around, he had a brandy snifter in each hand.

"Hello, John."

His jaw sagged in surprise. "What brings you to New Orleans?" he said. "Where's Albert?"

She walked to him and took one of the brandy snifters from him. "He's in Beaumont. On one of his get-rich schemes. I wish I'd had a chance to talk to you before you gave him any money."

He didn't reply. He looked nervously over her shoulder.

"You expecting someone?" she asked innocently.

"Oh, no," he protested. She smiled, resisting the temptation to say something smart about his always pouring himself two drinks at one time. Then he asked, wanting an answer this time, "What *are* you doing in New Orleans?"

"I was bored with Beaumont," she said. "I've been shopping."

"I've been with Charley Broadhead," he said. "You know, I like to pop in every now and again, unexpectedly, to see how things are going."

"From what Lucille says, your Charley is making money for you just about as fast as my Albert is spending it for me."

"Shame on you, Kate," he said. "As a loyal wife, you should believe that Albert is going to make us very, very wealthy indeed with his petroleum. If not in this century, then certainly in the next."

He tossed his drink down. "Have you had dinner?"

"While you did," she said. "While I was gathering my courage to come down here and announce myself."

"Why should you require courage to do that?" he asked. There was a sound in the corridor. He looked at the door nervously.

She took pity on him. "I gave her ten dollars and sent her away," Kate said.

"Oh, God," he said. "How on earth did you know?"

"I saw the bellboy tucking money in his cute little hat," she said. "I knew you hadn't sent out for whiskey or food. And then she appeared."

"Thank you, Kate," he said solemnly. "I don't think I could have lived with myself if I had done that."

"Don't be a hypocrite, John Wilton," she said.

He shrugged. "Well, Kate, what should we do now?"

She looked him straight in the eye. "Don't tell me you've never heard of a frustrated female."

"What are you saying?"

"I'm saying that while Albert Dennison is a perfectly nice man, whom I like and admire, he is not the answer to a maiden's prayer. I don't even remember the last time it happened."

That was an out-and-out lie. The last time it had happened was in Beaumont, a ritual coupling before she went to the station. He wasn't the answer to a maiden's prayer, but he did perform his husbandly obligations. But John Wilton would not easily bed a friend's wife.

"And I have the same ethical problems about it as you do," she went on. "The last thing in the world I would want to do, could do, would be to hurt Albert."

"Yes, of course, I quite understand," he said. "Is there something wrong with him? I mean, some disease or something like that?"

"There are people who have different needs," she said. "Albert doesn't have much of a need."

"How terrible for you," he said.

What you're thinking, you bastard, she thought, was how good for you. "Yes," she said softly, "it is."

"But we certainly couldn't . . . uh . . . do anything. Now, could we?"

"Neither of us is liable to boast about it if anything were to happen," she said.

"That's true, that's true," he said. "I take your point." He studied the brandy swirling around his glass. "You don't think . . . uh . . . that it would be, uh, *obvious* to anyone concerned, do you? The, uh, change, so to speak, in our relationship?"

"There would be no change," she said. She walked out of his sitting room and into his bedroom. She unbuttoned her jacket and shrugged out of it and laid it on a chaise longue.

"But there would be a change," he protested, coming to the door and leaning on the jamb. "Obviously, there would be a change."

She was working on the buttons of her blouse. She knew that his eyes were on her. She liked the feeling.

"God knows I've thought about you often enough," he said. "But I had no idea, no idea whatever . . ."

"Have you?" she asked, and was ashamed to realize she

was fishing for affection, some sign that she would be more to him than a half-hour in bed.

He put his hand on hers. "Let me do that," he said. When he had his hand inside her underclothes, his fingers touching her stiffened nipples, she pressed her body against his. He was hard.

John groaned, then picked her up and carried her to the bed. He pulled her skirt and petticoats down off her legs. And then he stripped himself quickly. Her eyes moved from his erection to his face.

"Would you forgive me," he said as he got onto the bed beside her, "if I said something to you I have no right to say? That I love you."

You don't love me, John, she thought. You just want to have sex. But thank you, my darling, for saying it.

"We'll have no talk of that sort of thing," she said. "Never again."

"Forgive me," he said, and lay on his back, not touching her. After a long moment, she sat up and straddled him.

"You feel marvelous," she said. "And I need it. Let's leave it at that."

She reached down and grabbed him and guided him into her.

I wonder, she thought, why he feels so marvelous, and why Al feels like an unwelcome intruder.

And then John had had enough of her esoteric arrangement of their bodies, and rolled her under him, and all she could do, before she abandoned herself to the sensations of their coupling, was to hope that neither Lucille nor Albert would ever find out.

32

The package arrived at Rancho San Miguel on January 10, 1901, more than two weeks after Christmas. Lucille's disappointment that it hadn't arrived in time for Christmas, or even immediately afterward, had been almost bitter.

It came in a wooden case of almost furniture quality, put together with brass hinges, and even varnished. Lucille's first reaction to this was that such packaging was absurd. But when she unfastened the hinges and took out the heavy saddle-leather case inside, the outer packaging seemed suddenly very appropriate.

Her letters to Messrs. Holland & Holland, the Strand, London, had ordered one best-quality rifle, on the Mauser pattern, in the newly developed caliber .30 U.S. government, plus a full set of accoutrements, engraved according to pattern furnished. As a result of their experience in the Spanish-American War, and at the prodding of "The Colonel" (who had just been elected vice-president of the United States) the U.S. Army, paying a royalty to Herr Mauser, had adopted the rifle used against it so effectively by the Spanish. They had developed a more powerful, slightly larger-caliber cartridge, .30 inch for the "new" weapon.

Somewhat reluctantly, at the insistent prodding of Captain John F. W. Wilton, the Honorable August Schulz had found himself a leading advocate of the new weapon in the halls of Congress. (Now that Roosevelt was to be vice-president, he of course was by no means reluctant to trade on this association.)

There had been, for three months, a case of one thousand cartridges for the weapon, from Union Metallic Cartridge Company, hidden in Lucille's closet. That was the last place John would snoop.

Moving somewhat awkwardly in her wheelchair, but refusing help from Dolores, the young Mexican girl who had become her nurse and companion, Lucille worked the leather case from the wooden crate and laid it on her father's desk. Then she unfastened the straps.

The case itself, and certainly the rifle as well, were works of art. The rifle and a cleaning kit of oil bottle and rod and brushes and swabs rested on what looked to Lucille like billiard-table cloth, each piece neatly fitted into a recess.

The wood of the stock was gorgeous. Lucille remembered that Messrs. Holland & Holland had written her that the "piece" was being stocked with a "rather nice blank of Circassian walnut." "Rather nice" was a gross understatement. It was beautiful.

She picked up the rifle and turned it over in her hands. On the bottom of the trigger guard were John's initials, engraved, intertwined. On the right side of the stock was a small golden plaque on which was engraved: "For Captain John F. W. Wilton with love from his wife, Christmas 1900."

Damn them, Lucille thought, for not getting this here in time for Christmas, or at least in time for him to take it deer hunting.

"Dolores," she said, "I think we'll take this to Captain Wilton. Will you have someone hitch an animal to the surrey?"

"Señora!" Dolores protested.

"Please, Dolores," Lucille said, but it was an order, not a request. Lucille laid the rifle back in its case and then rolled herself out of the office and down the corridor to their bedroom. She was going to get one hundred rounds of ammunition. But when she rolled herself up to the door of the closet, she knew there was no way, short of crawling on the floor, that she was going to be able to get into the closet and then open the case and take ammunition from it.

She waited impatiently for Dolores to return to her.

John had had the saddlemaker rig two sets of straps in the

239

front seat of the surrey for her. One strap went under her arms and over her bosom, and the second around her waist. It served very effectively to keep her from sliding down out of the seat.

She had never before gone so far as the eight-mile distance between the big house at Rancho San Miguel and the ranch house at Anglo-American Land & Cattle, but there was no reason she shouldn't. She could just as well spend the night at Anglo-American as come back here, whether or not John was actually at Anglo-American or up in the hills.

It was cold, but the sun was shining, and she could certainly wrap herself in enough buffalo robes. She would not be troubled with cold feet; she had no feeling in them.

She sat on her wheelchair on the veranda of the big house and watched as the leather-cased Mauser was put beneath the seat of the surrey. Under John's direction, a ramp had been built beside the veranda so that the floor of the surrey was level with it. With Dolores helping her, it really wasn't all that much effort to hoist herself into the seat of the surrey, although the springs sagged when she finally transferred all her weight to the surrey.

Dolores arranged the straps around her bosom and waist and then tucked buffalo robes over her. And when she slid beneath the robes beside her, Lucille flicked the buggy whip against the animal's rear, and the surrey pulled away from the big house.

When they got to the ranch house, no one came to greet them. John had probably taken them all hunting, and the women were probably engaged in putting up his kill. Getting out of the surrey and into the ranch house was more difficult than she thought it would be. No provision had been made here for a woman in a wheelchair.

Now that she had come to the ranch house, Lucille thought, John would have somebody tend to it. In fact, he would probably have to be restrained from having a ramp constructed today.

Finally she made it onto the veranda, and Dolores helped her crawl into the wheelchair.

"I think I will surprise Captain Wilton," Lucille said. "When you unhitch the horse, put the surrey and the horse in the barn, where he won't be likely to see them."

And then she rolled herself down the veranda and to the front door. She got the door, which was unlocked, open without trouble, but she had trouble rolling the wheelchair over the sill. All the sills at Rancho San Miguel had been substantially cut down and the doors rehung. That would have to be done here, as well.

There was no one inside, and Lucille had not expected there would be. But she was surprised to find the house in disarray. The dishes from last night's dinner were still on the dining-room table. The dishes and the bottles, Lucille saw. Three bottles of wine, empty, and a half-empty bottle of brandy sat on the table beside the dirty dishes.

Well, Dolores would have to clean it up, that's all there was to it. And she would have to see if she could find some more wine, and something to have Dolores prepare for supper. Something simple, but nice.

She wondered whom John had had dinner with.

It was at that point that suspicion first entered her mind. She sat immobile for a moment or two and then rolled across the dining-room floor into the parlor and then across the foyer to the corridor leading to the sleeping quarters.

The bed in John's bedroom, *their* bedroom, was unmade. And there was another bottle of brandy and two glasses on the bedside table. And two leather suitcases, not hers, not John's, standing against the wall.

She rolled the wheelchair toward the suitcases, and then she saw the nightgown on the floor. She rolled alongside it, and then reached as far as she could, finally catching part of it with a finger. But that was enough. In a moment, with movements that now seemed quite natural, she had the nightgown in her hand.

It smelled of perfume. Expensive perfume. Somehow familiar.

The tears came, and she put her hand to her mouth, the nightgown still in it. And then she saw it, where Kate had left it on the bedside table, the cotton blossom with the two-carat diamond in the center.

There was no mistaking it. No one else had a brooch like that. No one else, now that she thought of it, had perfume like Kate's.

Kate!

241

It would have been bad enough to come in here and find that John was . . . was . . . *finding physical release* with some Mexican girl. He had not, after all, lost the feeling in the lower half of *his* body.

But *Kate*? Kate was the only friend she had in the world!

And how long had it been going on? Before the horse fell on her?

She picked up Kate's diamond cotton blossom and squeezed it in her hand so hard that it hurt. She put her hand beside her head as if to throw it. But then she lowered the hand and carefully put the brooch back where she had found it.

She rolled herself back out of the bedroom and into the dining room.

Dolores had started to clean up the mess.

"Leave that!" Lucille said.

"Señora?"

"Leave it," Lucille repeated. "And help me back into the surrey. We're going back to the ranch."

John did not return to the big house at Rancho San Miguel that night, or the next, but on the morning following, leading a line of pack animals, eight of the twelve horses with deer carcasses, gutted, wrapped in cheesecloth, tied across them.

The kitchen boys saw him coming first, and ran to her, excited, to tell her. A wave of anger swept through Lucille. She rolled into the foyer and up to the window and looked out it, and saw him, tall and erect in the saddle, his usual battered and floppy sombrero replaced for some reason by a stiff-brimmed Stetson, with a creased crown, the brim tipped forward to shade his eyes from the sun.

She rolled the wheelchair into the office, and then, impatiently, back out of the office and into the foyer again, and finally back into the office. She didn't know how to face him.

She opened a drawer in the desk and put a ledger onto it, and took a pencil in her hand, and pretended to be working. She heard the sound of animals making their way around the house to the kitchen. She looked up at the bookcase, whose glass doors sometimes reflected what was outside the windows. She saw the haunches of the packhorses walk past. On the last animal (she hadn't seen this when she'd looked out the foyer windows) were the heads and antlers of three large

deer, wrapped in cheesecloth. She remembered that Wilton
had promised both Paul MacSwain and his brother Tom "a
nice head." A stuffed deer head was apparently the height of
fashion back East. Lucille couldn't imagine why.

"Doña Lucille! Doña Lucille!" Juanita cried in Spanish.
"Come see all the venison the master has brought home!"

I wonder when he found the time to hunt, Lucille thought.
But she put her pencil down on the ledger and rolled out of
the office and toward the kitchen.

The kitchen, and the porch outside, and the ground beyond
the porch, was a scene of sudden frantic activity. Juanita was
ordering other Mexican women about, having work space
cleared in the kitchen, ordering fires in the unlit stoves, indicating which of the huge pots she would require, ordering
spices and onions and garlic from the root cellar. On the
porch, and beside it, the animals were being unloaded, the
deer carcasses hung on the rafters of the porch, the horses
themselves being led off to the stable by the stableboys.

Wilton, his rifle cradled (almost *lovingly* she thought, an-
gered by that, too) in his arms, stood, visibly pleased with
himself and the world in general.

He didn't see, or sense, that she had rolled to the kitchen
door.

"You had a good hunt, I see," Lucille said finally.

"What ho, my dear!" he said, turning, smiling, bending to
kiss her. "Wait till you see the capes I got for Tom and
MacSwain."

She didn't reply. She was being cold and distant. He interpreted this to mean that she was preoccupied with the fruit of
his hunt. And she was, too, she realized. His hunting was by
no means solely for the joy of the chase. Venison was a welcome change from the diet of beef, infrequently pork, and
rarely, on great occasions, some kind of fowl.

There would be venison for everyone tonight. Haunches
would be put down for sauerbraten, the most satisfactory
means of preserving whole meat. They themselves would
have deer liver, a genuine treat. The carcasses would be
boned, mixed with pork meat, turned into sausage and
smoked in the smokehouse, the hides tanned.

Once he was satisfied with the work at hand, John

marched into the house. Lucille refused to look at him. She began to direct operations in the kitchen.

But as she watched the first of the carcasses being skinned, the furry skin separated with great skill, using a literally razor-sharp curved-pointed knife, from the flesh beneath, she realized that she wanted to face him. Literally face him. Look into his face, to see what it said, to see if she could see something she had missed before.

She told Fernando that if he marred the skin he was working on, she would skin him, and then spun the wheelchair around and rolled into the kitchen, and through it. John would be in their room, changing from his hunting clothes, taking another of his frequent shower baths. Wiping the essence of Kate off him.

But he wasn't in their room. He was in the office, and he had the crate from Messrs. Holland & Holland open, and the leather case within, and the rifle in his hands. Of course, she thought. He would have gone to the office first, to clean his rifle.

I'd like to take that rifle and bend the barrel around your head, Lucille thought.

And then he saw her at the door, and looked up, and he smiled at her with love and gratitude. "I must say, I didn't expect anything like this," he said.

"I'm glad you like it," Lucille said.

"Like it? It's a bloody work of art, that's what it is!"

He came to her to kiss her in thanks, and when he got close, she pushed herself as far as she could out of the wheelchair to take the kiss.

He's still mine, she thought. Except for *that*, he's still mine.

Kate opened the door to their suite in the Harlingen House and called her husband's name. There was no reply. She really had expected none, but she was grateful that he wasn't there.

It was easier, when she came back like this, if he wasn't there. He always wanted to take her to bed when she had been away, and she didn't like that when she came home.

If she could put him off until tomorrow, it would be easier.

She wondered, idly, where he was, and then there was a knock at the door.

A bellboy with a telegram.

"It was in your box since yesterday, Mrs. Dennison," he said. "And when you didn't stop at the desk, I thought I'd better bring it."

She gave him a dime, and tore open the envelope. Albert had found oil in Beaumont.

Kate read the telegram again. Albert said the well "blew in." A "gusher." He said it *had come in*. She did the arithmetic in her head. One-eighth of 100,000 barrels was 12,500 barrels. That couldn't be right. The last she'd heard, the going price for oil was a dollar a barrel. If she was to believe Albert, that meant $12,500 a day.

She'd better get right down there and see what was really going on.

PART TWO

33

Albert Dennison had become one of the richest Texas oil millionaires, attracting the Mellons, among others, as his intimate friends and business associates. On a cold December day in 1914, Albert, his wife, Kate, and Mr. and Mrs. John Wilton were in Pittsburgh, Pennsylvania, as guests of the Mellon family.

They had traveled east in Albert Dennison's private railroad car, and were using its luxurious appointments as a hotel during their two days in Pittsburgh. From there they would go to where Albert Dennison had just taken over a string of gasoline filling stations. John had come as an adviser and Lucille was along to see the museums in Pittsburgh and Boston. She felt up to it, she said. Kate didn't believe that for a minute, but there was nothing you could do about Lucille when she wanted to move about, and she *was* interested in museums and oil paintings and things of that nature. Really interested. They gave her a great deal of pleasure, and God knew the poor woman had precious little of that.

Albert had immediately gone off with one of the Mellons to play golf; John had been shooting with another of them, and the Mellon ladies, including the grande dame, had escorted Mesdames Dennison and Wilton to the museum. Albert had told Kate that the Mellons had given the museum to Pittsburgh. Kate had thought, but had not said, that they had probably given the paintings and the rest of that stuff to the

247

city of Pittsburgh to get it out of the house. The house itself was more like a museum.

The Mellon ladies had mentioned in passing that they were about to go to Philadelphia to a ball for some English lord. They didn't really want to go, but it was expected of them.

"Perhaps you'll be there, Mrs. Wilton," one of them had said somewhat awkwardly. Crippled women didn't go dancing. "I understand your husband has family in Philadelphia."

"He does," Lucille had said, "but you know my John. The only way you would get him to a ball would be in leg irons."

The others laughed politely, but Kate saw that Lucille really wanted to go to that ball and meet an English lord. So, come to think, Kate realized, do I. I wouldn't make a fuss over it for myself, but by God, if Lucille wants to go, Lucille is going. If sitting there in a wheelchair watching people dance will make her happy, she'll go to the damned ball.

She approached John about it that evening. "The Mellons told us they were going to a ball in Philadelphia and I think Lucille wants to go. I mean, *really* wants to go."

"To a *ball*?" John was puzzled. Why would Lucille, who couldn't walk, want to go to a ball? "Are we invited?"

"No," Kate said. "But if the Mellons are going to a ball in Philadelphia, I'll give you three-to-one your mother is going, too. Call your mother, John. Please. She'll know how to arrange it for us."

He sat down in one of the rotating leather overstuffed chairs and reached for the telephone.

Kate got him his drink, and then stood beside him.

"Mother? How are you, Mother?" he said.

Ten minutes later it was all arranged. "It's for the governor general of Canada," John said, putting the receiver back on its cradle. "Mother and Paul have a table. We have tickets."

"Lucille will be very pleased," Kate said. She could smell his after-shave, and his cigars, and just a hint of sweat. "It'll make her happy."

"Thank you, Kate, for thinking of this."

"Oh, *I* want to go too. I've never met a prince or a lord or a governor general, whatever he is."

"Most of them are arthritic old men with bad breath," John said.

"You're terrible," she said. Then, relenting: "Did you have a good time today?"

"Damned good time. I'm going to have to get a trap for the ranch. I'll teach you how, Kate. You'll really love it."

He drew her to him, unbuttoned her blouse, and slipped his hand inside. Her breast swelled at the touch of his hand.

She kissed the top of his head. "I was wondering if we were going to have the opportunity."

"So was I," she said. She pushed herself off him, and walked down the corridor to the master suite. After a few moments she heard him cursing in his compartment. She knew what it was. Stark naked, she walked into the other compartment and knelt, and pulled off his boots.

Kate got Albert alone later and told him they were going to a ball in Philadelphia before going to Boston, but would keep it a secret from Lucille. From Albert's reaction, she knew exactly what he was thinking. An unexpected stroke of good fortune. There would be a large number of wives at a ball like that: wives married to men who had by hard work, faithful service, constant study, and their noses to the grindstone achieved positions of success—vice-presidencies, even presidencies—and made as much money in a week as Albert Dennison made in a year. Or a day. Or spent on cufflinks.

Kate realized that she was in no position to cast the first stone. She was the whore on the road to wherever-it-was in the Bible. But it didn't seem like what she and John were doing was wrong.

Kate sometimes thought that it was entirely possible that John Wilton was, if that was the word, faithful to her. She had never heard of him with another woman. It pleased her to think this. Another woman's husband faithful to her.

There were times when Paul T. MacSwain was glad that he had sold the place in Wallingford to Thomas Wilton and moved back to the city, to the house at 14 Rittenhouse Square, and this was one of them. He had pushed the curtains aside in his bedroom upon arising and found the ground in the park in the square snow-covered and the air full of small hard snowflakes, indicating that it was going to continue snowing for some time.

It was hell, when there was snow on the ground, getting to the station in Wallingford from the house, and on a day like this it probably would have meant that when he finally did get home, he would have to walk to the house, as getting back up the ice-covered hill in an automobile was impossible, period.

When Paul turned from the window and looked at his wife, he saw that her eyes were open. "It's snowing," he said. "There is no reason for you to get up."

He walked to the bed and kissed her and then pulled the bell cord twice to announce in the kitchen that he was up and would require breakfast as soon as he had dressed.

He went into the adjacent room, closing the door after him, and started to dress. A suit had been taken from the closet by the butler and hung on a cherry-wood floor hanger. A shirt and tie lay on the bed, and so did a shoehorn, a collar and collar button, and cufflinks.

By the time he had shaved, dressed, and gone quietly down the hallway to avoid disturbing Margaret, she had gotten out of bed, brushed her hair, put on a robe, and gone downstairs herself. She was pouring her stepson Edward's coffee when Paul walked into the dining room.

"Good morning, Father," Edward said.

"I didn't hear you come in last night," MacSwain replied, taking the extended morning paper from his son's hand.

"I'm glad," Edward replied with a smile.

"Where were you?"

"Carousing around the Tenderloin," Edward replied, smiling even more.

"Paul," Margaret said, "he's twenty-five years old!" There she went again, taking Edward's side against him. But then Margaret turned and snapped at her stepson. "You should be ashamed of yourself, talking to your father that way!"

"As a matter of fact," Edward said, "I was in New Jersey looking for a piece of property." Paul realized that the information was directed more at Margaret than it was at him, possibly to reassure her that he really hadn't been in the Tenderloin, possibly for other reasons.

He hadn't believed for a second that his son had been out for a night on the town, and certainly not in the Tenderloin. The Tenderloin was Johnny's playground.

Paul MacSwain, although he disliked discord at mealtime, nevertheless rose to his son's challenge. "And did you find a piece of property?" he asked with sarcastic concern.

"I think so."

"And I hope you also found the money to pay for it," MacSwain replied.

Edward colored, and Margaret gave her husband a withering look.

"A successful businessman of my acquaintance," Edward said, a patently artificial smile on his face, "once told me—as a matter of fact, has told me again and again—that capital is always available to finance a sound business idea."

He was quoting his father, and that was doubly infuriating.

"I hope you can find a sympathetic banker," Paul said unctuously.

"I don't need a sympathetic one," Edward said, and now there was anger in his voice. "All I need is one who isn't afraid of you!"

"Stop it, the both of you. That's enough!" Margaret snapped. "I won't have it."

"I'm sorry, Mother," Edward said.

What you're supposed to do now, young fellow, his father thought, is jump up from the table and storm from the room. But he didn't, and his father didn't expect him to. He sat there and ate his breakfast. Storming out of the room would have been a childish, foolish, immature thing to do. And Edward was not, with one enormous exception, childish, foolish, or immature.

And being very honest with himself, MacSwain conceded that his son's idea was not bad at all. For someone else, it might have been a very good idea.

Edward had, God alone knows where, come up with the notion that he was going to make his fortune in the cheap-clothing business. Possibly, even probably, there was a fortune to be made in cheap ready-to-wear clothing, and just as probably, if Edward applied the hard work and good sense to such a business that he demonstrated at MacSwain Manufacturing, he could make his idea work.

What was foolish, childish, and immature about it was that he didn't have to go out and make his fortune. MacSwain Truck Manufacturing was going to be his one day. In case that had somehow failed to occur to him, Paul had carefully explained that he was not so much as *working* in the plant as *training* himself for the day when he would be MacSwain Manufacturing's chief executive.

He might as well have talked to the wall. Edward had said that he wanted the "challenge" of doing something himself. As if there was no challenge in directing a factory with more than four thousand employees, which damned well might grow to ten thousand or even more employees if they got some of the war business he fully expected to get.

Making sure there was enough money in the bank every week to meet a payroll with four thousand names on it was a challenge, all right!

He had tried and failed to enlist Margaret to make Edward come to his senses. She hadn't come out against him and for Edward, but very nearly so.

"What's bothering you is that your son wants to do something himself," she had said.

"He has an idiot idea. And I need him in the company."

"He doesn't believe you need him, and he doesn't think his idea is any more idiotic than your idea that a man could make some money with horseless wagons."

"The trouble with you, Margaret," he had said, suddenly quite angry, "is that you have an overdeveloped maternal instinct. Whatever that son of yours wants, you think he should have."

"He wants me to advance him some money, since he can't get it from you," she said.

"Margaret, I absolutely forbid you to lend him ten cents!"

"I haven't made up my mind, Paul," she said. "One of the two of you is going to be hurt by this. What I'm trying to do is decide how to cut down the hurt as much as I can."

Margaret had, without saying anything to him, apparently decided not to lend Edward any money. And cutting off other sources of financing had been so easy that Paul MacSwain was more than a little ashamed of himself. The banks with which MacSwain Manufacturing did business would not lend his son any money. And the other banks had apparently decided that if it was a sound idea he could have gotten the financing either from his father or from a bank with which MacSwain had connections.

So Edward kept working at the plant. On his salary he would be a long time putting aside enough money to start a business.

What he needed, what would probably put the whole business out of the picture, was to find a nice girl and get married. But he seemed to be just like his father in that regard, too. Paul had shown only a casual interest in the opposite sex until he'd met his first wife. And after she'd passed on, he had shown no interest at all until Margaret came along.

The more he thought about that, the more he become convinced that he was doing the right thing. Let things ride as they were, until Edward found the right girl. The right girl would quickly talk sense to him, and he wouldn't be out until all hours of the night, looking for property that he had no chance in the world of being able to rent, much less buy.

In the Pierce Arrow, on the way to the plant, Edward told his father that he had spent the previous day at the new plant in Allentown; that construction, despite the weather, was ahead of schedule; and that, if things went right, they could start casting blocks in late March, no later than the first of April.

Maybe, Paul thought, I could name him works manager in Allentown. Maybe that would put the cheap-ready-to-wear-clothes idea out of his head.

An hour before the MacSwain breakfast, Thomas Wilton sat down to breakfast with his family in the big house in Wallingford. Thomas now had a beard, grown in the correct belief that it would make him look older and more dignified. Martha was at the table, with Olga, George, and Alice.

Olga was at the University of Pennsylvania, a tall, erect young woman with bright, intelligent eyes whose resemblance to her father would have been pronounced had her father been clean-shaven. George was planning to go to Harvard. It had been decided to send him there, rather than to the University of Pennsylvania or to Princeton, to remove him from the influence of his older brother, Johnny. Alice was at Miss Porter's School. George and Alice had taken after Martha's family. Harold Tilley was very much aware that his grandson looked like him, and had already begun to extol the

253

virtues of the publishing business whenever he had the opportunity.

Alice was the beauty. She was a golden-haired blond, and already had the boys chasing after her. Olga was not unattractive, but neither did she seem to exude whatever it was that turned young men into suitors.

The absence of John F. W. Wilton II from breakfast was not mentioned at table. Johnny was at Princeton but was now home for the Christmas holidays. He had matriculated with the class of 1912, but had just about wasted his first year, and had been twice expelled for drinking, and was scheduled finally to graduate with the class of 1915.

Johnny was an object of adoration on the part of his mother; he had always been a spoiled child, and now he was just as obviously a spoiled young man. He was taller and larger than his father, and it was generally agreed that he was probably even taller than his Uncle John, although they so far had been unable to stand the two of them back-to-back to see for sure. John Wilton seldom came to Philadelphia.

When he was in town, there was only time for a quickly arranged dinner, and his namesake was seldom able to make the family get-togethers. This was not to suggest, Thomas Wilton realized, that John was uninterested in his nieces and nephews. In their regard, he was generous to a fault. Lucille remembered their birthdays without fail. The presents she sent, in her and her husband's name, were really too extravagant, even if all the tales told about exactly how much money had come to them from John's oil investments were true.

Thomas was making, he thought, nearly as much money as Martha could spend. That certainly was an accomplishment, for Martha spent money as if it were perishable. They had a position to maintain in society, she said. And it wasn't as if they had to put money away for their old age. When the children were gone and married, they could cut down.

That wasn't all she was implying. She was implying that she would certainly inherit her father's interest in the Philadelphia *Inquirer*, and that he would certainly inherit his mother's interest in MacSwain Trucks, which she held separately, plus what MacSwain would leave her as well.

Martha was suggesting that all they had to do was keep up appearances until the time when they would come into everything. She had even considered inheriting from John and Lucille. Thomas had been quite shocked by that little conversation—although, married as long as he had been to Martha, he supposed by now he should be past shock. Martha had pointed out that since poor Lucille obviously wasn't going to have any children, and as obviously wasn't going to be able to hold on much longer, her property would go to John. And since John had no heirs, that meant everything would come to them.

Thomas didn't go along with any of that. For one thing, Lucille seemed to be a perfectly healthy woman, with the exception of the damage from her injury. She was not going to conveniently pass away anytime soon. The odds were, if you were forced to think about that sort of thing, that John would go first. He would have a hunting accident, or fall off a horse, or get shot by an enraged husband, whereupon his property would pass to Lucille, rather than the other way around. And Lucille was not going to leave her property to a sister-in-law she clearly disliked.

There was, although he didn't like to think about it, a selfish, mean streak in Martha. He had sometimes wondered if the greatest mistake in his life had not been marrying Martha. If he hadn't forced himself on her (he wondered about that, too; obviously she hadn't been raped), she would not have become pregnant, and he would not have married her.

The other side of that coin was that she had become pregnant with their son Johnny, and Tom couldn't imagine life without Johnny, no matter what outrage Johnny committed that week. He sometimes thought, even now, when Johnny was really a man, that having him around was rather like what he remembered of his childhood. Johnny had always seemed, from the time he could walk and talk, more like a friend than a son, trailing after his father everywhere, much as Thomas remembered trailing after his older brother.

Genes were an amazing thing. The similarity between his brother and his son was sometimes astonishing. He tempered his affection for his son (which could and did get out of hand) by telling himself that at twenty-three Johnny had yet to earn a dime, or do an honest day's work, while his brother at that age was running a huge ranch in the Far West, *after* having served as a decorated officer in the army in India.

If Johnny was a wastrel, the fault was his father's. He had been so busy getting Lennai Mills on its feet that he hadn't spent enough time with his son in his formative years. Neither had he put his foot down to keep Martha from spoiling him.

The first time he had been expelled from school (from Episcopal Academy, even before he went to Princeton), Margaret MacSwain's unsolicited advice had been that he be sent out West for a year to John, and put on a horse, and informed that if he wished to eat, he would first work. Martha had thrown one of her spectacular fits over that, of course, a hysterical session in which Episcopal Academy had been flayed as the villain, laying temptation before Johnny like a chicken before a hungry lion. The solution to the problem was for the school to remove temptation from the paths of playful youths, rather than—God, you know I really do sometimes question your mother's sanity—send a child away from home and into the custody of a man who was doing only heaven knew what.

Thomas thought his mother's suggestion a little strong (he had been thinking more along the lines of getting his son out in the carriage house and letting him have a dozen swipes with a buggy whip, quickly, before Martha came rushing to his rescue), but for once he could not completely bite his tongue.

"At Sagamore Hill, Martha," he said, "I understand they call my brother by his Christian name at table."

There had been a photograph on the front page of the Philadelphia *Inquirer,* obviously given that prominence by Harold Tilley, showing a dinner given by the former president of the United States for his former Rough Rider officers. Mr. Roosevelt had been photographed with his arm around the shoulders of John F. W. Wilton.

"Roosevelt," Martha had replied, "is crazy. Everyone knows that. Roosevelt and your brother are two of a kind. There probably wasn't a gentleman within miles of Sagamore Hill."

Thomas had often thought later that what he should have done was whip Johnny, and then send him to New Mexico, and then given Martha a few cracks of the whip.

But that hadn't happened. Mr. and Mrs. Paul T. MacSwain

had visited the bishop of Philadelphia. The Episcopal Academy received a rather substantial gift from the MacSwains, and Johnny Wilton was readmitted on probation, academic and social. On his graduation, he had received a canary-yellow Mercer forty-six-horsepower runabout, with the congratulations and best wishes of Mr. and Mrs. John F. W. Wilton.

Olga's graduation gift had been a diamond brooch and a Ford Model-T coupe. Thomas decided that it probably gave his brother pleasure to make such gifts to his children; he had none of his own. And of course, there was no arguing with the fact that John could afford to give them anything that struck his fancy.

The telephone interrupted Thomas' reverie; he wondered who would be calling at that hour of the morning, and then the obvious answer occurred to him: one of the young bloods after Alice.

"Excuse me, Mr. Wilton," the housekeeper said, standing in the door to the sun porch, "it's the depot on the line. They want to know if they should park the car near a ramp, or whether you're going to have it moved."

"Did they say what car?" Thomas replied. Obviously there had been another error by the railroad. A car intended for Lennai Mills had been dropped off here at Wallingford by mistake.

"Why don't you go to the telephone yourself?" Martha said, and there was a sarcastic tone in her voice he didn't like at all. But he laid his napkin on the table and went. In two minutes he was back.

"What do you know about horses, Martha?" he asked.

"I have no idea what you're talking about."

"There is a cattle car at Wallingford Station," he said. "It contains seven horses and one accompanying handler. It is consigned to John F. W. Wilton II."

"I don't know if he's home."

"Martha, I thought I had made it quite clear to both you and Johnny that I cannot support him in the manner to which he wishes he were accustomed. I cannot afford polo ponies. Did you give him the money to buy any horses, or in any way imply that he could oblige me to pay for any?"

"The only thing I did was mention to Mother MacSwain

that it was important, socially speaking, for Johnny to move in those circles. I have no idea what she did, but it is possible, I suppose, that she mentioned it to your brother. He has more horses than he can count."

Thomas glowered at his wife, but then he was forced to smile. That explained, certainly, what the stationmaster was talking about when he said there were seven horses and one Indian.

34

The first twist of the doorbell, a grating, muted clanging, woke Mrs. Kenneth P. Hoover, and the moment she became aware of where she was, a fear gripped her, chilling her, actually twisting her stomach.

She was naked in a double bed in the bedroom of an apartment at 1513 Cherry Street in Philadelphia with a naked man not her husband. A stuffed mountain lion sitting on a chest of drawers against the wall at the foot of the bed snarled silently at her, and the glass eyes of an enormous deer mounted on the left wall seemed to be focused on her.

The strident ring of the doorbell did not disturb the sleep of her lover, who lay on his stomach beside her.

I will just ignore it, Ann Hoover decided. Pushing terror to the rear of her mind, replacing it with reason, she told herself that it couldn't possibly be her husband. Her father-in-law hadn't liked the idea of his taking three days off from the store during the Christmas season to attend the governor general's ball at all; there was no way he would have permitted Ken to come down from Hazleton a day early. And even if he had come down, even if he had gone to the house and found out she wasn't there, there was no way he could have found her here. No one knew where this apartment was. Ken simply couldn't be ringing the doorbell.

She had just decided that whoever it was at the door (a salesman, probably) had decided there was no one at home, when the bell was twisted again. Four rings this time, an even more strident summons than the first. It must be audible all over the building.

She pushed the naked man beside her. He shifted on the bed, groaned, and settled himself again. She had the somewhat immodest thought that he should be tired.

"There's somebody at your door," she whispered fiercely.

"They'll go away," he said sleepily. "Somebody selling something."

The bell was twisted four more times.

"*Will* you answer your door?" she commanded.

"I think not," he said after a moment.

She lay beside him on her back, the sheet drawn up to her chin in her balled fists. Thirty seconds later, the bell was twisted four more times again.

"God!" she said. Then she threw the sheet off her body and swung her feet out of the bed. She picked up her wrap from where she had laid it on the back of an overstuffed leather chair and put it on. She went out of the bedroom and into the living room. The bottle of champagne he had stolen (not without difficulty; it had been carefully guarded by the servants) from the party at the Frawleys' sat on a low table before an overstuffed leather sofa matching the chair in the bedroom. She remembered that they had sat there drinking it as he undressed her, that she had actually sat there quite shamelessly naked before he had had enough of the game and picked her up and carried her into the bedroom.

It didn't seem nearly so delightfully wicked now. It seemed like something a wife cheating on her husband would do when she was drunk; something a slut would do. She looked at the door to the apartment. There was a frosted-glass panel in the door, engraved in a scroll pattern, apparently designed to do what it was doing now, permit a somewhat indistinct view of whoever was standing outside the door.

She could make out a man's shape, a short man wearing a derby hat. At least it wasn't Ken. Ken was six-feet-two, and much heavier. This was probably a salesman, somebody selling something.

The doorbell was twisted still again. Up close, the ring was even more unpleasant; no wonder it had woken her in the bedroom.

She went to the door and turned the dead bolt and pulled

the door open. She would get rid of this persistent salesman immediately. The cheek of these people!

A soberly dressed gentleman stood there, immediately, on seeing her, removing his derby with a gray-gloved hand. He wore a necktie whose stripes she recognized as those of Harvard University. A Phi Beta Kappa key hung from a gold chain between the lower pockets of his vest. He was, incredibly, a Chinese.

"Mr. John Wilton II, please," the Chinese said without a hint of an accent. "I am expected."

She stared at him a moment, and then, as she closed the door in his face, mumbled, "Just one moment."

She ran quickly to the bedroom. At the door she called his name. "Johnny! Johnny!"

He didn't stir. She went and stood looking down at him. Damn him, he was sleeping like a baby. Suddenly furious, she slapped his face.

He woke angrily and sat up. "What the hell was that?" he snapped.

"There's a Chinese at the door," she said. "He says you expect him."

"Sam?" John F. W. Wilton II called out, almost a shout.

"On the landing," she clarified. "Outside."

"Jesus Christ!" Johnny said. "Why didn't you let him in?" He hurled himself out of bed and walked quickly to the door. She went to the bedroom door to see.

"I'm sorry, Sam," he said, holding the door open for the Chinese, who smiled, and nodded, and stepped inside. Then he turned and saw her. "Sam," he said. "This is Mrs. Hoover. Sweetheart, this is Samuel Long."

"How do you do?" the Chinese said, politely inclining his head, almost a bow.

How dare he introduce her by name? What was wrong with him, calling her "sweetheart" in front of this Chinese?

"Your telephone, Johnny," the Chinese said, "seems to be off the hook." He nodded his head toward the telephone on the table, its earpiece sitting erect beside the champagne bottle. He walked over to it. "That probably explains why your line was reported out of order." He hung it up.

"It has an unfortunate habit of ringing at the wrong time," Johnny said. That was a clear reference to what had happened, without interruption, on the couch. "I suppose you have some valid reason, other than curiosity, for coming here at this hour of the morning?"

Sam settled himself on the couch, crossing his legs. Ann Hoover saw that he was wearing spats. And good shoes. Expensive shoes. Ken had told her you could always tell a gentleman by his shoes. It could be, she thought, but it sounded like something someone who sold shoes would say. There was a large men's shoe department in Hoover's Department store in Hazleton, Pennsylvania.

"When Mother MacSwain was unable to reach you," he said, "she called upstairs and asked me to see if you were here, and if you were, to deliver two messages."

"Oh, God!" Johnny said. "Sam, do you want some coffee?" He walked into the tiny kitchenette and put water in a pot.

"I have to be getting to the office," Samuel F. Long said. "Thank you, no."

"What were the messages?"

"You have a rail car containing seven horses, presumably polo ponies, and one Indian at Wallingford Station," Sam said. "Your father said that you are to take care of them immediately."

"I had hoped to get them into the Rose Tree stables before he found out," Johnny said. "Lucille telephoned to say that they were coming, but they weren't due for another couple of days."

Curiosity got the best of Ann Hoover. "Polo ponies?"

"If there is one thing better than having a rich uncle," Johnny said, "it is having a five-goal rich uncle who likes to train ponies."

"Five-goal?"

"There is a handicap system, Mrs. Hoover," the Chinese explained. "Better players are given a goal handicap corresponding to their ability, as judged by their peers."

It was absolutely incredible having a Chinese, dressed the way he was, like a banker or a lawyer, and speaking perfect English, treating her as a social equal, and patiently explaining polo.

"How, may I ask, do you expect to pay for their board at Rose Tree?" Sam asked.

"I'll think of something," Johnny said. "Did my father think I was at Rittenhouse Square?"

"Mother MacSwain led him to believe you were there, innocently asleep," Sam said.

Johnny decided a further explanation was necessary. "For the obvious reasons, my parents don't know about this place," he said. "They are not nearly as understanding as my grandmother."

Ann felt her face flush. She had just been identified as the sort of woman who went to a love nest. It had been obvious to the Chinese, of course, from the moment he had seen her. But it stripped her naked of the pretense that this was a great passionate romance, one whose intensity permitted her to violate her marriage vows. She was now simply someone cheap, cheating on her husband in an apartment kept for expressly that purpose, and frequented by Chinese. She felt dirty and ashamed.

"You said two messages?" Johnny asked.

"I hope you have marked plans to attend the governor general's ball on your busy social calendar."

"Not on your life, Sam!" He waved his hand in Ann's direction. "Among other things, *Mr.* Hoover will be at the ball. I would just as soon not, thank you, run into him."

"Your Uncle John telephoned late yesterday afternoon, from Pittsburgh. He and Lucille, and the Dennisons, are now en route to Philadelphia. They will attend the ball."

"In that case, I wouldn't miss it for the world."

"Mother MacSwain suggests that you meet the *Prairie View*. It will be at the Thirtieth Street yards at three-fifteen."

"You're going to be there?"

"If at all possible," Samuel Long replied.

"You want me to pick you up?"

"You are wholly unreliable, and have left me stranded for the last time," Sam said.

"Okay, okay," Johnny agreed. "I'll see you there."

"Good morning, Mrs. Hoover," Sam said, getting to his feet. "It has been a pleasure to make your acquaintance." He turned and started out of the apartment.

"Sam!" Johnny called after him. "Thank you, Sam. Again."

A smile appeared, very faintly, at the edges of Sam's

mouth. And then he turned and walked out of the apartment, closing the door after him.

Johnny smiled at Ann Hoover and then walked into the kitchen. "I'm going to have to get moving," he called, "if I have to be at the yards at quarter past three."

"That was despicable of you," she said. "Letting that Chinese in in here, humiliating me like that!"

"Careful, sweetheart," he said, an unpleasant tone in his voice. "I am very fond of my Cousin Samuel."

"I should never have come here," she said.

He opened the icebox, peered inside, and then slammed the door. "There's not a damned thing to eat in there."

"I thought you cared for me," she said, then hesitantly, "loved me."

He poured a little coffee in a cup, examined it, and put the pot back on the burner. "There's a big difference between 'care for' and 'love,' " he said. "I never told you I loved you."

She met his eyes and then turned on her heel and went into the bedroom and started to dress. Her eyes were fuzzy with tears. She looked at the bed with shame and revulsion.

By the time she had dressed, she was angry. She walked into the kitchen. He was pouring himself a second cup of coffee. He raised the pot to her, offering her some.

"No, thank you," she said icily.

"I'm sorry you're so upset," he said. "I can't imagine why."

"Making a fool of myself over you, trusting you, believing you," she said, "is bad enough. But to have you humiliate me in front of that Chinese. . . . I would be very grateful if you would finish your coffee and then take me someplace where I can catch a taxicab to take me home."

"I'll take you home," he said after a long moment.

"How could you, Johnny?" she demanded dramatically. "How could you do this to me?" She put a handkerchief to her eyes.

"How could I do what to you?" he asked.

"*Exhibit* me to that Chinese?"

"Is that what's bothering you? Or did you come here with some childish notion that I would wake up in the morning—"

"I came here because I thought you loved me!"

"You came here because you've found out that if you take Ken Hoover's football and his collection of loving cups away from him, what you have is a storekeeper," Wilton said. "And storekeepers are not very exciting, in bed or out of it."

"Not as exciting as you are, is that what you're saying?"

"You are here, Ann," he said. "Aren't you?"

She glowered at him, hoping that he would crumble before the wrath and contempt in her eyes. He did not.

"Will you at least call me a taxi?" she asked.

"The number for Checker is on the phone," he said. "It takes them about five minutes to get here from Broad Street Station. Are you packed?"

She didn't answer him. She went to the couch and sat gingerly on the edge of it and gave the number of Checker Cab to the operator. When she had given the taxi dispatcher the address and hung up, Johnny was standing in front of the table.

"Aren't you being a little foolish?" he asked reasonably. "If Sam is what's bothering you, you can put it out of your mind. He's not going to say anything."

"What makes you so sure?" she snapped. "He hasn't when you've had other women here?"

He didn't reply.

"I think I have the right," she said, "to know exactly who that Chinese is."

"His name is Samuel F. Long," Wilton said. "He's an attorney. I think of him as my cousin because he was raised by my grandparents. If I didn't think of Sam as family, I'd say he was my best friend. Is that enough? Or should I explain the Phi Beta Kappa key? University of Pennsylvania, *summa cum laude*. He also went to Harvard Law. Now, let me see, what else? Oh, he owns this building."

She really hated him now. Her face showed her loathing.

"All things considered, sweetheart," Wilton said nastily, "you'd have done a lot better with my Chinese than with your football player. Not only is he a lot more fun, but I'm sure he makes a larger salary. And after a while, you don't see the yellow skin."

She stood up and walked past him to the bedroom and claimed her bag. He went to the door and held it open for her. She met his eyes, started to say something, and then changed her mind.

She went down the stairs and out onto the street. John F.

W. Wilton II went into the bathroom and ran water in the tub for his bath.

Edward MacSwain walked across Broad Street in front of the Bellevue-Stratford Hotel pretending he didn't hear the angry blast of the police whistle, calling his attention to his violation of the traffic laws of the city of Philadelphia.

He entered the First Philadelphia Bank & Trust Company building by the narrow entrance to the right of the bank's ground-floor operation and rode to the fifteenth floor alone in a large elevator. The elevator opened directly into the reception room of Cayman, Naileby, Boothe & Davis, attorneys-at-law, whose offices occupied all of the fifteenth floor and about half of the sixteenth.

The receptionist recognized him. "I know he's in, Mr. MacSwain," she said. "Shall I see if he's free?"

"I am about my father's business," MacSwain replied with a smile. "He shall have to be free."

Samuel F. Long, Esq., who was carried on the firm's stationery as "of counsel," devoted ninety percent of his time to three clients. MacSwain Truck Manufacturing, Inc.; Lennai Mills, Inc.; and the Dennison Oil Company. If he was tied up with another client, it would be some other Chinese in trouble with contract law. Since no bill would be rendered for such services, such clients had to stand aside when a MacSwain or a Wilton appeared.

Samuel F. Long, in his shirtsleeves, was being served coffee by a typist when Edward pushed open the door to his office.

"Very busy, Sam?" Edward asked.

"I have in hand a rental contract that will endure all tests and emerge intact," Sam said, waving his guest into an armchair. "I drew it myself, something I don't believe Messrs. . . ."—he looked at a letter—"McGarvey, McGarvey & Connors are aware." He looked pleased with himself. "The Canton Palace Restaurant, at Seventh and Arch?" he asked. "The owners have, I believe, a better offer from Horn & Hardart. Who are going to have to search for other suitable premises."

"God, it must be a strain, being that brilliant. How do you live with yourself?"

"Not as well as Johnny," Sam said. "He had a real beauty this morning."

"I tried to call him about half-past nine. There was no answer," Edward said. "I'm glad you found him."

"Mother MacSwain called me at six yesterday, and then again at half-past eight this morning," Sam said. "I was there at a quarter to nine this morning."

"Anybody I know? The girl, I mean?"

"Probably," Sam said with a smile.

"But you're not going to tell me who?"

"I am known for preserving confidences," Sam said.

"Touché," Edward said. "I don't suppose you really want to have lunch with Dad, do you? He is collecting a group of notables to pick their pockets."

"In that case, certainly not," Sam said. "What's the cause?"

"Underwriting the governor general's ball's losses," Edward said. "The Irish, Dad has just learned, are not almost like the English. They are staying away from the ball in droves."

"Maybe he has learned something you should."

"I don't think I like that, Sam."

Sam threw his palms above his shoulders, a gesture of surrender. "I was simply suggesting . . ."

"Sam, we're going to have a baby," Edward said.

Samuel F. Long, who had been leaning far back in his heavy oak chair, let it fall forward. He looked at Edward. "I was about to say something stupid," he said. "The lawyer, always protecting his client's interests."

"What were you about to say?"

"I was about to remind you that girls sometimes . . ."

"Say they're pregnant to get the man to marry them? Thanks a lot."

"If that were the case, my advice would be for you to marry her. But since you have already taken her as your wife, I really don't know what to say to you."

"How about 'congratulations, I'm happy for you'?"

"Is that why you're really here? To ask me what you should do?"

"That, and to ask you to cover for me at lunch again."

"When it comes out, and it will now have to come out," Sam said, "I don't like to think what your parents are going to think of my role in this."

"They will think you behaved as a big brother should," Edward said. "As you have behaved."

"I suppose it's occurred to you that if you just told them what you've done, they could roll with the punch?"

"I don't know who's worse, Mother or Dad," Edward said. "They'd as soon see me married to a black."

"Or a Chinese? I haven't found them as bad as you paint them."

"And as bad as they are, they're not half as pigheaded as the Herlihys." Edward looked right at Sam and announced, "I'm going to see if Uncle John won't lend me the money I need."

"That will pose an interesting question," Sam said. "Who is most disloyal—me, for what I've done, or your Uncle John, for giving you money your father doesn't want you to have?"

"I'm sorry I involved you in this, Sam."

"So am I," Sam said.

"But it would be the solution to the whole problem," Edward said. "It would get both of us out of Philadelphia. Tempers would cool, after a while, I mean. Mother would come to see Patricia for what she is, and after a while, after the baby comes, they'll soften. Mother and Dad, and Patricia's parents, too."

"And all will be sweetness and light?"

"You have any better ideas?"

"No, but I can let some of the wind out of your sails," Sam said. "What makes you think John Wilton will give you the money just because you ask for it? I can hear him going to your father. 'I dislike intruding in your affairs, old boy,'"—Sam did a very creditable mimicry of Captain John Wilton's clipped British speech—"but the thing is, you see, don't you know, that your boy, poor little chap, has got himself hung up with an Irish lassie. Really got him lassoed, so to speak. For all I know, he may have sowed the seed, so to speak. He came to me for money. Didn't give—'"

"All right, Sam," Edward said. "I get your point." He had to smile at the apt mimicry, but then the smile faded. "If he knew Patricia . . ."

"If he knew Patricia, nothing," Sam said. "Your ladylove's accent is worse than his. She sounds as if she got off the boat from County Cork last week."

"Dammit, Sam!"

Sam Long held up his hand to shut him off. "On the other hand, if Patricia were able to impress Lucille and Kate Dennison, Captain John would fall in line."

"Dammit, Sam, that's it!" Edward said. "But how are we going to get them together?"

"The *Prairie View* will be at the Thirtieth Street yards at three-fifteen. I don't think we'd have much trouble talking Captain John into a lobster. Can you get Patricia to meet us at Bookbinder's, to *wait* for us at Bookbinder's, from, say, four on?"

"You'll come along?"

"I'm in this damned near as deep as you are."

Edward picked up the telephone and gave the operator a number. Sam Long picked up an extension to listen.

"James F. Herlihy Construction," an operator said, coming on the line.

"Good day to ye, darlin'," Edward said in a quite authentic Irish brogue. "This is Father O'Hare. Would you be a good girl and put Miss Patricia on the line for me?"

"I'd be happy to, Father," the operator said.

"Accounts payable," a male voice said in an equally thick brogue.

" 'Tis Father O'Hare calling for Miss Patricia, Mr. O'Dell," the operator said. "Could she be coming to the line?"

After a moment Patricia's voice said, "Hello?"

"God love ye, darlin'," Edward said. "Ye know who this is?"

"Yes, of course. How are you, Father?"

"I was wondern' if your busy schedule would permit ye to have a bite of early supper with a poor lonely old man of the cloth?"

"You're not old, Father," she said.

"I'll never see sixty again, darlin'," Edward said. "That's how young I am. I'm thinking that since it's Friday, a bowl of Bookbinder's clam chowder and maybe a small piece of broiled fish would be nice. Could ye share it with me? Say, about four o'clock, give or take?"

"Thank you very much, Father," Patricia Herlihy said. "I'll see you then."

"I'll be waitin' for ye, darlin'," Edward said. "God bless you, darlin'."

He hung up. "Within five minutes," Edward told Sam, "my unknowing father-in-law will have a full report that his daughter is going to have a light, early supper with an elderly priest. Whereupon he will stop worrying for as much as an hour that his precious Irish princess will get contaminated by a godless Protty-stant."

35

James F. Herlihy's Packard limousine was outside the door of the James F. Herlihy Construction Company, Inc., when Patricia came out the front door, Timmy, the chauffeur, wiping at the chrome radiator with a chamois.

From the top of the stairs of the three-story red-brick building, Patricia could look down North Broad Street all the way to City Hall, with Pitt's statue on top of the building. She could see almost, within six short blocks, to where she was going to meet Edward.

She hoped that Timmy wouldn't be there waiting for her. Sometimes he wasn't, when her father was off somewhere. If she could have taken the streetcar, there would have been a period of transition between her two worlds, a chance to adjust from being Miss Patricia Herlihy and what she had become. She had not yet grown used to accepting that she was, at least according to the laws of the great state of Maryland, Mrs. Edward MacSwain, a married woman. God forgive her, she felt like a girl who had sinned and was in trouble.

Here, she felt that way. Once she got inside Bookbinder's, once she could touch Edward's hand, sense his physical presence, then she would feel like Mrs. Edward MacSwain. When she was with Edward, everything was different, everything seemed all right.

"Can I be giving you a lift somewhere, Miss Patricia?" Timmy asked, coming up the steps, touching his hand to the brim of his chauffeur's cap.

271

"My father won't be needing the car?" she asked, playing out the charade.

The car was there because either Patrick O'Dell or Mary Alice Feeney, the telephone operator, or both of them, had reported to her father that Father O'Hare had telephoned and asked her to Bookbinder's. If her father had to go somewhere, he would go in one of the company Fords. He felt much better if Patricia were protected from all the sin and wickedness in Philadelphia by travel in the Packard, with Timmy, two hundred pounds of red-headed devotion, behind the wheel.

"He said he'd be in the office all afternoon," Timmy said, running back down the stairs to open the Packard door for her.

"I want you to understand, darling," her father had said when she had first come to work in the company, "that you'll be treated exactly like any other employee of the James F. Herlihy Construction Company, not that I think for a moment you'd take advantage of your position."

And so she was. Except that the eyes of half a hundred faithful employees were always on her, aware that she was the boss's only child, the apple of his eye, his pride and joy, his little princess. And reporting to the boss, for example, about Father O'Hare.

Although Edward had made the name up, just like that, at the very beginning, there really was a Father O'Hare, a wizened, kind-looking little man, one of the priests at Saint Malachai's, not far from the James F. Herlihy Construction Company.

Her father had announced at dinner one night that he'd met *her* Father O'Hare, and Patricia's stomach had dropped to her knees, thinking the whole business was now exposed.

"I ran into him at the Knights of Columbus," James Herlihy went on. "He gave the invocation. I told him who I was, your father, I mean."

Somehow she got through that dinner, actually afraid that her father knew everything and was going to go along with her deception until she decided to confess all. She met Edward the next day for lunch at the Horn & Hardart cafeteria on Market Street and told him.

272

Almost immediately he chuckled. Edward seldom laughed out loud, but his chuckling was warm and contagious.

"What if he sees him again? What if he says he never heard of me?" Patricia asked.

"Admit that he doesn't know the only daughter of James F. Herlihy, grand exalted poohbah of the Knights? Close personal friend of the archbishop? Wild horses couldn't drag that admission out of him," Edward said. "There is probably another Patricia Herlihy, flattered, if somewhat baffled, at the attention the good Father O'Hare is now paying her."

"Edward, you're terrible," she said, but his reaction warmed her. Practically everything Edward did warmed her.

She'd met him nearly a year before in John Wanamaker's Department Store. She had noticed him before he spoke to her, and when she was honest with herself, admitted that she thought he was a handsome young man indeed, and well-dressed. *Nice*-looking.

She had gone to the purse department to buy her mother a purse for Christmas; he had gone to the purse department to buy purses, plural. When she first saw him, he had a dozen or more handbags lined up in neat ranks atop the glass display case and had a clerk and a floorwalker in attendance.

And then he walked over to where she was standing, took off his hat, smiled at her and said, "Forgive the intrusion, miss, but I need some help."

She wasn't used to being spoken to by strangers, but the floorwalker was right there, and seemed to be beaming at this young man.

"I need purses for my mother, two aunts, and two cousins," he said. "I am afraid that I am about to give mother-type purses to my cousins, cousin-type purses to my aunts, and so on. Would you be kind enough to come to my aid?"

"All right," she said, surprising herself, and walked over to where he had the bags lined up. "These are all very nice," she said. And they were all also expensive, which went with the nice way he was dressed.

"My mother," he said, "is what I suppose you could call a lady of some style. I mean, she is a morning-galloper-in-Fairmount Park-type mother."

273

She had to smile at that. She couldn't think of a thing to say in reply.

"My cousins are something like you," he said. "I mean to say, unmarried, attractive. Alice is still in school, and Olga in college."

"And your aunts?" Patricia had asked, not looking at him.

"One is your pillar-of-society-type aunt," he said. "She is liable to be the hardest to please."

"And the other?"

"Confined to a wheelchair," he said. "She is the one I would like most to please."

"I'm so sorry," she said, suddenly aware that he had told her a very great deal about his family. She picked out two purses she herself would have bought. "These would be nice for your cousins, perhaps."

"Wrap them up," he said to the clerk. "Mark one 'Alice' and the other 'Olga.' "

"I think the Misses Wilton will be very pleased with what Miss Herlihy has selected," the floorwalker said. There was something reassuring about the floorwalker knowing who he was. He was not, then, a masher.

"And what do you recommend for the old folks, Miss Herlihy?" he asked. She thought that he had picked up rather quickly on her name.

"I really shouldn't be doing this," she said, suddenly uncomfortable.

He chuckled. "In the world of the blind," he said, "the one-eyed man is king."

"Any of these are quite nice," she said. "I really feel uncomfortable. They may not like what I like at all."

"I'm sure they will be delighted," he said. "Since they normally steel themselves against the horror of what my packages are sure to contain." He turned to the clerk. "Wrap those up, too, marking them 'Lucille,' 'Martha,' and 'Mother.' "

"Would you like them sent to your office, Mr. MacSwain?" the floorwalker asked. "Or to Rittenhouse Square?"

That identified him. MacSwain of Rittenhouse Square. Old Philadelphia. Social Philadelphia. Tory, that is to say, *Protestant* Philadelphia. She was disappointed. It had been a foolish notion, of course, to think that she could meet a suitable young man at the purse counter in John Wanamaker's; things simply didn't happen that way.

"I stand in your debt, Miss Herlihy," he said.

"Not at all," she said, turned on him, and walked away. She kept right on walking, past where she had been standing at the other side of the purse counter, telling herself that she had to end this encounter right now. It could prove embarrassing to the both of them. What she would do, she decided, was go listen to the organ recital, a Wanamaker's Department Store Christmas-season noontime tradition, at least for a few minutes, and then return to the purse counter when he certainly would be gone.

A strange feeling of excitement had run through her all during the exchange, slowly leaving now, and then bursting back into life when she saw him standing thirty feet from her in the crowd, watching the organist. She felt his eyes on her, and was unable to keep from looking at him whenever she felt that he might be looking away.

And then she fled. She would have to get her mother something else, some other time. She was standing by the carriage entrance waiting for Timmy and the Packard when Edward MacSwain showed up.

He stood looking away from her for a moment, then walked up to her. "I hope I haven't run you off," he said, blurting it out.

"I don't know what you're talking about."

"I don't mean to frighten you. That's the last thing in the world I want to do."

"You don't frighten me, Mr. MacSwain," she said.

He chuckled. "You ran out of there like the devil himself was after you."

"I don't know what you're talking about," she said. "I left because I have to go to confession."

A deeper chuckle. "What in the world could you possibly have to confess?"

She didn't have to come up with an answer for that; Timmy rolled up in the Packard and the doorman held the door open for her. She felt Edward's eyes on her as the car rolled away.

"I have had carnal thoughts, Father."

275

"What kind of thoughts, my child?"

"I have thought about what it would be like to be with a certain young man, Father."

"Pray to God for strength to resist these thoughts and pray to him that He will bring you together with a good Christian man in the sacrament of matrimony."

"I will, Father."

"Is that all?"

"I am heartily sorry for having offended against God's holy law."

"Say a dozen Hail Marys, and pray for God's blessing."

The first time he called her, at the house, was three days later, the same day MacSwain Truck Manufacturing Company had let the construction contract for its new Allentown plant to Kramer & Schultz.

Her father had bid on the contract, and was convinced that its award to Kramer & Schultz was one more manifestation of the Masonic conspiracy against Roman Catholics generally and Irish Roman Catholics in particular. He had just finished delivering a five-minute speech at dinner about the evils of the Masonic order, and all its branches, when the maid announced that Miss Patricia had a young gentleman caller on the telephone, and she had told him that they were at dinner and to call later.

She had known, even before she heard his voice, that it would be him. When he called fifteen minutes later, the maid stood there watching after she handed over the phone, beaming in the belief thas it was a fine young man for Miss Patricia.

"Hello," she said.

"If you're really not afraid of me, would you have lunch with me?" Edward had said, not even offering "hello."

"Who is this?" she said, even though she knew perfectly well who it was.

"Edward MacSwain."

"Oh, hello, Mr. O'Connor," she had replied for some insane reason. "How are you?"

"Someone snooping, are they?"

"I thought I had made it perfectly clear that I had previous plans," she said.

"I'll wait for you tomorrow at Bookbinder's from twelve o'clock on."

"I'm afraid that's out of the question," she said.

"If I die, right there, of starvation, it'll be on your conscience."

"That's silly," she said.

"It'll give you something to confess," he said, and chuckled, and the line went dead.

And the next morning, at ten o'clock, Patrick O'Dell stopped by her desk. "Father O'Hare left a message for you, Miss Patricia," he said. "While you were away from your desk."

"Father O'Hare?" She didn't know a Father O'Hare.

"He said he was calling to confirm your lunch."

"Oh," Patricia said. "Yes. I had forgotten. Thank you."

Now what was she going to do? If she didn't at least leave the building at lunchtime, her father was sure to ask what had happened to her lunch with Father O'Hare.

Timmy and the Packard were waiting for her that first day, too. She decided that the thing to do was meet Edward MacSwain and make it perfectly clear that he had to stop this nonsense, and stop it right now.

She pushed open the door to Bookbinder's, and when her eyes adjusted to the darkness, she saw the lobsters in their tank, and the men standing at the oyster bar, and then Edward MacSwain.

"I was afraid you wouldn't come," he said, and thrust a dozen roses at her, so quickly that she took them before she knew what she was doing.

"You're crazy, you know that?" she said.

"It came on suddenly," he said.

"I've got your table for you, Mr. MacSwain," the headwaiter said.

"I can't be seen with you," Patricia said. "I came to tell you that."

The headwaiter winked at Edward. "A very nice table," he said, and waved them upstairs to a small room with a curtained door. As she walked up the stairs, very much aware of Edward's strong fingers on her arm, Patricia wondered why she hadn't just given him his stupid flowers back and walked out the door and told Timmy that Father O'Hare couldn't make lunch.

The waiter stood there.

"Clam chowder and lobster all right?" Edward asked. She nodded her head, unable to speak.

But when the waiter had left, closing the curtain, she found her voice. "What was that Father O'Hare business all about?" she demanded.

"After Kramer & Schultz got the Allentown contract, I didn't think calling up and giving my name would be a very good idea."

"Calling up at all wasn't a very good idea," she said. "It was a very bad idea."

"I had to see you again," he said simply.

"Whatever for?" she asked.

"I don't know," he said. "I just had to."

"That's crazy," she said.

"Isn't it?" he said. He looked at her, and she fell into his eyes. Finally, actually feeling dizzy, she closed them.

Six months later, she went to bed with him, without pretense, without false modesty.

By then, he had introduced her to Sam. He hadn't told her that his cousin Samuel F. Long was Chinese. Just that Sam was his cousin, and a lawyer, and he wanted to meet her, and that he had a Chinese cook in his apartment who prepared a lunch that was food for the gods.

He had a dual, perhaps triple, motive in getting her together with Sam. He wanted Sam to be proof that his family wasn't all that prejudiced. Sam told her how he had been sent east from New Mexico and educated by the MacSwains and the Wiltons. And he told her that no matter what her father thought about a Masonic plot, Kramer & Schultz had been given the contract for the Allentown plant of MacSwain Truck Manufacturing because they had offered a price, and a construction time, that was better than that offered by James F. Herlihy.

And of course, he wanted to show her off to Sam.

They regularly lunched at Sam's apartment on Cherry Street. It was just a walk of a few blocks from where Timmy dropped her off at Wanamaker's. And no one was likely to see them together at Sam's, whereas they would likely be seen at Bookbinder's or another restaurant.

They were kissing by then, a brief passionate embrace inside the door of Sam's apartment before going in to lunch, another brief embrace as they left. He hadn't told her he loved her. That had been unnecessary.

And then one day she got to the apartment and went in, and Edward kissed her, and then he said that the signals had been mixed, that neither Sam nor the cook had apparently expected them.

He didn't wrestle her to the couch or profess a love undying. He just looked at her, and she fell into his eyes again, and she had closed the door with her foot.

She'd made the bed afterward, but Sam must have known what had happened. He hadn't been surprised, only concerned, when they announced their intention to get married.

He'd argued against it, of course, recommending instead various means of making Patricia Herlihy a suitable mate for Edward MacSwain in the eyes of his parents and hers. He had gone over all the options, methodically, thoughtfully. Edward could convert to Roman Catholicism, which would make things easier with the Herlihys, and untenable at home. He found out from someone in the archdiocese chancellery the restrictions the Roman Catholic Church placed on marriage between a Catholic and a Protestant. Among other things, they included the execution of a document requiring that any issue from the union be raised as Roman Catholics, and the moral obligation on the part of the Catholic spouse to pray for, and urge the conversion of, the other to the One True Faith.

Edward said he had a conscience, too, and while he didn't care what Patricia did for her religion, he wasn't going to have his children reared as papists, with all the attendant mumbo-jumbo. He wasn't asking her to switch, and she shouldn't ask him.

That was a moot point. By then she knew him well enough to know that he would last about fifteen minutes in the forty-hour instruction program required of adult converts to Roman Catholicism.

Edward had a hard head. He was going to leave MacSwain and go into business for himself, selling inexpensive, sturdy, well-cut clothing to workingmen. His father thought he was insane, Sam thought he was ill-advised, and they all agreed that he was going to do what he wanted to regardless of what anyone thought.

"There is one final option," Sam had said. "With some preparation, it is possible to take the 12:05 *Congressional Limited* to Baltimore, obtain a marriage license, get married, and return to Philadelphia on the 4:17 *Manhattan Express*, arriving here at 5:21."

Sam had found a sympathetic Episcopal priest, a former teacher at Episcopal Academy now with a parish in Baltimore, to marry them. He had actually quoted Saint Paul, "it is better to marry than to burn," during the service. Sam had stood up as one witness; the priest's wife and the sexton had been the others.

Patricia never had a wedding night. There hadn't been time.

They had been married four months. Nothing seemed to have changed; everything hinged on Edward getting the money to go into the clothing business. They had never spent a night in bed together. One of the afternoon sessions had been enough, apparently, to put her in the family way, and even now, when there was no question about that, nothing much seemed to have changed. She was still afraid to face her mother and father. Adopted or not, that's what they were to her, and what she had done was going to break their hearts, and she just couldn't face up to it. And Edward was no closer to getting the money he needed.

The Packard rolled to the curb on Chestnut Street in front of Bookbinder's. Timmy pulled the parking brake on with its customary screech, jumped out, and held the door open for her.

She got out and walked inside. A Stutz Bearcat skidded to a stop on the cobblestones behind the Packard. She looked at it. Oh, my God, Johnny Wilton was at the wheel. Beside him sat a large man in a sheepskin coat and a wide-brimmed Stetson hat. When he swung his feet out of the car, she saw he was wearing ornately stitched high-heeled cowboy boots.

A Buick town car pulled up behind the Stutz Bearcat. The man in the broad-brimmed Stetson and the cowboy boots looked at her appreciatively, then waved at the people in the Buick.

Patricia saw Sam behind the wheel, and ducked into the restaurant. God, now what? There was no way she and Edward could eat in here now, without Johnny seeing them.

She walked just inside the oyster bar, looking at the main entrance while shielding her face. Sam came in, and then Johnny, and then another man in Western clothes, and then the one with the cigar and the cowboy boots, and then, incredibly, Edward bringing up the rear.

She ducked inside the oyster bar.

And then Edward was standing beside her.

"Come on, sweetheart," he said. "It's time my family met my wife."

36

The whole family had turned out to meet the train bringing John Wilton, his wife, Lucille, and Kate and Albert Dennison to Philadelphia. It had been previously agreed that the visitors would all stay at 14 Rittenhouse Square, with Edward MacSwain treating the male guests, along with Sam and Johnny Wilton, to a welcoming lunch at Bookbinder's. At the restaurant, Edward excused himself for a moment while his guests followed the waiter to a private dining room. A few minutes later, the curtains parted, and a tall red-haired Irish girl, well-dressed, obviously upset, was propelled inside by Edward. A slight smile flickered across her face as she recognized Sam, but vanished as John, Albert, and finally Johnny stood up.

"A pleasure, ma'am," Albert Dennison said, breaking the awkward silence.

"Uncle John," Edward said. "Mr. Dennison, Cousin Johnny. I would like you to meet my wife."

"You can let go of her arm, Edward," John said, coming around the table to stand before them. "I don't think she'll run."

Patricia looked up at him, met his eyes. She was a little afraid of him, by reputation, and physically, by his size. He was even larger than her father.

"I don't suppose Mother and Paul are aware of this union?" John Wilton said.

"No," Edward said.

"And you're Irish? And Catholic?"

"Yes," Patricia said. "Yes, I am."

"And your parents don't know, either, I gather?"

"No," she said barely audibly.

"You might as well hear all of it," Edward said. "We're going to have a baby."

Patricia averted her eyes, lowered her head, fought back tears.

John reached out and raised her chin. She met his eyes. "The first thing we have to do, obviously," he said, "is cancel the beer. Albert, run down the waiter and have him bring us some champagne. And then I think we'd better send for Mother."

He saw the frightened reaction to that in Patricia's eyes.

"Despite what Edward may have led you to believe, I assure you Mother doesn't have fangs."

That made her smile.

"Edward," Wilton went on, "would you rather go get Mother? Or should I send Johnny to fetch her?"

"Right now?" Edward asked. Patricia turned to look at him.

"Of course," Wilton said. "We might as well get this over with." He looked at Patricia again. "Now, who would you like to face first, your father or your mother?"

"I can't face either one of them," she said.

"Of course you can," Wilton said.

"I can't!" she insisted, turning and looking again at Edward for help.

Wilton pointed his finger at Sam. "I would be very surprised if you do not know who Patricia's father is," he said. "Your silence, so to speak, has spoken volumes." Sam looked uncomfortable. "Find a telephone, and get him down here."

"Are you sure that's wise?" Sam asked.

"Get him down here, Sam," Wilton said. "Right now!"

The waiter walked in with a pitcher of beer and half a dozen glasses on a tray.

"I distinctly remember canceling the beer and ordering champagne," Wilton said accusingly.

"Sir?" the waiter said, confused.

"Take that away and bring us champagne. The best you have already chilled," Wilton said. "And then bring us lobsters, all around. Bring us at least a dozen, to start. And some oysters, I think." He looked at Patricia. "You do like lobster, don't you, my dear?"

"Yes," Patricia said. "Yes, I do." There was something reassuring about this big man with the cowboy boots and the enormous cigar.

"Go on, go on," Wilton said, gesturing with his hand for the waiter to leave. "And you two," he said, taking in Edward and Sam. "Get going!"

Margaret Wilton MacSwain swept into the room thirty minutes later, pushing the curtain aside, her eyes sweeping the room. The table was covered with dishes, oyster shells, and lobster bodies.

The men stood up. Patricia looked at her, then lowered her head.

"Mother," John said. "Thank you for coming."

She ignored him and walked to where Patricia sat. "You haven't touched your lobster," she said. "I'm not surprised."

Patricia looked up at her.

"I'm ashamed of what my son has put you through," Margaret said. "Deeply ashamed."

Patricia stood up.

Margaret put her arms around her. "And you, Sam!" Margaret said furiously over her shoulder. "How could you?"

Patricia started to cry.

"We can't have that," Margaret said through her own tears. "Your father'll be here shortly, and he'll be enough of a problem without finding you in tears."

"Mother," John said, "will you have a glass of champagne?"

"Yes, of course I will," Margaret said. "And Patricia will drink hers." She took a glass from John and gave it to Patricia. "Go on," she said. "Drink it."

Patricia took the glass in both hands, forcing back her sobs.

The curtain was brushed aside again. Kate Dennison swept into the room, followed by Olga.

"We have been sent by the WCTU to make sure . . ." Kate said, and then saw Margaret and stopped in midsentence.

"Kate," Margaret said. "I'm really glad to see you."

"So am I," John said.

"Patricia," Margaret said, "this is our dear friend Kate Dennison, and my granddaughter Olga Wilton. Kate, Olga, this is Edward's wife."

"Aren't you . . . *weren't* you Patricia Herlihy?" Olga blurted, then added lamely, "We were at the university together, weren't we?"

"Yes, I think so," Patricia said.

"Now, that's a good Irish name, *Herlihy*," Kate said brightly, walking to the champagne. "My maiden name was Shaughnessy." And then the name struck her. *Patricia Herlihy.* Oh, my God! "Is your father in the brick business?" she asked.

"The construction business," Patricia replied.

Kate forced herself to continue sipping the champagne.

"We expect Mr. Herlihy momentarily, Kate," John said. "He has yet to learn the happy news." Kate looked at him. "Of either the marriage or the upcoming blessed event," John concluded.

Kate walked over to Patricia. "Everything's going to be all right, darling," she said. "Don't you worry about a thing."

And then she put her hands on her daughter's shoulders and leaned forward and kissed her on the cheek.

37

From the moment, an hour later, that her father walked into the upstairs room at Bookbinder's, his hat in his hand, a look of concern on his face, Patricia realized she didn't have to be afraid of him. From the very first moment, she only felt sorry for him.

"Is there a Mr. Samuel Long here?" he asked when he pushed the curtain aside, and then he saw her and stopped. "Princess," he said. "What the hell is going on?"

Captain John F. W. Wilton got out of his chair and started toward James F. Herlihy, but his mother beat him to it.

"I'm Margaret Wilton MacSwain," she said.

"I know you are, all right," Herlihy said. "What I don't know is what's going on here."

"Our children have married, Mr. Herlihy," Margaret said. "And we are to be grandparents."

"Holy Mother of God!" he said, and looked at Patricia. "Darling, is what she's saying the truth?"

Patricia couldn't talk; she nodded her head, and lowered it, and then met his eyes.

"When?" he asked, and for a moment she didn't understand the question. Was he asking when she had married, or when she was going to have the baby?

Kate leaped into the silence. "I'm Kate Shaughnessy Dennison, Mr. Herlihy," she said, putting out her hand, adding, Patricia was sure, a brogue to her voice. "A friend of the family who's thinking you could use a drink."

Herlihy looked at Kate and said, "My God, how am I going to tell her mother?"

Kate gave him a glass of champagne. "Will you join us in a toast, Mr. Herlihy?" she said. "To the young people, and their baby."

"Hear, hear," Wilton said.

"May God protect and keep you princess," Herlihy said, holding up the glass. "You and your baby."

And then he broke down and wept, the tears running down his cheeks. Patricia ran to him. He got control of himself in a moment, by taking deep breaths, by force of will.

"What you may not know," he said, "is that Patricia came to us from the good Sisters of the Poor. I've always said it made my wife a better mother than if she'd carried the girl herself."

"I'm sure the proof stands before us," Margaret MacSwain said, "that Mrs. Herlihy has been a splendid mother."

"But you don't know my wife," Herlihy said. "She's a *devout* woman." He looked at Patricia. "I've never told you this, darlin', but your mother's said many a novena that you would be called to the church." Patricia didn't reply. "What I'm saying is . . . is that . . ."

"She's going to be unhappy that Patricia has married a Protestant," Margaret said.

"You don't know how unhappy," Herlihy said.

"About as unhappy as my husband is going to be when he finds out that Edward has married a Roman Catholic," Margaret said.

"You're telling me he doesn't know either?" Herlihy said. "I didn't see him when I came in."

"Patricia told me that it was going to kill her mother when she found out," Margaret said.

"And it just might," Herlihy agreed.

"Which frankly is what I thought it would do to my husband when he found out," Margaret went on. "But when Patricia used the word, I realized that was obviously an exaggeration. It will *kill* neither of them."

Herlihy looked at her. "If it wasn't for the baby, I'd grab her arm and take her out of here and . . ." He stopped suddenly, and looked around the room, finally letting his eyes rest alternately on Johnny and Edward. "Which one of you is it?"

"I love your daughter, Mr. Herlihy," Edward said. "I love her and I married her."

"I had best not say to you what's in my heart right now," Herlihy said.

"We have been discussing the young people's future, Mr. Herlihy," Wilton said.

"I'm sure you have."

"Edward believes that he can make a go of the ready-to-wear-clothing business," Wilton went on. "We have—specifically, Mr. and Mrs. Dennison have—arranged for the necessary financing—"

"So that's the way it is?" Herlihy said. "MacSwain won't want him in his business, now that he's taken up with a Catholic, is that it? Well, you needn't worry about dirtying your gloves anymore. There's a place for him with me, and to hell with all of you."

"Will you have the courtesy to hear me out?" John said very slowly, enunciating each syllable, pausing between each word. Herlihy glowered at him but said nothing, and then he sort of wilted under John's glare in the long moment before Wilton went on. "Paul has found a suitable place to establish the business in Newark, New Jersey," Wilton said.

"*Newark?*" Herlihy asked, as if Newark were the other side of the world.

Wilton held his finger up imperiously, silencing him. "And it has been generally agreed that it would be a good idea for them to go there almost immediately."

"Why the hell should they go to Newark?"

"To avoid whatever repercussions are bound to be heard from Mr. MacSwain and, from what you have said here just now, from Mrs. Herlihy," Wilton said. "Mr. MacSwain, it has been decided, is not going to be told any of this until after the ball tomorrow."

"And am I supposed to just show up at the ball, with my wife, is that what you're saying? And with Patricia, married to him, and act as if nothing whatever has happened?"

"If you could carry that off, Mr. Herlihy," Margaret said, "it would solve a number of problems."

"When Pat and Edward do come back to Philadelphia,"

Kate said, pouring champagne into Herlihy's glass, "things will have calmed down somewhat. We can't have them leaving town with the families shoutin' at one another, can we?"

"I don't know what to do," Herlihy said to Kate. He sounded beat and miserable.

"Ah, sure ye do," Kate said. "Ye want to do what's best for the girl. And this is the best, Mr. Herlihy, you can trust me on that."

He turned to Patricia. "Is that why ye talked me into going to that goddamned ball, princess? Is that why?"

"Daddy . . ." she said. "Daddy, what I hoped was that maybe I could get you to meet him there."

"Well, now I've met him," he said. "I hope you're happy, princess." He put the champagne glass down. "Let's be going." She looked at him in surprise. "Your mother will be worried about us," he said. "She's got your dress for the ball from the dressmaker's, and she'll be wanting to have you try it on."

When Patricia kissed Edward, Herlihy averted his eyes and swept the room. His eyes stopped on Margaret. "You're a fine lady," he said. "I can tell that. I can only hope you passed some of it on to your son."

Waiters passed out champagne from trays in the lobby of the Bellevue-Stratford, and encouraged the guests to go directly to the main ballroom, which had been decorated for the occasion with crossed flags—Stars and Stripes and the Union Jack—and with an enormous British Lion carved from ice.

The governor general and his party emerged from the elevator, and smiling disinterestedly, walked into the grand ballroom. The governor general was in uniform. Harold Tilley privately thought he looked like a character from an operetta, but he also had to admit that the man cut a splendid figure. The ladies beamed at him.

Dinner was served, to the strains of Handel's *Water Music*.

"Mr. Tulley," the governor general said to him.

"That's Tilley," C. Harold Tilley corrected him with restrained indignation.

"Forgive me," the governor general said. "Mr. *Tilley*. Forgive me for asking, but is that fairly common in the United

States? Those boots?" He nodded his head toward table three, that of Paul T. MacSwain and party, where the alligator cowboy boots of John Wilton and the black-and-white calf boots of Albert Dennison where clearly visible.

"Those gentlemen are from the Far West, your Highness," Harold Tilley said. "Texas and New Mexico."

"Extraordinary," HRH Prince Arthur, Duke of Connaught and governor general of Canada, said. "That table is all from the West, you say?"

"No, your Highness," Tilley said. "Just the two gentlemen in the boots, and their wives. The others are Pennsylvanians. My daughter, my son-in-law, and friends of mine, actually. I'd be happy to introduce you."

"That won't be necessary, thank you just the same."

Goddamned snob, Tilley thought. Albert Dennison could buy and sell Buckingham Palace out of petty cash.

He was therefore more than a little surprised, when the speeches were over and the orchestra began to play for dancing, to see the governor general of Canada get up without warning and walk away from the head table, right toward table three.

Harold Tilley scurried after him, and got there in time to watch the Prince, Duke of Connaught, bow to Margaret MacSwain. "I believe, Margaret," Prince Arthur said, "that I have the honor of this dance."

Margaret got up, curtsied, and said, "Sir, I am delighted."

"Well, I'll be damned," Paul MacSwain said.

John Wilton looked at his brother, Thomas. Thomas looked baffled.

"He called her 'Margaret,'" Martha Wilton said. "Her first name."

"Yes," John Wilton said. "He did, didn't he?" It was the first thing he had said to Martha in the two hours they had been together.

"I don't know how I'm going to explain this to my husband," Margaret said as they whirled around the floor.

"Think of some nice white lie," Prince Arthur said.

"I don't lie to my husband, Arthur. Not this one."

"He's good to you, Margaret?"

"He's a very good man. I love him very much."

"Well, he's obviously taken very good care of you. You're as lovely as ever."

"Yes, he has."

"The one in the boots is John?" Arthur asked, and she nodded. "Extraordinary. And he's covered with medals."

"Please mention them," she said. "He's terribly proud of them."

"And the one with the beard is Thomas?"

"Yes."

"You've done very well with them, Margaret. Thank you."

"They have done very well for themselves," Margaret said. "I'm proud of them."

Back at the MacSwain table, Kate Dennison, who had stopped by Bailey, Banks & Biddle, the jeweler's, and come out with a diamond tiara "on approval," caught Edward MacSwain's eye and moved her head.

"Now?" he mouthed. The rest of the question went unsaid: With that guy about to come back?

She nodded her head firmly. Martha saw it, looked suspiciously between them and then with unabashed curiosity at Kate Dennison. Kate flashed her a smile. Edward got up from the table and marched across the room to where Patricia sat with her family.

"Miss Herlihy," he said, "would you honor me?"

"I don't think I've had the pleasure . . ." Mrs. James F. Herlihy began, but her daughter was already on her feet and in the arms of Edward MacSwain.

"I threw up before I came," Patricia said. "I thought you were supposed to throw up in the morning."

"Well, don't throw up now," he said. "I think you're about to meet the governor general."

"Why is he dancing with your mother?"

"I don't know what's going on. But they know each other. Probably back in England."

"I'm afraid to go over there," she said. Then: "Oh, my God, I think I'm going to be sick again."

"No, you're not," Edward said. "Don't even think about it!"

He stopped dancing and led her to the table.

The greetings were stiff, except from Mrs. Dennison and Mrs. J.F.W. Wilton.

"Please join us, Miss Herlihy," Kate said. "Two Irishmen are always better than one."

"You're the most beautiful girl here tonight," Lucille Wilton said.

God love you for that, Lucy, Kate thought.

The music stopped. Margaret and Prince Arthur walked toward the table.

The men stood up.

"Sir," Margaret said, "may I present my family and friends. My husband . . ."

"A pleasure, Mr. MacSwain," Prince Arthur said, and put out his hand, shaking Paul's warmly. Then he turned to John Wilton. "I know this gentleman," he said. "Lieutenant Wilton, late of the Prince of Wales's Own Bengal Light Cavalry, if memory serves."

"Captain Wilton, your royal Highness," Wilton said, bowing in the English tradition. "Late of the First United States Volunteer Cavalry."

"The Rough Riders?" Prince Arthur said. "By God, sir, I'm familiar with your exploits."

"My wife, sir," Wilton said.

The rest of the introductions were made, and then they came to the Dennisons.

"We're almost ex-countrymen," Kate said. "I'm Irish, and so is Miss Herlihy."

"Well, then, I'm especially glad to see the both of you here tonight," Prince Arthur said, beaming. "But you'll have to excuse me, I must return to my table. It was good to meet you all, and especially nice to see old friends."

When he had gone, Margaret, as she sat down beside her husband, said, "Prince Arthur knew your father, John, Tom. I was surprised that he remembered me."

He might have known my father, John Wilton thought, but I don't think he called him, as he called you, by his first name. Very interesting. What had really happened? He stood up and bowed to Patricia. "Miss Herlihy, one of the privileges of being the rogue uncle is dancing with nephews' girlfriends, whether or not anyone likes it." She flushed but got to her feet.

"What did he mean by that?" Martha hissed even before they were out of earshot. "Edward's *girlfriend?*"

"I think she's charming," Lucille Wilton said. "Charming, and exquisite."

"My God, look what he's done now!" Paul MacSwain said. They followed his eyes. John F. W. Wilton was at the Herlihy table, smiling from ear to ear, shaking hands with the Irishmen, kissing the hands of the Irishwomen. They were too surprised to do anything but smile back, nervous and ill-at-ease.

38

Johnny Wilton, shod by French, Shriner & Urner, shirt and tie from Sulka, hat from Dobbs, suit from Brooks Brothers, all in all, about three hundred dollars' worth of sartorial elegance, stepped from a taxicab in the section of Newark, New Jersey, known as "Down Neck" outside a brick building bearing a large red-and-yellow sign reading "A COMPLETE SUIT OF CLOTHES $11.95 ONE FLIGHT UP."

He turned and helped his sister Olga from the cab.

They were allegedly in New York—Johnny on some vague business in connection with Lennai Mills, and Olga, to visit Bonwit-Teller and other stores along Fifth Avenue.

"Good God!" Johnny said, glancing around him and not liking at all what he saw.

"Behave yourself," Olga said. She took his arm and propelled him toward a door at one side of the building. It was painted in the same flaming yellow and fire-engine red, with black lettering repeating the "ONE FLIGHT UP" message, with an arrow.

"It would appear, to judge from the arrow, that Edward's customers aren't exactly sure which way is up," he said.

"Be nice, Johnny," Olga said.

Patricia Herlihy MacSwain, visibly pregnant, sat on a stool behind a cash register. She heaved herself awkwardly off it when she saw Johnny and Olga.

Olga threw her arm around Patricia's neck and kissed her.

"How are you?" she asked, and there was nothing ritualistic in her question. She was obviously concerned.

"Very, very pregnant," Patricia said.

"I would never have guessed," Johnny said. "Where is the P. T. Barnum of the dry-goods trade?"

"Stocking the racks," Patricia said. "Go look for him. He won't know you're here unless you do."

The second floor was chaotic. Along one wall were changing booths, each with signs warning customers to guard their valuables. The floor itself was tightly packed with clothing racks, galvanized-iron-pipe structures ten feet long and mounted on small wheels, with just enough room for people to pass between them.

Each rack, crammed with suits on hangers, carried a large floppy cardboard sign with the size of the clothing it held and the constantly repeated legend, "A COMPLETE SUIT OF CLOTHES, $11.95."

Johnny found Edward vigorously scrubbing a spot on a suit-jacket sleeve. "I sort of like that," he said. "Does it come in a tweed?"

Edward looked up at him and smiled but did not stop scrubbing the spot. "What brings you here?" he said.

"Grandmother dispatched me to New York to chaperon Olga. And then just happened to mention in passing that if we got off the train in Newark, it wasn't more than a ten-mile walk to your place of business."

"There," MacSwain said, satisfied the merchandise was as clean as ever. He corked the bottle of naphtha and put out his hand to Johnny. "I'm glad to see you."

"I realize that you have to sell this stuff," Johnny said. "But do you have to wear it as well?"

"There's not all that much difference between what you're wearing and this. A little more expensive material, I'll grant, but more expensive does not mean better."

"Oh, come on."

"The standard markup in a regular clothing store is one hundred percent. If they pay ten dollars for a suit, they sell it for twenty. And the ten dollars they pay is not what the manufacturer gets. Salesmen get ten percent. That means the manufacturer gets nine dollars. Out of that nine dollars, he has to buy the material, pay the cutters and the sewing-machine operators, rent the loft. Take away that, and there's not much left."

"What are you paying for these?" Johnny was, just barely, curious.

"The returns and the overruns come in at a flat seven-fifty."

"What is a return and an overrun?"

"Are you really interested, or are you just being polite?"

"I'm fascinated," Johnny said. "Compared to watching the shuttles go slick, clock, slick, clock, slick, clock, practically anything is fascinating."

"I'm about to open another store. If you really want to hear . . ."

"Tell me about an overrun suit," Johnny said.

"Well, let's say one of the outfits that makes private-label clothing is making suits for a store in, say, Akron, Ohio. Say, twenty suits. The bolt of material has enough for twenty-one or twenty-two suits, but all the store in Akron, Ohio, wants is twenty. What to do with the extra material? They make the twenty-two suits, and I take the extra two off their hands for more than they can get from the remnants man."

"But what if you need *three* suits?" Johnny asked.

"Then I have to have them made, and they cost me a little under nine dollars. I go to them, you see—they don't have to put a drummer on the road and pay him."

"And you can turn a profit selling them for eleven-ninety-five?"

"We pay very little rent. We don't have fancy stores. We don't even do alterations. We have no salesman. It's me, an off-duty cop to discourage free sampling, and Pat on the cash machine. That gives us a gross profit of twenty-five percent, hereabouts."

"Versus, you said, one hundred percent in a real store."

"We sell a lot of suits, John. We're open from seven-thirty in the morning until ten at night. Sometimes even later."

"My God, what for?"

"Because the workingman doesn't get home until six at the earliest. By the time his wife can feed and talk him into getting a decent suit of clothes, it's seven-thirty, eight o'clock."

"But half-past seven in the morning?"

"Police and firemen, bakers, people like that, get off work when others are getting up."

"You sound just like a Jew, you know that," Johnny Wilton said.

He expected a laugh, perhaps even indignation. He got, instead, a pained look.

"It was a joke."

"You know where I get most of my stock?" Edward asked. "From a guy named Abraham Levy. And you know who's holding Pat's hand? His wife. I guess he told her about what's going on with Pat's mother. Anyway, she's been damned nice to us."

"What is going on with Pat's mother? You don't mean to tell me she's still convinced God's about to strike the two of you dead?"

"Her father came to see us a couple of times a month to tell me anytime I come to my senses, there is a place for me in Herlihy Construction. But her mother won't come. So far as her mother is concerned, Pat's worse than dead."

"That bad?"

"Pat tried to write her a letter. It came back marked 're-fused.'"

"Jesus!"

"I don't understand it," Edward said. "How a woman could treat her own daughter that way."

"How about your father?"

"Pat doesn't bother him. What bothers him is that I don't want to make trucks. That's what he's mad about, and that I can understand."

"I am something less than thrilled about Lennai Mills," Johnny said.

"Then get out before it's too late."

"I've been thinking about it."

Edward didn't believe him. He didn't doubt that Johnny had been *thinking* about doing something other than working for his father, but he didn't believe that this was more than idle thought. Johnny was not what Edward thought of as a self-starter. While he might think it would be nice to be independent, there were too many things that would have to be given up if he defied his father. The polo ponies would have to go, for example, and another job would really mean a *job*, not much money, and carrying with it the requirement to be someplace at eight o'clock every morning, five days a week, maybe six, instead of showing up at Lennai when the mood struck him.

It made much more sense for Johnny to stay right where he was. It was possible (if rather unlikely) that he would meet a girl who would give him some backbone, but right now, despite the brave words, all that Johnny was doing about getting out on his own was thinking about it. Nothing more.

Edward was wrong.

At four o'clock that same afternoon, after installing Olga in a suite at the Plaza Hotel, warning her to be careful if she strayed off Fifth Avenue while shopping, and promising to meet her at half-past-seven in the Palm Court in the lobby, Johnny took a taxi six blocks down Fifth Avenue and entered an old mansion above which flew the tricolor of France.

He had with him his passport and a document issued by the United States Department of Commerce in Washington, D.C., that licensed him as a pilot of airplanes. The assistant military attaché, who was expecting him, told Johnny that his physical examination indicated he was in superb shape.

At seven o'clock that night, Sergeant John F. W. Wilton II, having been sworn into the Service de L'Air de L'Armée de France, boarded the SS *Ville de Nancy*, under orders to proceed to the Lafayette Escadrille for training.

Although now that he thought about it, it had really been stupid of him. Johnny somehow presumed that he would be instantly equipped with a uniform; he had with him only the linen he would have needed to spend the night in New York.

And he had never, in his wildest dreams, imagined that when he sailed for France he would be expected to travel in steerage, eight men to a room. They were fed, sitting on stools, off a table eighteen inches wide suspended between two poles. The entire meal consisted of bread and a bowl of greasy soup with pieces of cabbage floating limply around in it.

"Ah wondah what has happened to that fancy French cooking we heah so much about?" the young man across from Johnny, one of his eight cabin mates, asked.

"I was wondering precisely the same thing," Johnny said.

The SS *Ville de Nancy* at that moment encountered the first swell of the Atlantic. The ship lurched and bobbed.

"This jes' won't do," Johnny's tablemate said. "This jes' won't do at all."

"What are we going to do about it?"

"I don't know about you, suh," the man said. "And I must tell you that Ah have nevah regarded mahself as my brother's keepuh, but what Ah intend to do is have a word with the steward."

"I'm with you, sir," Wilton said.

"Ah pro-foundly regret having to mention this, suh," the young man said. "But mah daddy tol' me there is only one way to deal with the French, and that is to give them money. Mah own funds, Ah regret to report, will not puhmit me to have you as a guest, so to speak, as much as that would give me pleasure."

"I've got money," Johnny said, getting to his feet. He put out his hand. "John Wilton."

"Braxton Bragg Long," the Southerner said. "Ah'm happy to make yoah acquaintance, suh."

Sergeants John F. W. Wilton II and Braxton Bragg Long completed the voyage in staterooms, 11c, 11d, and 11e, on the boat deck, first class. Two of the staterooms were equipped with double beds, and there was a couch in the third, their sitting room, large enough to accommodate a body. On a rotation basis, the six other young Americans bound in steerage for the Lafayette Escadrille and what they truly believed was glory spent alternate nights in first class, and augmented the steerage food with vast quantities of hors d'oeuvres and delicacies made available gratuitously to first-class passengers.

Well-tipped stewards and a kitchen crew aware that *les braves Americains* were on their way to fight for La Belle France saw to it that none of the eight lacked for creature comforts.

At Cherbourg, before they were loaded onto unheated, wooden-seated third-class coaches for transportation to the flying school, cablegrams were delivered.

Johnny Wilton received three:

YOUR FAMILY IS PRAYING FOR YOUR SAFE RETURN. LOVE, FATHER.

WE HAVE NAMED OUR SON AFTER YOU. EDWARD AND PATRICIA.

MAY THE STRONG RIGHT HAND OF GOD SUSTAIN YOU AND PROTECT YOU AND GIVE YOU VICTORY. WE'RE ALL IMMENSELY PROUD OF YOU AND I AM WITH YOU IN SPIRIT AS YOU MAINTAIN THE WILTON SOLDIERLY TRADITION. MORGAN BANK PARIS WILL HONOR YOUR DRAFTS. CAPTAIN AND MRS. JOHN F. M. WILTON.

"Ah like the long one," Braxton Bragg Long said after they had exchanged cablegrams. " 'Specially that part about the Morgan Bank. Ah jes' converted how much the French are going to pay us into real money, and we're going to need it. He always talk that way? Sounds like a preacher."

"Whatever my Uncle John is, he's no preacher," Johnny said. "He was a Rough Rider. In Cuba with Roosevelt."

"Well, Ah'll be damned," Braxton Bragg Long said.

Olga Wilton told her grandmother that she wanted to start back early, as she wanted to stop by Strawbridge & Clothier before she caught the train to Wallingford. The MacSwain chauffeur dropped her at the main entrance to the department store and ran ahead of her to push the revolving door for her.

She thanked him and went inside. She walked to the nearest counter, which displayed purses, and pretended to examine them until she was sure that he had enough time to get back in the Pierce Arrow and drive off.

Then she went out the revolving door and crossed Market Street to City Hall, an enormous building occupying the whole of the square at the intersection of Broad and Market streets. The building was quadrisected by passageways. She entered the passageway aligned with Broad Street and walked through the building and then up North Broad Street to Hanneman Hospital. She turned down Cherry Street, and at the intersection of Cherry and Fifteenth streets entered the Hanneman Delicatessen.

The Hanneman Delicatessen had only proximity to relate it to the Hanneman Hospital. It was, William had told her, inarguable proof of the inedibility of the food served in the medical-staff cafeteria of the Hanneman Hospital. The Hanneman Delicatessen, he had explained, had achieved the sort of success it wished by judicial pricing. It was a little too expensive for interns and student nurses, who would have cluttered up the place over coffee, and a little bit below the salt for the senior staff physicians. It was just right for residents and registered nurses, who were finally making a living wage and who were kept so busy that they gulped down the high-protein food and quickly made place for others.

William had brought Olga there the day they'd met. The day she had, she supposed, allowed him to pick her up on the train from New York. The day Johnny had run off and joined the Lafayette Escadrille.

A Western Union boy had delivered a telegram to her in the Palm Court of the Plaza. It had been typically Johnny: he hadn't wanted to face her.

She had caught the 8:55 *Congressional Limited*. There had been no seats, except in the extra-cost parlor car, and William had been in the chair opposite the one to which she had been shown.

She had modestly averted her eyes, of course, although she had noticed he was a nice-looking young man, well-dressed, with an intelligent face and somehow sad eyes, and he had been a gentleman for at least thirty-five minutes, or until they were pulling out of the station in Newark.

Then, out of the blue, holding his drink in his hand, he spoke to her. "You have all the earmarks of someone who expected to be traveling with someone, and is not," he said. "What did he do, miss the train?"

She looked at him, but of course she did not reply.

"You also have all the earmarks of a well-bred young woman who had been instructed never to talk to strangers in public places," he said. That made her want to smile. "My beloved mother," he went on (and made her wonder if she had smiled, and he had seen it, and saw it as encouragement), "made three exceptions when giving those wise instructions to my beloved sisters. They were permitted to talk to three categories of strangers when in distress. Policemen, clergymen, and physicians."

Olga had felt herself coloring.

"The first two, of course, one can recognize by their uniforms," he went on. "How Mother expected the girls to tell the difference between a bank robber and a practitioner of the healing arts was never very clear to me, however."

"You're a doctor?" she asked.

He fished a calling card from his vest pocket. William L. Galvin, M.D. "What happened to your boyfriend?"

"My *brother*," she said, "has joined the French Army."

"Oh, God!" he said. "Young men and their dreams of glory."

She had nodded, and he went on, "May I offer you something to drink?" When she apparently showed reluctance in her eyes, he added, "A Coke, if nothing else. Actually, I would prescribe a hot toddy."

"I really shouldn't," she said. "But thank you. I'm really afraid to go home."

"So am I," he said, and she sensed he hadn't intended to say that. She looked at him quizzically.

"I have just been informed that my wife will require hospitalization, or at least custodial care, for an indefinite period."

"I'm very sorry," Olga said.

"I have no idea why I told you that. I had no right to."

"Two unhappy people," Olga said. "May I ask . . .?"

"She lost a child, and went into what is known as postpartum melancholia," he said. "She's in a hospital in Hartford. I just came from there. They offered me a position on the staff. Her family, and mine too, probably, are going to wonder why I don't take it. But that's the point—I couldn't take it."

"What kind of a doctor are you?"

"An obstetrician," he said. "In Philadelphia. And what do you do?"

"I'm graduating from Penn June two," she said. "BA in music."

She had two (or was it three?) hot toddies on the train, but that wasn't the reason it happened. Why had it happened? It seemed preordained.

There were no advances on the train, no off-color remarks, nothing like that. At Broad Street Station she told him she would stay in town, "so I'll have to wake up my grandmother and spend the night with her. On Rittenhouse Square."

"Would you like something to eat first?" he said. "It's just a block or two in the other direction. It's open all night. A Jewish delicatessen."

She nodded, somehow aware that she was agreeing to more than something to eat.

It was the first time she had ever had chopped chicken liver on rye bread in her life. It came with half of an enormous dill pickle and a burning-hot white china mug of coffee. She had three cups of coffee so that she wouldn't be drunk.

"You're not expected?" he asked.

She shook her head, not trusting herself to speak.

"You know what I'm asking," he said. "Even if I don't have the courage to put it in words."

For the first time she touched him, shyly putting out her hand to rest her fingers on the back of his hand, and then closing her fingers over his.

He had a tiny efficiency apartment on North Sixteenth Street. "As the senior obstetrical resident, I am furnished with a place at the hospital." He laughed. "Fortunately, I'm rich and don't have to live there."

Afterward he said, "Good God, why couldn't you have been some well-bred slut? Why did you do it?"

He made reference to her lost virginity; he was a doctor—he knew.

"We needed each other," she said. She put her hand on his face, as shyly as she had put her hand on his hand. He caught it and kissed it, and she felt him start to cry, and held him to her, his whiskers rough against her breast, until he stopped.

It was simply presumed the next day that she had spent the night in New York and come out on the first train in the morning. She expected him to call, and when in six days he didn't, she went to the Hanneman Delicatessen and just waited until he showed up. And then they went back to his little apartment, and they didn't talk about anything at all until he had made love to her. And the second time was different from the first. The second time, it seemed to be the most natural thing in the world for her to do. There was no shame

303

at all. She knew that she gave him pleasure and peace, and she had never felt more alive in her life.

When she walked into the Hanneman Delicatessen, William, in a white coat, a stethoscope hanging from his loose white jacket, stood up when he saw her. When she sat down, he pushed a plate with a pastrami sandwich on it over to her. "Would you believe that I have four women up there?" he said by way of greeting.

"It doesn't matter, I can't stay anyway."

"It matters to them," he said. Their knees touched under the table. She smiled at him as she picked up the sandwich.

When she got home this evening, she vowed, she was going to work on her father again. He had said something last night about a war with Mexico. The Mexicans had massacred sixteen Americans. If there was going to be a war, there was going to be a need for nurses. There was no reason she could not be a nurse. Her father would see that, and her father would handle her mother. He seldom put his foot down, but he would now, because she was right. She was not going to sit out the war doing something stupid like knitting scarves.

She was going to do something that would permit her to spend more time with William. She had found her man, even if he was married to someone else.

39

An officer of the United States Army, booted, breeched, wearing a Sam Browne belt with brass fittings (but no sword), the insignia of a major, and the embroidered wings of a military aviator, walked out of the American embassy in Paris, returned the salute of the dress-uniformed U.S. Marine guard, and turned left toward the Tuileries Gardens and the Place Vendome.

On Rue de Castiglione, he turned into the Hotel Continental. He rode to the fourth floor in the wrought-iron cage elevator, and then walked down the corridor to 411–413.

He knocked at the door. There was no reply. He knocked again, this time with the hard end of his riding crop. This time there was a response. *"Pas d'entree! Allez avant!"* The language was incorrect, and the accent atrocious. The major pegged it as North Carolina.

He rapped on the door with the head of his riding crop again.

The door opened to reveal a tanned, hung-over American in a nightshirt. Even a nightcap.

"My name is Mitchell," the major said. "I'm attached to the French Army as an observer. I'd like to see Lieutenant John Wilton."

"You would like to ob-serve John Wilton?" Braxton Bragg Long inquired. He flung the door open, threw his arm wide. "Observe away, Major, suh!" he said.

Lieutenant John F. W. Wilton II, commanding officer of

the Troisième Section, Escadrille No. 103 (more popularly known as the Lafayette Escadrille) of L'Armée de L'Air, holder of the Medal Militaire, the Croix de Guerre with Palms, Officer de la Legion de L'Honneur de France, lay in bed. On this cold January morning in 1917, Lieutenant Wilton was on his back, stark naked, sound asleep, and snoring.

"Is there any chance we can wake him?" Major Mitchell asked.

Braxton Bragg Long walked over to the bed and spilled cognac on Wilton's head. "That will also serve to kill the cooties," he said solemnly.

Wilton woke suddenly and sat up. "You son of a bitch, what did you do to me?" he demanded.

"We have a visituh," Braxton Bragg Long said. "Who has been standing here, obsuhvun' you for the United States Ahmy."

Johnny focused his eyes on Major Mitchell. "Who the hell are you?" he asked unpleasantly.

"My name is Mitchell," the major said. "I'm a friend of Colonel John Wilton."

"Jesus," Wilton said. He scooted down the bed, climbed out, and walked into the bathroom.

"How long have you been in Paris?" Major Mitchell inquired of Lieutenant Long.

"Four, five days," Braxton said. "They give you seven days with the Legion of Honor."

"The Legion of Honor is very impressive," Mitchell said.

"It gets you seven days in Paris," Braxton said. "That's very impressive."

"You two fly together?"

"We used to," Long said. "I've always been his wingman. But now that I'm an officer, I suppose they'll make me take a section."

Wilton came out of the bathroom, wrapping a soggy towel around his middle. He looked at Major Mitchell. "What's this all about?"

"I brought you something from your uncle," Major Mitchell said. He handed Wilton a package wrapped in oiled paper, a foot long, six inches deep, three inches wide, tied with waxed cord. Wilton took it wordlessly and unwrapped a

Colt .45-caliber single-action Peace Maker revolver and a cheap, thin leather holster.

"What the hell am I supposed to do with this, do you suppose?"

"Your Uncle John and Lieutenant Patton went bandit-hunting in a Dodge touring car," Mitchell reported. "They came back with Mexican bandits on each fender, like deer, and a couple of pistols. That's one of them."

"My Uncle John is a goddamned fool," Wilton said. "He thinks war is . . . I don't know what, a fucking game!"

"He's a pretty good officer," Mitchell said.

"You were bandit-chasing with him?" Wilton asked. "He wrote they had a couple of airplanes."

"We used them mostly for observation," Mitchell said. "They were very useful for that. And for messenger service. When we could get them in the air."

There was no response to that from either Wilton or Long.

"The Mexicans, of course, didn't have any aircraft," Mitchell said, "so we didn't gain any experience in air-to-air combat. The only Americans who have it are the people in the Lafayette Escadrille."

"You ought to go talk to them," Braxton Bragg Long said. "I'm sure they'd love to talk to you. You go to Chalons sur Marne and—"

"I've been out there," Mitchell said, smiling. "They sent me to talk to you."

Wilton said, "I don't want to talk about flying with you, or anyone else. In two days we have to go back. I don't want to even think about airplanes until then."

"I've always liked to talk about flying," Mitchell said.

Wilton gave him a look of utter disgust. "There were sixteen guys who came over here with us," he said. "You know how many are left? You're looking at them."

"Then you must have been doing whatever has to be done right," Mitchell said.

"You know how much training we had? Since you like talking about flying. Six goddamned flights, that's how many. Then some Frog showed us what a dog fight was supposed to be. Then they sent us out. The guy who was supposed to be my flight leader had gotten himself shot down the day before I got there. So I didn't have anybody to show me what I was supposed to do. *I* was the flight leader, and Brax here was my wingman. Why we didn't get shot out of the sky in those first few days, I'll never know."

"What about the Germans? Are they good?" Mitchell asked.

"Good? You bet your sweet ass they're good. And that tri-wing Fokker makes square turns." Wilton grimaced. "Jesus, I have to get something to eat. Brax, get that fucking waiter in here and get us some food."

Brax walked to the door, opened it, and bellowed, *"Garçon! Gar-çon!"*

"I don't know what you mean by a square turn," Mitchell said.

Wilton flashed him a look of contempt. He held his hands in the air, fingers together; they had become airplanes. "I'll tell you what it means. You bust your ass to get behind and above him, because he's faster than you are, unless you're in a dive. And then you make your dive, and just when you get him in range, he makes a turn, a *square* turn." He demonstrated with his hands.

Major Mitchell knew he had won. He had got Wilton to talk about flying. Once he started flying with his hands, he wouldn't stop talking. Pilots were all alike.

40

In the car that carried him from the Penn Dennis Club, where he had lunched as the guest of Frederick J. Peterman, vice-president for traffic operations of the Louisville and Nashville Railroad, Albert Dennison, chairman of the board of the Dennison Oil Company, had experienced unpleasant indigestion.

It was surprising. All he had had to eat was a bowl of clear broth, a sliced tomato, and a small medium-rare steak. He was trying to lose a little weight, and a small lunch like that should have gone down smoothly.

The doorman held open the door of the Cadillac for him, and he walked quickly across the sidewalk, for the icy wind was cutting. He put his hand on his mouth and tried to belch. It didn't work, although he wanted to burp and could feel the pressure of the gas in his abdomen.

He had been heading for the desk to pick up his key, but turned and headed for the barroom. A little belt, washed down with a glass of soda water on the side, would quickly set things in order.

Two steps inside the barroom, Albert Dennison suffered a rupture of the carotid artery, which branches off the aorta and supplies blood to the brain. He was conscious long enough to sense that he was falling, to cry out, "Damn!" but he was dead long before the bartender could rush to his side.

Frederick Peterman, when he learned of Albert's death, attempted telephoning John Wilton, but Wilton was not in Dallas. He was out on his ranch. Then the mayor of Louisville called Colonel Wilton personally. Peterman had told him Wilton was not only the president of Dennison Oil but also Mr. Dennison's best friend, and the best man to tell the widow.

The colonel said if the mayor could have a local undertaker prepare the body for shipment and get it onto the *Prairie View*, he would take care of things from that point on.

Albert Dennison was carried aboard the *Prairie View* on a stretcher by two Louisville police officers. After a discussion with the steward, the body was laid on a bed in the master suite and covered with a royal-blue blanket on which were embroidered Dennison's initials.

Funeral services were held at Holy Trinity Protestant Episcopal Church in Dallas, a parish to which Mr. Dennison had made frequent and generous financial contribution, although he was seldom able to worship there of a Sunday. The bishop of the Diocese of Texas presided.

As large as Holy Trinity was, there was some trouble getting all the floral tributes into the nave; some spilled over into the aisles. The governor of Texas read from the Holy Gospel, and served as one of the ten active pallbearers (there were twenty names on the published list of honorary pallbearers). In addition to the white-and-black-robed choir of Holy Trinity, there was a purple-and-gold-robed forty-strong choir from the First African-Methodist-Episcopal Church of Dallas, who sang "Swing low, sweet chariot, coming for to carry me home" at the conclusion of the service, as Albert Dennison was carried down the aisle.

Albert got to make another trip on the *Prairie View*. Kate Dennison decided to bury him beside her first husband, in the small cemetery at Waxahachie.

Kate watched as the casket was loaded aboard the car, her arm on that of Colonel John Wilton, and then she bent and kissed the cheek of Mrs. John Wilton, who (understandably—it's a marvel that poor woman gets around the way she does) was not up to making the trip to Waxahachie. Then she got on the *Prairie View* and went directly to her compartment, leaving Colonel Wilton to see to the comfort of the pallbearers.

Albert was put into the ground in time for the pallbearers to catch the 6:12 local back to Dallas. Kate Dennison stayed behind, and Colonel Wilton remained to comfort her in her sorrow.

"You really didn't have to stay," Kate said to John in the parlor of the house at Waxahachie.

"I'll stay as long as I'm needed," he said.

"Or until we get to bed, whichever comes first."

"My God, Kate! How can you suggest—"

"Oh, stop it."

"Okay," he said. "Guilty."

"I was just wondering," she said, "when Albert found out about us."

"Good God! You really think he did?"

"Of course, he did. Albert was no fool, whatever else he was."

"I don't see where we're going to gain very much from pursuing this line of conversation."

"We never do pursue this line of conversation," Kate said. "All we do . . ."

"If I didn't know better, I'd think you'd been, well . . ."

"Drinking? Of course I've been drinking. What did you think I was doing in my compartment on the way down here?"

He didn't reply.

"And I did some thinking about us," Kate said. "You and me."

"What kind of thinking?"

"Maybe I was just flattering myself," Kate said. "Maybe all I really am for you is convenient sex." She saw his face stiffen. "Haven't you ever thought about Lucille, John? Haven't you ever wished you didn't have her around your neck?"

"She is my wife," he said. "I'm responsible for what happened to her. I don't think of her being 'around my neck.' "

"And you've never wished she weren't around?" Kate said. "That's what I thought. It's not very pretty, but that's what I thought; now that Albert's gone, if only Lucille were gone too . . ."

"You're drunk," he said. "You don't know what you're saying."

"Would you, John? If you were free, would you marry me?"

311

"I don't know," he said truthfully.

"That's better than an 'of course' that you wouldn't have meant."

"I suppose I would," he said. "Yes, I suppose I would marry you. But that's the end of the conversation. I've had enough of this."

She laughed nastily and walked from the parlor. "So have I, my friend," she said, pausing at the door. "That's what I was really thinking about on the train on the way down here. I've had enough of us, too."

"You're drunk," he repeated. It was all he could think of to say. "Be careful on the stairs."

The buckboard and two sturdy cowboys were waiting at the siding at Rancho San Miguel when Lucille returned alone from Dallas. The cowboys came onto the parlor car, and after first loading the luggage and the wheelchair onto the surrey, they made a seat with their hands and wrists, and Lucille sat on it, and they carried her, with practiced skill, off the train and to a place where they could shove and push her onto the seat of the surrey.

She fastened the straps in the back of the seat around her bosom and waist, and then took the reins. Before she went to the house, she went to the cemetery to see if the plants and trees had been watered in her absence.

Then she drove down to the house. Juanita and Dolores took the wheelchair from the rack on the back of the surrey and set it up on the veranda. Lucille hoisted herself from the surrey into the wheelchair and then rolled into the house.

She went to her bedroom and had Dolores help her undress down to her slip, then dismissed her. When the door was closed, she worked the slip up over her hips and pulled it off over her head. Then, naked, she rolled herself into the shower stall and hoisted herself from the wheelchair onto the bench John had built for her in the shower.

She usually avoided looking at her legs. The muscles and fat had long since atrophied; she was nothing below the waist but skin and knobby bones. She pinched some of the skin, and lifted it up, and then let it fall again, and shook her head. She had long ago vowed not to dwell on her physical condition.

She turned the water on, adjusted the temperature, and washed herself beneath the steady flow. Then she turned off the water and dried her hair vigorously, then hoisted herself back into the wheelchair. She rolled into her bedroom and put on a robe only; there was no need in the house to wear anything more, and the robe itself was enough trouble to get beneath her, and then to straighten, and then to button.

She rolled out of her bedroom and down the corridor to the office. There had been some mail in the few days they had been gone, and she opened and read it.

The longest letter was from Margaret MacSwain, who was sure Lucille was glad John was back from soldiering in Mexico. He was too old for that, and one John Wilton off at war at a time was more than enough.

Lucille wasn't sure about that. If she had her way, of course, neither her husband nor her nephew would have gone off. But John had come back reluctantly, despite his loudly announced relief that he was glad *that* was over. She knew him well, and as he had given her a day-by-day account of the Mexican punitive expedition, she had understood how much it had meant to him. The regulars, from General Pershing on down, had gradually come to accept him as one of their own. He was a good soldier, a good officer. Lucille wasn't surprised. John was a man of many talents, even if most of them were beneath the surface, hidden by an apparent childishness.

He loved being called Colonel. His new "Lt. Col. John F. W. Wilton, VC, DSC" calling cards had arrived at the ranch before he had. His friends smiled behind their hands. But the point was, he had earned that right. If circumstances were different, he was fully qualified to be a full-time colonel; it was not an affectation in polite society.

Lucille knew how much it had cost him to decline General Pershing's offer to continue on active duty and plan for the massive buildup of the U.S. Army the American entry into the world war would require. She believed John, despite what others said, that U.S. participation in the war was inevitable. He hadn't gone, or stayed on, because of her.

That might have been a blessing in disguise. With Albert gone now, John was going to have no choice but to take over the company. Not that Kate couldn't run it herself, woman or not, but because there had to be a man as titular head. John could run the company because he could run people.

She replied to Mother MacSwain's letter, describing the funeral and mentioning her belief that John would now have to take an active role in Dennison Oil Company. And she added a line that she was sometimes in pain.

She answered several other letters, unimportant ones, wrote a half-dozen checks, cleaned up the business on the desk. And then, after a moment's thought, she wrote a final letter.

Then she rolled herself over to the gun cabinet, took her father's Merwin & Hulber revolver, the one he had carried with the Second Georgia Cavalry, from its pegs. There was a can of DuPont's FFFG powder in the drawer, and a box of bullets, and a box of caps. She had a pleasant memory of her father, when she was just a little girl, showing her how to load it. Forty-one grains of powder was the most accurate load, she had been taught.

She thought again what a damned shame it had been that she hadn't been able to give John children. He would have been as good a father to their children as her father had been to her. And all he had was Thomas' children. It seemed to be their luck that the child named after John was the most useless of the lot. She had never said anything to John, of course, but she had never liked Johnny, even as a small child. He looked like John, and acted like John, but he was a weakling, and there was a mean, selfish streak in him. To which, of course, John was quite oblivious.

The measure screwed to the top of the DuPont can was already set for 41 grains of FFFG. She worked the measure, putting the powder in one of the chambers in the revolver's cylinder. There were no patches. She rolled herself back to the desk, took scissors from a drawer, rolled back to the gun cabinet, and cut a circle of cotton from what had once been a petticoat and had been cut up for use as patches. The round she cut was nearly a perfect circle, and of just the right size. She was pleased with it. She laid the patch over the chamber, pushed a 240-grain round ball against it, hard enough so that it was stuck in position, and then used the lever to ram the bullet home in the chamber.

Then she set a cap in position. She put the revolver on her lap, closed the drawer that held the powder and the bullets and the cotton and the caps. Then she rolled out of the office, down the corridor to her bedroom, through the bedroom, and into the shower.

She held the pistol in her right hand, and forced the hammer back with her left. Then she put the barrel in her mouth and pulled the trigger.

41

Paul T. MacSwain died of cancer on October 11, 1918, one month to the day before the armistice in France. He had complained most of the summer of arthritis, pains in his joints and muscles, and had begun to lose weight. In late August, with carcinoma of the liver the most probable diagnosis, an exploratory operation was performed. His condition was inoperable; he was closed up.

The pain was very bad toward the end, although he was given ever-increasing dosages of morphine and other painkillers.

The closest Margaret came to tears in his presence was when Edward and Patricia brought the baby to see Paul in his hospital room. He had refused painkillers so as not to be, as he put it, *foggy* when he saw his grandson for the first time. She knew (she *felt*) the agony he was in, especially when he had the bed cranked up to hold him semierect. He took the child and held him up.

"I'd leave you the company, little fella," Paul said, "if I didn't think your crazy father would liquidate it and use the money to expand his clothing empire."

There were now four Thrifty Scot clothing stores. But it was hardly an empire.

"Dad," Edward said, "if that's what you want, then, okay, I'll sell the stores and go to work for the company."

"Good God, sometimes I wonder if you're mine. I don't want you to run it for me. I want you to run it for yourself,

316

and for that child in your arms, and the one Patricia is carrying."

"Paul," Margaret said. "Do we have to talk about this now?"

"It'll be hard to talk about it when I'm in the ground."

"Father MacSwain!" Patricia said. "Don't say that."

They all managed to laugh.

"But if you mean that, Edward," MacSwain went on, "I'll have Sam Long draw up a will giving your mother the income from, and voting rights in, the stock during her lifetime or until such time as she decides that you are capable of voting the stock yourself. On her death, the stock will pass to your children."

"What you're saying," Edward suddenly said almost angrily, "is that you want me to run a company that won't be mine."

"You miss the point," his father said. "I don't own MacSwain Truck any more than you own your cheap-clothing stores. All I have is custody of it until it's time to pass it on. I want to impress that point on you, the responsibility that goes with ownership, or what they call ownership. You've never had to worry about meeting a payroll."

Margaret wondered why he had stopped, whether the pain had been too much. She wished this confrontation was over, even knowing that it had to have happened.

"What would you do with your rag business?" Paul went on.

"I'll find someone to run it for me," Edward said. "I have an obligation to the people I hired."

"Yes, you do. That's what it's all about."

"Haven't we talked about this enough for now?" Margaret asked.

"We've got to finish our business," Paul said. "Thomas was here to see me. To let me know he would accept the presidency of MacSwain."

"Paul!" Margaret was shocked.

"I think Martha was behind it," MacSwain said. "Since Lennai Mills closed, she's apparently had second thoughts about his cutting off his nose to spite his face. I told him that I had offered the presidency to Sam. I would have liked to see her face when he reported that to her. Anyway, if he weren't so pigheaded, the mills would still be open and he wouldn't need a job."

"He made the threat, Dad," Edward said. "He had to carry it out."

"Unions are here to stay," his father replied. "Tom should have known that. And he should have known that in a wartime economy, with jobs going begging, a threat to close the plant if they struck it was meaningless. And he was a damned fool to think I would turn my company over to him."

And then he groaned, as if a sudden wave of pain had come unexpectedly. With a motion of her head Margaret ordered the others out of the room and took her husband's hand.

"Good God, Maggie," Paul said. "I can't take much more of this. Why the hell doesn't God take me?"

Squeezing his hand, unable to trust herself to speak, even if she could think of something to say, Margaret reached for the button that would summon the nurse and her hypodermic of painkiller.

When Paul had had his shot, when his hand grew limp in hers, when his eyes hazed over and his mouth sagged open and he went into what was as close as he could come to sleep, Margaret went out in the corridor to where Edward and Patricia waited.

"We've talked it over, Mother," Edward said. "Pat can run the business. I'll just stay here."

Margaret kissed her daughter-in-law. "No," she said. "Thank you, but no. You go on home. When you get there, telephone Sam. Tell him what you and your father agreed. Make arrangements for your business."

Paul MacSwain died two weeks and three days later. Edward was with him every waking moment for the last five days of his life, but by then his father was so full of narcotics that they never had another chance to talk.

The Reverend Dr. Lawton Steele Houghton was brought from retirement to preside at the funeral, which was held across Rittenhouse Square from the house, in Holy Trinity, rather than at St. Mark's. Holy Trinity was a good idea—there would have been no way to get all the mourners into St. Mark's—but the Reverend Dr. Houghton was not. He was senile and had to be prodded through the service by "assisting" priests.

Margaret wasn't listening to what the old man had to say. She had come to her own terms with Paul's death and with God. She told herself it was a blessing he was gone, free of that agony. She believed that if there was a heaven, Paul was now in it. She was grateful to her God for having given her Paul for the years they had had. And if she was a sinner for wishing she could go with him, then so be it.

Edward sat with her, with Patricia and little Jeremiah on the other side. Tom and his family sat in the pew immediately behind, Martha weeping loudly from beneath a heavy veil. Directly across the aisle, in the pews reserved for the pallbearers, actual and honorary, unaware or uncaring, sat James F. Herlihy, defying the edict of the archbishop of Philadelphia that good Catholics do not participate in heathen worship services, even funeral services for worthy Protestants.

Halfway through Reverend Dr. Houghton's rambling funeral oration, there was a stir behind her. Margaret looked over her shoulder. Kate Dennison, her red hair swept upward against a black hat, a full-length ermine coat on her arm, walked down the aisle.

She laid a hand heavy with diamonds on Margaret's shoulder, and Margaret, through tears, squeezed her hand. There had been a telegram from Kate from San Francisco, and Margaret had automatically assumed she would not be able to get from San Francisco to Philadelphia for the funeral, that because of the distance, she wouldn't even try.

A wave of sympathy for Kate swept through Margaret. Kate had buried two husbands; she knew what it was all about, being left alone. And Kate was really alone; there were no children, no family. Margaret wondered again why Kate and John didn't marry.

Margaret MacSwain was pleased with what she saw when she came down the stairs at Rittenhouse Square after the burial. Harold Tilley, James F. Herlihy, and Kate Dennison (holding little Jeremiah on her lap) were standing at the bar set up in the drawing room. Paul had been Harold's best friend for many years, and he was taking Paul's death very

319

badly. Margaret had made a point of speaking to James F. Herlihy at the cemetery, asking him to come by the house. She didn't believe for a minute that he would come. But here he was, making Harold chuckle. Paul would like that, she thought. And the way Kate Dennison had taken over responsibility for Jeremiah from Patricia, who was so very pregnant, was doubly pleasing. It relieved Patricia of the nuisance of a baby, and it made Kate feel more a part of the family.

Martha Wilton intercepted her mother-in-law at the foot of the stairs. "I'm sorry you had to see that," she said. "I was about to take care of it."

"I beg your pardon?"

"A baby in one hand, and whiskey in the other. Telling jokes after a funeral. I suppose you should expect that from the Irish. But I can't imagine what my father is thinking."

Margaret didn't trust herself to reply. She walked across the room to the bar, the refectory table covered with a cloth, and with the cook's son pressed into service as bartender.

"I'll have a little whiskey, please," she said. Harold Tilley put his arm around her. Margaret reached out for her grandson. Kate gave him to her.

Martha came up, white-faced. "Give me that child, Mother MacSwain," she said. "I'll have him taken care of."

"He's being taken very good care of by Mrs. Dennison," Margaret said.

"Is something the matter, Martha?" Harold Tilley asked his daughter.

"I don't like to see my father and my mother-in-law making a public spectacle of themselves, is what's the matter with me."

"It seems to me that you owe my guests, not to mention your father and me, an apology, Martha. And I'll have one, too, thank you," Margaret said icily.

"Not from me you won't!" Martha said, and turned to her father. "You should be ashamed of yourself." She spotted her husband. "Tom," she called loudly enough to be heard all over the crowded room, "get the children and our things. I won't stay where I'm not welcome."

Three weeks later, Martha came calling, unannounced. Margaret had more or less expected her. She found Margaret on the floor of the parlor at 14 Rittenhouse Square, with Jeremiah beside her, beating on a saucepan with a wooden spoon.

"If you don't mind my asking," Martha said with a smile, "why don't you get him a drum? Since you apparently don't mind the noise."

"The saucepan is a compromise," Margaret said, getting up and allowing her cheek to be kissed. "What he really would like to have is a pile of mud."

"Patricia's gone out?"

"Patricia's in Newark," Margaret said. "Taking care of business."

"I thought Edward had come to his senses about that," Martha said. "But actually, I'm glad she's not here. I'd just as soon not have a witness to my humiliation."

"What could you possibly be humiliated about? Let's have some tea," Margaret said. "Or perhaps something a little stronger?"

"Tea, please."

Margaret, the baby crawling after her, went to the corridor and softly called to her maid to bring tea for Mrs. Wilton. Then she went to the bar and helped herself to a brandy.

"You are bearing up remarkably well, Mother MacSwain," Martha said. "We are all proud of you."

"I don't really have much choice, do I, Martha? Now, tell me what's on your mind."

"It's about finishing the children's education," Martha said. "I just don't see, in our changed circumstances, how we can manage."

Margaret didn't reply. She knew what was coming.

"And frankly," Martha went on, "we rather expected that they would be remembered by Paul in his will. They always thought of him as their grandfather, and I suppose they expected him to feel the same way."

"Paul loved your children, you know that."

"He did not mention them in his will." Martha put Margaret's notion to rest with that inarguable logic.

"If he didn't," Margaret said, "it was probably because he thought they were already comfortable, financially speaking."

"Well, they're not. There is absolutely no money at all."

Margaret exhaled. She bent over to the baby, put the

wooden spoon in his hand, and picked up her brandy. "Paul did, in fact," Margaret said, "look upon my grandchildren as his own. And when it became apparent that he wasn't going to be with us much longer, he had a talk with your father about them."

"Oh?" Martha said, brightening.

"They agreed that because of your reduced circumstances, they would take over the expense of the children's education between them. They were speaking of George and Alice. Olga's self-supporting in nursing school, or just about, and Johnny, of course, is a man. Unfortunately, Tom flatly refused their offer."

"That was only foolish pride speaking," Martha said. "Obviously, our income is not what it was when the mills were open. All we have is the rents from the houses."

"Martha, they could hardly argue with your husband."

"Tom has no idea what things cost."

"I don't know what to say," Margaret said.

"I was thinking perhaps you could let me have some money. No one would ever have to know."

"I couldn't do that, Martha. I couldn't go behind Tom's back. He would never forgive me if he found out."

"He wouldn't have to know."

"He would find out," Margaret said flatly.

Martha tried tears next, sobbing as she said she just didn't know what they were going to do. But when it became evident that Margaret was not going to change her mind, she stormed out of the house, announcing that her father would understand the predicament Margaret's fool of a son had put his family in.

42

Colonel John F. W. Wilton was obviously surprised to see the group assembled in New York to welcome him home from Europe. Margaret MacSwain was not at all surprised at the obvious. As a matter of fact, she had often thought it would be very nice indeed if Kate and John got together. The gathering in the Dennison Oil apartment in the Plaza Hotel included Kate, Tom Wilton, (Martha had stayed home), Sam Long, and even C. Harold Tilley, who shook John's hand for a full five minutes and said they had to have room service bring them up something to celebrate. Champagne, perhaps something even stronger.

"When is Johnny coming home?" Thomas Wilton asked. "For that matter, why didn't you bring him home with you?"

"It doesn't work that way, Tom," John said. "You come when the army sends you home. It'll be three weeks, maybe even four or five, before he even gets his orders."

"You're home," Tom said. It was an accusation.

John took offense, but chose to turn it into a joke. "I am both a colonel and an important civilian," he said. "I managed to convince General Pershing that if he failed to send me home *tout de suite,* the Dennison Oil Company would fail and throw the entire country into a depression. Johnny, alas, is nothing more than a hero, doomed to holding court in the Ritz Bar for his admirers, mostly feminine."

"I don't see why he couldn't have been sent home with you," Tom pursued. "You could have arranged it, I'm sure."

"I could have arranged it, Tom, by knocking some other young officer, equally anxious to get home, off the shipping list. I really couldn't work up a good deal of sympathy for Johnny. Spending six more weeks, whatever it takes, in Paris is hardly a hardship."

Kate Dennison was angry, and feeling the forty-five-year-old cognac John had brought home with him. "If the money he's spending is any way to judge, he's having himself a high old time over there," she said.

Wilton flashed her a warning look, but it was too late.

"I don't quite follow that," Tom Wilton said.

"It's a long story, Tom," John said. "And not really important. He'll be home soon enough in any event."

"I want to know what Kate meant by that."

"All right," John said. "Wars are not fought on the battlefield alone, Tom. Some of the most vicious battles are between allies, and fought over the dinner table."

Tom looked at him but said nothing.

"After doing his share, and then some, in the shooting war, Johnny was transferred to the political war. I don't want to go into details, but his duties required that he maintain a standard of living quite impossible on a captain's pay. I arranged for his expenses to be taken care of from funds the company had in France."

"I don't have the faintest idea what you're talking about," Tom Wilton said, "but I don't like the sound of it."

"I saw to it that he had an expense account. You can understand that, can't you?" John said, a little drunk himself, and tiring of the discussion. "Sam, tell Tom what an expense account is."

"I don't like the idea of Johnny taking charity from you," Tom said.

"Don't be an ass, Tom, it wasn't charity at all. Because he was my nephew, he was put into a situation where he would have been damned uncomfortable on his captain's pay. I saw it as my responsibility and I took care of it. I'm sorry it came up. I didn't expect any thanks, but neither did I expect to catch hell over it."

"Be glad," Margaret said, unwittingly pouring gasoline on the flames, "that John was there to see that he had the money, Tom."

"What's that supposed to mean? That I can't provide the money my family needs?"

"I meant nothing of the kind," Margaret said, but it was too late.

"I know what all of you are thinking," Tom burst out. "You're thinking I made a damned fool of myself with the mills—"

"Now that you mention it," Colonel John Wilton said.

"John!" Margaret said.

"Well, goddammit, Mother," John said, and now he was angry, "if closing down a profitable, smoothly running business doesn't make him a damn fool, what does it make him?"

"It wasn't smoothly running," Tom said. And then, furiously: "Don't tell me about business, you strutting peacock. If your girlfriend's husband hadn't found oil, you wouldn't be so high and mighty."

"You're right," John said, and he was angry now to the point where his voice was low and icy. "Without Albert, I would probably be down to my last ten or fifteen thousand head of cattle. But I'll tell you this, Tom: I wouldn't have shot the cattle and left them to rot on the prairie just because my ranch hands wanted to form a union. As stupid as I am, I know better than that."

"I've got one thing to say to you," Thomas Wilton said. "To *all* of you. I want you all to keep your noses out of my family's business. I want you to leave me and my children alone."

"Now, now," Harold Tilley said placatingly. "Isn't this getting a little out of hand?"

"You're damned right it is. It's gotten out of hand. It is out of hand. I will not have you going behind my back to my children! I just won't have it!"

"Oh, for Christ's sake!" John said. "What the hell is the matter with you?"

"What's the matter with me? What's the matter with me?" Tom shouted. "You all make me sick, that's what's the matter with me! Laughing behind your hands at me. Humiliating me!"

"How did anyone humiliate you?" Margaret asked compassionately.

325

"You know," Tom replied darkly. "You know very well." He looked directly at Sam but said nothing further.

"What you need, brother," John said, "is a little of this ancient French brandy."

"That's your solution to everything, isn't it? A little snort. Have a drink."

Wilton looked at their mother. "What the hell started all this?" he asked almost plaintively.

"Thomas, get control of yourself, you're saying things you don't mean," Margaret said.

"I meant every damn word I said," Tom said. He slammed his hat on his head and stormed out of the suite.

"I'll go after him," Harold Tilley offered.

"You can't reason with someone in that mood," John Wilton said. "Is he really losing his mind?"

"John, what a dreadful thing to say!" Margaret said, but she had been wondering precisely the same thing. "You set it off with that sarcastic remark of yours."

"What sarcastic remark?" he asked in honest confusion, and then remembered. "You mean when I agreed he had made a damned fool of himself closing the mills."

"You shouldn't have said that," Margaret said.

"It's true," Tilley said. "That's exactly what he did. He made a damned fool of himself."

"You're damned right he did," Wilton said righteously.

"Tom had his reasons," Margaret said loyally, aware that she was being a hypocrite. "What probably set him off today was his disappointment at finding his son hadn't come home with you."

"Your grandson, Mother," John said angrily, "has a lamentable tendency to use people. The reason he's not here is that I found out he used my name to have himself returned early from France. When I found that he'd done that, I arranged to have him declared essential. I also shut off his allowance."

"Oh, John!" Margaret asked. "Does he know?"

"I made a point of telling him," John Wilton said. "That scene was almost as uncomfortable as this one."

"I should imagine," Margaret said.

"The reason he wanted to come early was so that he could join the Dennison Oil Company," John said. "In a suitable executive position, of course. Since his father had cut off his own nose to spite his face, and Lennai Mills no longer needed a vice-president, he had to look elsewhere."

"And are you going to take him into the company?" Margaret asked.

"I offered him a job as a trainee," John said. "Either in Texas, at the home office, or in our international department. We're going to move into China, and into French Africa and the Belgian Congo."

"Well, I'm sure he'll do well," Margaret said.

"A trainee position is apparently far beneath Captain John Wilton's assessment of himself. It's probably just as well. Tom would have taken offense anyway."

"Well, he's young," Harold Tilley said. "He's just come through a war . . ."

"We haven't heard from you, Sam," John said. "What glad tidings do you bring?"

Sam held up his brandy glass. "Welcome home, Colonel," he said.

"Sam, why don't you and I go out to the ranch, make up a pack train, and spend a couple of weeks in the mountains?" John asked.

"I'd love to," Sam said. "I really would. But I can't get away right now. All the military contracts have been canceled, of course, and we're in the process of sorting things out. I just can't get away."

"No, of course you can't," John said, and smiled at him. "Just a crazy notion."

Margaret Wilton wasn't sure which of her sons she was most sorry for.

43

Johnny Wilton arrived home from France on an icy February day in 1919, to an equally chilly reception from his family. His mother spent most of her time complaining about their lack of money and her husband's lack of sense.

Thomas Wilton *was* a little odd, to be sure. He had announced that he was now retired, and planned to devote himself to the rose garden at Wallingford. Man-to-man, he told Johnny that he had enough put away, which, together with the rents from the workers' houses at the mills in Lennai, would be enough to put food on his table for the rest of his life.

He had, he told his son, with something of the fervor of a religious fanatic, spent the best years of his life turning a run-down factory into a successful business, supplying honest work at fair wages to an ungrateful flock of peasants, who had repaid his good works by forming a union.

He had told them, he said, that if they formed a union after all he had done for them, he would simply close the mills. They had, and he had. He had personally closed the valve feeding oil to the steam engine that powered, through a series of overhead pulleys and straps, the looms. Cloth still hung from the looms.

They could starve, for all he cared.

As delicately as he could, Johnny suggested that now the war was over, and jobs were scarce, his father could more than likely get the workers to come back.

"Never!" his father said. "Once burned is enough for me."

That was a pity, Johnny decided. It would have been nice to go back on the Lennai Mills payroll, at least until he got his feet on the ground. He had some money, his terminal pay, but it wasn't going to last long.

There would be no problem with any of the children, his father announced. Olga would graduate this spring as a nurse and would have no trouble finding employment. Alice would sooner or later marry a rich man. George had already gone to work for his grandfather's newspaper. "And you, of course, are a young man with unlimited opportunities before you," he told his elder son.

Martha decided that the answer to Johnny's future lay in a suitable marriage. She went down a long list of well-to-do young Philadelphia women whom she considered right.

He would take a wife, and with the wife, a suitable position. All he had to do was make his presence known. He was, after all, the scion of a very prominent family. That sort of thing counted. "You know how much money Paul MacSwain left your grandmother?" she asked. "More than she can possibly spend in her lifetime, and with more coming in all the time. And Grandfather Tilley is a wealthy man, too. And do you think either of them is willing to help us out, now that we've fallen on hard times? I went, practically on my knees, to them, and was flatly turned down. My own father suggested we sell the big house and move into an apartment in Philadelphia. Can you believe that?"

"Why don't you? What do you need this big place for?"

"Because of your crazy father, that's why. He has the notion that we have all the money we need. He won't hear of giving up the big house."

"I didn't think you wanted to."

"Well, how would it look if we did? How is Alice going to find a husband if everyone knows we're on our uppers?"

Johnny paid a call on Edward MacSwain at the offices of the MacSwain Truck Manufacturing Company, hoping Edward would make him an offer of employment. He did, but it wasn't what Johnny expected.

"I don't know what your plans are, of course. But if you'd like to consider managing one of our clothing stores until you decide, Patricia's always on the lookout for bright young men used to exercising authority and leadership."

Patricia was paying the bright young men she hired a beginning salary of $22.50 a week, a drawing account against commissions on gross sales.

There was nothing open at MacSwain Truck. They were, Johnny would understand, still pulling in their horns from the wartime days. They had to let go men they really wanted to keep. "The only thing I could offer you would be something on the floor of the plant itself, or as a clerk in the office. You wouldn't like it. Not after what you've done in the war."

"Just an idle thought," Johnny said with a smile.

"You'll find something, I'm sure," Edward said. It wasn't a put-off. The simple son of a bitch really believed it.

Johnny had been home two weeks when there was a telephone call from Braxton Bragg Long.

"How did it go?" Johnny asked Braxton about his homecoming in North Carolina.

"Ah don' even like to think about it. My Uncle Gowan wanted to put me in a Fo-hd automobile and send me around the country nailing up tin cigarette signs."

"What are you going to do?"

"Goddamned if Ah know. But Ah was sorta hopin' that you'd like to do it with me."

"Where are you?"

"In the Algonquin Hotel on Forty-fourth Street in New York."

"I'll be in just as soon as I pack a bag," Johnny said.

The hotel room was also occupied by a dog, a seventy-pound, heavily panting animal with liver-spotted fur who was, Braxton Bragg Long informed Johnny, a Morgan hound.

They sought employment in the afternoon. In the evening they drank, and in the morning they slept. There was not very much in the way of suitable employment available for young men whose only real talent was flying airplanes.

Johnny visited his Princeton classmates, but they were neither especially happy to see him nor interested in finding him a job. He was offered trainee positions (simply because he was Princeton) at a bank and at two stockbrokerage firms.

"A stockbroker is a used-car salesman," Braxton said, "who has learned not to blow his nose in a napkin."

330

Braxton found employment first. He was taken on as an assistant account executive with Porterfield, Braswell & Dale, Advertising.

"They were impressed not only with my academic record at the University of North Carolina," he said, "and my medals and silver wings, but with the fact that Uncle Gowan and Aunt Eloise own that tobacco company."

"They want that business and think you can get it for them?"

"There's as much chance of that happening as there is of you getting them the Dennison Oil account," Braxton said. "But, yes, that's what I've led them to believe. I've also put in a good word for you, pointing out that you are extremely close to your loving, childless uncle, Colonel John Wilton."

Johnny Wilton entered the employ of Porterfield, Braswell & Dale in the mail department. The salary was $17.50 per week, five dollars less than he had been offered to become a manager trainee in one of Edward MacSwain's off-the-pipe-rack clothing stores. But as Brax pointed out, not only was there a greater chance of advancement, but in their financial condition, $17.50 was a figure not to be ignored.

44

"Here she is, Kate," Margaret MacSwain said, sliding the door to the study at 14 Rittenhouse Square open. "What did I tell you she'd be doing?"

Patricia MacSwain, pregnant for the third time that spring of 1919 got awkwardly to her feet from behind a desk littered with invoices, cash receipts, and other business papers. A secretary, a mousy-looking young woman with her hair drawn tight against her skull, looked in awe at Katherine Dennison; she had never before seen a lady smoking a cigarillo.

"What's the matter with you, child?" Kate said.

"*Nothing's* the matter with me," Patricia said. "Did you get Uncle John off all right?" Margaret and Kate had just returned from New York, from seeing Colonel John F. W. Wilton off to Africa, where he would oversee the expansion of the Dennison Oil Company's small operation there.

"He sends his love," Kate said. "You should be in bed."

"I feel fine," Patricia insisted. She walked to Kate and kissed her on the cheek. "I don't want to be in bed. And besides, someone has to do all this." She kissed her mother-in-law. "Edward has his hands full at the factory."

"Your mother-in-law and I are about to have a drink of whiskey," Kate said, putting her arm around Patricia. "I wanted one on the train, but your mother-in-law was convinced that she would be mistaken for a painted lady if we went to the parlor car without gentlemen escorts."

"I said nothing of the kind," Margaret said, chuckling as she walked to the bell cord and rang for a maid. "What I said was that I was in mourning, and it wouldn't look right."

"You should be Irish," Kate said. "Tell her, Patricia, that being in mourning is all the excuse an Irishwoman needs to hit the bottle."

The maid appeared, and Margaret ordered drinks.

"Bring them into the sitting room," Kate ordered. "And we'll get the princess here into a chair, and her feet up on something."

"Aunt Kate," Patricia said, "I'm not made out of glass. I feel fine." But she allowed herself to be led from the study across the corridor to the sitting room.

"Let's keep it that way, then," Kate said. "If you don't give me any trouble, I'll give you a little nip of my whiskey. A little one."

"I'm not sure I should."

"The day John was born," Margaret said, "I had half a bottle of brandy."

"If I could be sure this would be the day, I'd drink half a bottle of brandy, too," Patricia said.

"What does the doctor say?"

" 'You're coming along just fine, Mrs. MacSwain,' " she said, mimicking the doctor.

"That's all they ever say," Margaret said, laughing. "I invited Sam for dinner," she added. "He'll be on the seven-fifty-five train, so we'll have to hold the food awhile. What I'm saying is, dinner will be late."

At ten minutes to eight the next morning, James F. Herlihy walked out the front door of his red colonial brick house in Jenkintown, acknowledged Timmy's cheerful "And a good morning to you, Mr. Jim" with a smile, and got in the backseat of the Packard. Timmy ran around the front of the car, got behind the wheel, and drove away from the house.

A moment after the Packard turned the corner, moving out of sight of the Herlihy home, a Pierce Arrow, which had been parked by the curb half a block away in the direction opposite from Herlihy's route to his office, came to life and began to move.

It turned off the street, past the brick columns and the steel fence, and drove up the curved driveway to the Herlihy home.

The chauffeur ran and opened the door. Kate Dennison got out, a small boy in her arms, warmly dressed against the cold. She marched up to the white-painted door, her mink coat scraping the stairs. She slammed the brass knocker twice, and then ducked her hand and tweaked the boy's nose. He giggled.

A black butler in a gray jacket answered the door.

"May I help you, madam?" His eyes took in the mink, and the hat, and the diamond stomacher, and the chauffeured Pierce Arrow on the drive.

"Katherine Dennison to see Mrs. Herlihy, if you please," she said.

"I'm not sure madam is home, madam."

Kate pushed the door open wide and pushed him out of the way. "I know she's home. You just go tell her I'm here." She stepped inside the vestibule, glanced momentarily around, and then walked into the foyer proper.

The butler went farther into the house. Kate adjusted the blanket on the boy, freeing his face and chest and arms. He grabbed for her earrings.

"Little devil!" she said, and tickled him again, making him giggle.

Mrs. Herlihy, in a dressing wrapper, came out of a door near the end of the foyer and walked until she was about six feet from Kate and the baby.

"Mrs. Dennison," she said coldly.

"Ah, Mrs. Herlihy. I'm glad that you remember me."

Mrs. Herlihy nodded.

"And this young fella is Jeremiah MacSwain," Kate said. "Patricia's boy."

"What is it you wish, Mrs. Dennison?"

"Looks something like her, doesn't he?" Kate said. "I thought I should give you a look at him, Mrs. Herlihy. I understand you haven't seen him before. Or his sister, Ellen."

There was no response.

"I'm taking care of him for a little while," Kate said. "It makes me feel something like a grandmother. It's a grand feeling, Mrs. Herlihy. A grand feeling."

"Will you please leave my home, Mrs. Dennison."

"The reason I'm allowed to take care of him is that at five minutes past six this morning, Patricia's water broke, and we took her to Hanneman Hospital to have her baby."

Mrs. Herlihy turned white, but she said nothing.

"Jeremiah's about to have a baby brother or another baby sister," Kate went on. "Whatever God wants him to have."

"Stay here as long as you wish." Mrs. Herlihy turned around and started toward the wide stairs leading to the second floor.

She was halfway up the stairs before Kate shouted, "May God damn you, you cold-blooded, blackhearted bitch!"

Mrs. Herlihy hesitated, but neither stopped nor looked back. The sound and the fury of Kate's curse scared Jeremiah. He took a sudden deep breath, squared his lips, and started to howl.

Kate, a look of shock on her face, quickly kissed him, and then, hugging him to her breast, half ran out of the house and down the stairs into the open rear door of the Pierce Arrow. By the time she settled him on the seat beside her, he was giggling again.

The official records would call what was happening an *ad hoc* meeting of the executive committee of the board of directors of the Dennison Oil Company, listing as participants Colonel J.F.W. Wilton (who was at the moment four days out of New York for Casablanca), chairman of the board; Mrs. Katherine S.S. Dennison, secretary; Mr. Samuel F. Long, counsel; and Mr. Marvin Shapiro, general manager, Eastern Region, the Dennison Oil Company, four members of the seven-man executive committee constituting a quorum.

What it consisted of, meeting in a small conference room on the tenth floor of a ten-story, narrow, somewhat old-fashioned building on East Forty-first Street in New York City, was Sam Long telling Kate of certain legal problems involved in the recent acquisition of the Howell filling-station chain (forty outlets) and Marvin Shapiro telling Kate of the practical problems and costs (replacing the Howell signs, for example, and repainting the service stations in Denco's familiar red-and-white color scheme) of getting in operation.

A similar meeting of the executive committee had been held in Dallas just before Kate had come with John Wilton to put him on the ship. The records of that meeting—concerning the acquisition of drilling rights on several hundred thousand acres of land in Oklahoma and Kansas and the setting aside of twenty-million dollars to finance the African expansion—showed that Kate, Wilton (who had actually been at Rancho San Miguel), and Charles Broadhead and Theodore Hallworth, president and vice-president of land management, had constituted a quorum.

Both meetings were actually the presentation to Kate of situations requiring a decision. There was discussion, and recommendations were expected, but it never would have entered anyone's mind to put a dispute or a decision to a vote. Decisions were made by Kate Dennison. It was presumed (correctly) that in making decisions she kept in mind her own intimate knowledge of how Wilton would have moved had he been present. It would have been wrong to conclude that she was acting independently because Wilton was neither concerned nor interested. Even when he was away, he had received notice of upcoming problems, and when his ship docked in Casablanca, there would be a coded cable or cables waiting for him, keeping him abreast of what had happened at this meeting or any others that would follow.

It would have been equally wrong to conclude that Kate was acting in his stead. They simply agreed on most things, most of the time. She had disagreed about spending all that money in Africa, for example, but that was the first genuine argument they'd had in some years. And Marvin Shapiro, when she'd asked him what he thought, had told her he thought she and the colonel were doing the right thing, and since she trusted Marvin's judgment, she was willing to admit she was wrong. Besides, John pointed out, the company didn't need both of them to run it.

Marvin had been the first employee of Dennison Oil in New York. Albert had hired him twenty years before, when they were going to need someone just to be in New York. Albert had been astonished at the large number of Jews he had met in New York, and decided that since the company would have to deal with them, the best person they could hire to do that would be another Jew. Thus Marvin Shapiro had been chosen, and installed in a one-room office, four months after his graduation from CCNY as an accountant.

In this very building. The first office was now a storeroom for the purchasing department, and the single room had grown to five of the ten floors in the building. Marvin's title, general manager, Eastern Division, which had been something of a joke when he'd joined Dennison as the only employee of the Eastern Division, had never been changed. It was officially recognized as giving him vice-presidential status, and unofficially as a bit more prestigious.

Eyebrows were sometimes raised by new executives in Dallas when they learned that Dennison was represented by a Jew in New York, but they were quickly given the word: not only did Dennison have a Jew, it also had a Chinese. Don't mess with either; there was nobody closer to the throne!

The question Mrs. D. was going to have resolve now, once Sam had laid out the facts for her, was whether to proceed with the Howell property as it was now, that is, about half company-owned, and about half rented, or whether to start on a program of either buying up the rented stations or closing them out when their leases ran out, and buying property to replace them.

Marvin Shapiro didn't care what was decided, he could handle it either way. And it was half a dozen one way and six the other. He was getting a little tired; they'd been at one problem or another of the Howell acquisition for four hours. It was time to break for lunch.

His secretary (a stenographer took notes in here; his secretary ran things when he was in conference) hesitantly opened the door, saw that he wasn't talking, and walked in and handed him a business card.

The card was printed: "John F. W. Wilton II, Executive Vice-President, Long, Wilton Advertising, Inc.," with a Madison Avenue address. This must be the son of the crazy brother, the one named after the colonel. Long, Wilton, *Advertising*? What the hell did he want?

Kate had seen his eyebrows raise in surprise. "What's that, Marvin?" she asked.

Marvin handed her the business card.

"Interesting," she said. "*Very* interesting. Executive vice-president? The last I heard, he was sorting mail."

John F. W. Wilton II looked convincingly surprised to see Katherine Dennison and Sam Long in Marvin Shapiro's office.

"Well, Aunt Kate," he said, "I really didn't expect to see you here."

She kissed him on the cheek. "Surprise, surprise, Mr. Executive Vice-President," she said. "I'm impressed."

"I'm in the advertising business. Don't believe everything you see in print."

"I don't. What do you want from Marvin?"

"I was hoping to see Mr. Shapiro alone," Johnny said. Then: "I didn't mean that the way it sounded."

"How did you mean it?" Sam asked. He was annoyed at the interruption.

"I wanted this to be strictly business."

"That's the way it will be," Sam said. "Shoot."

"Okay," Johnny said. "Mr. Shapiro, we've learned that Denco has acquired the Howell chain of service stations in New Jersey. And Long, Wilton would like a chance to get the advertising account."

"Long who?" Kate asked.

"My partner, Braxton Bragg Long," Johnny said. "We were in the Lafayette Escadrille together."

"What do either of you know about advertising?" Sam asked.

"Well, to tell the truth, I don't know very much. Oh, I've written some copy, but basically all I know about it is that it's a fine place to make a lot of money. Brax, on the other hand, really has a flair for it. He's one hell of an idea man."

Neither Kate nor Marvin Shapiro said anything. They waited for him to go on.

"We've gone out on our own, you see, away from Porterfield, Braswell & Dale."

"How are you doing?" Kate asked innocently.

"To tell you the cold truth, we only have one account so far," John said disarmingly. "Edward's pipe-rack-clothing stores."

"Well, I suppose you have to start someplace," Marvin said.

"When we get some solid experience behind us," Johnny said, "we hope to get the Carolina Tobacco account."

"Which just happens to be connected with Long in some way?"

"Well, yes, his aunt and uncle own it."

"Looks like you're set, then," Sam said. "What do you want from us?"

"I want the business of your new filling stations," Johnny said. "And when you hear my proposition, I think you'll give it to us. We'll do it for nothing. For expenses."

"How are you going to get rich doing that?" Sam asked, laughing.

"We're going to get rich from Carolina Tobacco. But we're not going to get Carolina Tobacco until we prove we can do the job."

"You're a schemer," Kate said, not unkindly.

"I guess so." Johnny smiled.

"So was the man this company is named after," Kate said. "That wasn't a criticism. There's only one flaw in your reasoning that I can see."

"What's that?"

"You don't have enough experience."

"We're going to buy that," he said. "Once we have the account, people who are working for companies like Bobson, Tree and Savage will be glad to come to us."

"I see you've done your homework," Marvin Shapiro said.

"So everybody comes out ahead," Johnny said. "You get at least as good as you've been getting . . . and I wasn't kidding about Brax. He's really an idea man, and you get him, too. We'll work at cost. And we're one step closer to Carolina Tobacco."

"Did you say you have Edward's clothing-store account?"

"Yes," he said, although that was completely untrue. He was going to get Edward's business *after* he had the Denco business. The Denco account would be his proof that somebody had faith in Long, Wilton Advertising.

"We have some rough ideas worked up," Johnny said. "Could I call back when you've had time to consider our proposal? I don't want to put you on the spot. What I'm really saying is, I hope you won't say no right now."

"Call Mr. Shapiro in a couple of days," Kate said. "It's his store."

"Thank you," Johnny said humbly. "And now that business is over, would you be interested in having dinner with a couple of eligible young bachelors, Aunt Kate? I'd like you to meet Brax."

"Oh, I'd like to, Johnny," Kate said, "but I'm going to have to get back to Philadelphia. I'm helping Margaret take care of Jeremiah and Ellen while Patricia's in the hospital."

"I'm going to try to get out this weekend," Johnny said. "Girl, wasn't it?"

"Seven pounds, four ounces."

"Splendid," Johnny said. "Well, I'll let you get back to work. And thank you, Mr. Shapiro."

45

Long, Wilton Advertising opened offices at 383 Madison Avenue, New York, one month and two days after Johnny Wilton called on Marvin Shapiro. Johnny circled the date in red on his calendar: October 5, 1920. After a moment, he added a large exclamation point.

He had not been surprised when he paid a second call on Shapiro and was informed that Mr. Shapiro had not only decided to give Long, Wilton the business to advertise the taken-over chain of Howell gas stations, but that Dennison would pay for the service "when billed." That is to say, in advance.

In his time in the mail room, Johnny Wilton had learned the advertising business was not all, despite popular belief, large highly skilled (and highly paid) teams of brilliant people engaged in the preparation of full-page advertisements in *Collier's* magazine or the *Saturday Evening Post* for multi-million-dollar corporations.

It was far more often one man in a small corner of an advertising agency sharing an artist with six people just like him, preparing small advertisements for marine pumps that would appear in *Coastal Shipping News*. Or advertisements for an ingrown-toenail medication that would appear in a column-inch of space on a back page of magazines and newspapers.

The people who did this sort of work believed, not without reason, that it took as much skill to prepare an ingrown-toenail-medication one-column-incher as it did to prepare a full-page ad for one of the variations of aspirin. They felt unappreciated and underpaid, which was often the case. As important, they had often established personal relationships with the manufacturer of the marine pumps or with the pharmacist who had concocted the ingrown-toenail nostrum.

After dinner in Johnny's and Brax's penthouse, with drinks on the patio overlooking Central Park; after hearing from Johnny Wilton his flattering appreciation of their skill; after hearing that the policy of Long, Wilton would be promotion from within; and that in recognition of their potential, they would start off as a vice-president, the people Wilton privately thought of as the gnomes were perfectly willing to believe that their future would be bright with Long, Wilton, even though (since they were just starting out) their salary as a vice-president wouldn't be much higher than they were presently taking home.

In a matter of months, Long, Wilton had enticed eleven account executives away from their previous employers, made them all vice-presidents, and added their fifty-seven clients to the growing roll of Long, Wilton clientele.

It had become progressively easier to solicit other business. The people they had hired were, in a surprising number of instances, quite capable of handling bigger accounts. What was even more surprising was that Brax actually turned out to be not just capable, but even brilliant.

Johnny regarded himself as the best possible judge of advertising. If an ad grabbed him, it was grabbing Mr. Average Customer. If it didn't grab him, it was no goddamn good. It was as simple as that.

The leaves had already begun to turn on the trees in Central Park the day that the Misses Alice and Olga Wilton got out of a taxicab in front of the apartment building and stood on the curb as the driver unloaded luggage from both the trunk and the baggage compartment beside the driver's seat.

The doorman carried the luggage inside the lobby. "May I announce you?" he asked.

"The Misses Wilton for Mr. Wilton," Olga said stiffly. "The penthouse, I understand."

The two women each picked up suitcases, one in each

hand, and walked to the elevator. The doorman quickly decided that it would cause a scene if he made them wait until they were cleared, and that the pair of them seemed to be who they announced they were, even if he wasn't sure whether the older one had said she was "Mrs. Wilton" or that they were the two of them, the Misses Wilton. He picked up his telephone and called the penthouse. "Two ladies coming up for Mr. Wilton," he said.

The butler was out, doing the morning's shopping. The door was answered by the Jamaican maid.

"Good morning," Olga greeted her. "Is Mr. Wilton up and about? I am Miss Olga Wilton."

"No, ma'am," the maid said. "The master is not up."

"Would you go to him, please, and tell him that his sisters are here?" Olga ordered. She handed the maid her coat, and turned to look at Alice.

Alice appeared on the edge of tears. "I'm so ashamed," she whispered.

Olga didn't reply.

It was several minutes before John F. W. Wilton II appeared. It had been necessary for him, on being informed that his sisters were *in the penthouse* (Christ, didn't they ever hear of telephoning first?), not only to get the woman with him dressed and out the service entrance but also to check in Brax's bedroom to make sure his playmate was gone. It was possible that since they had come together, Brax's friend would wait for the other one.

He was in the process of putting emerald links in the cuff of his shirt when he finally walked out of the corridor to the bedrooms and into the enormous two-level sitting room with the view of Central Park and the apartments rising on Fifth Avenue across the park.

"Good morning, girls," he said. "To what do I owe the honor?"

Alice started to sniffle.

"Olga, what the hell is the matter with her?" Johnny asked. "What's the matter with you, Alice?"

"Do you always get up this late?" Olga asked.

"Hello, Johnny," Alice said. "Your apartment is just beautiful."

"Alice is in a little trouble," Olga said.

He looked at Olga for a long moment, then at Alice, then back at Olga. " 'A little trouble'?" he asked. "Is that the same thing as 'in trouble'?"

"She's not pregnant, thank God," Olga said.

"Oh, Johnny," Alice said. "Don't look at me that way!"

He looked away in embarrassment. "You want to explain this?" he asked. He saw the maid. "Get me a cup of coffee, please," he said. "Get coffee all around. Everybody want some coffee?"

Alice started to sob again. Neither her brother nor her sister made any move to comfort her.

"There was a letter," Olga finally said. "To Alice. Dad read it."

"What kind of a letter?"

"From one of her boyfriends," Olga said. "A very stupid letter.

"A *love* letter, is that what you're saying?"

"In a way," Olga said.

"Was it or wasn't it?" Johnny asked. "What the hell, she's old enough to get a love letter. And Dad is upset? Is that what this is all about?"

"That's what it's all about," Olga said.

"Who's the guy, Alice?" Johnny asked. He was amused.

"Pietro Santelli," Alice said very faintly.

"Who?"

"Pietro Santelli," Olga repeated for her. "The rehearsal pianist at the Academy of Music."

"He's a tenor," Alice said, "not only a rehearsal pianist."

"A rehearsal pianist? Named *Santelli?"*

"The reason he wrote the letter," Olga said, "was that our baby sister stood him up. I gather she's grown tired of having him 'worship her magnificent breasts.' "

Alice began to cry again, more of a howl of anguish than sobs.

"And of whatever else she let him do to her," Olga concluded.

"Have you been . . ." he began, and stopped, and then went on, "sleeping with this fellow, Alice?"

She nodded her head.

Olga handed a thick six-page letter to him.

He had difficulty believing that Alice could have provided

the imaginative sexual gratification her "adoring Pietro" described in such flowing terms.

He asked the only question he dared: "How did Dad get hold of this?"

"He just took it and opened it," Alice wailed.

"And?"

"Got in the car and went into town and attacked him with a cane," Olga said. "In the foyer of the Academy of Music."

"My God!"

"She has to get out of Philadelphia," Olga said. "So we came here."

"Why can't she move in with you? If it's a question of money . . ."

"She has to get out of Philadelphia," Olga repeated. "And I . . . I'm already living with someone."

"What do you mean by that?"

"Just what I said," Olga said defiantly. "I'm living with someone."

"You mean with a man," he said.

"Yes, with a man," Olga said.

"What the hell am I going to do with her?" Johnny asked rhetorically.

"All you have to do is give her a place to sleep," Olga said. "Grandmother MacSwain says she'll pay for her to study here. *If* you give her a place to live."

"Grandmother knows too, huh? You really did it up brown, kid, I'll say that for you."

"Johnny, I don't know what to do," Alice said, looking at him through tear-filled eyes.

"She has to get out of Philadelphia," Olga repeated again. "And there's no place she can go except here. With you. You're her brother."

When he thought back on it later, Johnny Wilton realized that he had arranged for a voice teacher for his sister Alice, not out of any belief that she could sing (the only young woman he knew from his milieu who did anything serious was Olga, and Olga had always been strange; the others studied music and art and literature to kill time until they got married), but to keep her occupied. When he told his secretary to find voice teachers, he specified females.

He went with Alice to Carnegie Hall, to a large-bosomed

Hungarian, and came away from their conference in the belief that Madame Czerny was a genteel confidence artist. After listening to Alice sing, she had pronounced, "Zis childt, vit a lodt of hardt verk, a lot of study, can become a goodt zinger. Maybe nodt a great zinger, but a very goodt zinger."

Alice was enrolled at the Juilliard School of Music. That came to two hundred dollars for an enrollment fee, and a hundred a month. Madame Czerny was five dollars an hour, four hours a week. Six men from Steinway spent a full day erecting a block and pulley to haul a concert grand piano up the outside of the building. The only place the piano would fit was where the bar had been.

Johnny sent the bill for the piano to Rittenhouse Square. Three days later there was a check from the First Philadelphia Bank & Trust for more than the price of the piano, and a note from Margaret MacSwain:

> Dearest Johnny:
> I'm sure there have been expenses in addition to that of the piano. The check enclosed should take care of them. If you will send other bills as they occur directly to the bank, you will be reimbursed.
>
> God bless you both,
> Grandmother

Alice's presence in the apartment, although Johnny had to admit that she tried to accommodate herself to him and Brax, caused a number of changes. Obviously, it was no longer possible for them to bring young women of their acquaintance home after a night on the town. Tuesday through Friday, Madame Czerny arrived promptly at nine in the morning for Alice's lessons. That made sleep impossible. There was an implied obligation to provide her company, as well as the unspoken responsibility on Johnny's part to make sure she didn't bring home a piano player from Juilliard to play with.

Brax uncomplainingly assumed his shares of the baby-sitting, even taking Alice to the Metropolitan Opera and Carnegie Hall, for one cultural event or another that Johnny was willing to pass over, but which were important to her education.

Alice had been with them six months when she and Brax

came home from a Lotte Lehmann recital of Schumann lieder at Carnegie Hall with an announcement..

"We've got something to tell you, old buddy," Brax said.

"Now, hear us out, Johnny, before you start losing your temper," Alice said, and took Brax's hand.

Alice and Brax were married in a chapel of St. Bartholomew's Church on Park Avenue, Olga standing up for Alice, Johnny for Brax, and with Harold Tilley, Sam Long, Edward and Patricia MacSwain, and Mr. and Mrs. Marvin Shapiro as the wedding party. Marvin had arranged for the waiving of the three-day waiting period required by law, and it seemed only right to invite him.

The wedding present from Brax's aunt and uncle was a duplex apartment in a new cooperative building on Fifth Avenue at Sixty-first Street. Mrs. Gowan Bragg had a penthouse in mind, but that had already been sold. The twelve-room duplex was the next-best thing.

Two months later, Gowan Bragg brought five Pullman cars full of his friends to New York for the debut recital (Rossini and Verdi arias) of Alice Wilton Long at Carnegie Hall.

Johnny was only mildly surprised that they had a packed house at Carnegie Hall. The way that worked was you rented the whole damn place, and guaranteed so much money, whether or not they sold any tickets. He had told the management to sell as many tickets as they could, and to give the rest away. There were apparently large numbers of people who wanted to listen to Alice.

Neither was he surprised at the attention the newspapers paid to the arriving concert-goers. The Carolina Tobacco Company and its peers were in town, and so was MacSwain Trucking, the Philadelphia *Inquirer*, and Mrs. Katherine Dennison of the Dennison Oil Company. That was good copy for the Sunday rotogravure section. Kate and her stomacher were worth a picture anytime.

And he expected the long line of uniformed ushers carrying basket after basket of flowers down the aisle when Alice had finished singing. He himself had sent twenty dollars' worth of roses, and the basket from Kate Dennison was about as flamboyant as the lady herself.

What really surprised him were the reviews read during the

buffet supper he gave (at Grandmother MacSwain's expense) at the penthouse after the concert:

"Astonishing range and mastery," the *American*'s critic reported.

"Alice Wilton Long demonstrated at her debut a voice and an understanding of her material unexpected of someone of her youth. Brilliant!" The Brooklyn *Eagle*.

"One attends debut recitals with the faint expectation of finding hope for the future. Alice Wilton Long's voice and virtuosity tonight at Carnegie Hall portend a glorious career, for she is barely more than a child." The *Herald*.

"Alice Wilton Long broke the rules tonight at her Carnegie Hall debut. Her disciplined, magnificent voice forced the diamond-tiara set to listen to her instead of each other's gossip. At long last, a soprano with beauty to match the voice, and vice versa!" The *Daily News*.

46

Johnny had begun to feel like odd-man-out even before Alice's debut, and it grew worse when she signed on with the Metropolitan Opera afterward. She continued attending Juilliard, and to meet four times a week with Madame Czerny, and spent every afternoon at the Met or at a rehearsal hall being used by the Met.

There were a maid and a cook, and a full-time accompanist who also served as a companion-protector. There were, Johnny had learned, opera buffs who agreed with the reviewers, and wanted to become close to Alice before she made her Metropolitan debut. They had to be kept away from Alice, and Sonya, the accompanist, was accomplished at doing that. Within a couple of weeks of being hired, she had taken over Alice's schedule, and Johnny was very much aware that he was being fitted reluctantly into it.

Brax seemed absolutely delighted with married life. In all the time Johnny had known him, Brax hadn't indicated the slightest interest in music, classical or otherwise, but that had all changed with his marriage.

He was perfectly content, even happy, to spend practically every night at some musical event, or even to just sit and listen to Alice rehearse, and was politely reluctant to go out with Johnny for as much as a drink. Johnny had been offered a standing invitation to dinner, but that had quickly evolved into a fairly ritual Thursday-evening get-together.

Seeing Alice with Brax, still looking like a little girl, it was difficult to accept his baby sister on the broadside posters announcing the Metropolitan's offering of Mozart's *The Magic Flute*, with Alice Wilton Long making her debut as Pimina, the daughter of the Queen of the Night.

Almost for lack of something better to do, Johnny took a far more active role in the day-to-day affairs of Long, Wilton Advertising. It proved far more interesting than he would have thought. He came for the first time to understand why Patricia had not simply chucked Thrifty Scot and gone back to Philadelphia when her husband had taken over MacSwain Truck Manufacturing. The sense of accomplishment one found in running a business was immensely satisfying.

Patricia came into Newark, just across the river from Manhattan, for at least two days a week, and Johnny fell into the habit of going to see her, to take her to dinner, to drive her around between the stores when she "dropped in" on them.

While the thought of so much as looking at her body was out of the question, it did occur to Johnny that Edward MacSwain was privileged to take this astonishingly intelligent female to bed, and all things considered, it must be really splendid to have someone like Patricia to go home to, wake up with, just to be with on a permanent basis. To love, and be loved by. When he saw Patricia's face light up at the sight of her husband, when he saw the possessive, intimate way Edward hugged her to him, Johnny realized how alone he was in the world, that no one really gave a damn whether he woke up in the morning.

He was wallowing in self-pity, he thought, but couldn't get it out of his mind, and that is what really brought him to Marian Hayes. She had red hair, like Patricia, the first thing Johnny had noticed when he hired her at Long, Wilton Advertising. When he started keeping his long hours at the office, he became aware of Marian at her typewriter long after the other girls went home. She seemed determined to prove something as she worked harder, longer, and better than the other stenographers. Johnny offered to drive her home one evening, to (he discovered) a shabby little rooming house on the West Side. She didn't invite him in, but two days later she accepted his offer to drive her home again, this time with a bite to eat before. She seemed unsurprised when he took her that night to his own apartment, although he was astonished, despite his much-vaunted sophistication, to discover she wasn't a virgin. It was a relationship, steady, warm, comfortable, that continued for six months. And then Johnny Wilton married Marian Hayes, almost as casually as he had first asked to take her home, for want of anything better to do.

They were united in matrimony by a clerk of the city of New York, with Samuel F. Long, Marvin Shapiro, and Marian's mother and father as witnesses. Brax and Alice were in Toronto, and once he'd made up his mind to get married, Johnny didn't want to wait for them, nor did he call Edward and Patricia. And the last thing he wanted was his mother inquiring about Marian's social background.

Marian was uncomplaining, silently accepting Johnny's decision to wait awhile to meet his family. It occured to Johnny that they never talked about anything now that she was away from Long, Wilton Advertising. Later, he told himself the reason he hadn't introduced Marian to his family was that he wanted to avoid all the supersweet nonsense that inevitably would follow the announcement of his marriage. He had no idea that his sister Alice, or especially Patricia, who he previously had thought was the most levelheaded of women, would instantly decide that Marian had married him only for his money. Even George, goddamn him, had managed to convey the impression that he wasn't surprised Johnny had married a woman "like that." The only one who was decent to Marian was Olga.

Marian got the message, but didn't complain, as usual. They didn't need anybody else, she said. They had each other, and there soon would be a baby.

What she really wanted was a house, a nice house in the suburbs, where she would make a home for them and their child. He bought a house in South Orange, on top of the mountain, where you could see the Manhattan skyline from the backyard, and got rid of the penthouse.

"Billy" Wilton was seven pounds, six ounces, a fine healthy baby. Patricia and Edward came to the hospital. Alice and Brax Long did not. Grandmother MacSwain wrote Marian a nice letter, enclosing a check for a thousand dollars and a silver teething cup, and explaining she was having difficulty getting around, and she hoped Marian would understand. His parents sent an almost identical loving cup, and no check.

Katherine S. S. Dennison presented Billy Wilton with one hundred shares of Dennison Oil common, and another hundred shares arrived from the First National Bank of Dallas, presumably from Colonel J.F.W. Wilton. Dennison was traded on the New York curb exchange at 213 3/8 as of the date of transfer.

Marian's mother came to the house in South Orange the day before Marian and the baby came home. She was seldom gone from it for more than twenty-four hours thereafter, and generally she was accompanied by at least one brother, sister, aunt, uncle, cousin, niece, or nephew.

Johnny had never before thought of himself as a snob. He had been an enlisted man, after all, and even after he became an officer, he had gotten along splendidly with the enlisted men, even the French enlisted men, not just the American. And he had before and after the war known some people charity required that he think of as colorful.

Marian's family was somehow different. They bored him, and made him uncomfortable. He was often tired when he got off the train in South Orange and rode up the hill to find at least two of his relatives by marriage, and often four or more, waiting impatiently for him to have "supper." He disliked eating at six o'clock. The evening meal should be eaten at about eight or eight-thirty, after a cocktail or two, and it should be eaten in peace, not with whining children at table, and sundry relatives whose manners left something to be desired, and whose conversation was centered around baseball and moving-picture actors.

Marian had taken on twenty pounds when she carried Billy, and she had not lost them. Judging by the shape of her mother and her sisters, and the way she wolfed down pastries and the candy from dishes spread out all over the living room, she was not going to lose it.

Their sex life had degenerated after Billy was born. The trim body he remembered was gone, probably forever, and he was ashamed of himself for being selfish about this. And at the same time aware that his mother (not to mention Patricia MacSwain) did not seem to bulge nearly so much as his wife. Marian, furthermore, took to motherhood with savage intensity. He remembered quite clearly that his brothers and sisters had been placed in either the nursery or their own rooms from the time they were born. Marian insisted on having Billy in their bedroom, which necessitated making love in a strained and unnatural silence, as well as in the dark, so as not to disturb the baby.

There was a fight about that; the victory was Pyrrhic. Billy was moved out of the bedroom at night, but Marian's sulking and dutiful offering of her body reduced their coupling to the satisfaction of his animal desires. Marian had not, he realized, really touched him since she had become pregnant.

His dissatisfaction fed on itself. It was easy to make cynical observations about his situation. The house in South Orange became headquarters for Marian's family. Why not? The food was free. None of them had houses of their own into which all the others would fit at one time; they barely fit into his house.

Complaints to Marian about too much family were met with the cold rebuttal (which he could not deny) that since his family showed no interest in her or their child, he really had no right to complain simply because she had a family. What did he expect her to do, become a prisoner on the mountain, just waiting for him to come home whenever he could spare the time?

One Monday morning when Johnny went to Long, Wilton, actually glad to be inside the place, a refuge of calm and order after a family "supper" in South Orange the night before, Braxton Bragg Long was waiting for him.

With him were the firm's lawyers. Lovell, Swazey had made an offer to buy out Long, Wilton. Brax thought the offer should be accepted. Not only was the price offered more than the firm was worth, but he found the other conditions very satisfactory. Brax and Johnny would be taken into Lovell, Swazey as vice-presidents. Brax would have Carolina Tobacco as his only responsibility. Johnny would be primarily concerned with developing new business.

"I'm just going to have to spend more time with Carolina Tobacco, Johnny, you understand that," Brax said. What he was saying was that he would eventually take over Carolina Tobacco, inherit it.

"Or what they're willing to do, Johnny, is to make you a very nice settlement. Then you could go out on your own."

John went with Lovell, Swazey. He lasted six months. He

353

was given three months' salary as severance pay, and that, like the money from his share of the Long, Wilton partnership, went into starting a commuter airline, Aero Transit.

Scraping up all available cash, a down payment was made on two Ford "Stout" trimotor airplanes.

On July 17, 1925, Aero Transit Flight 103, New York–Hartford–Boston, Captain J.F.W. Wilton II, pilot, attempted to make an emergency landing in a thunderstorm near Darien, Connecticut, hit a power line, and crashed, killing all aboard.

47

The first indication that there were financial troubles came when Marian Hayes Wilton hysterically called Edward MacSwain at his office. There was a sheriff at the door, she wailed, who wanted to arrest her. Mr. Hayes, Marian's father, came on the line, and from him Edward learned that the check Marian had written the funeral director had been returned by the bank, marked "insufficient funds." Marian had told him that was obviously a mistake, and to present it again. He did, and when the bank again refused to honor it, the funeral director turned it over to the sheriff for collection.

Edward asked to speak with the deputy sheriff, identified himself as president of MacSwain Truck Manufacturing, assured him not only that there was some sort of a mix-up but also that he would personally guarantee the check. The deputy sheriff was unimpressed.

Marian was taken to the Essex county sheriff's office and held there until Marvin Shapiro could come over from New York with cash to redeem the check. Marian was not actually placed in a cell, but she was driven from the house in South Orange in a sheriff's car, and the experience was both humiliating and frightening. She also resented the Wiltons sending a Jew to get her out of jail, and not coming themselves.

As soon as he'd gotten off the telephone from talking to Marvin (who was the closest, most immediate source of cash), Edward had called Samuel F. Long, and Sam had caught the next train to Newark to get to the bottom of the problem. Edward was doing his very best to meet his obligations as male head of the family.

Colonel John F. W. Wilton was in Africa, Thomas Wilton would not have been any help, and Harold Tilley could not be thought of as having any obligation.

Colonel John F. W. Wilton was in Le Hôpital des Soeurs de le Sacre Coeur in Léopoldville in the Belgian Congo at the precise moment. Quite without warning, while he was having an after-dinner cognac on the deck of the Congo river streamer *Ferdinand de Lesseps,* he had suffered a heart attack four days out of Stanleyville from Léopoldville. One moment he was standing there watching the boat head in for the pier where it would tie up for the night, and the next moment he was writhing on the deck, suffering incredible pain in his right arm and chest.

There was absolutely nothing that anyone could do for him. There was no doctor at the plantation where they tied up. He was carried to his cabin, undressed, and placed in bed. If he lived through the night, they would put out again at first light, and since he was who he was, proceed directly at full speed to Léopoldville without making any of the scheduled stops. The captain of the steamer had several years before had dinner with the general manager of Denco-Congo, and seen the respect and deference with which that powerful man had treated *Le Colonel* Wilton. It was possible, even likely, that he would be dead long before they got to Léopoldville, but it would not be said that the captain hadn't done everything he could. A telegram was dispatched ordering an ambulance to be on *la plage* at Léopoldville when they arrived.

The general manager of Denco-Congo was also on the beach at Léopoldville when the *de Lesseps* nosed in. Colonel John F. W. Wilton received him in his cabin, white beneath his tan, if no longer in pain, and in full control of the situation.

It was possible, he said, that he would "expire"; only time would tell. If that should happen, his remains, suitably embalmed, were to be shipped home on the next Denco tanker to dock at Matadi. He was not to be buried here. His remains would be interred beside his wife in New Mexico. In the meantime, since there was nothing whatever that anyone in the United States could do about the situation, no word of what had happened was to be sent to the United States.

He presented the general manager with a letter which, should that become necessary, would serve as proof that the general manager had carried out his express wishes.

Only then did he allow the doctor from the Sisters of the Sacred Heart Hospital into his cabin, and ultimately to have himself carried off the *de Lesseps* on a stretcher. He was installed in a large, airy room overlooking the Stanley Pool. A Belgian priest, who was also a physician, explained to him what had happened. While it was possible, he was bluntly informed, that he would suffer another, possibly fatal attack at any moment, the fact that he had lived through the first couple of days was cause for some hope.

Had he made his peace with God? It was John F. W. Wilton's judgment that the only truly shameful thing he had done in his life was to tacitly encourage his wife to play polo, and was thus responsible for her crippling, and her finally taking her life, and he was prepared to suffer whatever punishment was appropriate for that.

"If you're asking, *mon père*," Wilton said, "if I am prepared to make a deathbed conversion to Romanism, the answer is no."

"I didn't ask that," the priest said, pouring some dark brown liquid in a glass and handing it to him.

"What's this?" Wilton asked suspiciously.

"Brandy," the priest said. "We're going to give you a glassful every four hours. It sometimes helps."

"I say," Wilton said. "If I had known that, I would have had a couple on the boat."

He was confined to his bed completely for two weeks, suffering what he considered the gross indignity of having to void his bowels and bladder into china appliances, and having himself sponge-bathed by glistening black Congolese student nurses who giggled at their work.

Starting with a few minutes out of bed (long enough to make it to the toilet and back), he gradually worked up to the point where he was out of bed most of the time, except for naps in midmorning and midafternoon, taking his brandy in Father Jean's office, and obliquely asking Father Jean, whom he had come to respect and admire, what his chances for survival were, over the long term.

"You may live twenty-five years, and you may die this afternoon," Father Jean told him. "It is in the hands of God."

"Splendid," Wilton said. "Nothing I like better than a precise answer."

He was having dinner (no fats, no fried foods, no heavy sauces, a tough little piece of Kivu Province beef called a "steak," rice, and some fresh tomatoes) when the telegram came saying Johnny had died in the crash of the Ford trimotor.

He was sorely tempted to tell Father Jean that it was his son, not his nephew, who had been killed. But he did not. There was no reason an uncle could not be deeply affected by the death, in the prime of his life, of a nephew.

The general manager of Denco-Congo informed him that a Denco tanker was a day out of Matadi. The captain was summoned to Léopoldville. The situation was explained to him, and the problem discussed in some detail. The dimensions of the door to the ship's freezing locker were obtained. A casket (somewhat smaller than normal) was ordered, shipped to Matadi by rail, and when a telegram confirmed that it fit through the freezer-locker door, Colonel John F. W. Wilton presented Father Jean a check for ten thousand dollars for the hospital and had himself driven to the railroad station for the 180-mile trip to Matadi.

Katherine Dennison, looking, Margaret MacSwain thought, like an eccentric cousin of the queen, descended regally from the MacSwain Packard limousine and headed for the steps of 14 Rittenhouse Square.

Margaret stepped away from the window and turned to Patricia MacSwain. "That's Kate, all right," she said. "Every time she makes Lester sound the horn that way, he cringes."

Patricia smiled understandingly, and got up. They were both facing the door when the maid slid open the door to the sitting room and announced, "Mrs. Dennison, ma'am."

Kate and Margaret went through a mockery of the female ritual of kissing cheeks; neither of them liked it, and they barely touched. But Kate's lips touched Patricia's cheeks when her turn came, and her arm lightly pressed the younger woman to her.

"And where's the brood, Patricia?" she asked.

"Jeremiah's sulking upstairs," Patricia said. "Grandma yelled at him for rouging Maureen into a painted Indian, and Ellen has put her in the tub to wash the rouge off."

"Tea should be here any moment," Margaret said.

"Tea isn't exactly what I had in mind," Kate said. She fished in her purse and came out with a pencil-thick three-inch-long cigar.

The door opened. It was Maureen MacSwain, whom Patricia had named for her maternal grandmother, in a futile gesture to make peace with her mother, who had nonetheless refused to show up at the christening, even though the celebrant has been his eminence the archbishop of Philadelphia. That had been the staw that broke the camel's back so far as Patricia was concerned. The following Sunday she had marched into Holy Trinity Protestant Episcopal Church, across Rittenhouse Square from number 14, on the arm of her husband.

She hadn't joined the Episcopal Church, and would not, but if her mother was going to be so unbending in her belief that her daughter had married a heathen and given birth to his bastards, she herself might as well accept the fact and go to hell down the aisle of a heathen church on the arm of her husband.

"Hello, darlin'," Kate cried.

"Aunt Kate!" the little girl said happily.

"Come and tell me what your terrible brother's been doing to you," Kate said, and, cigar in mouth, held out her arms. The child ran to her, and was scooped up, as the other two women smiled. Kate listened solemnly to the tale of painted forehead, and then announced that as soon as she had a little something to cut the dust, she and Maureen would go upstairs and throw Jeremiah out the window.

"Good God, Kate," Margaret protested. "She's going to believe you."

The little girl giggled and shook her head no.

She allowed herself to be cuddled on Kate's lap, playing with Kate's stomacher, the diameter of a coffeecup, a jeweled representation of a cotton blossom surrounded by a three concentric rows of diamonds. It had been, she had once told Patricia, her first piece of jewelry, a brooch given to her by the late Mr. Sawyer, and subsequently done over by Van Cleef & Arpels. On any other woman in the world, it would have been grotesque. On Kate, it seemed quite natural.

A maid rolled in a tea tray, on which sat two bottles of whiskey, a soda siphon, and a bucket of ice cubes in addition to the tea implements.

Patricia smiled as Kate told the maid she'd "take care of that" when the maid offered to mix a drink. Kate put ice and a maraschino cherry in a glass, sprayed soda on it, and solemnly handed it to Maureen then poured whiskey generously into two other glasses. She looked at Patricia.

"It's a little too early for me, thank you," Patricia said, slightly embarrassed.

"You're at the age, darling, where you should drink whiskey only before going to bed," Kate said.

"I don't have any trouble sleeping."

"That isn't what I had in mind," Kate said. Patricia blushed, and then blushed again when Margaret laughed.

"Kate, you're embarrassing Patricia," she said.

"I'm trying to preserve her happy marriage is what I'm doing." Kate said. "What do we hear about our world traveler? When does the boat dock?"

"Sam called just before you got here," Margaret said. "He's on his way to Chester now to pick him up."

"I don't want this settled between Sam and Uncle John," Patricia said very firmly. "Uncle John—and you know it—is just going to say, 'give her money.' And that's not a solution."

"Mr. Shapiro is with Sam," Margaret said, placating her. "They're all coming here directly from the ship. We can talk it over then."

"Am I going to be in the way in this?" Kate asked.

"Don't be silly," Patricia said. "You're family. And about the only one with a harder head than Uncle John."

"This has put Marvin on the spot," Kate said. "I know more about this than maybe I should. She's been going to Marvin for money. And he thought he should tell me."

"Marian obviously has to live, Patricia," Margaret said, gently chiding her. "Marian and the boy."

When Sam Long and Marvin Shapiro (and Edward, which surprised and annoyed Patricia since she hadn't known he was going to Chester) arrived with Colonel Wilton from the Denco marine terminal in Chester, they were almost immediately ushered into the dining room. The twenty-two-foot-long table had been stripped of the normal complement of candelabra and other decoration. There were paper tablets, pencils, and a telephone (not normally in sight) instead. A butler's cart held cups and a silver pitcher of coffee.

It looked, as Patricia MacSwain intended that it look, like a conference table in a boardroom, not like Grandmother MacSwain's dining room. She had something, a good deal, to say about "the problem," and she had no intention of being dismissed as only Edward's wife.

She made the point, at least visually, to Colonel Wilton.

"It would seem," he said, "that all we need is an ashtray for my cigar, and we can call this meeting to order."

Furious with herself for forgetting the damned ashtray, Patricia snatched a coffee saucer from the butler's cart and laid it on the table before him.

"There you are, Uncle John," she said. "Call the meeting to order." He had naturally, she saw, taken the chair at the head of the table.

"You want to know, apparently," Colonel Wilton said, "about what we're going to do about Johnny's widow and the boy."

"We want to discuss it, yes," Patricia said.

The facts were that Johnny Wilton had left no assets, leaving his son and widow penniless. The airline was mortgaged to the hilt, so there were its debts to contemplate. Since Johnny's death, the Dennison Oil Company, via Marvin Shapiro—with Kate Dennison's blessings—had issued Marian Hayes Wilton checks totaling $14,500. But handing Marian money as or when she demanded it was no assurance to the family that Johnny's son was properly taken care of, Marian being in the habit of handing over most of what she got to her own family.

"In a nutshell, I'll provide for their needs," Colonel Wilton said. "We all realize that the Hayeses are in no position to do so, and I don't think Tom and Martha are, either."

"If it was only a question of money," Patricia said, "I'd see to it that they had it."

Colonel Wilton didn't reply, but his eyebrows went up.

"My wife, Uncle John," Edward said, amused and proud, "has become a woman of power. She is now presidentress of Thrifty Scot."

"I told you, I don't think that's funny," Patricia snapped at him.

"Is *Madam President* of Thrifty Scot," Edward said, smiling at her.

"Listen to what Patricia says, John," Kate said. Wilton looked at her. She had Maureen on her lap. She apparently felt free to speak in this family conference.

So Patricia had figured it all out. John was impressed with her eye for detail. A trust would be established. A house, a decent house, but nothing as large as the house in South Orange, would be acquired, either purchased outright or rented, and made available, at no charge, to Johnny's widow. She would be given a cash allowance for out-of-pocket expenses, and arrangements would be made with various merchants to provide food, clothing, and other necessities. When the time came, Billy Wilton would be educated in suitable schools. "The sooner we can get him away from that woman and her family, the better," Patricia said.

She had planned, virtually to the last detail, a system that would ensure that Marian and her child would want for nothing reasonable, and yet which would not permit her to divert any funds to her family. Patricia would run the fund; she would be grateful if Uncle John would let her contribute half of its cost.

"I loved him, Uncle John," she said. "He was the loneliest man I ever knew. I'll keep an eye on his son for him. It's the least I can do."

48

Thomas Wilton died when Billy Wilton was nine years old.

Patricia MacSwain telephoned Marian with the news. Marian had three months before married Howard T. Davidson, the service manager of Brick Church Buick in East Orange. Marian and her son had moved to a three-bedroom frame house on Vernon Terrace in East Orange, and she had met Howard Davidson when she had taken delivery of the Buick Patricia bought for her.

"Marian, this is Patricia."

Marian didn't reply, just waited to see what Patricia had to say.

"I've got bad news, I'm afraid. Grandfather Wilton passed on last night. I waited until this morning to call you. I didn't want to upset you at night."

Again there was no reply. Marian was not going to be a hypocrite and say how sorry she was. So far as she was concerned, Thomas Wilton was as cold-blooded as the rest of the Wilton family.

"I think it would be a good idea for Billy to go to the funeral," Patricia said.

"He doesn't have anything to wear."

"What about the blue flannel suit?" Patricia asked. She had sent the suit, and a large parcel of other clothes, most of it barely worn. She had been sensitive enough about worn clothing to ask her husband and Margaret MacSwain. Grandmother MacSwain told her she didn't think Tom had ever

363

had a new suit of clothes until John reached puberty and shot up like a weed so that his discards were too large for his brother. Edward told her he clearly remembered a whipping he got from his mother for tearing a suit of clothes he had got hand-me-down from Sam Long and which was scheduled for Johnny Wilton. Patricia had been satisfied with that. If Billy's father had worn Edward's hand-me-downs, there was no reason Billy couldn't wear such clothes.

"It doesn't fit," Marian said. That was untrue. Marian was hurt and offended by Patricia's gift. It was one more indication of the scorn and contempt in which she and her son were held by the high and mighty Wiltons and MacSwains. She hadn't been invited to take Billy to the boy's department in Thrifty Scot. Not even that. What she got was hand-me-downs, and what she did with them was throw them out the day they came.

"I'm sorry to hear that," Patricia said. "Well, I'll just send for him a little early, and see what we can do in Thrifty Scot."

Sure you will, Marian thought. New clothes to take him to a funeral where somebody's likely to see him. No other time. She did not know, and probably would not have believed, that Patricia did not outfit her son at Thrifty Scot either.

"You'll send for him?" Marian asked coldly.

"I'm going to take the next train to Philadelphia. Marvin Shapiro said he'd pick up Billy when he goes. If you'll tell me where."

"I don't want him flying," Marian said flatly.

"I know, Marian," Patricia said. There had been a terrible scene a few months before. Billy had been at Grandmother MacSwain's for Thanksgiving dinner. Colonel Wilton had taken him to New York and sent the excited boy home with the story of his first airplane ride. Marian had not been able to find Colonel Wilton. She vented her fury and rage on Patricia, whom she could locate.

"Could I tell Marvin to pick him up after school?" Patricia asked when Marian did not volunteer any information.

"I'll have him ready at three-fifteen," Marian said. "When are you bringing him back?"

"In several days. I'll bring him back myself."

Marian hung up on her.

49

It was a warm June day in 1933 when the airplane, two of its four engines stopped, taxied across the waters of San Francisco Bay. It rose somewhat ungracefully out of the water up the ramp onto the shore, and then toward bunting-bedecked bleachers.

Quite unnecessarily, loudspeakers boomed, "Trans-Global Airways announces the arrival of Flight One-seventy-seven, the *Asia Clipper,* from Hawaii."

The engines were killed. The U.S. Army band from the Presidio of San Francisco began to play, first "Garry Owen" as the passengers (preceded by a motion-picture star with his trench coat worn over his shoulders, who, despite the bright smile on his face, had been airsick most of the way) debarked, and then, after they had formed a group with the crew, "The Star-Spangled Banner."

The governor of California, trailed by the mayor of San Francisco, shook hands with the motion-picture star while the newsreel camera whirred and the flashbulbs exploded, and then the mayor was handed a three-foot-long gold-painted wooden key, which he handed to the tallest member of the group.

"Colonel Wilton," he said. "The key to San Francisco."

Colonel John F. W. Wilton, chairman of the board of Trans-Global Airways, looked impatiently over his shoulder. The flight engineer thrust two small white boxes at him.

"Mr. Mayor," he said, "I bear this token of friendship

from your counterpart, the mayor of Honolulu." He took an orchid from the box. "Actually, I suppose he intended it for your charming wife."

There was laughter as the orchids were pinned to the mayor's and the governor's wives.

"The flight," Colonel Wilton said, looked into the lens of the Fox Movietone News camera, "was not entirely a success. We are fifteen minutes behind schedule. Captain Webster feels this is because he turned the controls over to me."

"And when is scheduled service actually going to begin, Colonel?" a reporter asked.

"Within three weeks," Colonel Wilton said. "The flights of the past four days have gone better than we hoped."

"And what for you now, Colonel? A well-deserved rest?"

"Not at all," Wilton said. "As soon as we refuel, we're continuing on to the East Coast. Not that I don't really appreciate the welcome we've been given, but this has really been a routine flight. I slept most of the way."

The colonel was in fact exhausted, but he was very much aware of the public-relations benefit of having the airplane immediately take off again. Neither had the flight been routine. It had been necessary to use four of the five fifty-five-gallon barrels of fuel strapped into the cabin, pumping their contents by hand into the wing tanks of the Sikorsky. The plane was going to the East Coast to have larger fuel tanks installed. But that information wouldn't sell tickets to the public. And there was more than enough fuel capacity to make it to New Mexico; there would be no newsreel cameras at Rancho San Miguel.

He had never flown one of the big Sikorskys into the ranch before. He was worried, a little, that the runway would not take all the weight, although engineers had assured him it would.

His approach brought him over Anglo-American Land & Cattle first. He clearly saw the ranch house, even saw someone come running off the porch to wave a pillowcase or something at them. Well, they didn't see that many airplanes around here, period, and this was the biggest airplane flying, so no wonder they were excited.

He came in over the rail siding, saw beefs in pens waiting to be loaded while horse-head pumps surrounded by fences sucked oil from ten thousand feet down. Goddamned pumps ruined the country, no two ways about that.

He remembered the boxcar they'd fixed up when Mother had come up from Philadelphia.

"One hundred miles," the captain said, reading out his airspeed.

"One-third flaps," Wilton ordered, and pulled backward on the throttles, all four of them in his hand.

The speed sank, and he picked up the nose.

"Ninety. Eighty-five. Eighty. Seventy-five."

He advanced the throttles.

"Two-thirds flaps," he ordered. The plane slowed, seemed to shudder.

"Full flaps." He ran the throttles forward against the pressure of the flaps in the airstream, and then slowly pulled them back. The *Asia Clipper* settled. He felt the wheel chirp.

"A greaser, Colonel," Captain Webster said, approving the landing. "A greaser."

"Watch who you say 'greaser' to out here, Frank," Wilton said. "Or you'll go back East singing soprano."

They taxied back toward the ranch house, fifty-gallon drums of aviation gasoline, oil for the engines, a truck with spare parts, and several automobiles waiting for them.

The engines were shut down. The colonel somewhat stiffly unstrapped himself and got out of his seat. He entered the cabin and took a small white box, six inches deep, a foot long, from the overhead luggage rack. He held it tenderly, like a rifle, in the crook of his arm, and walked down the aisle and jumped out the door to the ground.

One of Samuel F. Long's many cousins (he had no idea which one), dressed in Levi's and a deerskin shirt—a yellow redskin, he thought—came and shook his hand. Three cars were drawn up.

"Would you help these gentlemen, please?" Wilton said. "Take them to the house. Get them a drink and a bath, in that order. I'll be along shortly." He laid the white box on the front seat of a Ford convertible and then got behind the wheel.

He drove to Lucille's grave, saw that the grass around it had been raked that day.

He opened the box, took from it a dozen orchids, and laid them on the grave.

"Let it be known," he said aloud, as if he were talking to Lucille, "that no other woman has ever had a dozen flowers like those. Those are the very first orchids ever to be flown from Hawaii to the United States."

He debated a moment putting some of the orchids on her father's grave. The major wouldn't give a damn. He hadn't cared any more for flowers than John did. But Lucille's mother. He knelt and counted out six orchids and moved them to the other grave.

Then he turned and without looking back got into the Ford and drove to the ranch house. He went into the sitting room and made himself a stiff drink. The truth of the matter was, he was exhausted.

"You silly old jackass!"

He turned and saw Kate standing in the doorway.

"I didn't know you were here," he said. "Or I'd have saved one of the orchids."

"What orchids?" she asked.

"I flew a dozen orchids from Hawaii," he said. "They were just starting to turn brown, but they were still exquisite. Shall I send a *muchacho* to get one for you?"

"I don't want a flower from Lucille's grave, thank you just the same," Kate snapped. "My God, you really are a jackass!"

"Lucille, I'm sure, would want you to have one."

"No, dammit," she said. "Are you out of your mind?"

"To offer you a flower? Apparently I am."

"I meant about flying across the ocean, you damned old fool! You're sixty-one years old."

"I don't think it would be safe for me to play a chukker of polo at my creaking advanced age. But one sits down to fly, you see, and even we oldsters can do that."

"My God, you're impossible," Kate said.

"What brings you out here?"

"I came here to bury you," she said. "Presuming they were able to find your body."

"But here I am," he said. "Now what are you going to do, now that I've ruined your plans?"

They smiled at each other, and Wilton opened his arms and Kate came into them. He held her very close.

It must be nervous tension, he thought after a moment. I haven't had an erection in six months.

She hugged him, this time very tenderly. "I'm glad you got here safe."

At five minutes to seven the next morning, the telephone rang in the ranch house at Anglo-American Land & Cattle. The noise did not disturb John Wilton. It woke Kate Dennison. She crawled out from under his arm and picked it up.

"Colonel John Wilton, please. Long distance from Philadelphia."

"May I ask who's calling?"

"Edward MacSwain."

"Ask Mr. MacSwain if he will speak with Mrs. Dennison," Kate said. "The colonel is asleep."

Edward MacSwain told Kate that, forty minutes before, when Margaret's daytime nurse had come on duty and looked in on her, she found the old lady had passed on in her sleep.

By the time Kate had finished talking to Edward and hung up, John Wilton was awake and had pushed himself erect against the headboard. She could tell by his face that he understood.

"I'm sorry, John," she said.

"We can make it in two days if we leave in an hour or so."

"If you have any idea that I'm going to be flying anywhere in that machine of yours, you're out of your mind," Kate said. "I'll get a special locomotive, if necessary."

"I understand, Kate. Of course," he said. "There is no reason for you to come."

An hour and a half later, the *Asia Clipper* broke ground at Rancho San Miguel. Its sole passenger was Katherine Shaughnessy Sawyer Dennison. Firmly strapped into her seat, she said her rosary, eyes closed, until curiosity got the better of her, and she opened her eyes and looked around, and then finally, as if she was afraid she would somehow fall out, looked out the window.

Two minutes later, she appeared in the cockpit. Frank Webster, who was flying, nudged Wilton, who was staring thoughtfully out the window. Wilton looked at Kate and smiled.

"I don't suppose this flying palace of yours has got a bar?" she asked.

"As a matter of fact, Kate . . ." Wilton said, and got out of the copilot's seat. He and Mrs. Dennison went into the passenger compartment, where a wicker basket held bottles of Scotch and bourbon whiskey.

"Grandmother wouldn't leave the radio," Patricia Herlihy MacSwain said. "From the time she heard you were on the airplane."

"I upset her, you mean?" John asked.

"No, not at all, Uncle John," Patricia said. "She was thrilled. The only thing she said was that it was a shame Johnny couldn't be here. She said it would have been very nice if Johnny could have flown that plane."

Wilton, unhappy with the sudden surge of emotion, almost as if he was actually going to cry, changed the subject. "And speaking of John Wilton," he said, "where is Billy?"

He saw from the uncomfortable look on Patricia's face that he wasn't going to like what he heard even before she finally replied, "As a matter of fact, Uncle John, he's in jail."

"Jail?" Wilton replied with deceptive calm.

"Oh, not really behind bars. It's the same thing, though. The Essex County juvenile detention home."

"Reform school, is that what you're telling me?" Wilton asked.

"No. He hasn't been tried yet."

"The last I heard," Wilton said softly, but in cold fury, "the boy was in that school in Massachusetts, and things were under control. What has he done?"

"This time," Kate said, "he stole an automobile and ran the cops a merry chase before he smashed into a parked car."

"You are, Kate," Wilton said, "apparently privy to all the details." The accusation was unmistakable.

"I was going to tell you in New Mexico," Kate said. "That's the real reason I was there."

"And why didn't you?"

"Well, I thought it would wait until the morning," Kate said. "I didn't want to ruin dinner. I knew what you would have done if I'd told you then."

"Then tell me now," Wilton said.

"He was expelled from Saint Mark's," Kate said. "About a month ago. Academic failure and antisocial behavior."

"Such as?"

"If it matters, he beat up a kid who turned him in for smoking," Kate said. "Anyway, as late in the school year as it was, there was no place to send him, even if we could find a school to put him in. Marvin has been dealing with Marian. The thing to do, until other arrangements could be made, was let him go home to Marian. That's what he said he wanted. They put him in the public school there, and he lasted about a week."

"I should have been informed," John Wilton said.

"What would you have done?" Kate asked. "Marian is enough of a problem, without you getting involved."

"He stole a car?" Wilton asked.

"First he 'borrowed' Marian's car, and the cops brought him home. Then the day you left for Hawaii, Billy climbed down the drainpipe from his room. Marvin said that he heard he'd been whipped by Marian's husband, but she says not. Anyway, he went down the drainpipe, found a car with the keys in it, went for a joyride, and when the cops saw him, tried to run."

"I presume Sam is doing what he can," Wilton said. "To get him out of jail, I mean."

"Marian is his mother," Kate said. "She has declared him incorrigible. She doesn't want him out. Marvin feels that a lot more happened between Billy and her husband than Marian is telling."

"And what does the boy say?"

"When Sam went to see him, the boy told him to stick his nose out of his business."

"And everyone concerned is content to see him languish in prison?" Wilton said. "Well, dammit, I'm not! Where can I find Sam?"

"If you could get him out, and you can't, they have different rules for juveniles. You can get a bank robber out on bail, but not a kid. Anyway, what would you do with him?"

"Uncle John," Patricia said, "Sam and Marvin have arranged for him to come to the funeral."

"In handcuffs, no doubt?"

"No," Kate said. "With a juvenile officer. Marvin's going

371

to provide an automobile. They'll being him here for the funeral, and take him back immediately afterward."

"That's tomorrow, Uncle John," Patricia said. "There's nothing you could do today anymore, anyway."

Billy Wilton did not attend his grandmother's funeral. Colonel Wilton was informed of this change in plans by Samuel F. Long.

"Why not, Sam?" Wilton asked.

"I talked to the director of the detention home myself," Sam said. "And then to Billy." Wilton waited for him to go on. "Billy said that since 'the old bitch hadn't given a shit for him when she was alive,'" Sam quoted, "'He didn't see why he should come all the way here to watch her get buried.'"

O'Day, the fat mick screw who had slapped him around yesterday afternoon when he found the cigarette under his mattress, came and got him out of woodworking. He stood there, the fat slob, making sure that all the tools were put back on their hooks in the wall, until he'd brushed the wood chips off the bench, and then swept up the floor. Then he put his fat hand on his arm and marched him out of the woodworking shop and down the corridor to the storeroom. The dame in the storeroom handed him his civilian clothes, not what he'd been wearing when they brought him here, but a suit of clothes, still smelling of the dry cleaner.

Then O'Day took him to the shower room and sat there and watched him take a bath and get dressed, and then back to his room, where he combed his hair and tied his tie and hung up the khaki uniform in the wall locker.

Then he marched him down the corridor again, and through the locked door to the administration section. He picked up some papers, his "evaluation report" from the dame in the admin office, the report of his horrible crimes since he'd been in the center—smoking and profane language and disrespect to attendants, all that bullshit against him—and not one word about O'Day and the other screws slapping him around whenever the hell they felt like it.

Then O'Day took his arm and led him out the front door.

"Where are we going?" Billy Wilton asked.

"You'll find out," O'Day said, and unlocked the back door of a Ford panel truck. The truck said "ESSEX COUNTY

JUVENILE DETENTION CENTER" on the side. There were seats for six back there, and a steel-wire barrier separating the back from the driver's compartment. O'Day shut and locked the door after him and then went around and got in beside the driver. The panel truck moved off with a lurch.

Billy couldn't see too well out of the back, but he could see enough to guess where they were heading. Downtown, toward the county courthouse. He was apparently coming to trial.

He admitted now that he had made a mistake, telling Sam Long to go fuck himself. Sam was supposed to be a pretty good lawyer. Anything would be better than the jackass the court had appointed to defend him. Now, there was a real clod.

It probably didn't make any difference. He'd talked it over with the guys in the center. It didn't matter what you had done, so long as you did it before you were sixteen. What they did was remand you, whatever the hell that meant, to the Clinton Training School for Boys until your eighteenth birthday. What that meant was that you could get turned loose when you graduated from high school, if you hadn't been a disciplinary problem in the meantime. He was going up for two years and ten months, minimum.

The panel truck drove to an underground garage in the courthouse building, and O'Day, grabbing his arm so hard it hurt, led Billy to an elevator, and then put him in a room, *locked him* in a room, way up, maybe the eighth floor, with wire mesh over the windows. That was stupid. As high as the room was, there was no way anybody could escape, wire mesh or not.

And then Billy realized that the wire was there to keep people from *jumping* out, committing suicide. He thought about that. Maybe he'd wind up doing that.

O'Day came for him fifteen minutes later. He had the lawyer with him.

"You just keep your mouth shut in the judge's chambers," the lawyer said. "The only time you say anything is when someone asks you a question, and then you say, 'Yes, sir.' You understand that?"

"Yeah," Wilton said. O'Day jammed him in the ribs with his elbow.

O'Day led him down a corridor and into an office, not a

courtroom. Billy saw the social worker, and the other dumb
dame who'd given him those stupid tests, and the cop who
had arrested him, and some other guy. Probably another lawyer.

And then the door opened and Sam Long walked in, and
then Uncle John and Aunt Kate. What the hell did they
want?

"The Family Court of the County of Essex," another fat
cop said. "The Honorable Pasquale T. Romero presiding. All
rise."

The judge came in, in robes, and sat behind his desk, and
put eyeglasses on.

"Please be seated, ladies and gentlemen," he said. He
looked at the young guy. "Is the state ready?" he asked, and
when the guy said it was, the judge looked at Billy's lawyer
and asked him if the defense was ready.

"Yes, your Honor," the lawyer said. "May I present to the
court Mr. Samuel F. Long, an attorney-at-law admitted,
among others, to the federal bar and to the Supreme Court
of the United States."

"What's your interest, here, Counselor?" Judge Romero
asked.

"With the court's permission, your Honor," Sam Long said,
"I would like to assist Mr. Kelly."

"And where is the boy's mother? Why isn't she in court?"
The judge looked annoyed.

"Your Honor," Sam Long said, "I would like to introduce
at this time a document executed by Mrs. Davidson stating
her willingness to have her son, John F. W. Wilton III, the
defendant in this case, legally adopted by the child's great-
uncle and aunt, Colonel and Mrs. John F. W. Wilton, who
are present in the court."

Sam Long handed the papers to the judge, who read them.

"Your Honor will find, I think, satisfactory proof not only
of Colonel and Mrs. Wilton's ability to provide for the boy,
but testaments to the high regard in which they are held by
other jurists with whom your Honor may be personally ac-
quainted."

"Colonel," the judge said, and Colonel Wilton stood up,
and then Aunt Kate beside him, "I appreciate what you're
trying to do for this boy, and you, too, Mrs. Wilton, but

there's a lot more to this than just walking out of here with him."

"Your Honor," the prosecutor said, "the complainants in the matter of the auto theft, and the auto damage, have withdrawn criminal complaints, and have informed me that satisfactory restitution of damages has been made. Under those circumstances, the state is willing to *nol-pros* the charges of reckless driving, failure to heed a warning light, no driver's license, and resisting arrest, on condition that the defendant leave the state and remain out of the state for a period of no less than one year."

"And I suppose the juvenile authority has no objection to any of this?" the judge asked.

The dame who had asked all the weird questions (had he ever worn his mother's clothes?) stood up. "Your Honor, the juvenile authority believes that what the boy needs is a stable family environment, and has been convinced that Colonel and Mrs. Wilton are able and willing to provide such an environment."

"That leaves only the boy to be heard from," Judge Romero said. "How do you feel about all this, son? Would you like to go and live with your aunt and uncle? To have them be, in fact, your mother and father?"

Billy Wilton didn't reply for a moment. Then he looked at Uncle John. He was getting a dirty look from Uncle John. But not from Aunt Kate. Aunt Kate looked as if she was afraid he would say no.

"Yes, sir," Billy Wilton said.

"So ordered," the judge said.

"Is that all there is to it?" Colonel Wilton asked the judge, as if he were inquiring the time of day from a passing stranger.

"Yes, Colonel," the Honorable Pasquale T. Romero said somewhat testily. "That's all there is to it."

"Splendid," Colonel Wilton said. He walked over to the judge and put out his hand. "Thank you very much," he said. "If there is ever anything I can do for you, I would consider it an honor to be of service. Sam, here, always knows where to reach me."

Judge Romero looked at Samuel F. Long and saw him

cringe. And then he shook the colonel's hand. "Good luck with the boy, Colonel," Judge Romero said.

"Why, thank you very much," Colonel John F. W. Wilton said, and then he crossed over to Billy. "Let's get out of here," he said. "I find this place very depressing." He put a possessive arm around the boy's shoulder, and then gestured for Kate to precede them out of the room.

About the Author

Eden Hughes was born on Philadelphia's Main Line to parents who trace their ancestry back to Pre-Revolutionary British colonists. Educated privately and abroad, in both England and Germany, this novel is Eden Hughes's first attempt at fiction. Denying that THE WILTONS is in any way a fictionalized history of the Hughes family, Eden Hughes says, "It is a compilation of stories of Philadelphians.

Eden Hughes is presently working on a second novel, this one dealing with Philadelphians and Bostonians whose fortunes and reputations came from the days of the tall ships and the China trade.

Recommended SIGNET Reading

Buy them at your local

bookstore or use coupon

on next page for ordering.

More Bestsellers from SIGNET

☐ **ON THE ROAD** by Jack Kerouac.   (#E8973—$2.50)

☐ **THE DHARMA BUMS** by Jack Kerouac.   (#J9138—$1.95)

☐ **ONE FLEW OVER THE CUCKOO'S NEST** by Ken Kesey.
    (#E8867—$2.25)

☐ **THE GRADUATE** by Charles Webb.   (#W8633—$1.50)

☐ **DANIEL MARTIN** by John Fowles.   (#E8249—$2.95)†

☐ **THE EBONY TOWER** by John Fowles.   (#E9658—$2.95)

☐ **THE FRENCH LIEUTENANT'S WOMAN** by John Fowles.
    (#E9003—$2.95)

☐ **THE CRAZY LOVERS** by Joyce Elbert.   (#E8917—$2.75)*

☐ **THE CRAZY LADIES** by Joyce Elbert.   (#E8734—$2.25)

☐ **WINGS** by Robert J. Serling.   (#E8811—$2.75)*

☐ **KINFLICKS** by Lisa Alther.   (#E8984—$2.75)

☐ **THE MAN WITHOUT A NAME** by Martin Russell.
    (#J8515—$1.95)†

☐ **SOME KIND OF HERO** by James Kirkwood.   (#E8497—$2.25)

☐ **KRAMER VS. KRAMER** by Avery Corman.   (#E8914—$2.50)

☐ **UNHOLY CHILD** by Catherine Breslin.   (#E9477—$3.50)

* Price slightly higher in Canada
† Not available in Canada